Tiramisu Kiss

~ Book One in The Niles & Pikes Series ~

A novel by
Peter Breeden

*To Tanya,
Your training ROCKS!
Cheers,
P. Breeden*

Tiramisu Kiss

~ Book One in the Niles & Pikes Series ~

Galant Press©

The **Galant Press** logo is a registered trademark of **Galant Press**

All rights reserved. No part of this publication may be reproduced, stored in a retrieval system, or transmitted in any form or by any means--electronic, mechanical, digital, photocopy, recording or any other--except for brief quotations in printed reviews without the prior permission of the publisher.

Cover by P.W.B, Toronto ON

Tiramisu Kiss Copyright © 2013 by Peter Breeden

Published by **Galant Press**, Toronto ON

Paperback first published: January 2013

ISBN: 978-0-9877927-6-1 Library and Archives Canada

This is a work of fiction. Names, characters, places or incidences are a product of the author's imagination or are used fictitiously. Any resemblance to actual persons or to events or locales, living or dead is entirely coincidental.

DEDICATION

THIS BOOK WAS WRITTEN IN MEMORY OF MY SISTER, MARYLYNN KIMBERLY BREEDEN.

CONTENTS

	Acknowledgments	i
	Part I	**iii**
	Prologue	**1**
1	Phillip Niles	5
2	Angela Portman	9
3	Leave of Absence	13
4	The Weekend with Grandpa	19
5	Casa Loma and the Next Project	27
	Part II	**31**
6	The Hunt for the Flip	33
7	Château Français et Le Manoir!	43
8	The Hideous Mansion	55
	Part III	**67**
9	The Renovations Begin	69
10	Things Get Complicated	81
11	Mayor Madame Lapossie-Laporte	93

12	Unexpected Pleasures	107
13	Hovering over Southern France	117
	Part IV	**131**
14	The Arrivals	133
15	Day of the Party	161
16	Les Nuits d'Été – La Grande Entrée	179
17	Les Nuits d'Été – La Danse Autour de la Piscine	193
	Part V	**227**
18	Up with the Birds	229
19	Warm, Buttery Croissants	241
20	Destination Agde	259
21	Homeward Bound	283
	Part VI	**287**
22	Bubble Bath	289
23	Hammerhead	299
24	Dignity	303
25	Tiramisu Kiss	309
26	Sleeper Artichoke Tames the Legend	341
	Epilogue	**347**

ACKNOWLEDGMENTS

Thank you to my dear wife, Georgina, for reviewing my book, encouraging me to write and supporting me in so many wonderful ways. You are my November Rose. I love you.

PART I

Peter Breeden

PROLOGUE

Anybody I know would have told you that I was so full of life that death seemed unrealistic for me, even at the ripe old age of eighty. Well, death happens and there simply is nothing one can do about it except be a little pissed-off for a while, give in to the sorrow and eventually move on.

That's me down there, about to be lowered into a six-foot hole and covered with the very soil that is life itself. I know a thing or two about soil, given that I farmed artichokes for most of my life. Yes, I grew a weed, thistle to be exact, for a living. How can a person prosper growing weeds? Well, it turns out that artichokes are actually a gourmet food. I'll tell you more about my life growing thistles later. For now, I have a much more important story to share with you.

I'm up here, by the way, on the hill overlooking a section of Cypress Tree Cemetery in a rather beautiful part of Palo Alto, California. I'm watching my own funeral service. I figured that this spot offered the best view of the celebration below, or rather, 'of the world falling apart' as my grandson, Phillip, sees it. Looking down on my own funeral is not something I could have ever imagined and I am a little at odds about the whole experience, personally. I'll get over it, I suppose.

Angels really do have wings, but every angel has a different pair. My wings are invisible... permanently cloaked, ha hah. So, I appear normal. Nobody else can see me, though, only you. Those are the rules... for this story, anyway. When I expired, I was given Snowy Owl wings rated at light speed performance with zero visibility. In my old-timer's lingo, these are known as 'a nice set of wheels!' I can't show you the wings, but I certainly will show you *The Wheels* later.

I'm sorry. I forgot to introduce myself. Charles Niles, master artichoke grower and loving grandfather of Phillip Niles. Hmm. Have you, by any chance, tried slow-baked artichokes stuffed with a heap-load of pressed garlic and marinated in olive oil? This is my all-time favorite artichoke recipe. Home always felt homier when I smelled the baked artichokes cooking in the kitchen. I feel like Pavlov's dog right now, salivating in anticipation of something tasty. I digress, though, my apologies.

Well, I'm bored looking at myself down there, so let's head to my farm in Monterey. It's a short trip south of Palo Alto. This Grandpa can scoot so try and keep up! I'll soar at a comfy pace, though, as I would not want to make you sick—barrel rolling over the mountains and along the waterfront. I'm not comfy flying over the ocean, yet, so I'll point out the ocean side towns as we pass them. San Francisco and the entrance to San Francisco Bay are to the north. We are heading south, though, over the Monte Bello Regional Open Space and Big Basin Redwoods State Park. See the tall redwoods below? Magnificent trees! There's the small seaside town of Davenport, below. See right there? That's known locally as "The Hole in the Wall" and one of my favorite secret spots! There's the beautiful little town of

Capitola and, a little further down the beach, we have Watsonville, home of the world famous strawberries! Wahoo! I might as well grab a few on the way, especially since they are, you know, right there. California strawberries are huge! Imagine that there strawberry dipped in melted chocolate. Mmm, now that's a tasty fruity. Ah, and here we have Monterey Bay in all its majesty and Seaside below with the rolling surf. In the distance I can see Point Lobos National Reserve, a place I consider to be a treasure among all treasures. If we head a wee bit east of Seaside... here we are! Welcome to the Niles Artichoke Farm and Estate!

We own 500 plus acres of prime artichoke farmland. This farm has been in my family for over five generations, since California became part of the United States over 160 years ago, on September 9th, 1850 to be exact. I brought you here because I wanted to show you the family photo on the mantle. This is the perfect time to show you the picture because nobody is here right now; they are still at my funeral. How convenient! Hah ha...

That's me in the overalls holding the hoe. I was full of pep back then... at the ripe old age of thirty. I worked alongside my father from dawn until dusk building one of the largest and most successful artichoke farms in California. Ironically, my dear grandson, Phillip, is the same age now as I was then in this old family photo. He too is building an empire, one much larger than a 500 plus acre artichoke farm. It is his story that I want to share with you today. To begin this story, we need to look back to where it all unfolded. So, make yourself cozy, stretch your legs a wee bit, and enjoy this journey, a journey of determination, loyalty, trust and... love.

ONE – PHILLIP NILES

It's difficult to spend an entire day in an office knowing full well that the temperature outside is like the inside of a dry-sauna before it reaches the Too Hot zone. Add to that, an unobstructed sun sitting in a pile of blue and a tempting dry breeze gently massaging the bougainvillea vines dangling outside the window and a day in the office begins to feel a lot like captivity. One hundred degrees isn't so bad in Palo Alto, California, if you're the outdoorsy type. Actually, it can be rather tormenting if you have to watch it from an air-conditioned office overlooking a beautifully manicured garden and shaded pathway that runs around the entire company property. This is exactly how my grandson, Phillip, felt on the day that would change his life forever. He sat at his desk twirling his pencil around his thumb and stared aimlessly through his office window at a very inviting lawn and garden backspace.

Spontaneously, he pressed the receptionist button on his desk phone and broke the silence. "Nancy?"

"Yes, Phillip?"

He stood up abruptly from his desk and performed a rather awkward stretch towards the ceiling. At six feet tall, he is a very handsome man. He has my broad shoulders and dark hair. The hazel eyes come from his mother, God rest her soul. "I'm heading out for an afternoon walk. I should be back in half an hour if anybody needs me."

"Okay, don't forget that Andrew needs sign-off on the hardware purchase and new-hires sometime this afternoon. And you have the boardroom booked at 3:00 for the process mapping session with the Quality Assurance team."

"Right... Thanks."

If there's one thing I know for certain about my grandson, he just can't sit still one moment longer than God intended. Even while attending Stanford for his degree in software engineering, he had to be busy doing something more than just his regular courses. That's why he could never be an artichoke farmer. Doing the same thing year-in and year-out was not his thing. I realized this when he was just six years old. Instead of playing with the tractors and exploring the barn, he was building Lego structures on the sunroom floor. When he was building, the Lego pieces would be scattered everywhere. One day, I walked into the sunroom and saw the Space Shuttle sitting on its launch pad with boosters and fuel tank and even the Mobile Launcher Platform inside the Vehicle Assembly Building; all made from Lego and no instructions. The kid was nothing short of a genius!

Phillip reached for his cell phone as he climbed the stairs leading to the scenic pathway around the company grounds. "Hey," he said with annoyance.

Andrew detected the short tone in Phillip's voice and adjusted himself accordingly. "How's your walk?" he asked while watching him through his office window.

"Noisier than it should be. Cell phone pollution is congesting the airwaves and disrupting the call of the humming birds and the symphony of the swallows."

"Shit, that sucks! I'll fire the cook!"

"Huh?" Phillip said confused.

"Well, obviously someone spoiled your chili sauce because something's got you in a foul mood."

"Wanker!"

"Right. Let me make things a little easier for you. I need your verbal sign-off on these new-hires and extra lab servers. Skip the 3:00 and take the rest of the afternoon off. We'll meet up for sushi at 6:30. Deal?"

"Yeah, that sounds good. Sorry. Just a bit out of sorts at the moment," he said apologetically.

Andrew paused for an instant and then spoke. "Well, you can tell me about it over seaweed salad and raw fish, then."

"Thanks buddy."

"K, later Bubba."

Andrew and Phillip went to Stanford University together. They met in their sophomore year while rebuilding one of the lab servers. While they were reconfiguring a hard disk drive from one of the remaining redundant server drives, they made a wager on the San Francisco Giants game. Phillip lost the wager and Andrew won a free dinner at the most expensive and posh sushi restaurant in the Bay Area. They've been best friends ever since. As a matter of fact, it was over that sushi dinner that Phillip Niles and Andrew Pikes decided to create an Internet software company together. Six years later, Niles & Pikes is one of the largest providers of the One-Stop-All suite of software applications in the world with over 2 billion in revenue, and growing, each quarter. The software is actually installed as one very large application on a computer and is completely customizable by linking to the Internet. The user can choose what applications the N&P User Interface loads simply by selecting them from a list, agreeing to a universal Terms of Use policy and selecting a simple billing structure, of course. The software even has a fail-safe mode that protects the user's application and data even if the Internet fails. How they did it is beyond comprehension, at least for me anyway. The technical gurus seem to have it all figured out, though. Everything makes sense to them. Personally, I always felt intimidated by it because I never understood it all. Everything is connected and somehow this keeps everything working. That part I do understand.

TWO – ANGELA PORTMAN

You can tell a lot about a person simply by observing how dedicated that person is to doing a good job. Some people detest their work and it shows. Others are just there for a paycheck and leave at the end of the day, as soon as the clock hits 5:00, or sooner… Angela Portman, on the other hand, is dedicated to success. She has the torque of a diesel engine. Well, not really, but she is one robust woman. She's usually up with the birds most weekdays and, more often than not, on weekends too. Long workdays are the norm for her and she is not one to shy away from hard, grueling work. In her books, a woman who sweats is a woman in charge!

During her college years, she worked part-time for her Uncle's construction company, and managed to put herself through trade school where she learned everything about the fine art of house flipping. Her first flip was a run-down bungalow that she bought at the ripe old age of twenty-three in the community of West Hill, Toronto. It took her four months to turn a local eyesore into a lovely single family home, complete with beautiful landscaping and huge curb appeal. It sold "over asking" within a week of being on the market. Not bad for a first-time flipper! The best and most rewarding part was that she doubled her investment and could now buy a bungalow in Leaside, a community more central to downtown Toronto. In fact, that is exactly what she did and her progress on the renovations has been nothing less than stellar. Seven months in and renovations on her second flip are almost complete. Her certifications in plumbing and electrical work have paid off substantially. Even now, as she chips away at the old ceramic tile in the Leaside kitchen, she can't help wondering where she would be if she had not taken the extra training. Her courses in brickwork and masonry paid off handsomely on her first flip, as did the courses on framing and dry walling. However, there is one course she regrets not taking, the course on permits and local by-laws.

"I can't believe it!" she hollered from the messy old kitchen floor at the Rooster clock hanging on the kitchen wall. "I need a permit for everything in this town! Renovating a kitchen? Need a permit. Building a fence? Need a permit. I better not scratch my ass for fear the permit committee finds out and bills me for that, too!" she said with a sudden burst of irritation and threw a half-eaten muffin at the Rooster clock. "Piss off clock!"

And what a lovely bottom she has, too, dare I say. At five foot 9 and three quarter inches, Angela has it all: beauty, wit and drive! She is most comfortable in a pair of jeans and spends most of her time looking like a Tom Boy. I guess that makes sense given her career choice. But take my word for it, when she lets her hair down, slips into some fancy heels and a sexy, hot, heart-ripping little black dress, nobody would mistake her for a Tom Boy! With legs longer than the CN Tower, curly dark brown hair, hazel eyes and buttocks of mass destruction, this girl has the looks and complexion of a supermodel.

"I need a dog," she mumbled sorrowfully to herself. "One with big floppy ears and... expressive eyes... intelligent and playful, not overly talkative, hugs... yes, must be a good hugger!" I'll call him... *HB for heartbreaker!* She paused for a moment and whispered, "I could use a hug right about now." Rising up off the kitchen floor, Angela grabbed her tools and headed for the door. "That's enough for today, HB," she said to her imaginary dog. "Let's go home."

Peter Breeden

THREE – LEAVE OF ABSENCE

Andrew arrived at the sushi restaurant early and kept an eye on the famous School of Tuna clock from his seat near the tropical fish waterfall and palms section of the restaurant. 6:29... 6:30...

"You always choose the same spot!" Phillip complained as he took his seat at the table.

"And you, my friend, always arrive on time. Thank you for that!" he said with a side-glance and a smile.

"That's me. 'Mr. Punctual!' Mr. Hungry, too; I forgot lunch today."

"Ah ha! That explains a few things," he said, glancing at Phillip over the top of his menu. "Miso soup, salad and edamame are on the way. I ordered two large Cokes and some green tea for us, as well."

"You A-R-E my buddy!" Phillip declared with great enthusiasm for his dear friend. "I like Pepsi sometimes, too, you know."

"I know food makes you happy and... well, we'll talk about the other thing after supper."

"Happy? That's an understatement. What other thing?

This sounds serious. What's going on? Did something fail with the *Next Gen* software testing today?" Phillip had a look of worry on his face.

"No, but your happiness seems to have been flushed down the toilet."

"That obvious, huh?"

The waitress laid some items on the table and quietly slipped away.

"Phillip, you've been moping around the office for a week. You normally don't let Esther get a word in edgewise during conference meetings and I saw you pour honey in your tea, this morning. Very odd! Your mind just seems… elsewhere. Something's up and I want to know what."

Phillip sat in silence for a moment and stared into the miso soup in front of him. "I'm terribly bored, Andrew," he said to his concerned friend and business partner. "It was all very exciting at first, building the company and selling software, but now I seem to be doing the same thing, day-in and day-out, and it's just not challenging enough for me."

"Are you bailing on me, Phillip?" he asked, somewhat irritated.

Phillip looked at Andrew for a moment and slowly began to explain something he couldn't quite understand himself. "No, my friend. I would never do that to you. But I need to do something different, at least for a while. I need…" He paused for a moment and tilted his heavy head a bit in deep contemplation. "…a break."

A few moments pass in silence as Andrew attempts to process Phillip's unwelcome surprise.

"Good evening, gentlemen. Are you ready to order?" the waitress said confidently with a soft voice.

Phillip reached for the menu and spieled off his favorite selection of sushi. "I'll have the Chirashi sushi, Rainbow roll, Spider roll, yellow fin Nigiri sushi and another soda, please."

"Very well. And for you, Sir?" she politely asked Andrew with a nod of her head and a pleasant smile.

Andrew decided to go for his old stand-by. His capacitors were overwhelmed with Phillip's unsavory revelation. "Spicy Tuna hand roll, make that two, and the California roll, and uhm… another Coke. Thanks."

When she disappeared into the kitchen, Andrew felt an overwhelming need to clarify something. "But you're *'A Natural'* at this business, Phillip. What else could possibly be more interesting than running Niles and Pikes Inc.?"

Phillip hesitated for a moment, and then reached for the edamame. "Restoring a castle," he said in a serene, almost whisper-like voice.

Andrew took a moment to process the new information, and then threw his hands out and tilted his head back in disbelief. "Well, well now… I don't think Hearst Castle is for sale, at least not last time I checked!"

"Hah ha ha." Phillip let a few chuckles escape, even though he was deeply serious and passionate about his idea.

"All joking aside," Andrew continued, "we already have a new office building going up in Europe. Why don't you oversee that project? Maybe, take a month and head to London to ensure the final phase of the project goes smoothly," he said.

Andrew, feeling confident that he had found a solution to the problem, took another sip of his soda and pulled out the sports section of the San Francisco Chronicle to show Phillip. "The Giants are really kicking butt this season. Are you up for the A's game tomorrow night? The Braves are in town."

Phillip just stared at Andrew with a blank, unimpressed expression. The School of Tuna clock continued to tick away in the background. Phillip felt a tick-tock in the back of his mind. Time was running out.

The Japanese waitress returned with the sushi dishes and the demeanor of both men changed from solemn to happy in an instant.

"Chirashi sushi and rolls for you," she said as she served Phillip.

Phillip observed her beautiful traditional Japanese Yukata. He had seen women wearing these beautiful dresses when he was in Japan promoting his software. It was wonderfully refreshing to see that a country so technologically advanced continued to embrace its traditions with such passion.

"And for you," she said with a smile as she served Andrew the two Spicy Tuna hand roles and California role. "Will that be all?"

"Yes, thank you," they answered concurrently, practically drooling over the sushi in front of them.

"Oh yeah… best sushi ever," Andrew said with great satisfaction.

"Mmm. Yup! Uh oh, wasabi buzz!" Phillip exclaimed as tears flooded his eyes.

"Nice!" Andrew grins with wicked enjoyment at Phillip's moment of wasabi agony.

Phillip and Andrew continued in silence, enjoying their favorite food together. Then, Phillip answered Andrew's question.

"I'm not interested in doing that," he blurted out.

"Huh?" Andrew said as he stared vacantly at Phillip. "Oh, crap! We're back to *The Castle*, again?"

"It's an unrealized dream, Andrew. I need to pursue it and I am going to take a year off to make it happen." Phillip didn't waste any words making his intentions clear.

"Well, what about the company?" Andrew protested.

"I'll still be there, just not physically. If a crisis arises, I'll drop what I'm doing and come help," Phillip explained.

"So, you've made up your mind then. Six months of freedom."

"More like twelve months and, yes, I've made up my mind. I need this, Andrew."

A few thoughts ran through Andrew's head, but the most logical one was to set the falcon free. "Okay, Phillip," Andrew muttered reluctantly. "Spread those wings of yours and go find yourself a castle. We'll be fine here."

"I know you will. You're my best friend, Andrew."

"And remember that when you bring back a few cases of vintage Bordeaux wines for me!"

Later that evening, Phillip found himself at home sitting in his study. His mansion sat eloquently towards the back of the property on seven acres of land near the Fremont Older Regional Open Space trails, south of Palo Alto. Staring aimlessly at a mountain biking picture on the wall above the leather chesterfield, he remembered why he bought the place. During his university years, he frequently came to this part of the Bay Area to ride or walk the trails. It was his place to go when he needed... space. On a clear day, he could see the entire Bay Area from several different vantage points on the trails: San Francisco, Berkeley, Oakland, Hayward, Santa Clara, San Jose, Los Gatos and the mountains beyond the I-680. It was simply, extraordinary.

All these thoughts were running through his head as he twirled his pencil around his thumb, back and forth like a dancer twirls a baton. It was a habit that he picked up from a classmate during his high school days and signaled a deep train of thought. Three darts lay on the desk in front of him. He occasionally threw darts at the board across the room while coding a new piece of software on the computer. However, today things were a bit different. The screen on the computer showed a picture of a beautiful castle in Edinburgh, Scotland. At that moment, Phillip knew what he would do. He picked up one of the darts and threw it across the room at the wall-sized map of the world. He rose slowly from his chair, and walked apprehensively over to the wall map.

"France. Bloody hell!" Phillip muttered out loud. "I can't speak a word of French." The dart landed near a little town in France called Agen, somewhere between Bordeaux and Toulouse in southern France.

FOUR – THE WEEKEND WITH GRANDPA

The next morning, Phillip drove to Monterey in his 69 Yenko Camaro to visit... me. Hah ha. I don't know why, but Phillip turned to me more than he did his own father. I guess we developed a bond during his formative years; might have had something to do with me showing some interest in his Lego airplanes, hot rods and battle ships. Or maybe, he just felt I was his friend. Either way, I felt honored to be the one he trusted most.

Perhaps I'm deceiving myself when I say I was the reason he came to the family artichoke farm so often in those years after leaving home for the big city. It could have been the sheer joy of driving his midnight black, vintage 69 Yenko Camaro that brought him here so often. The ride from the Bay Area to the farm in Monterey was nothing short of extraordinary. Driving through the valleys and mountains and coast-side along the Pacific Coast Highway (PCH 1) in the Camaro was a rejuvenating experience, trust me on this one. I think that car added ten years to my life just by sitting in the passenger seat alone, not to mention being behind the wheel and giving her a little unharnessed encouragement with my heavy right foot on occasion. I say *her* because Phillip named the car *Carolina* after his beloved grandma, God rest her soul. I think he gets his hot rod blood from me!

Phillip pulled into the Niles Estate after completing the hour and a half drive from Palo Alto. His early morning departure at 7:00 ensured relatively quiet roads during the trip to the farm. It was a spectacular drive, especially since he had a chance to blow out the carbon—in the heavily modified, custom-built, V8 engine—on a quiet stretch of the PCH 1 before reaching Seaside. So, he was in great humor as he drove up the tree-lined driveway towards the barn adjacent to the old family home. Velocity, our full-blooded black stallion, cantered alongside Phillip as the Camaro rolled down the driveway. What a sight that was! Velocity, or Velly for short, knew Phillip's car and always jumped with excitement when Phillip arrived. I think it was his eager anticipation of the long runs he and Phillip would take at the back of the farmlands. I was excited to see my boy, too, and on this particular day, I was sitting on the veranda eagerly awaiting his arrival. Poor Velly. There would be no run for him today.

Phillip parked the car, waved at me, and then opened the hood to let the engine cool off. I watched him inspect the engine bay for any signs of trouble; something I taught him many years ago.

"You made good time," I said with a wise old smirk.

"Traffic was light… and the old girl needed her pistons cleaned," he said as he walked across the yard to shake my hand. He then sat on the steps and looked out over the fields in an unusual, pensive manner, which immediately told me something was up.

"I see," I said and paused for a moment to gaze upon my grandson, and then back at the supercharged V8 Camaro that we built together. "The new exhaust system sounds good, looks good too."

"Oh yeah! There's less back pressure and more top end torque now. She scoots!" he said looking back at me with big, proud eyes.

I smiled and took in the beautiful California morning. There was still a glimmer of dew on the bright yellow Ayres Turbo-Thrush S2R-T34 crop duster sitting pretty in the barnyard. Tyler, Phillip's father, flew the crop duster and managed to keep the artichoke fields bug-free with his low "Spray-on" passes and high G-force turns. His mind was always elsewhere though and, as usual, he was out-of-town for the weekend.

I thought to myself, as I took in the whole scene, that Phillip had something important to tell me. I could see it in his posture, hunched over a bit as he sat there on the front steps caressing Sandy and Comfy, our household cats.

Phillip, putting his own deep thoughts aside for a moment, asked me how my Plymouth project was progressing. "Any luck finding the parts for the RAM Air intake, yet?"

I smiled at him and took another sip of my morning tea, cherishing each moment of suspense as he stared back at me. I had been modifying my 93 Plymouth Acclaim for many years now; "a work in progress," I used to tell him. Somehow, I don't think I ever convinced him that my "Grandpa-mobile" would be anything more than a family sedan. "She's in the barn, if you want to have a look."

"No way! You're done, already?" he said with a look of shock and disbelief.

"You bet your ass, I am!" I said hopping out of the veranda rocker and off to the barn. "The RAM Air is for when I want to enjoy a little country drive. The RAM Nitrous, on the other hand, is for when I hand you your ass at the track next month!"

"Sweet Lord, my Grandpa has flung a lug nut!" Phillip hollered across the yard. "When did you finish?"

"Put the last clamp on the throttle body last night," I said as I peeled the dust cover off the car and popped the hood.

Phillip gazed into the engine bay with amazement and complete admiration at the work I had done to the engine. He kept saying "sweet" and "cool" and "unbelievable" as he moved his head in, under and around the engine bay. We both loved mechanics; engine modifications in particular. I think it stems back to the Lego…

"Where did you find the scoop?" he asked with his head underneath the air dam looking at the underside of the RAM Air assembly.

"The local Pick and Pull," I replied, leaning over the engine with a flashlight. "It's part of an intake from a Dodge pickup. I just trimmed it a bit and built a skeleton through it to handle 200 mph of wind shear."

"This is so fantastic, Grandpa! Can we take her down the run-way?" he asked with that boyish expression that men get sometimes.

"Wouldn't have it any other way, Lug Nut!"

I crawled into the passenger seat to ride "Shot Gun" while my grandson closed the hood and jumped into the driver's seat. Whatever it was that was on his mind was lost… at least for the time being. He did not suspect that I was inconspicuously observing him, searching for clues that would reveal what was bothering him. I watched him start the car and tap the gas. "Whoa ho ho ho…" he said as the rumble of the engine turned a rather quiet barn into a rock concert.

"Where's the nitrous button?" he said eagerly.

"I'll show you the nitrous system at the track. For now, we'll just test the RAM Air intake."

"But where's the button?" he said perplexed.

"This isn't a movie, Lug Nut. There are no pretty buttons on the steering wheel. Instead, the nitrous kicks in at wide-open throttle, but you first need to open the nitrous bottle, which is in the trunk, engage the system with the toggle switch, wait for the bottle heater to heat the nitrous oxide, purge the system, and then…" I paused for a moment and grinned at him. His eyes were the size of footballs. I saw nothing but pure love for brute horsepower and torque written in bold letters across his face. "It's all about the RPMs," I continued. "I'll show you when we take the cars to the track next month. We'll run the quarter mile, side-by-side, just for fun. Deal?"

Phillip paused for a moment, and then shrugged off the disappointment. "Deal," he said, extending his hand and giving me a good old fashioned, knuckle-wrenching handshake.

I sat back in my seat and watched Phillip shift through the manual 5-Speed transmission (A543 housing with 568 gears) that I had custom-built by a MOPAR transmission expert on the East coast.

"I love these gears… feels like a TANK!" he said, showing sincere interest in the car.

Then he opened up my sweet Isabella, as I so fondly referred to her, and my head and shoulders instantly became firmly embedded in the seat. What a great feeling; being held back in your seat by the fury of an engine. I couldn't even reach up to scratch my nose. "Okay, Dale Junior… easy on the thunder!" I said as the fields of artichokes flew by in a blur and the end of the runway quickly became a little too close for comfort.

"Woo hoo hoo! Yeah, baby!" he shouted at the top of his lungs and smiled at me with that rare look of pure joy one seldom witnesses. At that moment, Isabella's rear end started to drift as the combination of a dry, grassy runway and a little bit of brake made her loose. Phillip overcompensated and the car began swerving back and forth like a drunk donkey. The donkey-swerve soon became a dust-tossing three-sixty flat spin before the car came to a complete halt at the end of the runway.

Phillip stared at me with a look of shock and sincere remorse for his aberrant driving. As the dust storm he created gradually began to settle, I managed to utter a few words. "Are you trying to kill us, boy?"

"I... uhm... sorry," he managed. "I thought I had her."

"What you had," I said sternly, grabbing his arm, "was a loss of control. You lost control of the damned car! Did you forget that I'm eighty years old?"

Phillip knew he had surpassed the limits of my patience. He looked deeply embarrassed and disappointed with himself, as he should be, but I couldn't be too hard on him. Something like this can happen to anyone, even the best of drivers. He managed to mumble something incoherent as he sat there in the driver's seat with his head hanging low.

A few moments passed before I began digging for the true source of the problem. "What's going on, champ?" I said in a friendly, old-man sort of way. Then I just waited for him to collect his senses.

"I need a break from work," he said, looking at me with glassy, sorrow-filled eyes. "I need time away to do something... fun. Work has become the same old crap, day-in and day-out. It's not rewarding for me to spend my time repeating, B-U-L-L-S-H-I-T, anymore. My creative flare has disappeared into a gigantic black hole, never to be found again! I don't care about broken code, human resource issues or winning conference call battles. I've created a wonderful new software language that is fully encrypted and unhackable with a good friend and business partner, and now I feel I need to move on to something else."

"Okay... move on then," I whispered emphatically. "Find another dream and go make it into something unbelievably real!"

Peter Breeden

FIVE – CASA LOMA AND THE NEXT PROJECT

Every Castle seems to have a sad story written on the bricks and mortar. Casa Loma, meaning "the house on the hill," is a magnificent, century old castle built on a knoll overlooking the Toronto harbor front. It's original architect and owner, Sir Henry Pellatt, art aficionado and financier, built the castle in the early 1900s to entertain royalty. One of his most notable accomplishments was building the Canadian hydro-generation station in Niagara Falls. Unfortunately, he was unable to keep the castle and it eventually fell into the hands of the City of Toronto and is now a popular tourist attraction in the city; one which Angela visits frequently. There are places in life that bring us great joy and peace within. For Angela, Casa Loma is such a place.

At the same time Phillip and I were doing three-sixties on the crop duster runway, Angela was touring the famous Casa Loma with her childhood friend, Holly MacGibbon. Holly grew up with Angela and they have been best friends since grade two. Unlike Angela, Holly chose a career as an Emergency Room Registered Nurse. With long, curly, glazed-walnut hair, shiny green eyes, witty smarts, and an hourglass figure, Holly always seemed to have a date, but never managed to find 'Mr. Right.'

"I bet there are ghosts in here," Holly whispered to her friend and confidant as they strolled through the Great Hall and peered through the grand windows at the magnificent gardens beyond.

"You might be right, Holly," Angela said with a smidge of trepidation. "There's an unfinished indoor pool in the basement that is quite spooky. I once felt a nasty little pinch on my shoulder in that room. Odd thing was that nobody else was in the room at that time, just me. When I turned around and looked into the empty pool again, a cool shiver ran down my neck, almost like something was running the cold bones of skeleton fingers down my spine.

"Stop it! You're creeping me out!"

"Oh, it gets better, darling. I once saw…"

Holly took a step back and stared at Angela with huge, horrified eyes, wondering what awful story she was going to tell next. She did not like spooky stories, not even the friendly ghost kind. It all stems back to a stormy night when she was home alone. Her parents were out for dinner in celebration of their 15-year anniversary. Holly had convinced them that she was old enough to look after herself at home, and she *was* old enough, at least right up until the doorknob from the attic started turning in the movie she was watching. "You stop it, Angela, or I'm leaving you here in your haunted castle by yourself!"

Angela knew it was time to stop teasing her friend. So, she offered a compromise. "Okay, I'm sorry. Let's head down to the cafeteria and get some hot soup and sandwiches."

"Alright then," Holly agreed after an awkward pause. "No more ghost stories."

"It's right beside the pool and I can show you the... I'm teasing!" Angela laughed as she hugged her horrified friend. "Don't worry," she said, "ghosts are afraid of ME! Besides, I have something important I want to share with you... a secret."

Holly's eyes squinted a bit in doubt before surrendering to Angela's offer of lunch. They headed off to the cafeteria, talking about everything except Angela's secret. By the time they had ordered and sat down for lunch, Holly could no longer contain her excitement. "So, what's this big secret? Found a guy?"

"Ah, no," she said quickly, "but I did manage to sell my second flip!" she continued with a big, shiny smile on her face.

Holly could hardly contain her excitement. "Oh! That's great news, Angela! I'm so happy for you," she screamed, reaching over to hug and congratulate her best friend.

Angela's face turned bright red in embarrassment at the scene Holly had created in the restaurant. Angela, being reserved and quiet in nature, preferred to be an observer rather than the center of attention. She had a particular disdain for people who continually demanded the attention of others. You know the type, "I'm important because everybody loves me." Yeah, whatever you say, s-u-p-a-h-s-t-a-r! Angela learned to always measure a person by how that person behaved around others, especially around individuals who could not benefit that person in any way. It all comes down to one very vital ingredient; love. Everybody is capable of showing it.

In this particular circumstance, however, Holly was just excited for her. She occasionally forgot her surroundings when things became exciting.

"Thanks," she said quietly, "but that's not my secret. I have something else to tell you, something much bigger!"

Angela stared at her friend with suspenseful eyes. "What on earth have you got yourself into now, honey?" Holly exclaimed.

"Well, nothing yet, but I am planning something much more challenging for my next flip."

"Yes…?" Holly said with an air of caution.

"I want to buy a run-down mansion… in France!"

"Oh my goodness… a mansion… in FRANCE! How romantic, Angela." Holly sat back down and immediately began to wonder if she would lose her closest friend and confidant. "How long do you think you will be gone for?"

"I'll probably need eighteen months to flip a mansion, but I'm sure it can be done sooner if I prepare properly for it and buy a mansion that can be easily restored."

"Why a mansion, and why in France? I'm sure there are mansions here that need some TLC!" Holly replied.

"I was researching my Family Tree the other day and noticed that my great-great grandmother, Simone Giroux, lived in a little town on the main route between Bordeaux and Toulouse in the province of Aquitaine. She was the wife of a prune farmer, of all things," she laughed. "Never underestimate those prunes! The farm is no longer in the family, though. I thought I would visit the place anyway and, maybe, if I like the area, find a mansion to flip in the process."

"So, you haven't bought a mansion, yet?"

"Not yet…"

"Whew!" Holly exhaled her pent-up breath, and then took another deep breath of relief. "Hah ha. Angela, I almost thought you were leaving tomorrow or something crazy like that."

"I am," she said, watching Holly's face drop and smash to the floor.

PART II

Peter Breeden

SIX – THE HUNT FOR THE FLIP

Being an Angel (or Heavenly Spirit if you prefer) has its perks, like snooping into the past or present events of peoples' lives, even the future. You might think of that as spying, but I like to look at it as the only honorable way to tell a story. I can scroll back and review any event in a person's life as often as I please to get the facts straight. And believe me, some events were closely examined. Of course, *The Big Guy* is always watching me, as well, so there is a fine balance here. I hope you are not offended by the liberties I have taken to tell you this story. In fact, it is much too lengthy to tell in one sitting anyhow. For now, I'll weave together the first part of an incredible journey that will eventually become a small part of a magnificent tapestry.

The trip to Lester B. Pearson international airport the next day was not quite the happy experience that Angela thought it would be. Holly was in quite the foul mood, being a little bit selfish and difficult, despite agreeing to drive Angela to her terminal. It was obvious that Holly was upset about the idea of her friend taking on such a huge project at the spur of the moment. The root of the problem, however, went much deeper. Holly had come to rely on Angela for emotional support during times when life had become daunting and disconcerting, which seemed to be happening more often this past year. Angela was, in effect, Holly's security blanket and big sister. For Holly, everything seemed to come to a halt with the news of Angela's departure.

"How do your parents feel about you running off to France?" Holly blurted out as she looked for a parking space at the International Departures terminal.

Angela rolled her eyes and chose to ignore the offhand, potentially explosive remark. She was too exhausted to continue arguing. "There's one," Angela said, pointing to a perfect corner spot near the terminal entrance.

Holly pulled into the spot, parked the car, and then motioned Angela for an answer to her question.

"They're both fine; actually very excited for me and my ambitious endeavors."

Holly shook her head in disbelief and stumbled out of the car. She made no efforts to hide her anger or the intentional slamming of the car door. "Fine, I hope you find a lovely French man to help you *flip your flip!*" she stammered, and then unloaded the luggage from the trunk, a concentrated effort to hide the puddles forming in her eyes.

They walked side-by-side to the ticket counter. The only words that passed between them as they walked came from Angela. "The seat sale was only good for today," she muttered.

Holly stood quietly beside Angela during check-in. A little quiver ran across her lips as the agent weighed the luggage and issued the boarding pass.

"Gate twelve. Have a good flight!" The flight attendant's voice echoed in Holly's mind like the jackhammer pounding of a Palliated Woodpecker attacking a bug infested, rotten old tree stump.

"Thanks for the lift, Holly. I'll call you when I get there. It might be a couple of days, though. I need to drive from Bordeaux to Agen and then settle in. I'll call regularly, and you can call me, too, any time. I promise to keep you up-to-date on my progress."

"Okay, Angie. I'll call, as well. I might become a cell phone pest. I apologize in advance," she said stepping forward and wrapping her arms around her friend. "I'll miss you!"

"You could always come with me…" Angela offered with a hopeful smile.

"I have three weeks of vacation coming up. If you buy the mansion, I'll come and help you renovate for a while. I hear France is quite lovely this time of year."

"I *am* buying a mansion. So, I expect to see you soon!" Angela waved good-bye and only looked back once with a big smile and excited expression on her face. Nothing, it seemed, could stop her from going on this trip.

Angela's flight landed on time at Charles De Gaulle international airport in Paris. She made haste making her way to her connecting flight to Bordeaux international airport in Mérignac, in the southwestern part of France, which left on time an hour later. She thought about spending the night in Paris, but it would take one day out of her busy schedule, a luxury she could not afford quite yet.

When she finally landed in Bordeaux, it was late and dark outside. The warm midnight air at the car rental facility was refreshing and fragrant. The combination of fatigue and soothing breezes made her very sleepy. Then reality set in. She was in Bordeaux, France. Without question, the most famous wine region, and producer of the best wines, in the world. Angela, of course, had her biases, but she knew her wines and Bordeaux's were her favorite.

The car rental agent gave her directions to the Vin Extraordinaire Bed and Breakfast ten minutes down the road. She jumped in the little black Renault Twingo rental car and immediately knew she would need to return it and lease or buy a pick-up truck when she finally began renovations on this mansion she had yet to find. "It will do for now," she muttered to herself.

The next morning, Angela awoke to the smell of freshly baked baguettes wafting through her room and the sounds of birds chirping outside her open bedroom window. The sun was shining and a warm summer's breeze gently lifted the curtains framing the old leaded glass windows. The view through the double windows was extraordinary and could very well be the inspiration for an oil painting. Angela crawled out of bed and walked over to the windows in her black silk nightie, half stretching and yawning at the same time. Slowly, she began to open both windows for a full view of the sun-drenched rolling hills with row upon row of well-manicured grape vines stretching out towards the untouchable horizon. "Magnifico!" she whispered to herself.

A loud thumping on the bedroom door startled Angela out of her dreamy, all-consuming state at the bedroom windows. "Allô, American... Are you going to sleep all day?" came the voice on the other side of the door. "Voulez-vous manger quelque chose... hungry, eat something, n'est ce pas?"

"Ah... yes, Oui! I'll be right down," Angela managed.

She had not yet flipped her state-of-mind-linguistic-switch from English to basic French conversation. Nor had she ever been called an American, before. It actually felt... refreshing. Angela didn't mind one way or another. Her father often brought his American colleagues and friends' home when they were in town. It all seemed... normal to her. A glance at the clock on the wall, showing quarter past ten, motivated her to jump into a pair of jeans and comfy shirt, throw some water on her face and pull her hair back into a pony tail.

She walked downstairs into the kitchen and greeted Madame Larose, the proprietor of the B&B. "Bonjour," she said simply and took a seat at the table.

"How would you like your eggs, ma chérie?" she said with a loving smile and a basket of warm baguettes in her outstretched hand.

Angela was on the road before the clock struck eleven. She had a wonderful breakfast with Madame Larose and was eager to start the hunt for the mansion she envisioned in her dreams, a complete eyesore in need of major TLC. As she pulled away from the B&B in her ball cap and shades, the little Twingo quickly responded to her heavy foot and rapid shifting through the gears. "Hmm, not bad!" she acknowledged aloud. "Sexy sunroof, too!" she continued and placed her cell phone in the innovative, spongy, non-slip dash tray.

She arrived safely in Agen shortly after 1:00 pm. She parked on Boulevard du Président Carnot outside the real estate office and hurried inside for her appointment.

"Allô! Bonjour! Comment est-ce que Je peux vous aider?" inquired the openly gay man at the front desk.

"Bonjour. Mme Beaujolais, s'il vous plait."

At that moment, Mme Beaujolais entered the room and,

for Angela, the world in which she lived all of a sudden paused to take notice. "Angela, my darling, it's so nice to finally meet you. And please, call me Caroline."

Caroline Beaujolais was the daughter of one of the most prominent plum and prune farmers in the region. Her reputation as a businesswoman and renowned real estate agent stretched far beyond the borders of France, itself. At six feet tall, including her four-inch pumps, she stood 2 inches taller than Angela. Four-inch pumps were, of course, a woman's right and Caroline used them to her advantage. Slender yet curvaceous, well groomed, fashionable and very sexy in her business lunettes, Caroline was, to say the least, a full-blooded Parisian Tease!

"Nice to meet you, as well, Caroline," Angela said reaching out to shake hands with the pretty lady.

"Come with me to my office," she said, motioning to the back hallway of the office. "I'll load some properties on my computer for you to see."

"Excellent," Angela replied. She followed Caroline's beautifully shaped—and satiny sheathed in designer pantyhose—legs to the back of the office. "Those have got to be the most incredibly long, silky legs I've ever seen," Angela whispered quietly to herself. She couldn't help thinking, *Lucky for me I'm straight and female; otherwise, I'd be… conquered!*

"L'Université De La Sorbonne!" Caroline said in passing as she sat down on the leather swivel stool behind two 24-inch screens and loaded the real estate listings she had book marked on her computer.

"Pardon?" Angela replied.

"You are wondering how I came to speak English so well?"

"Yes, actually."

"I attended La Sorbonne for my degree in translation.

So, I am comfortable serving you in English, if you like."

"That would be lovely, Caroline. Thank you." Somehow, Caroline made Angela feel very important and now she felt obliged to behave accordingly, speak favorably and present herself in a more polished manner than usual.

"Come. Sit beside me. What do you think of this one," she said pointing to one of several mansions displayed on her giant dual screens and pulling up another swivel stool for Angela.

Angela sat down beside Caroline and inspected the property listing. The mansion seemed to be in rather pristine condition, which sent alarm bells ringing in her head. "It's very nice, but I was thinking of something a little less expensive and in need of some pretty serious renovations."

"Yes, the kitchen in this one needs some serious renovations to bring it up to modern standards. Of course, I can recommend several contractors to help you with this work; not for a lady to be doing such… manual labor, no?"

More alarm bells rang in Angela's head as she stared at the kitchen photos and immediately fell in love with the beautiful styling and 'old world charm' of the layout. She wouldn't change a thing in that kitchen.

"Uhm… It's not really what I'm looking for. It is beautiful, though. Yes, very pretty, indeed."

"Okay, my dear. How about this one? It resides on two hectares of beautifully landscaped gardens and the grand entrance includes a spectacular oval driveway! Et voila…only €850,000! Bargain!"

Angela pondered what a hectare might be, or how it would translate into acreage. "Hmm. I'm looking for something in much *worse* condition, Caroline. There is not much I can do to improve this property. Show me something for around €500,000 on at least three acres of land and requires extensive renovations."

Caroline turned towards Angela and stared at her over the rim of her lunettes rather impatiently. "What do you mean, ma chérie? I am not going to show you something… *h-o-r-r-i-b-l-e*. Now, let me show you something a little smaller around the €600,000 price range." Caroline typed the new search criteria into the application and pressed Entrée to retrieve the results.

Several moments passed by as Caroline scrolled through numerous listings that did not measure up to her stringent requirements. One of the listings, however, jumped out at Angela. It was an old, run-down property with overgrown weeds and no landscaping to speak of. The building itself had great potential, but in its current state was more unsightly than a heap of overgrown busted-up bricks.

"How about that one?" Angela asked.

"Oh yes, yes! I like the farmer's manor, too," she said and enlarged the property listing to full view. It's a bargain at €650,000."

"Not that one… This one!" Angela pointed to the small icon of the hideous mansion at the bottom of the screen.

"Oh, no No NO! Not that disgusting, mound of abomination… That will not do!" Caroline said emphatically as the hideous mansion property listing came to full view on the screen.

"Why?"

Caroline threw a blank, frustrated glance at Angela. "Is it not… obvious? It's a mess! Many bugs, broken foundation and unsightly bricks, many leaking spots throughout and nobody has lived there for over two decades. It has Les Fantômes… Ghosts!" she said with big, scary eyes and a very convincing expression. Perhaps she saw one once…

"Perfect! I want to see that one ASAP!"

"I will show you the farmer's manor first. If you still

want to see this stinking old wreck afterwards, I will show it to you.

"Excellent, Caroline. When can I see it?"

"I'll call you tomorrow. I need to make a few phone calls first."

"Okay, I'll use this time to get myself settled in. See you tomorrow, Caroline." Angela was excited about the old mansion, but at the same time, she knew that €600,000 was a little beyond her comfort zone, especially given that the massive amount of renovations would swallow every bit of her available capital.

Caroline walked Angela to the front door and waved good-bye. Her instincts told her the young lady would choose the hideous mansion over the much more suitable farmer's manor. What Angela did not know yet, however, was that many contractors had walked away from the mansion in the past. There was a reason why the local bank still owned this property after so many years. Nobody wanted it… until now.

Peter Breeden

SEVEN – CHÂTEAU FRANÇAIS ET LE MANOIR!

The in-flight Internet service proved to be very helpful for Phillip. He found three stately castles for sale, as well as a real estate agent during the overnight flight to France, which began at San Francisco international airport, connected at John F. Kennedy international airport in New York, again at Charles De Gaulle international airport in Paris and finally landed at Bordeaux international airport in Mérignac at 10:35 the following morning. The red-eye flight took a toll on him, but not before he let everybody know about his success. "J'ai trouvé trois châteax!" he said aloud and very persuasively during his flight, much to the displeasure of those relaxing or sleeping around him. He was learning to speak French using the Berlitz Self-Teacher French paperback. My grandson has always shown an unyielding passion for his dreams, the type of passion that often rockets a person toward incredible achievement. For Phillip, the process of realizing a dream was the astonishing and incredibly fulfilling journey that fed his soul.

Phillip landed in Bordeaux a day after Angela had settled into an enchanting B&B, Le Pruneau en Vol, in Agen. He purchased a brand new, limited edition, ground pounding, quad-turbo W16 Bugatti Veyron Super Sport (with dual black intakes) right off the Bordeaux Exotic Car showroom floor and c-a-l-m-l-y drove it to Agen. This car was… ferocious. At the back of his mind, he had already convinced himself to unleash the Little Monster on the famous Autobahn in Germany once it was properly broken in. He was now ready for the next big adventure in his life to begin.

Phillip arrived in Agen at 4:00 that afternoon. He decided to stop off at the local grocery store for some toiletries and other miscellaneous items before checking into his room at the Palais des Pruneaux. He pulled up to L'Épicerie Gregoire on rue Voltaire and parked the Little Monster at the back of the lot away from the other cars. "Please save me from the door ding gremlins," he whispered in prayer as he scanned the parking lot for hostile autos.

Feeling reassured that Little Monster was strategically parked well enough to fend off the gremlins; he jogged across the parking lot to the entrance of the grocery store, unknowingly cutting off Angela at the store entrance in the process and capturing the attention of several teenagers skateboarding into the parking lot.

"Nice one Slick," she mumbled to herself, and then entered the grocery store. Curiosity captured her senses as she watched him running about the store, quickly gathering items in his arms and dropping them just as fast. She picked up the Tylenol and toothbrush that he dropped as he hurried around the corner into the next aisle.

"Pardon, monsieur? Allô," she said as the man, obviously not French, finally turned and stared at her with a bewildered expression. "Uhm… you dropped your deodorant," she said bending down to pick up the item off the floor, "and your Tylenol and toothbrush, as well."

"Oh, thank you! Sorry. I was in such a rush to…" Feeling overly embarrassed to say he was in a rush to get back to his hot little sports car, he, instead, remained at a loss for words.

"No worries," she said with an amused smile, handing him the dropped items. "Have a nice day."

Phillip returned the smile and watched the lovely woman with the very long legs as she turned and headed towards the fruit and vegetables. Her cell phone rang at that instant and he overheard her short conversation: "Hi Caroline. Yes, tomorrow morning at 8:30 is perfect! See you then. Bye." She then bent down to pat a Seeing Eye dog that, for obvious reasons, seemed to adore her.

Door ding gremlins crept back into his mind as he stood there a moment longer. He then made a mad dash for the cashier, paid his bill and hurried out the sliding door to the parking lot where Little Monster sat with a number of high school students standing around her in awestruck admiration. "Too late… finger and paw prints everywhere," he mumbled to himself as he approached the young bandits with his well contrived "cool dude" smirk stretched across his face.

Phillip spent the following morning meeting with his agent, Ben, short for Benoît, to discuss the castles he wanted to inspect, while Angela was across town meeting up with Caroline at the real estate/immobilier office. Angela pulled up beside Caroline's beautiful red convertible.

"Are you ready to see some lovely manors, ma chérie?"
"Yes! I'm very excited, actually. I can't wait!"
"Good. Let's go. We'll take my car."
"This is a beautiful convertible. S-e-x-y too! Italian?"

Caroline smiled and adjusted her sunhat. "It is a 2010 Alfa Romeo 8C Spider," she said as they drove off to the farmer's manor on the outskirts of town. Angela absorbed everything as it passed by: the beautiful town of Agen with its age-old architecture, the fragrant and appealing countryside and the locals navigating their way through the day. It was a delight to the senses.

Angela's eyes widened with excitement as they drove into the farmer's mansion. It was a beautiful seven-bedroom mansion on about five acres, or two hectares, of land. The property belonged to a well-to-do plum farmer before he sold everything and retired. The gardens and trees were well manicured on the lot and the front of the mansion showed very well. There was no work to be done here, but it was a good example of what her hideous mansion flip would look like when renovations were complete. Angela toured the property, inside and out with Caroline, knowing full well she wouldn't buy it. She did get some great ideas, though: the well balanced landscaping with trees and rose gardens throughout, the Koi pond, the stone work and leaded windows were nice, and the grand staircase was very well done in marble and solid acacia wood. The windows, however, looked naked without shutters.

Caroline noticed that Angela was taking notes as they passed through each room of the old place. When they returned to the grand foyer together after several hours of intense property inspection, she was curious to know what Angela thought about the mansion.

"So, tell me what you think?"

"It certainly is beautiful. I like the grand staircase, and the stonework around the exterior of the house is very appealing. I want to see more mansions before I make my decision, if that's okay? I'm looking for something that I can make my very own, put my own mark on it, you know?"

"Okay, then. How about some lunch, and then afterwards we can tour the run-down mansion?"

"Excellent idea," Angela confirmed as they walked back to the car.

Phillip and Ben decided to look at Le Beau Pruneau Château first. It was the largest and most awe-inspiring castle on his list, and the only one that ran goose bumps up his spine. The magnificent four-century-old Renaissance château sat facing southward from the top of a gently sloping hill in the middle of one hundred and four hectares of pristine land. The lengthy driveway to the château was lined on either side by evenly spaced, tall coniferous trees that faded into open land as the castle came into full view.

"Good Lord! That's HUGE!" were Phillip's first words as they approached the colossal château.

"Welcome to Le Beau Pruneau Château, Phillip."

"Sold!"

"Mon Dieu! Sérieusement, Phillip? You are joking, right… n'est-ce pas? You have not seen the place, yet. Phillip… Phillip!"

Phillip could hardly believe what he was seeing, which apparently interfered with his ability to hear Ben. When the car finally arrived at the front of the château, he jumped out of Ben's mint condition vintage Mercedes Bens' sedan and slowly turned three hundred and sixty degrees, recording every detail of the property in his photographic memory. The château stood commandingly behind him much like a medieval battalion of troops stands behind its fearless leader before the battle. A spectacular three-tier fountain with horses and statues stood between him and massive front grounds that stretched far beyond a scattered cluster of trees in the distance. When he finally found his tongue, he looked at Ben and simply said, "Show me everything!"

"But, of course, Phillip!" Ben agreed euphorically with happy thoughts of a big commission payday running through his head.

Angela and Caroline arrived at the run-down mansion sitting on three hectares of wildly overgrown property early that afternoon. A pungent odor of foul, rotting fruit greeted them when Caroline opened the front door.

"I think I am going to lose my lunch," Caroline said with a look of noxious retreat painted across her face. "Let's leave now and forget we ever saw this place," Caroline suggested.

Angela's nose twitched at first detection of the odor. She reflexively pinched her nostrils to lessen the stench. However, she wasn't about to let a little stinky smell, okay… a *big* stinky smell scare her away.

"Let's check it out. We're here now, anyways. It might not be a serious issue at all."

Caroline just laughed in disbelief and proceeded inside with her client. She covered her nose and mouth with her expensive Hermès scarf, which she would immediately send to the dry cleaners before the day was done.

Angela quickly located the source of the odor in the cellar. "Broken prune juice bottles," she said, pointing to the fallen shelves of prune preserves. "That's an easy fix," she continued.

"Some dirty beast of an infected wild animal must have crawled through that broken window and contaminated everything down here," Caroline said and pointed to the damaged window by the pile of broken crates along the cellar wall.

"I think you are right, judging by the stench and mess of things around here. The foundation seems solid, though. No leaks, and I could make a fabulous wine cellar down here. Let's head back to the main floor. How many bedrooms are there?"

"Twelve."

"Wow, five more bedrooms than the farmer's manor. Bathrooms?"

"Ten," Caroline said reluctantly.

"Nice. Show me the kitchen," she said, observing the filthy doublewide grand staircase made of solid marble as they passed.

"The kitchen is this way. Did you notice that the staircase and second floor banisters are wobbly and unsafe, ma chérie; see?" she said and grabbed a hold of one handrail, swinging it back and forth. The entire handrail and second floor balustrade began to creak and move like a snake. A decorative baluster shook loose from the second floor balustrade and ricocheted off the ground floor.

"Yikes! That's not very good," she agreed. "The steps are made of pure marble, I see. This is something I would have installed myself at great cost. The banisters are obviously damaged, but they can be replaced with a much better choice of hand crafted wood or custom designed wrought-iron railing with a more appealing, modern design."

"This is true, but that won't be cheap."

Angela nodded her head in agreement as they made their way to the spacious kitchen at the back of the mansion.

"Oh my, my... This is very doable," Angela commented as she entered the huge cobweb-infested kitchen with a series of bright, airy windows facing the tangled mess of overgrown weeds, shrubs and trees in the backyard. "This kitchen is enormous!"

"Disgusting!" Caroline remarked and frowned at the

unsavory state of the kitchen. She glanced down to make sure she hadn't stepped in something undesirable in her $800 pair of black web-strapped satin heels.

"I l-o-v-e, absolutely love, Love, LOVE the antique spiral staircase," Angela said ardently and ran her fingers along the beautiful, cobweb infested, dust covered wrought iron railings.

Angela scanned the moldings around the floor and ceiling and immediately fell in love with the design. She then inspected the hard wood floors, counters, sinks, faucets, and ovens and finally looked at the window frames. Peering through the window, beyond the tangled mess, she saw what appeared to be the most magnificent castle she had ever laid eyes upon.

"That is one HUGE castle!" she whispered just loud enough for Caroline to overhear and walk over to the window beside her.

"Yes, it is very impressive, indeed. Le Beau Pruneau Château, currently for sale at just over €55 million. Interested?" Caroline said with a carefree chuckle.

"Hah ha, maybe in another lifetime. It's a smidge over my budget, unfortunately."

Both ladies looked at one another and smiled in that daydream state of mind that so often accompanies the "If only I could have that…" wish of a lifetime.

Back at Le Beau Pruneau Château, Ben and Phillip had managed to partially inspect three of the five levels of the château. The East and West Wings, towers and turrets of the château would have to be inspected tomorrow. The East Wing included the quarters for the landscape, orchard, maintenance and equestrian crews while the West Wing was home to the Butler and Chauffeur, as well as the culinary and cleaning crews.

Phillip had already spent the better half of a day walking through the first three levels with Ben, including the first level that opened up from the Grand Ballroom onto a spectacular backyard terrace and Olympic sized pool. He was starting to feel hunger pains and exhaustion was beginning to set in.

The stairs to the fourth level led them to an spacious Recreation Hall with a sizable indoor pool and lounging area that opened up to a rather large and undeniably beautiful walkout overlooking the expansive backyard of the property. Suddenly, Phillip was no longer tired!

"Oh, I like this wide open area, Ben," he said, stepping into the cavernous hall and walking by the pool towards the walkout. "Nice touch with the indoor pool, too."

"And quite the engineering feat, as well. The entire West side of this floor is a water purification and treatment area, which sits directly below the water tanks," Ben explained, pointing to the doors at the end of the hall. "The rooftop is designed to capture rainwater and funnel it to several large holding tanks on the fifth floor, which is directly and conveniently above the purification area."

Phillip nodded and amusingly clasped his hands behind his back as Ben continued describing the unique features.

"The water is then used for multiple purposes, which include servicing the bathrooms, pools and château maintenance activities. There are also several wells, which supply the entire safe drinking water needs for the property. As you can see outside, there is a stream that winds around the plum orchard toward the back end of the property. This water is used to irrigate the orchard and gardens throughout the property."

"Heck, with all this water we could start a business," Phillip replied. "We'll call it Agen Spirits and flavor it with prune nectar!"

"Hell yeah," Ben agreed, totally missing Phillip's sarcasm and need to simply take it all in without the fancy tour guide spiel.

"The East side of the fourth floor is an expansive library that actually continues via a spiral staircase from the third level. The entire fifth floor including East and West Wings is the observation level of the château. You can see the full perimeter of the property from this floor without having to go up on the roof or to one of the six turrets. This is what I call The Men's Den!"

"Fantastic, Ben! And where is The Women's Den?" Phillip replied.

"You're standing in it!"

"What? The ladies get the Recreation Hall?" he said with a look of disappointment.

"Well... Phillip... it's a little comfy this room, no?"

Phillip laughed and sauntered out onto the spacious walkout. The view was simply incredible, except... there was some hideous building at the far end of the property, and it was ruining the view!

"Ben, what is that junk at the back corner of the property? That's not a garbage dump, is it? It's destroying the view."

Benoît looked at the run-down mansion in the distance and grimaced. His worst fear, that he would lose the sale, was coming true. He had a plan though...

"This old piece of property, nobody wants, Phillip. The bank would be happy to sell it to you for pennies, probably only €400,000. You could then do as you pleased with it." Ben looked intently at Phillip for a favorable answer.

"Alright then. We'll leave it for now and I will think about what to do with it. In the meantime, I want to purchase this lovely *undersized* château today. Let's get it done!"

"Okay, monsieur Phillip. This is great news. You won't be disappointed, I promise you."

Ben was all smiles as they headed back down the stairs to the car. Phillip was already making plans to improve the château and that ugly mansion… it had to go!

"Oh, I forgot to mention that the underground garage is accessed through the hidden remote doors," Ben said nonchalantly, pointing to the hidden doors as they were getting into the Mercedes. "The contents of the château, including the old cars in the garage are included in the list price of the château."

"Old cars?" Phillip paused and looked at Ben intently over the roof of the Mercedes.

"Yes, apparently there are some old rusty bolts… excusez-moi, rust buckets, stored in the garage and a recently purchased Peugeot. Unfortunately, there is nothing to get excited over, as far as I understand. A car is a car, no?"

Phillip nodded his head in acknowledgement, and then jumped into the car as he added another note to the list on his cell phone application: "Inspect the garage and old cars." The top priorities were to have his lawyers in Palo Alto inspect the property title and relevant paper work, then purchase the estate and organize the contractors to begin renovations. The château, though very impressive, would need extensive repairs throughout.

Peter Breeden

EIGHT – THE HIDEOUS MANSION

Angela and Caroline wrapped up the mansion inspection later that afternoon, and then headed back to the office to work on an offer for the property. Caroline was not that surprised that her client chose the run-down mansion, but was a little concerned about the amount of work that lay ahead for the young, adventuresome lady.

"D'accord, ma chérie. The bank is asking €625,000 for the property. I personally know that they will sell for much less just to get it off their hands."

"I agree, Caroline. Let's make an offer of €400,000 As Is. That's my best and final price and it's good until the end of the day."

"Excellent. I'll send the offer to the bank right away. I need you to sign these papers first, and then I'll get started!"

Angela sat in the posh real estate coffee room watching France and Spain battle one another on the large screen plasma TV while Caroline began negotiations with the bank. The excitement of FIFA World Cup Soccer had everybody, including Henry, the office receptionist, glued to the action. Angela was already feeling passionately connected to the French team, even though they were behind by a goal. Caroline walked in just as France tied the game.

"OUI! Score for France!" Henry hollered and clapped fervently for his favorite player. "Oh la la… mes beaux hommes… mes joureurs! Fantastique!" he shouted and did a little arms-in-the-air booty-dance in front of Angela.

"Henry! S'il vous plaît!" Caroline said sternly and pointed in the direction of Henry's desk. The poor fellow slumbered back to his desk and received a firm pinch on the ass when he passed Caroline.

"Ouille!" he exclaimed in protest and kept going. Caroline and Henry were best friends since childhood. Their friendship and love for one another was like the ties under a railway track, solid and supportive.

"The bank has rejected your offer, Angela. They returned at €500,000 and the offer is good until the end of the day."

Angela showed her disappointment as she rose from the butter-soft leather couch. "Well, it's a good thing I don't fall in love with a piece of property before I buy it, then." She reached out to shake Caroline's hand. "Thank you for your time today, Caroline. I'll call you tomorrow to schedule… "

"That's it! You mean to say that you are no longer interested in the mansion?"

"That's correct. It would be far beyond my budget at €500,000 given the extent of the renovations. We can look at other properties, though. I'll give you a call in a couple of days. Hopefully, by then I will have a better idea of what is out there."

"Alright, I'll let the bank know. I think they might be a little shocked with your decision."

"They shouldn't be… the papers did say 'best and final

price,' right?"

"Yes, but everything can be negotiated in France, darling," she responded with a sweet smile and a reassuring gesture of her hands.

"Well, I guess that's good for me then. Hey, where can a girl get a …"

Angela was interrupted by Caroline's cell phone. It was the bank calling to see if there was any progress.

"Allô! Non, elle n'accept pas, malheusement. Mais… Pardon? Oui… Attendez un moment," Caroline placed her cell phone against her breast and snapped her fingers to regain Angela's attention.

"Angela! Angela, great news! The bank will accept your offer of €400,000, as is. Is this agreeable to you, ma chérie?"

"Yes, Caroline. Sold!"

"Magnifique!" Caroline rejoiced aloud with Angela and confirmed the sale over the phone with the bank representative. "Elle l'accept, Au revoir! Oui, Je rappelerai!"

"It's official, Angela. Congratulations, the hideous mansion project is all yours!"

"Thank you so much, Caroline."

"Come see me tomorrow morning, my darling, and we can finish the business then, okay?"

"Perfect, bye for now," she laughed and skipped out the door.

The next day, Phillip found himself at Ben's office on a conference call with his lawyers and Andrew.

"Yes, everything looks pretty solid, Phillip," boomed Jake and Gillian's voices over the conference speakerphone from the law offices in Palo Alto. "The Beau Pruneau estate was put on the open market when the owner died last year," Gillian continued. "The proceeds from the sale of the property are to be split equally among his surviving children."

"Thus, everything, including the vintage cars in the garage, is included in the sale price," Jake added. "Judging from the vehicle ownership descriptions, you might want to mosey on down to the garage and have a look at your… rust buckets," he said jovially.

"One other thing that you might not know," Gillian continued. "The estate also comes with ten highly prized, purebred Arabian horses. You l-u-c-k-y *bastard!*"

"Nice, hah ha," Phillip managed.

"The horses are currently residing at the Agen Equestrian Park, which is managed by an old friend of the previous owner. The stables on the castle grounds are fully equipped to handle fifteen horses at any given time. So, when you're ready, you can go retrieve your *rust bucket* horses from Monsieur Sebastian Riviera at the equestrian park!"

"Thanks Gillian. I know how much you love horses. When I get this place under control, you and Jake can come and see the place… the horses."

"Yes, sign us up for that trip, Phillip. Thank you!" Jake and Gillian's excited voices bounced back and forth over the conference phone.

"What about me!" Andrew protested. "Am I just a pee-on here or what?"

"Come anytime, buddy. You don't need an invitation," Phillip said reassuringly. "Actually, I could use your…"

"Okay, stop right there…" Andrew responded. "In case you forgot, I *am* running a major international software company here… ALL BY MYSELF!"

"Alright, alright. I do, however, expect you to travel here in a couple of months when I have the place in a respectable state."

"Sounds good, Bubba," Andrew replied.

"I have one last concern, folks," Phillip continued, as he moved closer to the conference microphone. "There's a run-down piece of property that I want to purchase and clean up. It's at the end of the estate and is actually a major eye-sore."

"Okay Ben," said Jake, "can you please forward the respective paperwork for this property today?"

"Absolutely. I'll send that to you immediately, and also open negotiations with the seller, the local bank. Hopefully, we can wrap this one up fairly quickly. The bank would love to unload this property, *tout de suite!*"

"Excellent, Ben. Thank you," said Gillian quickly in an effort to wrap up the call.

"Okay, folks… if there's nothing else?" Phillip said as he reached for the disconnect button on the speakerphone.

"No, nothing. Have fun, Phillip, and remember to keep in touch, compadre!" Andrew added affectionately.

"Right. Later!" he said, and then disconnected.

Phillip smiled at Ben and shook his hand. "Congratulations on a job well done, Ben. Don't spend it all in one place," he continued in reference to Ben's rather large commission payment.

"Oh, monsieur Phillip, I won't. I might have a petite drink tonight in celebration and maybe purchase the local hot spot café tomorrow."

"Good plan, mon amis. Call me when the deal for the abomination at the corner of my property is finalized."

"Yes, boss. I'll get right on it."

Angela made her way back to her newly purchased wreck and parked in the driveway with the full view of the manor facing her.

"Lord in Heaven! What have I got myself into?" she said,

staring at the massive building and slowly being squashed by the hefty weight of renovations weighing down upon her.

She immediately dialed her parents on her cell phone, but there was no answer. "Must be at the movies," she mumbled. She left a brief message on their answering service: "Hey Mom and Dad. I bought a mansion today. It's huge... fifteen bedrooms on three hectares, or rather, six and a half acres of land. It's beautiful and has great potential, but it's got a few issues with it..." she began to sob and immediately disconnected the call to avoid further embarrassment.

Feeling the overwhelming need to talk to Holly, she pressed her speed-dial buttons to quickly connect to Holly's home number. It was about 9:00 in the evening in Toronto.

Holly instinctively picked up her vibrating, bagpipe-chiming cell phone lying beside her on the bed. She was wearing her favorite pink and white nightie with cotton stuck between her toes and the latest Nora Roberts romance novel in her hand. She looked at the incoming call display-message, hoping it was Angela. *Sexy Senorita Calling* flashed across her screen. "Yay!" she cheered and answered the phone.

"It's about time you called!" Holly bellowed.

"Hi," Angela managed with a sob.

"Okay, what pile of manure did you step in now?"

"I bought a mansion..."

"You found one already? Congratulations! Why are you sobbing?"

"It has a few... minor issues..."

"Yes, like what?"

"It's kind of ... broken all over."

"What? You bought a broken mansion?"

"I can fix it!" Angela snapped defensively, wiping away

the tears.

"Uh huh! I can see that clearly now, judging from all your sobs. Just how broken is it? Send me a picture!"

"Hold on," she said climbing out of the car to take a picture of the front of the mansion with her cell phone camera. "I'm sending it now," she said and sent the picture to Holly's cell phone suddenly realizing that maybe it wasn't such a good idea sending it afterall.

"F-u-c-k, that's ugly!"

"Shut up!"

"You shut up! I'm sending this picture to your papa. He's soooo going to boot your arse!"

"Send that picture to anyone and you'll have one less friend to bitch at!"

The two friends carried on over the phone, bantering back and forth. This call was shaping up to be one of those lengthy three hour conversations. Angela buckled in for the long haul as she was not about to let Holly believe that she had made a huge mistake.

Phillip was standing on the fourth floor walkout inspecting the the rear westside tower and the backyard stables through a pair of binoculars, when he received the call from Ben. "Magnificent," he muttered to himself as he zoomed in on the heavy tractor equipment through one of the stable windows before he finally answered his bothersome cell phone.

"Hello."

"Hi Phillip. It's Benoît, here."

"Bonjour Ben. Everything okay?"

"Ahum, well… merde! I have some bad news, Phillip. The run-down mansion is sold. Some crazy woman paid 400,000 for it."

Phillip's eyes quickly shifted from the stables to the

hideous mansion at the far end of his property.

"What?"

"I'm sorry, Phillip."

"Ben, how could you let this happen? Crap! Who is she? Where can I find her?"

"You can call her agent, Caroline Beaujolais, at Beaujolais Immobilier (Real Estate) downtown. Apparently, the new owner is a foreigner and she wants to keep the mansion. She's going to renovate it... merde!"

"Awe, that's *j-e-e-e-e-u-s-t* beautiful! I need to deal with this mess right away, Ben," he said and ended the call.

Phillip ran out of the château and drove straight downtown, laying a bit of rubber in the process. He stormed into Beaujolais Immobilier and glared at the fellow behind the desk with the painfully correct sitting posture.

"I'm looking for Caroline, please."

Henry, detecting an overbearing, rude, opinionated, heterosexual man, decided to give him a hard time.

"En Français, s'il vous plait!" he insisted with an air of authority.

"Huh?"

"Exactement! Elle n'est pas la!" he stammered just as Caroline walked into the reception area to see what all the commotion was about.

"What's going on here?" she queried.

"You are a mess of a man!" Henry sniveled with a face resembling someone who just came across the most foul odor known to humankind.

Phillip's witty, irritated sense of humor kicked in. "I love you too, teddy bear."

Henry, infuriated now, was about to explode when Caroline pulled him to the side and sent him to the back office to take care of some filing.

"He's my guard dog. Pay no attention to him," Caroline

said passively as she reached out to shake Phillip's hand.

Phillip shook her hand and, in the process, couldn't help noticing the beautiful lady. She was every bit a supermodel with her fashionable form-fitting dress and stylish strappy four inch heels. *Beautiful stockings*, he thought to himself, *and the hair… a river of silk*!

Caroline, noticing that Phillip was attracted to her, quickly put the fire out. "And this is my Italian boyfriend, Maurizio," pointing to a picture of herself and her very beefy boyfriend hanging above the water cooler.

"Pardon me, Caroline. You are very beautiful."

Appreciating his honesty and a compliment, Caroline continued as if nothing had happened. "Thank you. Now, how can I help you Mr.…?"

"Phillip… Phillip Niles," he said with a polite smile, and then proceeded to his reason for coming. "I need to buy the run-down mansion behind Le Beau Pruneau Château."

"Well, you must be the new owner of that gorgeous little cottage on the hill."

"Indeed, I am. And now you can understand why I need to purchase and tear down that hideous pile of garbage!"

"Where were you last week…" she mumbled.

"Huh?"

"You are too late, monsieur! The property is sold to a very ambitious lady."

"Where can I find…"

"Angela? You might find her at the mansion, if you're lucky. She moves fast! Good luck to you, Phillip!" she said as he took off out the door.

Phillip drove directly to the run-down mansion from Caroline's office, occassionally losing the rear end around some sharp hillside corners in his haste. He pulled into the pot-holed driveway, making every effort to avoid bottoming out in his brand new Bugatti sports car, and cursing every inch of the way.

"Dambed pot holes… Holy Moses, look at that."

Standing before him was a tall woman in tight form-fitting jeans, leaning against her car. She was facing the building and talking on her cell phone.

Angela did not notice Phillip pull up behind her and get out of his car. When he stood beside her, removing his shades to see the decay of the building clearly, she jumped and quickly said goodbye to Holly.

"Hello," she said to Phillip, trying to remember where she had seen the fellow before.

"Hello again," he said with a look of incredulity on his face when he recognized her.

"I recognize you from somewhere."

"Uh huh… the grocery store. You were following me."

"That's it. What? I certainly was not following you. You dropped your load and I simply made you aware of your oversight."

"Right. Thank you again for that. I was rather preoccupied at the time," he said with a smirk. "This your place?"

"Yup! Just bought it. Why?"

"Nice, needs a bit of work, huh?"

"A bit…"

"I'm your distant neighbor, Phillip Niles, from down the road about a mile."

Angela stretched out her hand to greet the young fellow and noticed the sporty car parked behind her rental car from the corner of her eye. Must be daddy's money, she concluded. "Angela Portman. Nice to meet you. That your car?"

"Yup."

"Very nice ride."

"Thank you. So, can you envision gourmet meals in your kitchen, yet?"

"Hah ha. No, at least not yet, anyway. There's too much work to do."

Phillip chuckled. "Why don't you just tear it all down and start with something fresh, perhaps a modern manor?"

Angela, a little offended by the remark, snapped back. "That would be kind of a waste, don't you think... hot shot?"

"Nope," he said simply.

Angela felt the overwhelming need to defend her new home, but was determined to keep a civil mind.

"The foundation and structure are still in pretty good shape. And the inside has a lot of potential, not to mention some very valuable materials and craftmanship."

"Hmm. I would rip it down. It looks unsafe."

Angela studied him for a moment before responding. "Afraid of a little risk, aren't you?" she said calmly. "The cautious type, huh?" she added with an accusatory bite.

"Easy now, Peanut."

"Don't call me Peanut... Do I look five years old?"

"I'm just trying to be neighborly, Angel."

"It's Angela..." she said obstinately, squinting her eyes and shifting her position against the car.

"Sorry... A-n-g-e-l-a," he said appologetically. "Look, if you want to tear this place down, I'll help you. It a bloody eyesore and..."

"Why would I need your help?" she asked point-blank.

"Well, it's there if you need it," he said walking back to his car. "I'll drop by in a few days... see how you're doing..."

"Maybe you could use some help with that... pot belly," she added with an evil smirk across her face.

Phillip chuckled at the rather personal remark, and

nodded to Angela as he climbed back into his car. *I deserved it*, he thought to himself, acknowledging that he had gained a few pounds recently.

It might have just been bad luck, or maybe even a sign from above, but the moment Phillip took off in his shiney new sports car, Angela turned in shock to witness the rumbling and tumbling of a large section of the front west side, including the load bearing corner of the mansion.

"Awe... SHIT!" she managed pathetically and gave way to a heaving, sobering sob.

PART III

Peter Breeden

NINE – THE RENOVATIONS BEGIN

First thing the next day, after collecting her senses, Angela headed out to pick up a tarpaulin to cover the gaping exterior hole. She also ordered the matching stones, cinder blocks, mortar mix and a cement mixer to begin the repairs. She was surprised when the foundation repair specialist at the local hardware store said the materials would be delivered within the week. These things normally take longer in a small village. She also picked up a few things to begin the clean-up and repairs in the cellar, including new glass for the broken window where Caroline's so called 'dirty beast of an infected wild animal' entered unlawfully. In the spontaneous blend of events throughout the day, she chanced upon a sign along the road, 'Chiots à Vendre' and surrendered to the unrelenting barking of an old friend at the back of her head.

"Oh heck!" she mumbled. "It can't hurt to look."

She drove up the quaint farmhouse driveway and parked in front of the fancy trimmed porch, decorated with a stunning arrangement of weeping flowers swaying gently in their hanging baskets in the summer breeze. And then she saw the puppies, frolicking about as happy as can be, under a shady front yard tree.

"Awe... look at you Mr. Buckets of Love!" she whispered adoringly and bent down to pick up the Great Dane puppy jumping at her feet.

Needless to say, she ended up buying that Great Dane puppy and a second one, his sister, who spontaneously tackled her foot until Angela stopped snuggling her brother. The twosome soothed her wounded spirits. Sure, it was one more problem, two actually, to add to the mound of issues she was experiencing in her life, but the need for them overruled the day. Allow me to introduce you to HB, short for *Heartbreaker*, and his sister, BG, short for *Bodyguard*. At three and a half pounds each, the pair could melt your heart in two seconds flat!

Angela still missed her childhood dog, but also knew there would come a day when she would have room in her heart for another canine companion. It had been eight years since old Gusty laid down his head for the last time. Since then, the time never seemed to be quite right to replace her beloved golden retriever. I guess the old fellow was speaking to her today. "Time to move on, sweetheart," echoed at the back of her head. "I miss you Gusty," she whispered aloud.

Phillip was settling into the third floor Grand Master Suite of his château when the construction crews and landscapers began to arrive and congregate outside.

"Pot belly!" he bellowed as he unpacked his suitcase lying on the enormous four-poster complete with full canopy and curtains. "Hot shot!" he continued, throwing his boxers in the antique dresser drawer. "Bitch!" he shouted and paused when he saw his disheveled self in the dresser mirror. "Pull yourself together, old man," he mumbled to himself and realized at that moment, he had not yet toured the Grand Master Suite.

The expansive chamber was furnished with period furniture throughout. It had a separate lounging area with dual walkouts overlooking front and back yards.

"I bet she's from the mid-west," he said pensively as he strolled through the lounge, past the grand marble fireplace and out to the walkout. He looked across the expansive property toward Angela's mansion and noticed that there was a huge blue tarpaulin pinned against the corner of the old house. "What the…" he started to speak and stopped to pull the binoculars from his side pouch. "Oh, I see. Making the place pretty, are we? Unbelievable!" he said, shaking his head and walking towards the private study on the other side of the suite. The study connected to the third floor library through a secret entrance, which Phillip poked his head through and made a brief comment, "Nice!"

The Grand Master ensuite bathroom had a central open fireplace surrounded by an oversized Jacuzzi tub and two separate shower stalls. There was also a separate entrance to a huge 2000 square foot dressing room on the other side. Phillip stood in front of the expansive vanity mirror to inspect the French-style double basins elegantly embedded in the marble counter top, and then hastily turned towards the toilet and bidet, and pulled down his trousers.

"Allô… Allô?" echoed a voice from the other side of the wide open double doors. Phillip, dumbfounded by the size of the roomy bathroom, forgot to shut the ensuite doors.

"Yes?" Phillip growled, annoyed about being caught in the middle of a wiz.

"I am applying for the Butler position," replied the steady, calm and dignified voice.

Phillip took a few moments to process the distinctly

French accent. The fellow was well dressed in fashionable trousers, unshaven and a little disheveled, much like he was a few minutes earlier. Judging by the hair and the skin, he must be around 53 years of age.

"Well, come back tomorrow then."

"My name is Réginald Beauchamp," he continued. "I have worked here at the château for the last thirty-five years assisting my father, François, the Head Butler."

"So, why don't I just hire your father, then?"

"You have three construction crews downstairs glaring at each other and various other landscaping and housekeeping candidates standing by for the available château positions. I could take care of that now for you. I know where to send the contractors and which of the workers to hire based on reputation and performance. My father is dead."

"Oh! I'm sorry."

"He died making love, so there is no sadness. Too much French wine and a shockingly beautiful woman, we think…" he said with a hint of a smile.

Phillip chuckled, and then quickly ran through the list of urgent jobs on his cell phone notepad:

a. Hire fulltime Butler and Housekeeper.
b. Hire fulltime cooking and cleaning staff.
c. Hire fulltime Head Landscaper.
d. Hire fulltime Head of Maintenance.
e. Inspect and repair all windows.
f. Polish the Ballroom floor.
g. Repair damaged lighting throughout.
h. Patch interior cracks and paint where required.
i   Secure any loose railings, banisters and piping.
j. Repair all leaky plumbing.
k. Update draperies and carpets where required

l. Inspect electrical systems.
m. Inspect boiler room and radiant heating system.
n. Inspect all fireplaces.
o. Install first aid stations throughout each level and purchase modern pool safety equipment.
p. Inspect the exterior of all buildings, top to bottom.

"Send me your list, monsieur, 05.55.32.42.52," Réginald said, waving his state-of-the-art cell phone at Phillip and giving him his number. "I can hire everybody through my sister's employment agency downtown. Makes things very simple for us, no?"

"Very well, Regi. You're hired! Send me your sister's information before the day is done. I expect a full briefing tomorrow morning at 8:00 in the main foyer."

"Bon! I will address the confusion downstairs and provide a very brief update in two hours."

Phillip watched the funny fellow leave. He had an unusual way of walking, almost like he was trying to hurry, but something was holding him back by the shorts. Perhaps his father had reached out from his place of rest and tied a harness around his son's waist to slow him down. Overly ambitious people spend their time rushing through life, with one eye fixated on the second hand of a stopwatch, and tend to forget that the world won't stop spinning if all is not done by the end of the day. Tomorrow is coming. One cannot stop that from happening. One can, however, spend a lifetime rushing around and never really know what it feels like to enjoy the myriad of roses that bloom in the summer… until it's too late.

Phillip walked across the bedroom with his laptop by his side, up a few steps to the raised study and sat down at the desk.

"I need some maps in here," he said, looking at the walls, "and a dart board!"

He powered-up his computer and connected to the local wireless network to access the Niles and Pikes Inc. secure intranet site. He worked for a while addressing company concerns and responding to emails. Then that subconscious force we call Thoughtlessness smacked him upside the head, and he reached for his phone to call… me!

"Niles Estate Premium Artichokes, Charles here," I bellowed from a phone in the barn where I was working on the Plymouth. It was evening and I had decided to work under the hood a bit before calling it a day.

"Hello Grandpa," he said affectionately when I answered the phone.

"Lug Nut! I was just thinking about you. You had me a little worried."

"Sorry, sorry. I got caught up in things here and one thing led to another. Everything okay there?"

"Well, do you want the bad news first?"

"Uhg! No, give me the good news first."

"Alright then! I'm fit as a fiddle according to the doctor; a little constipated, but apparently that's normal."

"Excellent! Have some prunes!"

"Hah ha. Okay."

"What's the bad news?"

"It seems to me we cracked the power steering high pressure tube on our little test drive the other day. There's a slow leak and no power steering."

"Yikes! I guess your massive forearm strength is out of the question, huh?"

"Yes, except for when I pop you on the noggin for breaking my Isabella."

"Sorry."

"No worries. I was going to drop the engine soon anyways. What's going on in your world?"

"I bought a huge castle. When are you coming?"

"Hah ha. Atta boy! I'll come when you have things in order and a sexy masseuse on the payroll to rub my achy back."

"Okay, Gramps. Give me a month."

"Oh, and one other thing…"

Uh huh?"

"Find some time to date a few ladies."

"I've already met two. One is already spoken for and is quite happy with her massively built Italian boyfriend."

"Sounds like trouble. Who else you got?"

"The other one is all hisses and nails and loaded with venom! An absolute nightmare if you ask me."

"Hmm… That's the one, boy. Find her inner weakness and go win her heart."

"What? You suck at matchmaking!"

"Okay, then. Prove me wrong."

"Forget it. I'm not touching the Fire Ant Queen!"

"Suit yourself."

"I'll think about it. Hey, I've got someone knocking on my door. I'll call you soon."

"Alright…"

"Love you gramps," he concluded and then disconnected.

I hung up my barn phone and slowly turned around to stare at the engine in my old Plymouth. The boy has a tremendous amount of ambition, I thought to myself, perhaps even too much.

The first major project Angela tackled after covering the gaping exterior hole with blue tarpaulin was to eliminate the fermenting stench in the cellar and do an overall clean up and repair of the area down there. She began by removing and relocating all pruning jars, broken or otherwise, to the two dumpsters, which were delivered that morning to her front yard. Each trip she made to the dumpsters allowed her to reinspect the exterior condition of the building and strategize how to fix the ugly stains, vines and cracks along the walls. It was then that she noticed the huge stump on the west side of the building and concluded that, at some point in the history of the building, the huge century-old coniferous tree that once stood there, fell on the mansion and compromised the integrity of the structure. She would have to do a complete visual inspection and repair of the walls and foundation.

"Awe SHIT!" she moaned aloud, capturing the attention of the puppies playing in the yard.

She immediately grabbed her phone and ordered an industrial sized sandblaster and a lift capable of reaching all three stories. The rock walls needed to be thoroughly cleaned so she could inspect the condition of the mortar holding everything together. She then made a note to purchase a heavy duty generator and return the rental car. It was time to buy a pickup truck.

The broken cellar window frame was still in good shape. It needed a fresh coat of paint and some caulking, but that could wait for a while. The new sheet of glass fit neatly into the frame, as expected.

"Et Voila!" she said, happy to have the window fixed.

She left the cellar windows open to allow the industrial sized fans to blow out any remaining odors lingering in the cellar. In one afternoon and evening, she had managed to remove the unwanted rubbish from the cellar and pile it in a safe place where it could be burned. She also disinfected the entire unfinished basement from ceiling to floor, including the area where the preserves had been and moved some old stinky furniture to the garbage bins. The couch was too heavy and its removal would have to wait until she found some help. Judging by the impression in the corner of the couch, the unlawful beast had made its bed right here. On closer inspection, she discovered the couch was covered in fleas.

"You've got to be kidding!" she shouted, stamping her feet on the concrete cellar floor. "A flea infestation!" Subconsciously, she began scratching herself.

She immediately threw all the couch cushions and pillows out the window, and then ran upstairs, returning a few seconds later with an axe. She didn't stop chopping until the entire couch was in easily movable pieces, which she then quickly threw out the window or carried outside to the fire pit.

When she had finished throwing the last of the flea-infested cushions into the garbage bins, she sat on the front steps with HB and BG and wiped the sweat away from her forehead.

"Mommy needs to clean a room on the first level tomorrow so she can move out of the B&B and into… our new home! What do you think about that?" she said as little tails and bodies wagged back and forth in delight.

Phillip woke up early the next morning and headed straight for the Recreation Hall pool on the fourth floor. He decided to restart his regular swimming routine each morning. That meant at least 40 minutes of front crawl swimming at a medium pace each day. Swimming was also a great way for him to plan his day; he rarely thought about swimming while he was swimming. Instead, he planned his day as he swam along the black line at the bottom of the pool.

I need to inspect the towers today, he thought to himself as he approached the end of the pool and performed a flip-turn. *I also need to inspect the stables, call Sebastian at the Equestrian Park and touch base with Réginald's sister at the employment agency.*

What else? Hmm, oh yes, remember to put the remote garage door opener in the car so I can get into the garage.

The first thing Phillip saw when he climbed out of the pool was Réginald.

"Morning Regi," he said, and took the towel hanging from Réginald's arm.

"Good morning, monsieur! Can I take your order for breakfast?"

Phillip tossed Réginald an amusing glace. "You cook, too?"

"Oui, monsieur, but not today... I have hired the Head Housekeeper and housekeeping staff, including the kitchen staff. They are waiting for your breakfast order and any special meal requirements that you may have."

"That's fabulous, Regi. Thank you. I'll have fried eggs, fried tomatoes, hash browns, two slices of toast with tea and orange juice. Oh! And HP sauce, please."

"Very well, then, anything else for you, monsieur... a newspaper, perhaps?"

"Yes thanks... Uhm, I don't like turnips or parsnips and I'm allergic to pork... makes me stinky." Phillip added.

"Bon! See you in the dining hall in fifteen minutes!" he said and promptly walked out of the Reception Hall to relay the information to the kitchen staff.

Phillip stepped out onto the walkout and glanced over at Angela's place. No activity yet this morning, he noticed. *Lazy bum*, he thought amusingly to himself. "Someone needs her beauty sleep," he muttered aloud.

Angela had been on the go since 6:00 that morning, contrary to Phillip's wild assumptions. She checked out of the pet-friendly B&B after an early breakfast and dropped the puppies off at the mansion before heading out to the local Ford dealer to inspect the pickup trucks. Her uncle, a professional contractor for over 40 years, used Ford trucks exclusively. So, she test drove, and then purchased, a blue Ford Ranger Wildtrak, which would be delivered the following day to her front doorstep. She then dropped off the rental car at the local car rental outlet and picked up some groceries and fine Belgian chocolates before making her way home in time for lunch.

"You bought this place?" the taxi driver commented as they pulled up the driveway. "It has ghosts, non? Boo, ahah ha!"

Peter Breeden

TEN – THINGS GET COMPLICATED

"I want this place in good order within a month!" Phillip told Réginald at their 8:00 morning meeting.

Réginald looked at Phillip with a concerned demeanor and unconsciously twitched his shoulder. Then he scratched his freshly shaven face and made a gesture with his hands.

"Might I suggest a different approach, monsieur?"

"Of course, what do you recommend?"

"Pick two areas of the château that need the most attention, and fix those areas first. Then we move onto something else."

"Nah, it would take far too long to finish all the projects on my list. Let's get it all done now, this month, tout fini! I want to invite my family and friends here at the end of July."

"Oh la, la, monsieur! Ce n'est pas possible! You will never have this château fixed completely in your lifetime. It's far too big."

Phillip stared at Réginald with a disturbed, pissed-off disposition, and then decided to make things difficult for him.

"Why?"

Réginald, an astute man of 56 years and knowing full well what Phillip was up to, responded with a deeply passionate, head bucking, hair-tossing Oscar-worthy performance.

"Do you want to have contractors fighting in the hallways? Do you want all the toxic fumes in your lungs… our lungs, we live here now too, Mon Dieu! The château cannot cope with heavy electrical demands and water would run low very *rapidment*. And, do you expect me to direct everybody without major problems? *Catastrophe!!!!* Merde… Merde!"

"Ah… F-U-C-K!" he responded, throwing his Tilley hat to the floor. He stared at Réginald with a look of defeat and felt a sob coming on. His eyes went a little glassy as he scratched his head in thought, but he managed to escape embarrassment by quickly ending the conversation. "Alright, Regi. You have my list of projects. Let's get the important ones done first: the Conservatory and the Ballroom."

"Right, monsieur," he said quickly and they both started off on their separate ways.

"Oh, one more thing," said Phillip turning quickly.

"Yes?"

"Where is the garage door opener?"

"You will find it in the Peugeot sports car parked in the garage downstairs. Go this way," he said, pointing to the double doors at the back of the main floor grand staircase.

Phillip made his way downstairs and turned down a hallway leading to the entrance of the garage in the East wing. He entered the garage through a series of doors, probably designed to keep the fumes from entering the upper floors of the château. His jaw dropped when he entered the enormous underground garage equipped with a full mechanics bay including car lift and tools, tools and more tools.

"Oh my, Lord. This is... Hey!" he said suddenly, noticing the five cars parked side-by-side in six of the twenty available parking spaces. The shapes underneath the car covers were starting to give him goose bumps!

One-by-one, he uncovered each car and performed a funny little celebratory dance in front of each as he continued down the row of immaculately maintained antique gems.

"A 1926 Rolls-Royce Phantom I," he gasped for air.

"A 1939 MG TB Roadster," he whispered. "Grandpa would love *rolling* in this."

"Wow! A rare 1948 Tucker," he stumbled and nearly knocked off the side mirror.

"A 1937 Bugatti... No way," he bellowed, jumping back in disbelief.

Given that there were only seventeen of these models ever made, I'd be dancing too. In fact, when I found out, I did a silly dance and wrenched my ankle in the process.

"I know what this one is," he said looking at the silhouette of the next car. "Oh my, my," he said as he gently pulled the cover off the 1965 mint condition Ford Shelby Cobra. "What a find!"

The last car was a brand new Peugeot RCZ Limited Edition sports car. He climbed in, pressed the button on the remote garage door opener attached to the visor and cranked the engine.

"Nice," he said driving up the ramp into the front driveway through the doublewide garage doors.

Pulling his cell phone from his belt clip, he pressed the quick dial keys. "Hi Grandpa." he said.

"Hello, Lug Nut."

"Guess what I found in the garage?" he said coolly.

Angela was parched and starving. The early afternoon sun was heating up her sand blast helmet, roasting her head within and dehydration was beginning to set in. She was so tightly caught up in sand blasting the exterior walls that she forgot all about lunch. She was covered in grime from head to toe and grumpiness was beginning to show its ugly head. *Twenty more minutes,* she thought to herself, and she would stop for lunch. She had managed to completely sand blast two of the four walls, top to bottom, by lunchtime. She was so involved in her work that she didn't notice Phillip pull into the driveway and get out of his car.

"G-o-l-l-y, what a huge difference," she said leaning back on the lift to look at the clean wall.

"Missed a spot…" bellowed the deep voice behind her. Phillip pointed to the dark area under one of the second story windows.

"Were you born this annoying?" she replied coolly. "Go find a sandbox to play cars in. I'm busy here."

"How about this sandbox, hot shot?" he said bending down to pick up some dirt.

"Hah ha hee hee!" she giggled looking down at Phillip from her pneumatic lift. "Sure, you can play there if you like… as long as you don't mind doggie poop."

Phillip grimaced and wiped his hands on a rag sitting on the workbench.

They looked amusingly at one another for a moment, and then Angela lowered the lift, deciding to be more hospitable to her nosey neighbor.

"Have you had lunch, yet?" Phillip asked.

"Yes, I love the taste of freshly sand blasted rock wall. Would you like to sample some?" she offered, handing him the blaster gun and stepping down from the lift.

"I was thinking more on the lines of steaks, potatoes and freshly baked pie and ice cream," he said, watching her remove the sandblast gloves.

She slowly wiped the sweat from her forehead with her forearm without losing eye contact, and then went inside. A few moments later she reappeared with HB and BG.

"Meet HB and BG. If you can entertain them for about fifteen minutes, I'll clean myself up. Then we can go get a couple burgers. Sound good?"

"That's fine," he said, taking the puppies in his arms.

"We'll take my truck," she added before heading inside.

Phillip watched Angela vanish through the old double-door entrance to the mansion, and then looked at the puppies fidgeting in his arms.

"You two like burgers?"

He set the puppies down to play and took a closer look at the front wall that Angela had just finished sand blasting. Underneath all the stains and vines there was a beautiful stone wall façade similar to the walls of his château. He walked around the corner of the building with the puppies bouncing at his feet, and inspected the damaged wall covered by the tarp. He was no expert, but judging by the massive fractures running in several directions from the crumbled section of the wall, the entire stonewall on that side (southwest side) would need to be rebuilt. He then examined the size of the stones in the rubble and concluded, after picking one up and cursing, that this would be a job for a team of heavily built masonry contractors.

He continued walking around the perimeter of the wall to the back of the building and looked across Angela's overgrown backyard, over his plum orchards to the back of his château in the distance. *She can see everything*, he thought to himself. In fact, he noticed through all the overgrown shrubs that there appeared to be a side trail coming from one side of his orchards into the back of Angela's small grove of plum trees. Phillip made a note to ask Regi about the hidden trail. Perhaps at one point, this home belonged to a previous owner of the château.

Phillip continued inspecting the back stonewall of the building and noticed a beautiful walkout coming from what appeared to be the kitchen area. The row of leaded glass kitchen windows with stained glass trimming was nothing short of spectacular. Through one of the windows, he saw a spiral staircase winding from the kitchen to what was most likely the master bedroom above, with a balcony on the second level.

"That's beautiful," he said aloud, unaware that Angela had snuck up on him while he was admiring the architecture.

"I thought you wanted to tear this place down," she said standing there with her arms crossed. "I recall you saying something to the effect of 'unsafe… a bloody eyesore…' if I'm not mistaken."

Phillip tried to hide the look of surprise on his face, but failed miserably. "I see you are trained in the fine art of ambushing unsuspecting prey," he managed, and then continued. "This place has some fine architecture, I agree. On closer inspection, I must admit, it would be a shame to tear it down. I see you have a nice view back here," he added and looked towards his château in the distance.

"Yes, that castle is almost five hundred years old. Isn't it magnificent?" she observed. He nodded and smiled back at her.

"It is quite something, indeed."

"The view is even better from the kitchen and the master bedroom above."

"Where are you located, Phillip?" she asked.

"Well, I'm renovating a place just down the road from you, similar to what you are doing here."

Angela immediately remembered the old manor down the road with construction material and some workers in the yard.

"Oh yes, I think I know the place. You don't look like a renovator to me. Are you managing the project?"

"Yes, that is what I do… manage projects."

Angela nodded and smiled with what appeared to be an ounce of respect thrown in Phillip's direction. "Cool, shall we get some grub?"

"Sounds good. All this renovation talk has made me hungry."

Over the course of take-out hamburgers and milk shakes in the park, Phillip learned that today was actually Angela's birthday. She was twenty-six years old, had never been married, or even engaged, and it didn't matter. She was in love with her passion, house-flipping. And she was good at it, too. Phillip, however, was beginning to sense that Angela was feeling a little overwhelmed. She had jumped into a leaky rowboat thinking she could patch the holes before the boat flooded and sank. So far, the boat was still afloat, but the bubble gum wasn't plugging the holes. Someone on the outside looking in wouldn't suspect a calamity approaching, though. Not when all they saw was Angela as happy-as-can-be chasing her puppies around the park fountain.

"My Rocks and Mortar!" said Angela as they pulled into the driveway after their burger outing.

Phillip looked at the huge load of rocks and skids of mortar mix, and then at the cement mixer in the background. The sight of it all made him a little nauseous.

Thoughts of Angela hurting herself, or scaring her lovely long fingers moving those heavy stones around, made his stomach ache. Even more difficult, however, was Angela's beaming face staring back at him with jubilant eyes. She couldn't wait to start working on the foundation and wall repairs.

"That's a huge pile of stones, my dear," he said trying to be polite and excited for her at the same time.

"It sure is, but I can handle it," she replied confidently. "That wall will be fixed in no time."

Phillip looked at her sideways and tossed her a reassuring smile.

"No sweat," he said emphatically.

Phillip left for home shortly thereafter, knowing that Angela was anxious to get back to her sand blasting. Pulling out of her driveway, he made a quick phone call to Regi to make arrangements for a little help. He decided to give Angela a practical birthday present, because he was a practical person, after all. Regi agreed to arrange for some of the château masonry workers to head over within the next couple of days to help Angela rebuild the broken wall. He then proceeded to inform Phillip of certain issues with the Conservatory and Ballroom renovations.

"I'm almost home now, Regi. I'll meet you in the Conservatory shortly and we can discuss it."

"Okay," he responded dolefully.

When Phillip walked into the château Conservatory fifteen minutes later, he immediately understood the pressing issue that Regi had alluded to on the phone. A wooden plank from the third story scaffolding had come loose and caused extensive destruction below. Somehow, one board managed to shatter eighty percent of the glass panels along the roof and damage many of the tropical greenhouse trees and plants below.

"Anybody hurt?" he asked as he approached Regi and the cleaning staff.

"Luckily, no," Regi said with relief. "Everybody was at lunch.

"I thank the good Lord for that," he said looking at the heavy wooden plank.

"This is what I mean by too many projects, monsieur."

"Agreed. Have the maintenance crews remove all scaffolding around the Conservatory immediately. I need you to get a crew on site as soon as possible to repair the glass roof."

"Oui," Regi replied as he pulled out his notepad.

"Save as much of the greenery as possible, although, judging by the amount of broken glass everywhere, you might need to send it all to the landfill. What a waste," Phillip continued. "Hire some greenhouse experts to determine an appropriate resolution here. We need this place fully restored and operational within a month; top priority."

"What about the fountain, monsieur?" Regi said, pointing to the damaged two-century-old Pegasus fountain at the center of the Conservatory.

Phillip examined the stately horse standing tall on its hind feet with one broken wing lying on the marble floor.

"A horse can't fly with only one wing," he said pensively. "Have it professionally reattached and give the whole fountain a facelift," Phillip continued, looking at Regi with exhaustion. "Anything else?"

"Unfortunately, yes. I need to show you something in the Ballroom."

"A lovely ballroom dancer, perhaps?"

Regi caught the joke and smiled as he scratched the day old stubble on his face. "Malheureusement, non, something a little less… tasty."

"What then?"

"Please come."

Phillip moaned and followed Regi down the hall to the Grand Ballroom. From what he could see, it was coming along very nicely. The stage area looked polished and well dressed with antique red curtains trimmed in gold lace and tassels. The elaborately designed marble floors were polished to a silky shine and the chandeliers lit up the room and vaulted ceilings with the pizzazz of bubbly champagne. The solid marble columns stretched upwards like massive Olympian forearms to the second story balconies above. Intricate moldings and period artwork wrapped around the Ballroom like ornate ribbons wrapped around cascading chandeliers. *Nope! There's no major catastrophe happening in here*, he thought, and breathed a sigh of relief.

"Look over at the stage, monsieur," said Regi, pointing to the front of the stage.

"Seriously, Regi, call me Phil or Phillip…"

"D'accord… Phillip, what do you see?"

"I see a very appealing handcrafted stage with rather interesting marble work and vintage stage curtains."

"Correct, the stage curtains…"

"What about them?"

"They need to be shipped off to a museum where they can be properly cared for."

"Museum?" Phillip questioned irritably.

"Oui! They are heavy, need extensive repair and do not meet current fire regulations. They are stinky… damp-fishy-toilet-bowl odors," Regi continued, plugging his nose for emphasis. "You need modern curtains with a main valance and main curtain in addition to a fire curtain and modern motorized curtain tracks with a walk along. And, le track moteur… is broken," Regi said, throwing his arms in the air.

Phillip reached out and slowly ran his hand along the fabric. Images of parties long forgotten mysteriously passed through his mind: a cabaret, fundraisers and other major social events.

"Okay, okay. Fine. Let's get a new drapery system installed within the next month."

"I wish to say to you... bonne chance."

Phillip looked pensively at Regi for a moment before unloading his witty comeback. "So this task has conquered you, then?"

Phillip stared at Regi with a despondent expression and Regi felt the sting.

"Well, I can try, Phillip," said Regi at last.

Peter Breeden

ELEVEN – MAYOR MADAME LAPOSSIE-LAPORTE

P̲hillip, entranced by the finely orchestrated window repairs and phenomenal overall progress in the Conservatory, did not hear his cell phone ringing at his side. Réginald looked at him with increasing agitation after each ring.

"This would be your phone ringing, non?" said Regi with a perturbed expression. It was still early in the morning and he was suffering a mild headache from too much *Bordeaux vin rouge* the night before.

"Oh, thanks," said Phillip answering his phone. "Hello."

"I don't *w-a-n-t* your help, Phillip," Angela declared over the phone.

"It's a birthday gift," he said cheerfully. "Happy Birthday, CG."

"I can take care of this myself."

"I know. You're very capable of putting that wall up. You're actually doing me a favor, though, as I have three extra masonry workers standing around twiddling their thumbs. I hope you don't mind… It's the most practical birthday gift I could think of and I know you are Ms. Practical when it comes to getting things done."

"I am that, for sure. But this is an additional expense that I was not…"

"It's a birthday gift. FREE, darling. If you feel like it's too much, maybe invite me over for dinner when you get that monstrous kitchen of yours renovated. Deal?"

Angela thought about it for a few moments. She really did need the help and her hands had already become blistered from al the sandblasting. "Alright then. I can live with that. I hope you like escargots, calf liver and sautéed onions."

"Ooh… lovely! Okay, talk later, bye," he said, ending the call and pointing at the renowned artist working on the fountain.

"I recognize him from somewhere…"

"Yes, that is the great David Archambault, Sculptor Extraordinaire," replied Regi.

"This is fantastic. Regi, you are awesome. You're doing a fine job, my friend. Keep up the good work," he continued and intensely studied the master sculptor as he methodically repaired Pegasus' broken wing.

"You have a guest."

"Huh?" replied Phillip after a few moments of being lost in admiration for one of the greatest artists of all time.

Réginald looked at him in disbelief of the short attention span this morning. "I said, you have a guest," and pointed to the pensive old fellow leaning against the doorframe at the entrance of the Conservatory.

I thought about phoning ahead, but then decided, *heck, I'll just show up and they'll just have to deal with me.*

"Grandpa!" he shouted and jogged over to give me a big hug.

"Hello Lug Nut," I said, returning his hug.

"How long were you standing there? When did you arrive? I wasn't expecting you for…"

"I know, I know. I got itchy feet and came a little early. I thought you could use… a little help," I said as I gazed around at the construction projects underway in the Conservatory.

"You guessed right, pops. I need all the help I can get. I am so glad you came early."

"Me too, boy. Now show me my room before I pass out on the marble floor here."

"Hah ha, yes, you must be tired… and hungry, too. Come with me," he said, throwing his arm around my shoulders.

Phillip motioned to Regi, "Can you please get everything set up in the Presidential Suite for my Grandpa?"

"Right away, monsieur."

"Merci beaucoup, monsieur," Phillip replied.

I woke up for dinner, and then went straight back to bed afterward, completely wiped-out from my travels. The artichoke farm in California seemed so far away now and being at Phillip's plum orchard in Southern France seemed surreal. Later that evening, while I was in a cozy-warm bed lost in reverie, Phillip found himself entertaining another guest, Mayor Solaina Lapossie-Laporte on the fourth floor Recreation Hall walkout. They were at a table overlooking the massive backyard of the estate, sipping vintage Bordeaux, compliments of the Mayor, and munching on cheese and crackers.

"I see you have settled in quite nicely, Phillip," Solaina said as she inspected the legs steaming down the inside of her wineglass.

"Yes, indeed, Solaina. You have a beautiful community here in Agen. Everybody is so helpful and full of good advice."

"Thank you, Phillip. For me, Agen is a paradise. It is too small to attract the tourists so it remains quietly hidden by the enormity of Bordeaux and Toulouse and every popular vineyard in between. We are a small commune here and we all know one another very well. We are very happy to have you here."

"It's nice to be here, Solaina," said Phillip, lifting his glass to make a toast. "Cheers."

"À la santé!"

There is something very captivating about French businesswomen, or all French women, for that matter. They are brought up to be very caring of their skin and deportment. It is a source of pride, I think. Their skin is smooth and healthy from using sunscreen and other skin care products from an early age. It is an enigma; how they seem to eat whatever they like while remaining slim at the same time. I've learned that many French women reduce their calories when their clothes begin to feel tight. Smart. I guess it's not just a glass of wine each day to keep a body healthy. It's a way of life. Perhaps there's a fine balance here. Enjoy life; yes, but also take preventative measures when things start to… expand, if you will. And never underestimate the value of a sunhat.

"So, tell me, is there anything I can do to make your project more efficient?" she continued, charmingly. Anything you need?"

"Hmm. I can't think of anything at the moment," Phillip replied, "but I certainly will let you know if I need something I can't manage myself."

Solaina nodded her head in acknowledgement and then shifted her gaze over towards Angela's mansion. "I wouldn't want anything to get in your way here," she said pointedly. "You have brought significant employment to our community, Phillip, which is greatly appreciated in these difficult times."

Phillip smiled and reached for another cracker loaded with Brie cheese and Beluga caviar.

"I can make the hideous mansion problem disappear for you," she continued. "I was told you were very upset, furious actually, when the old place was purchased from under your feet."

Phillip sat back in his chair and smiled at Solaina with his fingers crossed underneath his chin. "I see there are very few things kept secret in this town."

"Let's just say, I know the right people."

"Well, thank you for your kindness and efforts to make things go smoothly for me. I think I have the hideous mansion issue under control though. So, no help needed there. She's a sweet girl… the owner." Phillip saw Solaina's eyes fire up with curiosity, but quickly put a damper on the conversation.

"What am I going to do with all these plums!" he said, changing the topic to something a little less… political.

After Solaina left, Phillip found himself sitting in his study looking out the window in the direction of Angela's mansion. A full moon on a clear, starry night lit up the landscape and the silhouette of the mansion could be seen clearly in the distance. His laptop was open and his inbox was full of emails from Andrew that needed his attention.

When I asked where the Master of the Castle was, Regi gave me directions. However, I made a right turn when I should have gone straight and ended up in an old storage room with a pile of leather bound books. I bent over and blew the heavy layer of dust off one, and then picked it up. "Voltaire," I mumbled, "Candide." Underneath it was another gem. I ran my finger across the title, "Le

Misanthrope," I whispered, "Molière." *I wish I knew more about other cultures... languages*, I thought as I grabbed both books and walked out of the room towards Phillip's study.

Maybe I should prepare my Capellini Pomodoro dish for her instead, he thought. The idea of escargots and liver turned his stomach. Maybe she was kidding, he pondered. Nice. Witty girl, that one, he mused.

"Deep in thought?" I said walking into his fancy study.

"Hi Gramps," he replied and pulled up a chair for me.

"Let me guess... Ms. All Hisses and Nails and Loaded with Venom!"

"You're good. How did you guess?"

"You're my grandson. By the way, where's that sexy masseuse you hired for me? My back is achy."

Our Head Housekeeper, Dominique, is a licensed masseuse. Lucky you. I'll let Regi, her loyal, loving husband, know you want to book an appointment with her for the pressure point massage. You'll love it."

"Sounds good. Sign me up. Now, show me the babies in your garage!"

"Hah ha, yes," said Phillip jumping out of his chair. "Which one do you want to drive first?"

"The 1948 Tucker. We'll take a spin to see your girlfriend tomorrow morning. Let's see what she knows about cars."

"She's not my girlfriend, Pops."

"We'll see. The Master Counselor chose your wife long before air graced your lungs. His plans will be unveiled soon enough."

"Well, it's not her. I think we could become good friends in time, though."

I smiled back at him with a reassuring nod and let my wisdom waft through the air.

The next day rolled around soon enough and by lunchtime, Phillip and I were rolling into Angela's driveway in the 1948 Tucker sedan. What a sweet ride. The car's smooth lines and chrome accents were a testament to the engineering of the time. The masonry workers were toiling away with the wall repairs. The wall was almost repaired now and the exterior looked brand new after all the sandblasting. Progress had been made in more ways than one, I noted as an interesting scenario unfolded before me. Phillip immediately saw Angela conversing with a handsome young fellow, not one of the masonry workers he had sent, and pointing to the dilapidated, semi functional, window shutters. A shiver ran up his back.

"Looks like you've got competition," I said as I observed Angela smiling and joking with the spry young carpenter.

"Can it, Old Timer!"

I guess I deserved the rebuke given that I hit a nerve. Looks like my boy Phillip might be falling in love after all.

Angela waved at Phillip as we slid out of the car and walked over to the far side of the house where they were supposedly discussing window shutters. Angela immediately noticed me, the spry old fellow, and quickly opened the conversation.

"Who's your handsome friend?" she inquired with a big smile.

I wasted no time introducing myself.

"Charles Niles, my dear; world traveler and sports car enthusiast. Oh, and Superstar Grandpa when the occasion permits."

"Hah ha, nice one, Tiger," she replied, holding out her hand.

"This here is Lug Nut."

Angela looked at Phillip, affectionately, and responded. "Yes, we've met. I'm going to have some fun with that nickname, I'm afraid."

"That's LUG nut, in case you need clarification. It refers to the bolts on a race car wheel," Phillip hastily clarified.

"Well, that would be LUG NUTS, wouldn't it?" she replied with a sly smile.

"Funny girl…"

"This here is my new window shutter contractor, Damien," she continued. "Damien, meet Phillip and Charles."

What Angela omitted was the fact that Damien was actually Caroline Beaujolais' nephew. Caroline was playing matchmaker.

"Nice to meet you Damien," said Phillip and gave the young fellow a hearty handshake.

"Ah oui, oui! You are the new owner of Le Beau Pruneau Château, n'est ce pas?" Damien said, pointing in the direction of Phillip's château.

Phillip's angst was quite apparent. His eyebrows contorted with an enormous frown and his face turned a light shade of pink. It was quite obvious that his cover had been blown. No more Mr. Project Manager from the place down the road.

"Yes," he admitted reluctantly.

"Ma soeur, she works for you, Bridgette, oui? She is a cook."

"Well, then, Bridgette is a mighty fine cook indeed. I've gained 10 pounds in the last two weeks."

Having said that, Phillip noticed Angela was looking at him differently, now. It was exactly what he was trying to avoid, the 'oh you have a cushy life, you don't need to work anymore' look. He absolutely detested people who misjudged him this way.

Despite being pissed, he still wanted to ask her out to lunch. "Grandpa and I thought we would take you out for lunch, if you're not too busy, Angela."

"Sorry Phillip," she replied firmly. "I've already made plans to have lunch with Damien. We're going to discuss my newly designed window shutters."

"Okay," he replied, nodding his head in acknowledgement. "The place looks great. I see you finished the sandblasting. And the wall… it's almost done," he continued.

"It should be by tomorrow. Thanks for the wonderful birthday gift, Phillip.

"You're welcome."

"When's your birthday?" she asked immediately.

"Hah ha," I laughed. "Good luck getting that out of him."

"On that note, CG," said Phillip, "give the puppies a big tumble and smack on the butt for us, will you?"

"CG…?" Angela inquired.

"Oh, that's just code lingo… you know, something to run alongside BG and HB."

"What's it mean?"

"Well, it's a code, silly. You have to break it," he said with a smile as he walked back to the car.

"I'm not much for breaking codes," she shouted at us. I waved as Phillip pulled out of her driveway.

"She didn't even notice the Tucker," Phillip said despondently.

"She did alright, but I think it got squashed with the shock of your… château. I guess she didn't know, huh?"

"I would have told her in time. I thought I would just get to know her a bit first."

"And likewise for her… you know where SHE lives, right?"

It was a quiet ride back to the château.

That evening, Phillip spent his time handwriting the invitations to the unveiling of his Le Beau Pruneau Château estate in Southern France. He sat by the poolside in the backyard facing the stables. The sun was quickly sinking towards the horizon and the sky was turning the colors of pink and indigo and even crimson red as the light reflected off the bottom of the wispy clouds scattered here and there across the sky.

The poolside marble table was evenly covered with all the invitation cards. He invited his entire family, including his father, with whom he had grown distant over the years, especially after the death of his mother. They never really understood one another. Phillip didn't have the heart to exclude him and hoped that someday his father would change.

He invited Andrew, his best friend, and of course, Jake and Gillian, his lawyers and good friends from high school. They were destined to be something great together and everybody at school knew it. Together, they lead the entire division of corporate law for Niles and Pikes Inc. As he was pulling out an invitation for Angela, his cell phone beeped. It was a text message from Angela.

"There's a big difference, Phillip, between living down the road in a place under major renovations and living in the large estate château after which the road was named."

Phillip responded to her text message a few minutes later after deciding to surrender, at least for today.

"Agreed. Sorry."

Angela's reply came almost immediately.

"Don't be sorry... just be honest with me, even if the truth hurts. Okay?"

Phillip thought about her statement for a few moments, and then replied.

"Okay, CG. Sleep tight."

Angela's witty response flew across his cell display.
"You too… Lug Nuts."

Phillip stared at Angela's blank invitation, wondering how to write it and if she would bring Damien along. He decided to keep things simple and open.

Peter Breeden

Dear Angela and Guest,

𝒫lease join me on the

1ˢᵗ Saturday of August at
19:00 hours for a celebration of
Beau Nuits D'été in the
Grand Ballroom of
Le Beau Pruneau Château at the crossroads (Agen)
between Bordeaux and Toulouse.

Your Host,
Phillip W. Niles

"Hmm, who else?" he mumbled to himself as he opened another blank invitation. "Oh yes," he remembered and continued writing invitations to Benoit, his real estate agent, and Caroline, Angela's real estate agent and, of course, Mayor Madame Solaina Lapossie-Laporte and her husband. Midnight quickly rolled around and he was still writing invitations. The sky above was loaded with stars and, every now and then, a shooting star would bedazzle the satin black, diamond-speckled night. In no time, his pile of invitations had grown into a mountain on the poolside table.

"Would you care for another Jack and Coke, Phillip?"

Phillip's head popped up at the sound of Réginald's voice. He was half asleep in his comfortable cast iron chair.

"No. I'm good, Regi," he said popping in and out of consciousness. "I'm a little sleepy."

"Bon, off to bed then. I will send these invitations out in the morning. Is Next Day delivery okay, monsieur?"

"Yes, that's fine… thanks Regi," he said and slowly began making his way into the château. "Good night."

"Bonne nuit, mon amis" he whispered and watched Phillip almost lose his balance through the main patio doors.

Peter Breeden

TWELVE – UNEXPECTED PLEASURES

Angela's kitchen renovations were progressing quite nicely. The ceiling, moldings and walls were spotless now and all the windows had been thoroughly cleaned and resealed where required. The old ceiling fixtures were removed and rewired for modern satin nickel track lighting and Angela mounted an antique chandelier made of Czechoslovakian crystal above the dining room table. The grand entrance antique chandelier, a larger version of the one hanging in the dining room, was on order and should arrive within four weeks. The spiral staircase to the master bedroom only required some light dusting and lemon oil polishing of the solid acacia wood steps. The twisting staircase was, by far, her favorite feature in the house and one of the very first jobs she completed on her lengthy list of renovations. The cozy wraparound railings were very comforting for her. Perhaps it was the direct access between the master bedroom and the kitchen that put her mind at ease, or the appeal of having a fancy wrought iron railing spiraling upwards to her cozy master suite in the clouds. Either way, the feng shui was working for her, and that was all that mattered. There wasn't much left to do in the kitchen now, except for polishing the wood floors, her current activity at the moment, and replacing the old sink faucets with designer satin nickel ones to match her new French door refrigerator. The fresh pine scent of the wood polish reminded her to open all the windows in the kitchen to air the place out.

"I picked up some lunch for us," said Damien as he entered the kitchen to a full view of Angela's shapely bottom drifting back and forth as she pried open the kitchen windows.

For some reason, at that moment, Angela remembered her promise to cook Phillip a meal in her new kitchen. Her heart sank a bit when she realized that this young window shutter carpenter, Damien, working shirtless in her front yard, might be falling in love with her. She had no time for men and their amorous flirtations right now. But she couldn't afford to be rude, either. Her primary concern was restoring the mansion and flipping it as soon as possible. All of her money was tied up in this project and she was beginning to feel a sense of urgency.

"That's kind of you, Damien. Thank you."

"You have a very hot ass."

That was unexpected, Angela thought to herself. But then again, he's only 22 years old... and probably swimming in hormones. And French.

"Well, thank you. You've got some pretty tight abs going on there yourself," she replied, trying to stay in the spirit of things, and acknowledged his well-developed six-pack with a nod of her head. "How are the shutters coming along?"

"Very nicely. I have eleven, no... twelve more to complete and I'm done."

"That's great news. Let's take lunch outside and you can show me your work," said Angela walking out of the kitchen toward the foyer.

"D'accord," he replied, following closely behind. "Oh, my aunt Caroline is having a family dinner on Sunday and I was wondering if…"

Shit, don't panic, she thought to herself.

"Would you join me?"

"How lovely; however, I don't think," she began, but was cut off by Damien's amorous persistence.

"Please," he said with big insistent blue eyes and pulled her into his well-formed, hot, sweaty arms. "I must have your company on Sunday."

"All right, then," she gave in.

"Oh merci, Angela, merci" he continued and gave her a slow, tender kiss on the lips.

Oh my goodness, Angela thought to herself as she held onto him. *How long has it been?* She found herself yearning for more. A second kiss, more passionate and deeper this time, was the tipping point. She wrapped her leg around his thigh and pulled him in closer with one hand tightly gripping his firm butt cheek and the other wrapped around his muscular shoulder. Her jeans stretched tight around her ass. A French kiss… a real one, very nice. His lips wandered… across her cheek they galloped and around her neck on both sides. Then his tongue trespassed across her collarbone and down towards the silky softness of her chest. *Yah, nice try you horny little bugger*, she muttered to herself and slowly pushed him down to the floor between her legs and promptly sat herself down on his chest, knees tight against either side of his shoulders. She looked down at him between her thighs and smiled.

"Nice smooch, Romeo."

"Marry me, great goddess of the earth!"

"Hah ha. Not today, buckaroo. We've got work to do," she said pulling him up off the floor and leading him outside to the window shutter workbench.

That afternoon, Caroline dropped by to see how Angela was progressing with the renovations. She couldn't believe what she saw when she pulled up the driveway. The hideous mansion had undergone a major transformation in the last month. It was no longer an ugly eyesore, she concluded as she wandered around the perimeter. The exterior walls were beautiful. There were no vines, stains or cracks anywhere to be seen around the home and the damaged exterior wall was flawless. Even the stones and mortar matched the original construction. The shutter repairs were still in progress, but Caroline could see the glossy black ones that had been finished and remounted on the window hinges. "Magnifique," she whispered to herself.

Caroline found Angela in the backyard playing with her adorable puppies that seemed to have doubled in size since her last visit.

"I am so jealous," she said, walking up to Angela and her two Great Dane babies.

"Bonjour Caroline. Ça va bien?"

"Très bien, ma chérie, merci beaucoup. Are you coming on Sunday… for dinner?"

"Yes, of course. Thank you for the lovely invitation."

Caroline nodded and smiled back at Angela, who was covered head-to-toe in dust.

"What can I bring?" Angela continued.

"Oh, just yourself. We have everything we need. Your place looks fabulous. You've really made good progress here."

"Thank you, but I can't take all the credit myself. Phillip sent some fellows to help put the wall up. They did a remarkable job, didn't they?"

"They did, indeed. There is no sign of any prior damage

to the wall."

"Would you like to come in for tea?"

"Not today. I'm meeting a client down the road in five minutes for a showing."

"Phillip?"

"No, monsieur Riviera, Sebastian Riviera, pourquoi?"

"I'm never quite sure what *'down the road'* means anymore…"

"Oh, I see. Sebastian owns the equestrian park five minutes down the road from the main intersection."

"Ooh, I love horses."

"Well, you've come to the right town then, darling. Well, I'm off. See you on Sunday?"

"Yup."

Angela watched Caroline stroll away. *Now that's a classy-sexy woman*, she thought to herself. "I need to find a pair of those satin chocolate heels," she whispered to her puppies.

Angela spent the rest of the day on the phone ordering the grand staircase custom wrought-iron railings and second and third floor balustrades she found on the Web. Caroline wasn't kidding when she said it would be expensive, €32,450.72, to be exact. Ouch. The design was inspiring, though, and matched the wrought-iron railings on the spiral staircase in the kitchen. She didn't want to skimp on the design given that the home required continuity and warmth throughout. But her funds were quickly disappearing and this worried her. She still had three floors to renovate and three hectares of property to landscape. *I might need to take out a loan*, she thought to herself.

Later that evening, Angela found herself snuggled up in bed with HB and BG at either side while she read a story in Architecture Digest, one of her favorite property magazines. She had a long, tiring day and was exhausted from all the excitement. Having a young buck working around the house during the day was also something new to her. *What a romp*, she thought to herself. *What a bod.* Reliving the heated encounter made her thirsty. Crawling out of bed, she made her way down the spiral staircase to the kitchen and turned on the kettle. Being a big fan of flavored teas, she stared at the selection in front of her for several moments before deciding on a combination of chocolaty chai and chamomile. She walked over to the fridge and pulled out a garlic and onion bagel and some cream cheese and made herself a little snack. She started humming the tune to *My Favorite Things* and sat down in the dining room with her cup of tea sweetened with honey and the cream cheese bagel. "Comfort food," she said aloud and took a bite of her bagel. She noticed the mail on the table and began flipping through the pile until she reached the invitation.

Ms. Angela Portman
100 Rue Beau Pruneau,
47000 Agen, France

The return address:

Mr. Phillip W. Niles
1 Rue Beau Pruneau,
47000 Agen, France

Wondering what Phillip was up to, she immediately opened the envelope. On the face of the card was a picture of two unsaddled Arabian horses in full chase with their long mains spread out wildly like an open wing behind their necks. Magnificent, she thought. She opened the invitation and read it aloud.

Dear Angela and Guest…

Oh, how lovely, she thought. *Now I get to see his place or château rather… E-x-c-u-s-e me!* She walked out onto the veranda and stared out across the orchard at Phillip's château. It was all lit up and looked gorgeous. "I'll need those fancy heels now, for sure, and a new dress, too," she mumbled to herself. "I wonder what it's like inside?"

At that moment, the phone rang and knocked Angela out of her château-in-the-clouds stupor. It was Holly.

"I hate the cheating bastards!" she cried over the phone. "Every one of them. They can putrefy in toxic waste as far as I'm concerned."

"Breathe Holly, inhale… deep breath, exhale," said Angela in a reassuring voice.

"Shut up."

"What? Bitch!"

"I just found out from Melissa that Ken was still dating Nancy when he took up with me. He denies everything, but even Nancy confirmed it to be true."

"And he still denies it?"

"Yes, he said there was nothing serious going on with Nancy. Ugh!"

"Baaastard," Angela exclaimed.

"Moron."

"Turd, I know!"

"Dirt bag."

"Exactly, Sewer Rat."

"Coward."

"Butt Sniffer."

"What?"

"Oops. Did I say that out loud?"

"Yes."

"Sorry. Not really… I'm just … angry."

"I know. Sorry."

"Humph."

He's not worth your anger. Move on…"

"Well, I've got a plan, my dear. I've booked my ticket and I'm coming to see you; three whole weeks of me babe."

"That's awesome," she shrieked with excitement. Holly was exactly what she needed. When?"

"I arrive a week Thursday."

"Excellent. Send me your itinerary so I have the exact times. You'll be here just in time for the Nuits D'été at the château. Want to go?"

"Hell yah! That sounds exciting. Whose château?"

"Phillip Niles," she said and poured another cup of tea, hazelnut vanilla this time.

"Phillip Niles from Niles and Pikes Inc., the largest software company in the world?" said Holly in disbelief.

"Well, I don't know, actually. He seems to spend his time driving around in expensive cars and managing constructions crews. So, probably not."

"Is he an American from California, about 30 years of age with broad shoulders, curly black hair and hazel eyes?"

Angela paused halfway up the spiral staircase. "That's pretty scary, Holly. Have you been spying on me?"

"No silly. Go to Niles&PikesUniversalSoftware.com."

"Hold on." Angela ran up the stairs to her bed where the laptop lay sitting beside two sleepy puppies.

"You there yet?" said Holly impatiently.

"Almost… yes."

"Okay, click **Company Profile** on the top right, and then click **Phillip W. Niles** and tell me if that's him in the picture.

"Oh my God…"

"You're kidding."

"No, that's him."

"You're looking at one of People magazine's most eligible bachelors under 30 years of age. Any other secrets you've been keeping from me?"

"One steamy encounter with a young, horny French carpenter working on my window shutters."

"You have been busy. Details please…"

"He's my real estate agent's nephew."

"Hot, ripped, big shoulders…?"

"I'm not sure how I feel quite yet. I'll fill you in when you get here."

"I'm packing right now, honey."

"Don't forget your sarong and string bikini."

"Right, bring sarong and string bikinis," Holly replied as a reminder to herself. "Now, off to bed young lady. I'll send you the itinerary and we'll chat again early next week."

"Okay, sounds good."

"Bye Doll."

"Later Chiquita."

Peter Breeden

THIRTEEN – HOVERING OVER SOUTHERN FRANCE

Phillip decided that Regi was to join him every morning for breakfast on the fourth floor walkout, weather permitting, for their daily meeting and progress reports. It was Phillip's way of bringing Regi, his confidant and 'master of château' affairs, into the family. Phillip only let people he trusted into his inner circle and I was somewhat jealous knowing that I would have to share Phillip's attention with Regi, a fellow quickly becoming more like a father figure than a butler. When I stepped out on to the walkout and walked towards the breakfast table, I knew immediately that I would need to become Regi's friend, as well.

I began salivating when I passed the buffet breakfast and assorted morning beverages lined up neatly to one side of the walkout.

"Good morning, all," I said, nodding at both of them and the buffet staff attending to the food.

"Morning Gramps."

"Monsieur Niles, good morning to you," said Regi

immediately pulling out a chair for me and commenting on the weather. "You like this sunny French morning in the prune yard, non?"

"Indeed, Regi. Please call me Charles. The view from up here is extraordinary and the morning breezes are…" I take a deep breath and continue, "Delicious."

"Perhaps that is breakfast you are smelling," said Dominique, the Head Housekeeper and Réginald's better half as she placed my freshly squeezed orange juice, bowl of prunes and black tea on the table in front of me. "Can I interest you in some French toast this morning?"

"Oh, you certainly can, my sweet, and a mushroom and cheese omelet, as well, please."

Dominique smiled. "Vous avez faim ce matin, mon cher," she said and walked back to the buffet.

"Working up an appetite these days?" asked Phillip, half amazed, half shocked at my appetite.

I just smiled and nodded in agreement. The prunes were calling my name this morning.

"Do you like horses, Charles?" asked Regi.

"Love them," I said with huge eyes. I always wanted to breed horses, but farming artichokes all my life left little time for other expensive, time consuming interests… dreams.

"Bon. You can help me with the Arabians today."

"Arabians? Today?" Phillip said, puzzled.

"Oui Phillip, oui," said Réginald with panic in his eyes. "It is Saturday morning. Did you forget?"

Phillip, squinting his eyes, slowly nodded his head in acknowledgement. "I thought that was next Saturday."

"Sebastian brings the horses at 10:00 this morning. The stables are ready and the equestrian crew has their orders."

"Okay then," Phillip replied, "as long as it does not interfere with the helicopter tour we booked for Grandpa tomorrow."

"It will not."

A moment of silence ensued. Regi, having developed some fondness for the horses, couldn't help reminding Phillip of their importance. "Your horses are well taken care of, Phillip. No worries there, mon bon ami," Regi replied, reassuringly.

"Whoa! Helicopter tour?" I said.

"Yes, I thought you might enjoy an aerial tour of the château, and then head south along the coast between Montpellier and Marseille for a bit."

"Well, that sounds mighty fine. I'll bring my shades and digital camera."

"Holy smokes, Grandpa… a digital camera? That's rather high tech of you."

"I had no choice in the matter. The young lady behind the desk thought I was teasing when I asked for a roll of 24 exposure film."

Phillip and Regi chuckled.

"She handed me something called a memory card," I continued, "and told me to insert it in my memory slot!"

"The nerve, mon Dieu!"

"I know! And if that wasn't enough, she handed me the latest 15 megapi… magpi…"

"Mega pixel," Phillip chimed in.

"Yes! A 15 mega pixel digital camera! She said if I didn't have one of these in my pocket I wouldn't be cool."

"Blasphème!" Regi exclaimed.

"I can take movies with it, too. It has a zoom lens, a full four-inch screen and stereo surround sound."

"Awe, is that all it does?" replied Phillip with a hint of sarcasm.

"What else should a camera do?"

"It should have one-touch wireless internet access so

you can immediately email your photos and movies to anybody, anywhere in the world: even have a streaming connection so everything is transferred live, as it happens."

"Honestly," he continued, "I don't know why we can't bundle modern electronic technology into one convenient and lightweight portable side unit with a full accordion-type collapsible keyboard and four 4x4 inch swing-stack screens. Basically, a one-stop shop for all your primary portable electronic needs, much like our software application caters to a universal audience."

"Wow, you're good. You should sell that idea. What's a steaming connection?" I mumbled. "Swing-stack…?" I continued with interest. "That sounds fancy."

Phillip pulled out his cell phone and sent Andrew a text message: *Let's develop a lightweight portable all-in-one side unit, budget 2 billion.*

"Andrew and I will figure it out. We need this tool, *now*."

I nodded and dived into my breakfast. "MmmMmmMmm, Dominique, your French toast is heavenly," I said and tossed her a flirtatious wink.

The Arabians arrived later that morning. Regi and I were standing by the stables when the prize-winning horses rolled up in the trailers. Phillip was nowhere to be seen. I guess he had complete confidence in Regi and me to leave such a huge delivery in our hands. I was excited beyond belief and the equestrian staff could not stand still. They moved about with harnesses and buckets and threw more hay into the ten stalls, each individually identified with a nameplate. There were four generations of horses in the group of ten Arabians. The mother and father (Pearl and Rafale) were now 15 years of age. Their four colts were born three years apart: Ouragan and Tempest are ten years old and their younger siblings, Amethyst and Potpourri, are seven. All four colts went on to breed champion Arabians, four of which remained in the family. Dynamite and Turbo (each four years old) and Rose Bud (two years old) were already superstars. Turbo sired the youngest colt in the herd, Quattro. At the ripe old age of three months, he was already causing a commotion in the horse industry.

The moment Sebastian walked Quattro off the trailer, my mind and heart leapt backward to the day Velocity (Velly) our black stallion at home, was born. That was only five years ago. Nothing could hold him back. At two days old, he was running, jumping and wiping out all over the place. At one and a half years old, every breeder in America wanted to borrow him.

"Bonjour, Sebastian," said Réginald.

"Bonjour. Le petit a arrivé."

I could tell there was some sadness in Sebastian's voice. He was going to miss the horses.

"Sebastian, this is Charles; le grand-père de Phillip."

"BON jour," I said utilizing my exceptional French vocabulary.

"Welcome to Agen, Monsieur Charles. Do you ride horses?"

"I do, yes."

"Formidable. I recommend for you, Pearl. She rides like the wind and will not try to buck you off. I recommend that you do not try to ride Dynamite or Turbo. They will try to toss you off, unless, of course, you, hmm, what do you Americans say… burn rubber, non… drive fast?"

"Hah ha. Yes, that's it. These days, though, I prefer to burn rubber in my Plymouth rather than on a champion racehorse. I guess real horsepower comes with an element of surprise, huh?"

"Oui, oui. Pearl est là," he said and pointed to the beautiful, silky white Arabian being led out of the second trailer.

"She's... magnificent," I said and walked over to her side. I learned that you should never look a horse in the eyes at first. So, I just ran my hand down her front shoulder blade and whispered her name. I didn't know it then, but the whole time, Phillip was watching everything unfold from the walkout above. It seemed to be one of his favorite places in the château. I guess he could see everything he needed to see from there: stables, horses, pools, plum orchards, maintenance buildings, the mansion...

I spent the rest of the day helping the stable crew get the horses settled into their respective stalls and properly fed. Turbo managed to put his mark on his old stall with a hefty double hind-kick against the dividing wall that sent a roaring thud down the stable corridor. *I'm home*, he snorted, and let loose a hefty whinny and stable-clearing FART. He looked right at me and dared me to saddle him up. If I was sixty years younger, maybe...

Phillip knew the horses would bring me great joy. It brought him such comfort to see me with the horses. I guess, inside he needed to know that I was happy. I was. I didn't want to think about returning home, but I knew I would have to return sooner rather than later to ensure everything was running smoothly on the farm and my sons hadn't strangled one another. Sons fight. That's just how it is. Only one Rooster on the farm crows at sunrise; otherwise, there be WAR.

Later that afternoon, Réginald sent Phillip a text message to rendezvous in the Grand Ballroom. Réginald stood in the center of the ballroom and gazed in awestruck admiration as he absorbed the majesty of the truly unique, fully renovated chamber. Everything was spotless. The marble glistened like moonlight dancing across lake waters. The new stage curtains were beautiful, fully functional and safe. Everything from the moldings and artwork down to the ornate designs in the marble floor balanced nicely. There was nothing left to do here except throw a party.

"What do you think?" asked Réginald, beaming proudly at Phillip as the young man sauntered towards the oval center of the Grand Ballroom.

"I think you did it, Regi. This looks… phenomenal. Oh, what's this spot here?" said Phillip pointing towards the bottom of one of the pillars.

Agitated beyond belief, Réginald skipped over to the column, hair flying all directions of the compass in the process, and pulled out his hanky. "Where?"

"Oh, sorry. Must have been my imagination," replied Phillip with a jovial look of "gotcha" written across his face.

Réginald, half bent over in front of the solid marble column, sat down on the floor, ran his fingers through his hair and responded with his witty sense of humor.

"Well, I… I have a little bad news. Unfortunately, Pegasus lost his other wing this morning," he said, tossing his arms in the air. "Broke off while the new wing was being reattached. It will take another month to fix."

The look on Phillip's face was priceless. "What? Another month? I can't wait another month. The wing broke off… completely off? Regi…"

Réginald began to smile as he watched Phillip anxiously shift his feet and place his hands on his hips. Slowly, he reached up to scratch the stubble on his face. "Well, maybe it didn't really break…" he said finally and reached out for a hand up.

Phillip, knowing his silliness had backfired, simply replied, "Touché," and pulled him up off the floor.

The sightseeing helicopter landed in the front yard just beyond the château fountain at precisely 9:00 Sunday morning. I was sitting on the edge of the fountain in my hip shades; backpack slung over one shoulder and my digital camera, held about three inches from my nose, recording everything. I even captured Phillip in the movie, leaning against the fountain and engaged in a fired-up cell phone debate about something or other business related with Andrew. I was so proud of him. *I must tell him that. I must tell him how much I love him*, I thought to myself as I was filming. At that moment, Phillip hung up the phone and looked over at me.

"You ready for some *Adventure*, Grandpa?"

"Hah ha... more like, is *Adventure* ready for me?"

The whole day was an exhilarating and breathtaking thrill ride. It was all so magical and overpowering. All I could do was sit back and just be amazed by it all.

We lifted off that beautiful, sunny morning at 9:09 sharp. The pilot, an Indian immigrant from Mumbai named Akhila, greeted us with friendly, welcoming chatter. After ensuring we were safely in our seats and prepped on aircraft safety measures, she effortlessly maneuvered the helicopter into the air and hovered in front of the château.

"What does Akhila mean?" asked Phillip.

"It means 'complete' in Indian," she replied with a huge smile. "You have a beautiful home here Mr. Niles," she commented and continued hovering up and over the Westside towers.

"Thank you. It's growing on me."

As Akhila hovered towards the end of the property, Phillip saw something he wished he hadn't seen.

"Those two look like they're having fun!" observed Akhila pointing her head towards the backyard of Angela's mansion. "Is that part of your property, as well?" she continued.

"Hmm," I mumbled and looked straight at Phillip. "Your girlfriend is rolling around in the grass with the window shutter contractor."

"That's my neighbor," Phillip said at last and turned his head away from the scene. "Can you fly us around the plum orchards and back towards the front of the property?"

"Sure can," replied Akhila.

Phillip turned to me as we flew back over the château. "How about a tour of the French Riviera?"

"Sounds good to me, partner."

"How quickly can you get us to the coast, Akhila?" inquired Phillip.

"I'll kick-in the afterburners," Akhila replied with a mischievous smile. "We can be there in time for an early lunch."

"This thing has afterburners?" I replied.

"Well, not exactly," Akhila clarified, "but she scoots quicker than a hare dodging a pack of Greyhounds."

I was a little worried about our pilot at this point. Did Phillip notice the concern etched across my face? She had that scorching look in her eyes, the kind of flaming intensity that, in the world of dragsters and funny cars, is usually backed up by twin-turbos, a supercharger or... *nitrous oxide.* The later was originally designed to increase aircraft engine performance during World War II.

Phillip remained subdued and pensive during the flight to the coast. I could tell he was depressed about Angela and probably wished he had been a little quicker to win her heart. That wasn't his nature, though. He took his time with things. I once told him that racecars were meant to go fast, but the journey of life itself was meant to be absorbed. Much like the scenery one enjoys (or detests) during a

Sunday afternoon drive in the country, life taps your emotions in so many different ways that you can't help but slow down to process it all.

When we reached the Mediterranean, we flew along the coast from Marseille to Nice enjoying the wonderful villas along the bluffs, mega yachts anchored in the coves and inlets, and picturesque towns along the way. The water was the color of azure and the sun sparkled off the rippled surface of the water like diamonds. Every beach had a myriad of vacationers either swimming, sun tanning or engaging in many different forms of water sports. Our tour along the coast delayed our arrival in Nice by about half an hour, but it was worth it. We still had plenty of time for lunch, recreational activities and dinner at the world famous *Digne d'Admiration* restaurant.

"What time do you want to head back today?" asked Akhila from the cockpit.

"How about 19:00 hours?" asked Phillip. "Does that sound okay?"

"That's perfect. It will give me time to prep the aircraft for our return flight and do some shopping for my husband. It's his birthday, so he gets me in some sinful lingerie and I get the heavenly box of Debauve & Gallais chocolates!" Akhila said with an undeniable twinkle in her eyes.

"Sounds like a plan, sistah!" replied Phillip.

"Go git 'em, girl!" I said throwing my fist in the air like I was fifteen years old again.

We walked off the flight field and took a taxi into Nice. The ocean air carried the warmth of the sun and the sand sunk into our sandals as we strolled along the waterfront for a bit, and then picked a quaint little café style restaurant for lunch. Everybody around me was happy and doing something fun. Even the street vendors were smiling and enjoying their work. I couldn't help thinking that the French know how to have fun. Or maybe they just pick the right sandbox to play in. I don't know. The mood here was undeniable, though: sun, fun and love.

I had some French onion soup, a tuna sandwich on pumpernickel bread and *tarte aux pommes à la mode* for dessert. Phillip had a spoonful of his onion soup and left the rest. Looks like Angela really sparked a cylinder within him. No woman made him feel this way before, that I know of anyhow. Ah, the heart. It's a stubborn mule-donkey-ass, I think. It won't listen to reasoning and it takes it own sweet time crossing the meadows of life. Every now and then, it stops under a shade tree for a while, a much-needed break, but eventually moves along to a sweeter pasture.

"Want to go parasailing?" Phillip said out of the blue.

"*Not bitchen likely*," I said, rather irritated that he would ask me to do something that crazy and on a full stomach, too. "I'm eighty years old. Find yourself another donkey to ride."

That afternoon, we went tandem parasailing. What a blast!—Shit my pants and screamed my ass off, but what a rush. It was worth it to see Phillip laugh again. By the time dinner rolled around, he was his old self.

Our candle-lit table at the *Digne d'Admiration* beachside restaurant was quaintly situated in a bay of windows overlooking an expansive curved beach covered with smooth, sun-warmed pebbles. People were walking barefoot along the waterline, patiently waiting for the sun to set. It was very romantic. I decided to be bold and attack the heart of the matter with Phillip.

"This is very romantic. You should bring your girlfriend here sometime."

Phillip looked directly at me.

"If you're referring to Angela, she's not my girlfriend, but yes, this is quite a romantic spot, indeed."

"If you keep thinking that way, she won't ever be your girlfriend."

"It's reality, Grandpa."

"Ask me what reality is, Lug Nut, and I'll tell you."

Phillip contemplated the question for a few moments as he looked over the menu items. He took a sip of his chilled water with two lime and lemon wedges squeezed together on the rim. He glanced at me a couple of times and scratched his head. Then the waitress came and took our orders. The whole time, Phillip was contemplating what my version of reality was and then, as I expected, he gave in.

"What's reality, Grandpa?"

I leaned back in my chair and looked out the bay windows across the beach and at the tugging sea beyond. I saw a young couple walking together, holding hands, laughing and leaning on one another.

"Water eventually draws everything into it. It's like a liquid magnet; it meanders and eventually ensnarls its prey in its watery web. We can't survive without it, and thus are drawn to it. It's the romance that pulls us in, the *love*. Life is the pursuit of everything we love."

I looked across the table at Phillip to ensure I had his attention, and then continued.

"Sometimes, Phillip, love just happens. You resist it for so long that you just give in to the moment when you're most vulnerable. Angela might have found true love with this young fellow, or she might have simply found a moment of lust... physical attraction. A universe of difference resides between the two. *True Love* lasts a lifetime. *A Fling* fizzles out or implodes after a short period because there is no depth to it. Let time solve this dilemma of the heart for you, but don't count out Angela simply because she appears to love another man. If you know in your heart that the only one for Angela is you, have patience, and let that peace of mind guide your way."

Phillip nodded his head. It was a lot of one old man's wisdom for him to process, but I think he understood. Of course, my big ego gets loose on occasion and stokes the embers in the fire. The hard part is the patience and I could tell he was struggling with that. We kept the rest of the dinner conversation light. The food and wine were fabulous, the ambiance was nourishment for our souls and the dessert simply obliterated any of that unpleasantness in life that weighs us down. Today was a milestone in my life, and Phillip's as well.

Both of us slept on the helicopter journey home. The day of adventure and revelation had wiped us out. The next morning, Regi showed us the Conservatory. The renovations were complete and it felt like we were walking through a tropical rainforest.

"Your Pegasus is masterfully repaired, Phillip," said Regi, proudly.

"It looks great, Regi," replied Phillip.

I tossed a coin in the fountain. I think you know what I wished for.

"Thanks for contributing to my retirement fund," Phillip joked.

Later that afternoon, Phillip jumped in his ground pounding, Bugatti Veyron supercar and headed to Germany for a few days. It was the Autobahn that was pulling him this time…

Peter Breeden

PART IV

Peter Breeden

FOURTEEN – THE ARRIVALS

I am a heavenly angel, remember, which means at some point in this story I die and my soul ascends into Heaven. I have returned to you upon God's request to tell this story, which has an important message.

An angel, or spirit if you prefer, is similar to a prophet or prophetess. Both are responsible for fulfilling a specific duty assigned by God. They fulfill their orders from God in different ways, however, with unwavering loyalty. A prophet is an inspired teacher who foretells the future according to the will of God. Be wary of the false prophet who claims to speak for the Lord, but is not a prophet of the Lord, for his prophecies wither and die like a diseased animal. An angel is an assistant of God and usually has a message to share. More often than not, angels are in disguise and you don't realize your paths have crossed until much later. For example, think of the fellow who ran through the red light with you in the car and remarkably, a hole opened up in the traffic allowing you to pass through unharmed. Angels carry out a variety of duties including protecting God's children from harm. The breath of an angel can save your life.

I don't know why God chose me to tell this story. Perhaps it was my unconditional love for my grandson or my passion and respect for life. I do know one thing for certain, though. God needs something from us, and that is our love and for us to extend our love towards others. For without love, we are but a dead bramble bush blowing across the empty, dry dessert. Ah, but I digress, on with the story...

Angela pulled into Caroline's driveway for Sunday dinner around the same time Phillip and I were enjoying dinner at *Digne d'Admiration* in Nice. At first, she was reluctant to accept Damien's invitation to Caroline's family dinner, but after spending a lovely afternoon with him picnicking in her backyard, and enduring a full-on tickle ambush in the long grass, she decided there was no reason to worry. She was learning to open up to a man again after a serious relationship in her past had gone sour. It made her feel vulnerable, but she also needed the companionship and love. He was teaching her some Parisian French, which was a major bonus.

Oddly enough, just as she pulled the knocker on Caroline's door, she remembered a helicopter flying around Phillip's orchards that afternoon. *I wonder if they saw us rolling around in the grass*, she thought to herself. *Shit, shit, shit... I hope Phillip wasn't in the helicopter!* Angela began to panic. The last thing she wanted was a bad reputation. She didn't want people referring to her as Damien's girl, because she most certainly was not. He was, at best, a companionable friend. And that's how she wanted others to see it, as well. Personally, I think she just needed time to resolve the void in her heart.

"Bonsoirée, Angela.
"Allô, Caroline. Ça va bien?"
"Tout est bien. Entrée, ma chérie, s'il vous plaît."
"Merci. Your home is lovely."
"Thank you. It is my sanctuary," she replied and smiled, all-the-while admiring Angela's outfit for the evening. Caroline was wearing an ivory one-piece swimsuit with a gorgeous silk wraparound that outlined her luscious long legs.

"That is a cute pair of form fitting slacks, my dear," observed Caroline.

"Oh, just something I had hanging *dans ma penderie*," she hastily replied, knowing full well that she spent over twenty minutes deciding which pair of slacks to pick from her limited wardrobe.

"Navy blue is my favorite color," said Caroline with an approving smile. "I have a beautiful Hermès scarf" (pronounced *air-may* for all you gear-heads out there) "for you that will match *oh so nicely* with your pretty silk blouse," continued Caroline, reaching out to feel the material and give Angela a sisterly squeeze on the shoulder.

"Thank you. I love Hermès scarves. Can't afford them, but certainly do admire them."

The two ladies walked through the house toward the backyard patio. Renaissance artwork adorned the walls of the winding staircase, living room and family room. Caroline was obviously a big fan of the Renaissance period and art in general.

"The one at the top of the stairs is a Titian. I also have a Raphael hanging on the wall at the head of my bed."

"Very impressive, Caroline; you have a wonderful selection of artwork."

"Do you know the Renaissance Period or the Impressionists?" she asked.

"Well, I've heard of Picasso, Monet and Van Gogh... and I really like that *half glass of red wine* painting hanging in your dining room. It's wonderful how the candlelight accents the wine glass and broach on the scuffled tablecloth," continued Angela, walking over for a closer look.

"What do you like most about it?"

Angela thought about the question for a moment and struggled with an answer. There were so many emotions tied up in that one painting, she thought.

"The carefree romance of it all," she said finally.

"Hah ha, well spoken, my dear. Come, I'll introduce you to the family."

Angela followed Caroline out onto the semi-covered patio that overlooked a long infinity pool with elevated hot tubs at either end. Beyond the infinity pool, a lush green sloping valley, with sporadic clusters of trees scattered here and there, gave way to rolling hills meandering aimlessly toward the horizon. An old castle that sat on a distant hilltop appeared to be floating on the infinity pool when viewed from the exact angle. *It would make a beautiful painting*, Angela thought.

Maurizio, Caroline's Italian boyfriend, was cooking up a storm on the delux charcoal/gas/smoker barbeque tucked cozily inside the outdoor kitchen. Damien assisted him with the marinated steaks and waved at Angela standing on the poolside with Caroline and her parents. Caroline introduced Angela to her brother, François, and sister, Sophie, and their respective partners. She then embarassed each of her nieces and nephews, six altogether, playing in the pool by individually pointing them out and shouting their names. A mad water frenzie ensued with high powered water pistols drenching everybody within seconds. Caroline was not impressed and jumped into the pool to round up the hostile renegades. Young Damien thought this was his chance to impress Angela and ran over, picked her up and jumped into the deep end of the pool, despite Angela's horrified screams to put her down. The kids laughed, but everybody else remained frozen in pin-drop silence. Not a peep.

The gasp for air when Angela surfaced was enough to paint another sort of unforgettable painting, one titled *The Biggest Dumbassed Move of the Century*. Even the kids fell silent as Angela struggled out of the pool, still heaving from the water that had gone down her trachea. Sophia, Damien's little sister and Sophie's youngest daughter, began crying. Caroline and Maurizio were horrified and immediately rushed to help Angela. Damien crawled slowly out of the pool and quickly came to realize the teenage stunt that had won him considerable popularity with the girls, had backfired catastrophically this time around.

Maurizio was the first to address Damien, half focused on Angela and intermittently glancing back to glare at Damien standing behind on the pool side.

"Perché?" he shouted at Damien in Italian with an angry hand gesture. "You're momma taught you better!" Then he blew him off with a single handshove that sent Damien flying into the pool for a second dip. That seemed to wipe the silly grin off his face, but also made him wonder if seeing Angela's nipples through her lovely wet indigo silk blouse was worth the inevitable wrath that would ensue.

"Come with me, ma chérie," Caroline said, taking Angela's hand and leading her into the house. "Let's get you into some dry clothes."

Angela followed Caroline across the patio and glared back at Damien standing there unappologetically… pathetically to her, before she entered the house.

It wasn't the journey into the pool that upset Angela as

much as it was the unpleasant realization that Damien went ahead and did it anyway, despite her sincere warning not to throw her in the pool. Is this the way it would be with him, she wondered? Is he the type of man that thinks a woman means yes when she says no?

"Here, try these on," said Caroline, handing Angela an ivory silk skirt with slip, green silk stockings, new undergarments and a georgeous cashmere sweater.

"Merci," she said taking the clothes and returning Caroline's smile.

She loved swimming, but you ask any lover of the water if they want to be in the water when their heart is focused on dry land and they will tell you; *absolutely not.* It's like going scuba diving in the rain. It's just not fun.

Dinner was an uncomfortable affair. Caroline and Maurizio did most of the talking while the kids kept the rest of the conversation entertaining. Caroline and Maurizio sat at opposite ends of the table with Angela sitting on Caroline's left and Damien on Maurizio's left.

During dessert, Damien managed a snide remark, about somebody in particular not being much fun, that stung Angela and left her mostly silent for the rest of the evening. When it was time to go home, Angela politely thanked everybody for their hospitality, hugged Caroline and slapped Damien across the face when he tried to say goodnight. She waited all evening for that moment, and boy did it ever feel good!

The next few days around Angela's place were frankly, kind of awkward. Damien was almost finished with the window shutters and Angela was anxious for him to be on his way.

"Are you still here? It's five o'clock, go home."

"I want to say, I love you," he replied as he packed up

his tools for the day.

"Do you normally drown the women you love?" she replied sharply.

"Yes, in kisses, roses and chocolate."

She kept things businesslike even though Damien made many attempts to apologize for his juvenile behavior the other night. Angela did not appreciate being embarrassed in front of everybody, especially amongst a bunch of people who still thought she was crazy to undertake such a huge renovation on a ramshackle, haunted mansion all on her own. It would take some serious groveling from Damien to undo the damage.

"I'll ask next time, before I throw you in the pool... d'accord?"

However, as the days passed, it seemed more and more unlikely that Damien had it in him. Perhaps, he realized this and was somehow hoping for a miracle.

When Angela pulled into the driveway with Holly MacGibbon, who had just arrived all the way from Toronto, Canada, Damien was hard at work, shirtless as usual, in the front yard with Heartbreaker and Bodyguard chasing a ball around the yard. He had been playing with them while he worked. This touched Angela. Somehow, she might be able to forgive him after all, she thought.

"What a gorgeous mansion, Angela. It's a lot bigger than I imagined, too," observed Holly.

"Thanks. She's a work in progress."

"Oh, is that the fellow?"

"Yes, that's Damien."

"He's handsome. Nice Abs," she continued, nodding her head in approval. "Look at those mountainous shoulders."

"Oh, he's a charmer, all right," replied Angela. She had not yet told Holly about Damien's misdeeds. It was something she just wanted to forget about entirely.

Damien turned and waved at the ladies as they climbed out of the truck.

Holly put her hand above her eyebrows to shield the sun and get a better look at Damien. Noticing that he was looking straight at her, she smiled and hollered across the front yard for some assistance. "Working hard over there, Slim? How about some help with these bags?"

Damien stopped his work and walked over to say hello. He whistled at Holly in his normal flirtatious manner as he approached the truck and proceeded to pull Holly's suitcases out of the back. Holly thought it was odd that he didn't spice up his gal Angela first before showing the newbie all the love.

"Welcome to France, darling," he said with a suitcase in each hand and an obvious adoration of her hourglass figure and wavy glazed-walnut hair. "You are a supermodel, non? Je t'adore, ma belle."

"Why, thank you Damien," replied Holly as she bent down to play with HB and BG, and in the process, revealed a very lacey black G-string camouflaged underneath whiskey colored pantyhose peeking out the top of her silk skirt. "Your puppies are so adorable, Angela. Look at the huge paws."

"Yes, my loyal companions. They're going to be huge," Angela replied, and then noticed, as her stomach began turning in knots, that Damien was checking out Holly. At that moment, she knew; he had to go. The guy was simply... shallow.

Damien followed the ladies to the front entrance, with suitcases in both hands and arms, and eyes wandering everywhere a respectable *unavailable* man's eyes would not. He was lusting after Holly. *Boy,* Angela thought; *if he only knew what Holly thought of men who behave like him!* Angela cringed when Damien stepped inside her home with

Holly's suitcases and, this time, Holly sensed that things were messed up.

"You can leave those there, merci beaucoup," said Holly to Damien. "Back to work with you now… 'Time is money', Slim."

Damien smiled at Holly and put down the suitcases. "If you would like a personal tour of Agen, perhaps this evening, I can…"

"Your boyfriend is a rather horny little punk, eh?" replied Holly, glancing at Angela before unleashing some wrath on Damien. "Are you still here?" she snapped. "Go hammer some shutters."

Damien, a little miffed, returned to his shutters. He only had two more to complete. However, it was time for him to go.

Half an hour after Holly sent him back to work Maurizio showed up, packed up Damien and his tools and drove away. Damien protested a little, but that only resulted in Maurizio's boot in his arse. His resistance was reduced to whimpers from that point on. All it took was a quick call to Caroline. Angela said she felt awkward with Damien around. His behavior around Holly was the last straw. Of course, Caroline was mortified at what had happened and apologized profusely. She thought Damien had grown out of his adolescent hormone-charged behavior, but that obviously was not the case. The young lad was still a boy.

Phillip arrived home later that afternoon from his road trip to Germany's famous Autobahn where he unharnessed his Bugatti Veyron supercar. He found Andrew busy at work in the study of his master bedroom. Andrew had two laptops open and Phillip's desktop computer powered-on with three 24-inch flat screen monitors, all flashing key pages from *Niles & Pikes* quarterly results.

"You're here!" yelled Phillip when he saw him slaving away and showing no obvious signs of jet lag.

"Of course I'm here, a little early, but here none-the-less," replied Andrew. "What's the verdict?"

Phillip, knowing exactly what Andrew was referring to, supplied the numbers from his test drive on the Autobahn. "First gear, zero to sixty in 3 seconds flat, zero to a hundred in a mindboggling 5.8 seconds and a top speed of ... wait for it..."

"C'mon!"

"...four hundred and eighty-four miles per hour!"

"Okay, Mr. Joe Pesci! And I suppose that was before you engaged the side booster rockets propelling you to a hood warping 800 miles per hour?"

"Hah ha, okay; I managed to hit 189 mph before I ran out of room."

"*N-I-C-E!* Is it still in one piece?"

"Yup."

"Where?"

"Follow me."

Phillip and Andrew spent the rest of the day in the garage, tinkering with the cars and taking a few for a test drive. Andrew, like Phillip, was very much a car enthusiast and even though he liked all of the models in Phillip's garage, the one he favored most was the red 1965 Ford Shelby Cobra with white racing stripes. I joined them for a bit, and then backed off into the driver's seat of the Rolls Royce Phantom while they had their heads under the hood of the Cobra. They quickly forgot about me as I watched them fumble around between the cars. I understood completely what drew them in. It was not only a friendship based on common interests and business, it was a brotherly love. It fueled their loyalty and trust of one another, much like the fuel and oil that fed the engines of each one of those mint condition, highly sought after, automobiles. Without the love, or the fuel and oil, the engines aren't much good. Man, I love a great engine.

Holly spent part of the afternoon catching up with Angela before giving in to the jet lag. She took a four-hour nap in the guest bedroom Angela had just finished renovating the day before. The bedroom, situated adjacent to the master suite, was cozy and illuminated with a warm champagne-color light from an antique chandelier that Angela found at a local Mom and Pop shop. The drapes complimented the bedspread and an old walnut cedar chest with a rose-themed quilt folded neatly on top sat at the foot of the Queen-sized bed. On either side of the bed stood two eighteenth century French oil lamps, one on each bedside table. Above the bed hung an unsigned oil painting of a Shepherd tending his flock of sheep in a grassy meadow that merged with the rolling hills in the distance. There was an antique desk and chair off to one side with a pad of paper and a pen on the desktop. A pair of Francesco chairs and matching ottomans sat at right angles facing a beautiful fireplace framed by two large windows on either side. An antique, wrought-iron fire screen with beautiful stained glass angels in long flowing dresses covered the open fire pit when the fireplace was not in use. Through the open windows lay an orchard of plums and in the distance a magnificent castle rose up to touch the clouds. The summer breeze lifted one of the curtains and the swish gently awoke Holly from her slumber. The breeze tickled her nose with a lock of her long curly hair, which she wiped away with a finely manicured finger. One leg edged slowly out from underneath the blanket and rested over the side of the bed. Then the other leg followed suit. With blurry-eyes, she managed to sit up on the edge of the bed and gaze through the open window. Her pink satin nightie caught on her right hip as she slowly eased herself up, revealing silky smooth legs and a shapely bottom wrapped in fashionable cotton panties.

Adjusting herself, she walked on tiptoes to the open window. *What a beautiful evening*, she thought. The sun had painted a river of golden marmalade, indigo and pink hues across the wispy cloud sky that flowed into the horizon beyond. In the middle of the sky-river sat a cluster of diamonds, which were actually the chandelier lights beaming out the windows of the château at the other end of the plum orchard. Holly, enchanted by the beauty, leaned her head against the window frame and lost herself in a reverie. Just at that moment, two men on Arabian horses popped out of the orchard in the distance and cantered up to the château pool. *That must be him*, she thought. *Who might the other fellow be*, she wondered?

"Le crépuscule à arrivé," she whispered to herself. The hunger pangs in her belly suddenly registered as the scent of honey-garlic chicken reached up and touched her dainty nose.

"Indeed, my fair lady. Evening has arrived and dinner is in the oven," Angela said softly, leaning against the bedroom doorframe with a whimsical smile. "Hungry?"

"Starving," replied Holly, dancing like a ballerina across the room to give Angela a big hug and kiss on the cheek.

"Good, me too."

"I'll bake a chocolate cake if you have the ingredients."

"I was hoping you would say that. Not only do I have all the ingredients for your prize-winning chocolate cake, I even have French vanilla ice cream to top it off," continued Angela as the two strolled down the hall, passing through the master bedroom and down the spiral staircase to the kitchen.

"Mmm, smells good in here." Holly immediately went over to wake up HB and BG from their afternoon slumber in the dog pillows by the patio doors.

"They've been napping all afternoon, the lazy bums," blurted Angela.

"Hey, I thought siestas were part of the European lifestyle."

"Forty-winks, yes, but four hours my dear is half a good night's sleep."

"Well, I certainly enjoyed my four hour nap, honey. I'm fully recharged and… Hey! There's a black cat outside your patio doors."

"I don't own a cat," replied Angela, walking over to have a look. Sure enough there was a black cat staring straight up at them through the patio doors. A white dove perching on top of the backyard shed caught her eye. It was staring at her with a calming, yet piercing gaze. This was no ordinary dove. This was Mother.

Holly, still in her pink nightie and bare feet, opened the door and in came the scrawny cat, meowing, purring and affectionately winding itself between the legs of the two young ladies. The puppies were not surprised to see the cat, which means they had seen it before. Indeed, they had.

Allow me to share the story with you. The cat was, unfortunately, dumped on the roadside near a farmer's field. It spent the first two days hidden under a bush before hunger set in and lured the desperate animal out into the open. Several vicious catfights ensued with the local felines before the front bumper of a transport truck stole pretty much eight of his nine lives. He managed to crawl to safety under Angela's backyard shed. His wounds consisted of a broken canine tooth, fractured skull with head lacerations, broken ribs and a pierced rear paw. It was BG who first discovered the injured cat. She crawled under the shed, HB in tow, and spent part of each day with the cat. They had become friends.

"Hello there, handsome," said Holly, bending down to take a closer look at the animal.

"Careful, it might have fleas, ticks or even worse… rabies."

"No, there's no sign of rabies here," Holly said as she touched the scabs on the feline's head. "He's not breathing heavy or foaming around the muzzle. Nor fatalistic behavior usually found in rabid animals. Let's have a look at you my friend." She carefully examined the cat as she would a patient at the hospital.

"Hmm, there's trauma to the head, for sure. There's nerve damage around the left eye and lower jaw… a broken tooth. Yikes, he has some half-healed broken ribs, see here? And they are tender to the touch, too."

"Oh, my goodness…" Angela bent down to stroke the cat.

"He's emaciated, poor fellow. His back paw is infected. I think we need to take him to the vet in the morning. Oh, and yes, you were right… fleas and ticks."

Huge vet bills started tumbling around at the back of Angela's mind. She was already in a tight spot with finances. *Oh darn*, she thought to herself. Ticks, fleas and more bills… merde. It was all too much to fathom.

"This sounds expensive, Holly. It's not my cat. Maybe someone is missing it?"

"There will be signs posted around the neighborhood if someone is looking for him. We can look around after dinner and call the local Pound and SPCA," she continued. "Don't worry about the fleas and ticks. They will stay on the cat until we get some medicine. Do you have some milk?"

"Yah, I've got plenty of that," she said and filled a bowl

for the scrawny little fellow. He launched into it like he hadn't eaten anything in days. Actually, it had been over a week with nothing but rainwater for the sick cat. Ironically, the previous owners had named him Panthère. A Panther will jump into the water to catch its prey, whereas most other cats are afraid to go in the water. Water, rainwater to be specific, saved this cat.

"There are no missing cat signs posted around here. I would have seen them if there were."

"Looks like you have an new friend, then. He chose you."

At that moment, the stove bell rang.

"The chicken's done. Let's eat," said Angela. "And I'm holding you to that chocolate cake, missy."

"Give me ten minutes here and I'll have it in the oven. Where's your cake mix?"

Angela pointed to the cupboard, and then pulled the chicken out of the top unit of her brand new, dual satin nickel ovens. The honey-garlic aroma permeated their lungs and made them salivate uncontrollably.

"So, what are you going to call him?"

Angela gave a heavy sigh. Here she was about to name a cat that was not part of her worldly plans. Darn feline was an unexpected hurdle that appeared out of nowhere to block her well planned passage to that ultimate destination of glory. Well, that's usually how life works, isn't it? Just when you thought things couldn't get much worse… I just happen to know that when God wants you to have something, be it good, uninteresting or bad, He delivers and that's how it is. I also know that what might appear to be burdensome could end up being something quite different in the end.

A name suddenly came to Angela.

"*Dovely*," she said and wondered if Holly had seen the

white dove on the apex of the shed.

"I like it. Where did that name come from?" she asked.

Angela walked over to the patio doors to see if the dove was still there. It was gone. Holly walked over and followed Angela's gaze into the backyard.

"What are you looking at?"

At that moment, Mother flew across the backyard from a lone olive tree and disappeared in Phillip's plum orchard in the distance.

"That."

"Oh my... Angela, that is... heavenly."

It was at that moment that Angela broke down and gave into her biggest fear; that the mansion was too big for her to finish.

"I'm never going to finish this fucking house," she cried out. "It's too damned huge! There's at least another year of solid work to do before I can put it on the market and I don't have that time... or money."

Holly, shocked at Angela's revelation, said nothing at first. Then she simply tilted her head and walked over to hug and hold on to her dear friend. They both sat down in silence.

"You'll find a way, Angela. You always find a way to complete your renovations, your dreams. This one is no different, it's just... it will take a little more time."

"I know," she whimpered, her eyes beginning to show the glassy sheen of hopelessness. "It's just a lot bigger than I thought it would be and I never factored in the strain of a failed romance, fling, messed-up thingy or whatever the hell you call it."

"Life," replied Holly, reaching out to console her dear friend.

A few moments passed while the two ladies reassured one another. As the sun's rays gradually broke through the thick clouds above, so too did Angela's confidence begin to resurface through the gloom.

"Are you baking me a cake, or are you just going to stand there and take pity on this willful Canuck?"

"Double fudge?"

"Yes!"

Everything seemed to be mended for the time being. Angela licked the icing off the spoon, and in no time the double-double chocolate cake went into the oven and the girls sat down to a honey-garlic chicken dinner and a fine bottle of red wine. They caught up on lost time over supper and dessert, but Angela spent the whole time pestered by a gnawing irritation at the back of her mind. Phillip's party was only two days away. It was over two weeks since they last spoke, when Phillip showed up on her doorstep with me in tow… and Damien standing there shirtless.

"I think I blew things with Phillip," she blurted out.

Holly dropped her fork and stared at Angela bewildered. "You had a thing with Phillip?" she asked.

"No, well, not exactly. We had what could be considered the start of a good friendship."

"What happened?"

"Damien."

"Angela! Are you crazy? Where's your common sense; where's your prudence?"

Angela glanced remorsefully across the table, and then down at her plate. "A moment of weakness, I guess…"

"Did you say something unkind to him?"

"No, but I passed on lunch with him and his grandfather to be with Damien."

"Okay, on a scale of one to ten, how important is the grandfather to Phillip?"

"One billion."

"Well…" she replied throwing her hands in the air. "You

are one dumb ass."

"Shut up."

"Well, you should be spanked for this strategic blunder, missy. Where's my mixing spoon?" continued Holly half-serious, half-teasing as she ran toward the sink to find the wooden spoon she used to mix the icing sugar for the cake.

"Don't you dare spoon me!" replied Angela running over to wrestle it out of Holly's hand.

"Somebody needs to smarten you up, lassie. Might as well be me," Holly shouted with three quick slaps of the spoon on Angela's derrière.

"Ouchy… Now you've done it. Prepare for your doom, missy."

A wild chase around the house ensued with loud screams and reassurances of retribution by both parties. Holly got her ass slapped and retaliated with a barrage of couch pillows. However, that only resulted in a mad dash up the spiral staircase into the master bedroom where the girls sprayed one another with lavender and ocean breeze air fresheners. Choking on the pungent aroma, they grabbed the pillows from the bed to fan the air, occasionally whacking one another in the process. They both ended up on the bed, laughing uncontrollably at their folly.

"Oh, what am I going to do?" Angela said, sitting back cross-legged on the bed, frustrated with the entire mess of things.

Holly blew her hair from her face and smiled across at Angela, both of them exhausted from their youthful exuberance. Then the timer on the oven rang and their faces lit up with big smiles. *The chocolate cake was ready!* They jumped with excitement and scrambled down the stairs.

"You're going to take me to that party of his, and were going to blow their minds with our beauty, wit and charm," replied Holly as she stopped the timer and pulled the cake out of the oven.

"Their minds?"

"Yes, I saw the two lads riding horses earlier today—Phillip and his friend whom you are going to introduce me to, right?"

"This is new. Who could that be? Do you think...?"

"I don't think, I *know*. It's his best friend and business partner, Andrew. He must be in town for Phillip's big bash," Holly continued, as several mischievous ideas popped into her head. "You take Phillip, I'll take Andrew, deal?"

"Hah ha. Okay, whatever," she agreed. "I have nothing to wear."

"We'll take care of that tomorrow, right after we drop Dovely off at the vet."

"Sounds like a plan."

"And this time, don't be so darned independent. It pushes people away."

"How?"

"Law of Attraction, my dear. Google it."

"You're so smart," replied Angela with affection and admiration.

"Thank you. Now, help me ice this chocolate cake already."

"I think I can manage that."

Back at the château, Phillip and Regi were reviewing the final details for the party Saturday evening, which was only two days away. Everything was falling into place quite nicely. The gardeners were busy pruning, weeding, planting and trimming to make the front and back yards presentable. The magnificent front yard fountain had been scrubbed down and new submerged lights were added to illuminate the *waterfall effect* at night. The rose garden surrounding the fountain was bursting with fragrant roses of many different hues and the grand entrance to the château with its quad stone pillars and towering double doors stood in splendor for all those who dared to enter. The outdoor kitchen BBQs were lined up ready for action in the backyard, as were the tables and chairs that would soon be placed around the pool deck. The chandelier lamps scattered around the pool deck were polished to a glistening shine.

Inside the château, the Grand Ballroom and Conservatory were in pristine shape for the big event. The world-renowned symphony orchestra that Regi booked for the evening, L'Orchestre National du Capitole de Toulouse, was busy setting up the Ballroom stage for Saturday's festivities. Soon there would be the sounds of Pachelbel, Haydn, Saint-Saëns, Mozart, Beethoven, Stanley, Schumann, Chopin and so on, resonating throughout the Ballroom and languidly meandering out the open archways to the backyard terrace to the clusters of guests gathered around the pool deck. The thought of live classical music permeating the château sent goose bumps up my back. I knew exactly where I would be for most of the night, too—sitting in my favorite poolside lounger sipping an icy-cool *Jack & Coke*. I was excited for Phillip. He had made a second home here in France, and some pretty good friends, as well. Regi, I think, will be a lifelong friend for Phillip. Watching them together as they struggle with various château issues is quite entertaining actually, like two cartoon characters trying to fix a leaky faucet. I don't think they realize it yet, but someday these two fellows will come to know and trust one another deeply.

"You've done it, Regi. We're finally ready for our guests," said Phillip triumphantly, leaning on the baluster of the main floor Grand Staircase.

"Well, almost… merci, Phillip. We still need to set things up and hire some more people. We need, let me think… oh yes, valets and extra security for our guests. We must also close certain areas of the château so our guests don't get lost or injured."

"Injured?"

"Oui, injured. The hallway carpet on the upper floors is shredding apart in many places. It's old material. People could trip. The library has loose banisters. Some steps are loose. Some rooms have leaky plumbing that creates slippery spots on the floor."

"That sounds serious."

"Not really if we take precautions."

Phillip wasn't convinced.

"Our out-of-town guests need someplace safe to sleep."

"Yes, I know. I have been stressing over this for the last month. I will put them in the West Wing of the second floor. There are eight pleasant suites in that area with very lovely views of the front and back yards. They will be happy there. The East Wing of the second floor must be blocked off as do the upper floor bedrooms."

"Okay, cordon off all entries to the upper floors, except the second floor for our out-of-town guests, and any unsafe areas on the main floor. No guests should enter the towers under any circumstances. Let's keep everyone confined to the Conservatory, Ballroom, patio deck and backyard."

"Oui. What is cordon? *Cordon bleu* cuisine, non?"

"Block off."

"Ah, oui, oui."

"How many more months of renovations do you think we need before we're done?" pestered Phillip once again.

"Oh, let me think," said Réginald rather sarcastically.

"Probablement, ehmm... most likely... well," he continued, shifting his feet and looking up with the occasional hand gesture thrown in for good measure. "All of them."

A blank look appeared on Phillip's face. "All of what?"

"All of the months."

"Ah fuck, Réginald."

At that moment, Andrew appeared. He had been working for most of the day in the study.

"Hey, let's go for sushi," he said to them. Andrew was hungry and had been craving sushi since deciding during his morning shower that it was time for some raw fish and a wasabi buzz.

The two fellows stared at him, bewildered. It was quickly dismissed as they refocused their attention back on one another.

"Let me explain," Regi continued.

"The Louvre is a big building, non?" continued. "It is the *Très Grand Palais* that has been over eight centuries in the making. They call it a work-in-progress for a very good reason. Do you know why?"

Phillip glanced over at Andrew and rolled his eyes, and then finally succumbed to Regi's question. "Because it's never finished?"

"No, it's finished. It took eight centuries. Mon Dieu, pay attention, Phillip."

"Yes, omnipotent commander of all things grand and castle-like."

"Be nice, now," Andrew said, poking Phillip in the shoulder.

"It takes several architects, including a resident building architect in addition to an in-house maintenance crew, to service the daily needs of the Louvre."

"And that's all of the months?"

"Yes, all of them," replied Réginald as he turned and promptly walked away.

"Okay, you done? Can we go for sushi now?"

"Yes, I can use a good wasabi buzz right about now."

"Okay, I'm driving. We're taking the Cobra."

"Like that one, huh?" replied Phillip as he snagged the keys from the key cabinet and tossed them over to Andrew.

"It's a sweet machine, my friend."

"Yah, that 'bout sums it up."

The two friends pulled out of the garage and made their way to downtown Agen in the red and white Shelby Ford Cobra convertible. They were both wearing scruffy jeans and button-up dress shirts hanging loose around their waists. Andrew stepped on the gas pulling out of the main driveway and Phillip lost his cap in the torrent of wind that came instantly from the throttle mash. They laughed together as Andrew stopped the car and Phillip ran back along the dusty road to retrieve his San Jose Sharks ball cap. Andrew's LA Dodgers cap seemed to be cemented to his crop of blond locks, probably because he adjusted it beforehand. His cap didn't budge an inch when all eight cylinders in the Cobra went ballistic.

Remarkable cars bonded these two fellows in the same way muscle cars bonded Phillip and I. Cars and water do pretty much the same thing, I've noticed. They both lure their mesmerized prey by assaulting the senses (visual, auditory, tactile, olfactory, taste, as well as *'the wow'*) until you're completely absorbed by the overwhelming enjoyment of it all. Yes, the lure of the crashing waves on a tropical beach with the suspended misty smell of salt drifting through the evening air can be just as enticing as the smell of a new car when you drive it home off the dealership lot.

"You smell something?" Phillip queried as they pulled

into town.

"Yup," replied Andrew, immediately pulling over to the side of the busy street and popping the hood.

"Smells like burning oil."

"There," Andrew said pointing to the exhaust manifold. "The valve cover gaskets are done. Oil is leaking out the gaskets and onto the headers. Looks like a slow leak. We need to take it easy going home." Andrew looked disappointed.

"Agreed," replied Phillip.

"We should pull the valve covers and replace the gaskets before taking her out again."

"Well, that's not going to happen anytime soon with the party this weekend and you heading back to San Francisco next week."

"I'll come back next month. We need to fix this."

"Okay. Next month it is then."

"Hey," blurted Phillip as his gaze fixated on a young, hip fellow standing in the square with an alluring young lady.

"See something?"

"Yes, I think that fellow there is Damien, Angela's guy."

"Well, he shouldn't be kissing the neck of that hot woman then."

"No he shouldn't," replied Phillip. "But it's none of my business," he continued. "Let's go get some sushi. We can walk there from here. It's only a couple blocks."

"Alright. So… tell me more about Angela," continued Andrew. "Does she like cars?"

"Maybe. I don't know, actually. Probably not given that we pulled up in the Tucker the same day she declined on my lunch invitation."

"Oof! Your timing's off."

"Are you saying I need a tune up?"

"Well…" said Andrew looking down at Phillip's belly

and giving a little chuckle, "actually, no. It just wasn't the right time."

"I figured out that much."

"That's part of the past; a minor glitch that will autocorrect itself going forward. Wipe the slate clean and start fresh at the party."

"It's not that easy."

"Sure it is. Don't even try to make things happen. Don't do it. Just let things fall into place naturally. If she has any interest at all, she'll want to talk. Throw her one of your puppy dog smiles and she'll not be able to resist."

"Okay. What about you?" Phillip asked as they entered the sushi restaurant.

"Ah, God has someone picked out for me. I just haven't met her yet."

"Maybe Saturday night is your big night, my friend," teased Phillip. "Double or nothing?"

"Let's just focus on the sushi, *Mr. I Have a Kick-ass Car Collection*."

Earlier that morning, Angela and Holly found themselves downtown at the animal hospital. I happened to be right next door at the men's tailor shop to pick up my tailored tuxedo for Saturday's festivities. I saw them walk into l'hôpital des animaux carrying Dovely. That poor cat had been through hell and back, but nobody knew his story, not even me until the Lord Almighty gave me my wings. That was my Day of Revelation, where I learned what was what and about Mother, the magnificent white dove. Ah, enough about me. This isn't my story; well, it's not supposed to be anyway.

I parked the Peugeot and decided to say hello to the ladies before picking up my tuxedo. Perhaps I had a plan, perhaps not, but my intuition pointed me in their direction that day.

I overhead the ladies talking to one of the doctors as I walked up behind them. The conversation was in French, so I didn't understand much of it, then, but now I know everything. The Veterinarian recommended a full examination including blood work, x-rays and surgery. Angela would need to leave the cat there for a few days. The estimate was huge, €2,680.00. Both Angela and Holly stood in shock when they heard.

"Good morning, Angela. Is everything okay?" I asked. She turned around and looked at me. Her face was pale and she did not immediately recognize me.

"It's Charles, Phillip's grandfather," I continued.

"Oh yes, of course," she replied. Good to see you again," she said finally and reached out to shake my hand. I smiled and looked over at her friend, Holly, who smiled back at me. At that moment, the Vet took the cat and said something quickly in French.

"Nous nous téléphonerons vous demain soirée, d'accord Angela?" said the Vet.

"D'accord," replied Angela.

Holly and I both looked at one another during the brief exchange with the doctor. I noticed a level of anxiety in her smile. I didn't want to impose on the ladies so I decided to remain silent instead of ask a bunch of likely insensitive questions.

"What brings you to town this morning, Charles?" Angela asked as we walked out the door.

"I'm picking up my tux for tomorrow's big fling."

"Oh, how rude of me," she said apologetically, placing her arm around Holly. "Sorry, this is my best friend Holly. Holly, meet Charles Niles. He's come all the way from California to visit his grandson, Phillip."

"Well that's lovely," Holly replied. Nice to meet you,

Charles."

"Likewise, my dear. I'm looking forward to yours and Angela's company tomorrow evening. You are coming, right?" I said, looking intently at both of them.

"Yes, of course!" said Angela.

"We wouldn't miss that for anything, even a tour through Willy Wonka's Chocolate Factory!" added Holly, whose passion for chocolate was as great as Casanova's passion for lovely women.

"Like chocolate, do you? Hah."

"We'll be there all decked out in our dresses and arriving in style too, in my lovely Ford Wildtrak," replied Angela with a hint of sarcasm.

I immediately put two and two together and concluded that Mr. Abs., AKA Damien, would not be joining Angela at the party. Instead, it would be the lovely Miss Holly. Fabulous!

"A truck? Good for you. You can get a lot done with a truck," I said. "How about I pick you ladies up at around 7:30 instead? This way, you don't have to worry about getting to the party and you can give this old man the privilege of having two lovely young ladies to show off."

"How sweet of you. You don't mind?" asked Angela, pulling her sunglasses out of her side bag.

"Not at all."

"Awe, you are so sweet," added Holly. She leaned over and pinched my cheek. I cracked a joke, made her laugh and chalked up another morsel of affection with a sweet kiss on my other cheek.

"That's settled then. See y'all tomorrow."

"7:30 right?" Angela confirmed.

"You got it." I waved good-bye and headed off to the tailor shop next door. My day was made. Tomorrow, I would escort two beauties to the event of the summer and walk both of them across the boys' sandbox, accidentally of course. Hey, sometimes you just have to spell things out for the young ones, in BIG BOLD LETTERS.

FIFTEEN – DAY OF THE PARTY

It was the morning of the big party. Andrew and I were both up early for breakfast and to get the day started. The warm sun danced brilliantly across the fourth floor walkout and through the crystal glasses at each place setting on the outdoor breakfast table. Andrew asked me about the Plymouth and when I was heading back to the track to test the new modifications. I told him next week and invited him to join me for an evening of Wednesday night racing at Infineon Raceway. He took a sip of his freshly squeezed orange juice and said he wouldn't miss that for the world. *What a good kid*, I told myself.

A few moments later, Phillip dived into the pool inside the sliding doors for his morning exercise routine. I smiled at Andrew and snorted something about His Highness being up, and then reached for the San Francisco Chronicle that was one of several international papers delivered to the front door each morning. The aromas of pancakes, scrambled eggs, hash browns, muffins and buttery croissants drifted from the buffet table behind us. What a spectacular morning. We could hear Phillip swimming lengths; a coughing and wheezing sound broke the regular pattern of leg kicks and front crawl splashing. We left the table and calmly strolled onto the pool deck for a closer inspection. Phillip squeezed out an embarrassingly loud high pitched cough a few more times, muttered something about water in his trachea, and then continued swimming. Dude breathed in a little water during his laps, not a common occurrence for him to lose his concentration like that. Réginald was always within eyeshot of the pool each morning to ensure Phillip didn't sink and drown during his workout. I guess, since there was no lifeguard, he considered it his duty to ensure The Boss remained afloat. He stood there over the pool with a wee grin on his face as Phillip continued his laps. *It's a good feeling when your persistence pays off*, Regi thought to himself.

Andrew grabbed a croissant and loaded it with cream cheese. I was back into my paper, so he walked over to the railings with his orange juice and peered over the backyard and plum orchard stretching out into the distance. *What a beautiful spot*, he concluded, and tapped the railing with his hand a couple times. *Phillip did well to find this place. Perhaps*, he thought to himself, *I should throw a dart at my wall map, as well, and see where I end up.* Just then, Gillian and Jake Fountain, the company lawyers, appeared from the stables with a couple of horse trainers walking alongside Ouragan and Tempest. Both champion Arabians were saddled-up and ready to go. Andrew waved down at them when he caught Gillian's eye, and then watched them as they rode off into the orchard. At the back of his mind, a gnawing irritation kept pestering him to be more proactive. "Perhaps I should start dating again," he mumbled and walked back to the breakfast table.

I was watching him standing over there by the railings; my newspaper was only a decoy. I sensed something was off with Andrew this morning. When he returned to the table, I decided to act upon a suspicion.

"Speak up boy. I can't hear a word you're saying," I bellowed.

"I didn't say anything," he replied, avoiding all eye contact.

"Ya mumbled something now, I heard ya. Speak your mind."

After a moment of silence, the truth came out.

"I'm tired of going to parties without a date."

"Well then, do something about it."

"About what?" replied Phillip as he approached the breakfast table, tugging on one ear and dripping wet from his swim.

I glanced up at Phillip standing there in his blue swim trunks with raccoon rings around his eyes from his goggles. I knew it was difficult for the boys to find their mates. It wasn't like the good old days when you went to a local dance and found someone, a gal that you already knew something about at least. Things were much more complicated now, especially given the boys' success in life.

"Mr. Magnificent here is whining about being dateless," I replied.

"Cheer up, mate. You're in good company. We're all dateless tonight."

Andrew nodded his head and took another bite of his French toast dripping in maple syrup.

I looked at both of them amused, and then decided to drop a bomb of my own.

"Well, speak for yourselves," I said mysteriously and pretended to continue reading my paper.

The boys looked at one another. Andrew stopped chewing and sat back, his eyes opened wide in astonishment. Phillip smiled.

"You have a date, Gramps?"

"Two, actually," I added casually.

They just stared at me blankly. Somehow, I think the news was a blow to their ego. Good. That should smarten them up a bit. *A good boot in the arse without the boot*, I thought to myself.

"You've only been here two weeks," said Phillip.

"Well, it only took one day," I replied. "I met them downtown yesterday when I was picking up my tux; lovely ladies, too. Their poor cat needed some medical attention at the animal hospital and I offered some moral support."

Andrew lost his appetite and excused himself from the table. Phillip returned to his room to change into something more appropriate for breakfast.

The stage had been set. If all goes according to my grand plan, I'll soon be able to sleep soundly again knowing that I've done all I can do to get these boys back on track.

Later that morning, Réginald and Phillip walked around the grounds inspecting the place once again in preparation for the evening festivities. They met at the front yard fountain, which was surrounded by a spectacular garden of well-tended rose bushes. The fragrances from all the roses conspired to confuse the senses and hypnotize one's sense of being into that of heavenly bliss.

"What's the plan for greeting the guests tonight?" Phillip asked Réginald.

"Our guests pull into the driveway at the front here where they will be greeted by valets. The valets park the cars at the West Wing tower in an organized fashion on the lawn. Five hostesses stand by to lead each of our guests to the security post at the front entrance. Their invitations will be cautiously inspected before access to the party."

"You mean carefully inspected, not cautiously inspected,

right?" Phillip clarified.

"Oh, escusez-moi, you are correct."

"What if something goes wrong?"

"Security will notify me immediately through these," he said tapping one ear. "Here, try one."

Regi reached into his midnight black tuxedo pocket and pulled out a spare, tiny wireless earpiece.

"Very cool," replied Phillip as he inspected the tiny translucent device that wrapped inconspicuously behind the ear. "How does it work?"

"It's very simple. All earpieces operate on the same frequency with a range of 1000 meters. To speak, you simply press the receiver, which inconspicuously clips on to—and hides behind—any piece of clothing. See?" Regi pulled the middle button back on his tuxedo jacket to reveal the tiny donut-shaped receiver hidden underneath.

"Nice," Phillip replied. "I want three of those for tonight."

"Pas de problem, monsieur."

Everybody was buzzing around the château, getting last minute chores out of the way. Many members from the orchestra had arrived the day before to set up the Ballroom stage and settle in for the big event. Some musicians were rehearsing in the Conservatory beside Pegasus. The warm Agenais sun and refreshing morning air ambled through the open louvers above. As Réginald and Phillip strolled through, an arrangement of John Stanley's Trumpet Voluntary filled the Conservatory with Heavenly splendor. It was my favorite classical composition. Violins, violas and cellos, arranged around the fountain under the watchful guard of Pegasus, called out to trumpets, French horns and oboes nestled somewhere behind the palm trees and bougainvillea vines at the far corner of the Conservatory. A film crew captured it all on video and promised to mail me a copy of their new Christmas DVD in the fall.

"Is your daughter here yet?" inquired Phillip as the two men sat down on a bench, situated between two Conservatory palm trees, overlooking the backyard terrace, pool and stables.

"Non."

"She's coming, right?"

"I hope…" he replied with a silky layer of dampness coating his ocean blue eyes.

Regi knew that his oldest daughter, Noella, might not make it to the party. He missed her dearly and all week he and his wife prayed for her schedule to free up so she could attend the party.

Noella was in her fifth year as a Resident Intern at Hôpital Bicêtre in Paris and was only one year away from receiving her Doctor of Neurosurgery. Regi was so proud of her. It had been nine months since her last visit… way too long. She grew up at Le Beau Pruneau Château along with her other siblings and, at times, the fond memories at every corner of the estate were overpowering for Réginald and his wife. Her fifth birthday celebration, a pool party, was particularly memorable. She kissed a playschool friend, David, for the first time that day. Looking out at the very spot where the crime was committed made him tear up. Her best friend, Élise, was incredibly jealous and her friend's mere expression of displeasure about the whole boy-kissing incident prompted Noella to plant a big one on Élise, as well. Immediate problem solved, or so Noella thought. It was more like the beginning of a lifelong rivalry, judging from the glare Élise tossed at David as Noella blew out her birthday candles.

The most heart wrenching memory was the loss of their family home when Noella was just three years old. The mansion at the far corner of the property, formerly known as the hideous mansion, now Angela's beautiful renovation project, had been in the Beauchamp family for generations. They moved into the servants' quarters at Le Beau Pruneau Château when part of the roof caved in, the part above Noella's bedroom, sending her to the hospital with two broken legs and a concussion. Réginald's father sold the place for very little money shortly thereafter. The new owner replaced the roof, but ran into money problems with the remaining renovations and ended up abandoning the home after his wife died. The bank couldn't sell it, so it lay in ruins... until Angela arrived.

"There are lots of memories here for me, Phillip. I've spent a lifetime both at that mansion down there, formerly my father's, and here in the château."

"That used to be your home, Regi?"

With a gentle nod of his head, Réginald answered the question.

"What happened?"

"Malchance, malheureusement," he mumbled. "A little bad luck along the way."

He turned and smiled at Phillip. Rising, he tapped Phillip twice on the shoulder and said, "Let's go. We've got work to do yet."

Later that afternoon, when all the arrangements and preparations for the soirée were finalized, Andrew and Phillip decided to go horseback riding on the extensive trails around the property.

"You ready for this?" asked Phillip as he approached the stables.

"I've been ready for about two hours now. What took you so long?" Andrew retorted, standing with both hands on his hips between the open stable doors.

Phillip, annoyed by Andrew's bitchy bite, fired back a

bitchy volley of his own.

"Took the Cobra for a spin around the block. Think I blew the head gasket, too, darn it."

Andrew's face went blank, pale white actually, as Phillip strolled by.

"What?" he said sternly, following Phillip over to Turbo's stall.

"I thought we were going to wait? I wanted to fix the valve cover leaks first."

"Saddle-up, Sweet Pea, we're going for a *ride*."

Andrew's anxiety began to waft throughout the stables like a horse fart.

"You broke it. You fix it!" he wailed.

Turbo and Dynamite, sensing the excitement became excited themselves. Their heads popped over the stalls to check out the two odd, out-of-place lads.

"Think you can handle Dynamite?" asked Phillip tauntingly.

"No, on second thought, don't you fucking touch it. I'll fix it myself."

"Fine, you do that, Spanky," replied Phillip.

"Hey, guys. Can you saddle-up Turbo and Dynamite for us please?"

The stable hands looked at Phillip like they would a mad man.

"Monsieur, I don't think is a good idea, non," replied Sebastian, who was on hand today to train the equestrian and stable staff.

"Damned horses need to run and, by golly, we're going to run 'em!"

"By golly, please don't," begged Sebastian, knowing full well that the green lads would be better off riding well behaved Hanoverians than feisty Arabians with bad attitudes.

Phillip tapped his watch and looked at Sebastian, who in turn groaned and nodded at the trainers to saddle-up the prize-winning horses.

Phillip and Andrew fell silent when Turbo, then Dynamite, sent a thunderous hind kick against their respective stall walls that rumbled down the entire length of the stable. These horses knew they were going for a *run*.

"Ah, I'm having second thoughts, Phillip." Andrew's apprehension wafted through the stables. "Maybe we should ride Amethyst and Potpourri instead," he replied, pointing at their stalls.

The trainers walked Turbo and Dynamite out of their stalls where they could be saddled properly. The horses looked at Phillip and Andrew, whinnied to one another and bobbed their heads. They were plotting something. Indeed, they had a plan.

"Afraid of REAL horsepower, are we?" Phillip retorted.

"I don't think today is a good day for eating dirt."

"Then don't fall off," snorted Phillip.

"You're in a foul mood, dude."

"Good reason to blow off some steam then, I reckon."

"Haven't you done that already… with the Cobra?"

"Shut up."

Phillip and Andrew followed Sebastian and the two horses out the far side stable doors into the paddock. Phillip saw Turbo and Dynamite for the first time up close. Their chests and hindquarters were massive. He ran his hand along Turbo's shoulder, but didn't look him in the eye. Turbo, however, was looking at him with wicked thoughts in mind, and nipped at his butt as he passed by.

The boys mounted their respective rides and calmly sauntered around inside the Paddock.

"This isn't so bad," blurted Andrew. "I think I'll be fine."

"Yah, they look intimidating, but when you mount them,

they're just a couple of pussy cats."

Sebastian muttered something indiscernible, but his facial expressions said it all. Nobody knew these horses better than Sebastian, and Sebastian knew these boys were in for the shock of their lives.

"Open up the gate, Sebastian. We're going for a run."

He nodded and reluctantly unlatched the wooden gate. The horses didn't even wait for the gate to open fully. When there was enough room, both Turbo and Dynamite hit the afterburners. Well-behaved horses, my arse! The two Arabians torn down the dirt road like two F-16 Falcons at full throttle, manes and tails fully extended in the headwind. A contour cloud of dust growing steadily down the dirt road was the only evidence that something powerful had just been unleashed.

"Donnez-moi Amethyst et Potpourri," grumbled Sebastian to his two trainers. "Mon Dieu, Mon Dieu. Les jeunes Américains," he said shaking his head and flicking the dirt with his boot.

When Sebastian and his sidekick, David, caught up with the boys, the two horses were grazing unattended in a field on the far side of the creek. Phillip and Andrew, on the other hand, were soaked head-to-toe in the creek.

David rode Potpourri across the creek to round up Turbo and Dynamite, but not before tossing both Phillip and Andrew a nasty frown on the way by.

Sebastian and Amethyst stared amusingly at the two pitiful boys. Sebastian, briefly looking in the opposite direction, couldn't help mumbling something disrespectful under his breath.

Then he finally broke the silence. "That is a beautiful black eye you have, monsieur, for your party tonight," he observed.

"Shit," replied Phillip as he reached out to touch the

bruise under his right eye.

Andrew, at a loss for words, simply glared at his friend. There was no eloquent way to express his feelings or perhaps there was, but he was too embarrassed and infuriated to speak.

"And you, there, Blondie-boy... Nice scrape along the side of your face; looks like it is swelling, too." Sebastian leaned in for a closer look. "Oui, that is a big bump on your face," he concluded with a wry smile.

Phillip glanced at Andrew with an apologetic look on his mug.

"For the record, I didn't take the Cobra for a spin. I was just *razzing ya*. She's still sitting in the garage where you last parked her."

Andrew, still half in the creek and leaning on the bank, leaned over and gave his friend a squeeze on the shoulder. All trespasses were forgiven.

Sebastian allowed the boys to ride Amethyst and Potpourri back to the stables and used the opportunity to lecture them the entire way back. If that wasn't bad enough, the lads ran into me when they tried to sneak into the château through the Conservatory.

My favorite spot in the Conservatory was a bench between two palm trees that faced the pool and stables beyond. I watched the young lads take off on the horses from this spot, Sebastian and his companion riding after them and their pitiful return about twenty minutes later. My day was running according to schedule, so I was not pressed for time by any means. I was just passing away the day until I could head out to pick up the ladies. When Phillip and Andrew hurried into the Conservatory, they weren't expecting to see me there, lounging on the bench in my tuxedo.

"Howdy boys," I said casually.

They froze on the spot and stared at me like two Bucks caught in the headlamps. I smiled, chuckled a bit, and simply said, "Perfect."

They ran off shaking their heads, mumbling something about a crazy old fart. That's what all the young ones say when their elders know something they don't.

I looked at my watch and decided it was time to head down to the garage and fire up the Rolls Royce Phantom. What a sweet ride. And what sweet ladies I'm chauffeuring, too. Angela and Holly are perfect matches for Phillip and Andrew. When they see the boys all wounded and embarrassed, my job will be done. Hah! It's triple whiskey night for me.

An hour later, I arrived at Angela's doorstep even though she was only five minutes down the road. I took my time polishing and warming up the Phantom before I left. The girls were naturally running late and I had arrived a little early just in case my exquisite fashion sense or handy common sense was required.

"Hi Charles. You're early and we're running late," Angela said as she opened the door, gave me a quick hug, and then ran back into the kitchen in her pink silk housecoat and matching slippers.

"I see your wrought-iron railings have arrived. Beautiful design!" I shouted from the main entrance foyer. The railings were stacked beside the grand staircase, waiting to be unpacked.

"Yes, thank you. I'm going to install them next week. Make yourself at home, Charles. We're going to be at least another hour. Is that okay?"

"That's fine. I'm in no hurry," I replied. Actually, I was a little hungry.

I stood in the vaulted foyer for a moment and had a good look around the house. It was quite big. The grand staircase split elegantly at the second floor and continued to the third floor. The spacious kitchen, dining and family rooms were to my right and on the left were several other large rooms. I walked through what appeared to be the living room with bright windows and a wood-burning stone fireplace at the far end. This room was filled with paint cans, brushes, moldings and other renovation supplies. A section of the wood flooring had been ripped up in the corner of the room and there were several different colors of paint patches on the wall.

I walked through an opening to the next room, which was filled with elaborate cherry wood shelving along the walls and another wood burning fireplace. This must have been a library at one time. I walked through a pair of elegantly restored French doors from the Library into a private study with a large office desk, probably from the early eighteen hundreds, which was positioned against an expansive window facing the backyard. A drowsy black cat was sleeping on top of some cushions piled on the desk. As I approached, I realized it was the same cat that was at the pet hospital the other day with the ladies. It stretched one paw out to greet me, and then barrel-rolled, daring me to reach in a give him a belly rub. As I leaned in, I noticed that his front leg was shaved and the rear leg had a rubber cast on it. His yawn revealed a missing canine and some stitches at the back of his head.

"Charles, meet Dovely, Dovely, this is Charles," replied Holly as she slipped a cup of steaming coffee into my hands and gave me a peck on the cheek.

"Thank you, darling," I replied. "And a pleasure to meet you, Sir Dovely."

Holly smiled and gave Dovely a scratch on the butt. She,

like Angela, was also still in her housecoat—a short, silky black knee-length negligee—with a side split down her hip that revealed satin root beer pantyhose latticing down her legs and into a pair of cozy woolen socks on her feet. What a beautiful lady.

"Help yourself to snacks and refreshments in the kitchen, Charles. We're going to be a while yet. There's a TV in the next room."

Just as quick as she came, she was gone.

"The next room?" I pondered. "There's another room on this floor?" I mumbled.

I walked through another set of French doors into a great room that ran behind the grand staircase; The Party Room, according to the letters on the stained glass light fixture hanging above the billiards table in the center of the room.

"Wow! This room is fantastic," I said in amazement.

An expansive teak bar with eight anchored stools sat alongside the wall opposite the billiards table. My eyes continued traveling around the walls of the room, along the series of panoramic windows facing the orchard in the backyard to the far wall where a lone picture of a sexy cabaret performer, singing her heart apart, hung in the center of the wall. I didn't know it then, but I can tell you now that I was looking at an enlarged vintage photograph of a young Édith Piaf, born Édith Giovanna Gassion, singing ballades of tragic romance on stage in Paris circa 1936. I walked towards the black and white picture elegantly enclosed in a mahogany wood frame and examined it closely. This woman, whoever she was, I thought, had an incredible story to tell. I reached out in hopes of catching Édith's cheek in my open hand at the very same moment Angela burst through the Party Room doors from the kitchen on the other side.

"I just finished restoring that picture," she commented. "That woman could sing!"

"She's beautiful."

"She certainly is, Charles. This room seems to pull people in."

"Is that so? Perhaps she has a few more songs to sing for us," I said, looking back at the picture.

"You sure look handsome in that tuxedo," said Angela, brushing off a few cat hairs from my shoulders and sleeves.

"Thank you, darling. You're still in your robe, I see."

"Yes, we might be a while longer, unfortunately. We're engaged in a hair, wardrobe and cosmetics extravaganza upstairs. Come along into the kitchen… I'll refill your coffee cup."

I wasn't in any rush. The adventure of discovering a new home was keeping me entertained. Angela was incredibly passionate about her renovation project and it showed in every room.

"Sounds good to me, sweetheart."

When I walked into the kitchen, Angela's two Great Danes were there to greet me.

"The lads are growing quickly," I commented.

"I don't think BG would be overly offended with the term *lad* as she is very much a Tom Boy in her ways. She prefers to rumble and tumble rather than sit in the background and watch the boys play."

"BeeGee? Is she a good singer?"

"Hah ha. She can certainly howl, especially when it's time for dinner, but no… BG stands for Body Guard."

"Oh," I said, taking a second look at the puppy with feet as wide as a saucer. "Why Bodyguard?"

"She tackled my foot when I picked up her brother," she said, bending down to give the dogs an ear massage. "I wasn't taking HB home without her coming, as well. She made that quite clear."

"Ah, the way it should be. And HB?" I asked with pensive eyes.

"Heartbreaker."

I nodded my head and gave each dog a scratch behind the ears. "Animals are a gift that we should protect and respect."

"Amen," she replied, and then suddenly bounced up the spiral staircase when Holly called her name. Golly, it's been forever since I had that kind of bounce in my legs. When you're old, the only thing bouncing is your ass when it hits the sofa.

"Coffee's in the pot; help yourself to cookies on the table," she hollered from the top of the stairs.

"Thanks."

What a great idea… a spiral staircase from the kitchen to the master bedroom. Now I know why she went with the custom wrought iron railings for the Grand Staircase. The front foyer theme continued in the kitchen with the elaborate wrought iron design built into the spiral staircase. Smart.

I refilled my coffee cup and sat down at the kitchen table. Freshly baked oatmeal cookies caught my attention and the eyes of two hungry puppies sitting very well-behaved facing the cookies on the table. Their glossy eyes swayed between the raised cookie platter and me. When I reached for the cookies, their mouths closed, ears stiffened and eyes widened. I paused for a moment to give them a big smile, and their tails began pounding the floor. When I lifted the glass cookie cover, BG huffed and stood up.

"Can I interest you both in a… COOKIE!" Both dogs jumped up in excitement and barked as I gave them each a king sized oatmeal cookie.

A voice from the second story came booming down the

staircase, "Don't feed the dogs Holly's prize-winning oatmeal cookies."

"Too late," I mumbled, and grabbed one for myself. "What good is a cookie if you can't eat it?" The dogs agreed.

Peter Breeden

SIXTEEN – LES NUITS D'ÉTÉ
LA GRANDE ENTRÉE

Despite the obvious bruises decorating their faces, Phillip and Andrew remained resolute and stood in the main foyer greeting their guests as they arrived. If anything, it would all add up to more juicy conversations during the evening festivities. They were brave lads.

"Welcome to our little soirée Madame, Monsieur Lapossie-Laporte," said Phillip, reaching out to take Solaina's hand.

"Word travels fast in Agen, Monsieur Niles," replied Solaina as she pulled out her spectacles for a closer look. "You boys look disgraceful. Have you nothing better to do than play Cowboys and Indians all day?"

Andrew, who was the quicker of the two lads with witty retorts, politely replied, "Well, my prized King Cobra escaped, no thanks to Phillip here, so naturally I had to scalp him for his misdeeds."

Solaina instantly froze. She detested snakes with a passion. There was nothing in this Universe that smelled worse, or propelled itself in a more spine-chilling manner, than a serpent. It didn't help that she woke up one morning to find a rattler coiled up right next to her face. That was the last time she went *camping*.

"*Trou... trouv... trouvez-vous le serpent?*" she stuttered, grabbing her husband's neck while dancing on her tiptoes and gasping for air.

"Yes, not to worry my dear," replied Phillip reassuringly. He's safely parked in the basement, for now..." he continued, and then glared at Andrew for upsetting his guests.

Shortly thereafter, the ladies and I pulled up to the main entrance of the chateau in the Phantom. It hung in front of us like a shiny Christmas ornament dangling from the Heavens above. No, I wasn't drunk and hallucinating. Perhaps, too many cups of coffee made everything appear more surreal. I was, however, anxious to get the show started and dive into my first *Jack and Coke* of the evening.

As we pulled up the drive, the chateau lights illuminated the shiny white silhouette of the Rolls and bounced along the chrome finish like a waterfall of sparkling diamonds. I left the car running and climbed out. My stomach heaved somewhat at the site of the valet standing there. I didn't want to surrender the car, but the ladies were waiting to be properly escorted from the car to the Ballroom. Reluctantly, I signaled for the valet to take the car, but not before ensuring that extra special care was taken.

"No mishaps," I repeated, looking back at the valet (with semi-concealed apprehension) as I assisted Angela out of the car.

When I took Angela's hand in my own, a silky leg pampered in transparent black nylon slid through the open slit of her sapphire blue dress as her foot, elegantly showcased in an open-toe three inch pump, slowly extended towards the pavement below. An old man, I am, but void of hormones, I am not. A beautiful woman always makes a man's heart skip a beat as it stumbles to regain its composure. My heart missed a couple beats, and then just kept backfiring. As I took Angela's hand and guided her out of the car to my left arm, her hair swished and enveloped me in a bouquet of mesmerizing floral fragrances. How can a man think? The Scarlet effect had me dumbfounded! I stumbled… almost fell on my arse, too. Angela caught my arm.

"Thank you, doll," I whispered as inconspicuously as I could. She smiled and hugged me with those huge hazel eyes.

Holly eased her way across the leather seat to the edge, pivoted and popped both feet out the door. Gracefully, both of her four-inch spaghetti strap stilettos hit the pavement, one foot angled delicately in front of the other. Both of her hands grabbed the top of the doorframe as she adjusted herself on the edge of the seat. Her large, liquid green eyes glistened and pulled me in with one shiny side gesture.

"My turn, cowboy," she said playfully with an outstretched hand bent at an angle, fingers flared Audrey Hepburn style to showcase the invisible diamond ring on her finger.

I took her delicate hand and gently pulled her out of the car. Her bunched up chiffon evening dress, a luscious olive oil color, slid down her honey colored nylon legs as she stood up. A ribbon of curly, glazed-walnut hair dangled from her Bridget Bardot style chignon and lightly danced upon the whiskey colored cashmere shawl wrapped around her shoulders. I felt like a young man again. How was that possible? *There was life in me, yet,* I thought. Perhaps, I should put the *bucket list* away for another year…

"First time in my life I lassoed two angels in one go," I

said with a big smile on my face.

"Easy now, Gramps," whispered Holly. "We're not in the building yet and those are some hefty steps in front of us."

"And try not to… ahem, BACKFIRE," added Angela.

I pretended to be embarrassed, but in all honesty, my one mistaken fart couldn't be helped. A fine bottle of wine improves with age, as does an honorable person. The two ingredients complement one another, handsomely. Let me clarify: an evening of finely aged Bordeaux wine to satisfy the palate and my company, that of a finely aged, honorable fellow, is the recipe for abundant laughter and good cheer, the overall effect, of which, is delightful satisfaction.

"Ah, you must be referring to my heart for it has indeed skipped a few beats today," I responded, that finely aged wisdom finally coming to fruition.

"Nice one, Casanova," replied Holly, sharing a smile with Angela.

"Thank you, my dear."

The ladies turned heads from all directions as we proceeded up the steps towards the imposing double doors. Their dresses were an instant hit judging from the facial expressions of the greeting staff and security. Despite only showing a conservative amount of skin, their allure pulled us all in. A touch of silky cleavage was enough to tantalize the imagination and send everybody into a whirlwind of pheromones after the moment of composed admiration had passed. We walked straight past the security staff without having to show our invitations. Réginald was nowhere to be seen. Of course, I winked at my new buddy, Henri, Head of Security, as we passed through the doors into the cavernous foyer. He had a huge grin on his face and was nodding his head with approval, almost as if I had won the World Cup or something similar. Indeed, I had won.

The crowd gathered in the foyer fell silent when we stepped into the limelight. The boys' eyes immediately locked onto Angela and Holly, mouths slightly agape, their faces hypnotized by the ladies' mesmerizing beauty. In the background, the sounds of Queen of the Night from Mozart's Magic Flute drifted outwards from the Ballroom. L'Orchestre National du Capitole de Toulouse was firing on all cylinders, filling the halls with unprecedented splendor. The high notes from the soloist sent spine-tingling chills up my back. Trays of fancy hors-d'oeuvres and cocktails, Champagne, were being passed around; everyone looked busy doing something.

"You go, girls!" shouted Caroline, who arrived only moments after us and was watching our entrance with a keen eye the whole time. Of course, she brought her entire extended family including Maurizio, her brother, François, sister Sophie, and their respective partners, as well as her six adorable nices and nephews. Damien was not among them.

Angela, Holly and I immediately turned around to welcome Caroline and her crew. Caroline walked confidently in our direction, with those long, luscious supermodel legs, and stopped in a pose, hands on hips, directly in front of us.

"Well now," she said, inspecting the ladies fashion ensembles, top to bottom. "Very S-e-x-y," she exclaimed nodding her head with approval. "*Très chic.*"

Their legs lifted in that fashionable lady-like manner as they group hugged one another. Of course, I ended up in the middle of the hug, given that both Angela and Holly were still attached to my arms. Ah, the wonderful fragrances of three lovely ladies. Caroline was wearing a diamond cross necklace that somehow stuck to my cheek during our hug. I didn't mind. She was wearing a little black dress that showcased her fabulous legs and jazzy stilettos.

At that same moment, I saw Réginald from the corner of my eye and my momentary bliss quickly faded. He was solemnly gazing out the foyer window as the guests arrived, desperately hoping to see his beloved daughter step out of one of the cars. As the minutes turned into hours, his hopes faded into the canyons of despair seated firmly at the back of his mind. I could feel his sadness. The slump of his body and the occasional blink of his melancholy eyes seemed to resonate loudly in my mind. Why didn't anybody else notice his sorrow? Maybe they did, I don't know, but I had to do something. I immediately walked over to the boys with my delightful company clasped on either arm.

"I trust you both will take good care of these two lovely ladies tonight," I said with a good hearty bellow, passing Angela over to Phillip and Holly to Andrew. The boys were still in shock; their faces were priceless.

"My dears, thank you for escorting me safely up those treacherous stairs. There'll be no dislocated shoulders or broken limbs for me tonight. It did happen once, you know," I continued seriously. "Got myself all busted up falling down some steep stairs."

"Only once, Pops?" replied Phillip with a penetrating grin.

I grinned and fired back. "Easy now handsome, I'm not the one wearing a shiner tonight." That shut him up. Phillip shook his head and looked at Andrew for some support, but he didn't get it. The ladies tried to suppress their giggles, but that only amounted to heartier laughter.

"Angela, Holly, I must now leave you in the hands of these two rather banged-up buffoons of mine while I tend to a pressing matter. I hope you're not offended by my rudeness."

"Not at all, Charlie," replied Holly, reaching out to give me a big cheeky kiss.

"Go take care of business, Charles. Make sure to save a dance for me tonight," replied Angela with a tender kiss on my forehead.

Holly's eyes locked on to Andrew's and her cheeks flushed as they stood eye to eye.

"I recognize you... from the plane, right?" she whispered softly.

"Yes, hah ha... that's me."

"You were much handsomer then. Good God, what did you do to your face? That's quite the massive welt!"

With a triumphant smile, I quickly bowed out and walked over to check on Réginald.

"Where can an old man get a whiskey around here?" I said cautiously, trying not to be intrusive.

He turned towards me from his attentive position at the window, still deep in thought. After a brief moment, he stepped back into the real world.

"Ah my friend, come," he said putting his arm around my shoulders and leading the way. "Let's go get a *real* drink."

A big smile crept across my face. "Finally, someone who speaks my language!"

Phillip watched Réginald and I exit the foyer in the direction of the Ballroom. For a host, he was acting pretty aloof with his guests. Caroline reached up and gave him a big kiss on either cheek to regain his attention.

"Oh my goodness, welcome Caroline. It's good to see you again. This must be your... your entire family, I see."

"Yes, Phillip. I hope you don't mind. Children add so much life to a summer party."

"Of course I don't mind. We're delighted to have you all here on this very special night."

"Merci beaucoup, Phillip. Vous êtes très gentil, mon ami."

"Benoît... you remember my real estate agent, right?"

"Of course, he is a pain in the ass. What about him?"

"He is anxious to talk to you about something; he asked if you would be here tonight. I believe he is in the backyard by the pool."

"Yes, I know exactly what he wants and he's not going to get it. I'll speak to him later, thanks."

"Maman, maman... la piscine, la piscine! Où est la grand piscine?" shouted Sophia anxiously tugging on her mother's hand. Caroline's little niece had been eagerly anticipating the party at the Grand Château all week. The pool, of course, was the main attraction for all the kids, especially Sophia. If there was a fish in the family it was Sophia, the beautiful Royal Gramma stealing all the attention in the tropical fish tank. Yes, Sophia would one day become the World's fastest Butterfly swimmer, not once, but for three consecutive Summer Olympic Games.

"Du calme, Sophia. Prendre patience, mon petite poisson rouge," replied Caroline with a mother's loving caress across the child's cheek.

Angela shared a smile with the little girl who had been admiring her since arriving. Sophia's eyes spoke to Angela what she dared not say aloud for fear of embarrassment...*you're so pretty*. Her bright young eyes twinkled at Angela; a new friendship had begun.

"Shall we make our way to the Ballroom for some refreshments?" Phillip asked. He smiled at Angela as she grabbed onto his arm. The two hadn't said much, yet, but their body gestures and eye contact enticed a conversation on a level of its own. The two were obviously delighted to be reunited once again. As they all strolled, en masse, to the Ballroom, the beautiful music of Italian composer Ennio

Morricone eased its way into everyone's hearts like a basket of roses drifting down a gently flowing river winding its carefree way around a picturesque countryside. It was The Mission - Gabriel's Oboe composition, definitely an unparalleled masterpiece and ambrosia for the soul.

The Ballroom was packed with guests from all walks of life, both local and from America. Even Réginald's family had taken the evening off to enjoy the festivities. Everybody was elegantly dressed and nicely polished—good behavior all around. Many of Phillip's and Andrew's colleagues and friends were there. Important people from Agen's business community were also there. Noella was the only one missing.

We soon found a table on the side of the Ballroom that opened up onto the backyard terrace and pool. The kids' eyes grew to the size of watermelons at the sight of the pool all lit up under the glorious evening sky and chandelier lamps. They ran impulsively out onto the terrace to play. Perhaps a combination of the pool and enticing smells from the BBQs drew them away from the Ballroom, or more simply, being free to roam as they pleased without adult supervision. Phillip, Andrew and Maurizio found themselves at the bar ordering drinks for everyone.

"Morricone is my favorite composer. He is the Lamborghini of composers," he stated with gusto.

"Not Ferrari?" asked Andrew.

"Ferrari, yes… but I drive a Lamborghini."

"Ah, well spoken my friend," replied Phillip. "At the end of the day, it's what's under the hood that makes a painter paint the masterpiece."

"Painter? You mean racecar driver?" replied Maurizio with a puzzled look on his face.

"Racecar driver, Painter, Composer, Pilot, Nurse, Doctor…"

Andrew looked at Phillip with a newfound appreciation for his friend. "Nice one, Da Vinci, very cerebral of you."

"Voulez-vous quelque chose à boire, messieurs?" interrupted the bartender.

While the men were ordering drinks for the ladies, Réginald was showing me his secret stash of booze.

"This is my private collection," he said as he opened the cellar door leading to a secret room in the basement of the East Wing. "This one here is the very first bottle of Bordeaux that my father earned while working here, a yearly gift of a case of premium Bordeaux wines from the owner of the château." The layer of dust was so thick on the bottle that I couldn't make out the label or date.

"How old?" I asked.

"She's pushing half a century."

"Wow. Got any Jack Daniels?"

"Non, malheureusement, but I have a Cognac that will not disappoint. Want to try?"

"Sure, I'll give it a go. I never understood the difference between the two, though, other than the taste difference."

"Hmm, Whiskey does not grow old in the bottle, only in the barrel. It is not like a bottle of Bordeaux wine."

"Whiskey does not improve with age once it's in the bottle?"

"Non."

"And Cognac does?"

"Non, only in the barrel. Whiskey is made from malt barley. Cognac is made from superb French grapes exclusively from the Cognac region," Réginald explained as he poured two glasses of Cognac, neat. He handed me one and made a toast.

"À la santé."

"À la Cognac," I replied.

The Cognac was smooth and rich and reminded me of a very fine brandy that I tasted in a Napa Valley Brandy Distillery many years ago. The business was sold and operates under a different name now. The taste, however, of that magnificent brandy will remain with me always. I bought a case of it that day and only one bottle remains. This Cognac must be incredibly good for it to retrieve such warm memories from my past.

"Well, what do you think?" Réginald asked.

"I think I need a defibrillator to restart my dazed heart."

"What, Bon Dieu. Something is wrong with your heart?" he replied, leaning in to support my tilting shoulder.

I grimaced at Regi in disbelief. "No, you old fart. Your Cognac is shockingly good."

"Oh, you like it then."

My old heart was trying to recover from the astounding impact of all the Cognac flavors. It was indeed one fine drink.

"C'est magnifique," I replied, exhausting my very limited French vocabulary. "I won't miss my *Jack and Coke* tonight." I licked my lips and held out my glass for another shot. "More please."

"You are a very funny man, Monsieur Charles," he replied, jovially pouring more Cognac into my glass.

"Come, we walk to the rose garden fountain," he continued. "Perhaps my daughter will show up after all, maybe not. But I hope very much for her to come tonight."

"Is this why you look so sad?"

"I am very proud of my Noella. She is very... hard working."

"Ambitious?"

"Oui, merci. But we never see her. Always working so hard... Never any time for her family..."

I nodded my head and began to think about Phillip

when he was going through school and starting the company. He didn't have much time for me then. He did, however, make it back home every now and then to catch up. He was dedicated and committed to his work. He didn't love us less; he was just determined to make his dreams a reality.

"When she does come, you will enjoy the time together twice as much," I commented as we approached the fountain. In the distance, I could see the dim headlights of a small car enter the long driveway. It looked like a taxi. I took another sip of Cognac and pulled myself up on the lip of the fountain.

"I will scold her for being so inconsiderate to her family."

I laughed, half to myself and half aloud. My friend had a broken heart.

Yep, it was a taxi all right.

"Here come the crates of Escargots we forgot to order."

I wasn't so sure about that. We both watched the little taxi pull up to the front entrance. When it stopped, the taxi driver ran out to open the back seat door. Nobody, however, got out of the car. He just stood there perplexed for a few moments looking into the car. Finally, out popped a slender lady talking feverishly on her cell phone. Réginald's demeanor changed in an instant.

"Bon Dieu! She has come."

I watched him run over and hug his daughter passionately, like all French fathers seem to do with their kids. He paid the taxi and looked back at me with tears running down his face. How quickly a broken heart mends, I thought, and smiled back at him. They hurried into the château and disappeared. I took another sip of my Cognac, eased down off the edge of the fountain and picked a rose for my lapel. The stars in the sky were shining very bright tonight. I reached up to touch them and took a deep breath. It doesn't get better than this.

Peter Breeden

SEVENTEEN – LES NUITS D'ÉTÉ
LA DANSE AUTOUR DE LA PISCINE

Only Andrew, Holly, Phillip and Angela were left at the Ballroom table. Caroline and her family had migrated to the poolside tables to keep a close eye on the children who were entertaining everybody with their lively drama around the pool. In the background, the orchestra played some vivacious pieces from Bach's Brandenburg concertos and even though it was still early in the evening, some couples were already warming up the dance floor.

The tension slowly faded away into the recesses of the night. The combination of music, affluent surroundings and chivalrous company made everyone feel at ease.

"Do you like to swim?" Phillip asked Angela as he watched his guests move effortlessly around the dance floor.

"Yes I do. I had a regular swim routine back in Toronto."

"Lengths?"

"Forty-five brutal minutes of the front crawl, three times per week at the Leaside Community pool."

"So you can hold your own in the water then?"

"Yes, I can. You're safe swimming with me, Phillip."

"Well that's good to know. I won't worry about you drowning now from inhaling water during your morning swims," Andrew said to Phillip.

Enlightened by Andrew's comment, Angela's eyebrows raised a tad, which she tried to conceal by taking a sip of her wine.

"That's a funny one, Bumper, seeing as I was the one who pulled your ass out of the creek this afternoon," Phillip replied.

"Easy now, Dream Boy. We're on the same team, remember?"

"Bumper? That's a cute nickname," Holly cut in, lifting her Brandy Alexander to her luscious lips for a sip, and then spontaneously reaching over to steal Andrew's Martini olive.

"Inhaled a little water, did you... Dream Boy?" whispered Angela, slowly running her finger around her wine glass.

Angela immediately caught Phillip's attention. Arousal inched its way up his spine, his eyes flash-dilating.

"That's okay, darling," she continued softly, slowly leaning towards Phillip and gently caressing his chin with the tip of her finger. "I'll just have to resuscitate you if it happens again."

"Ahem, hm, hmm." Phillip cleared his throat before responding. "You're more than welcome, Angela, to join me for a daily swim. Drop by anytime."

Angela smiled in her sophisticated flirtation way, and then flashed her long eyelashes at Phillip.

Andrew chuckled, slightly embarrassed by the romantic turn of events.

"That's my Angela," Holly said, holding up her glass to

toast her. Cocktail glasses chimed around the table.

"Anybody up for a stroll around the pool, maybe grab something from the BBQ feast brewing out there?" proposed Phillip.

"Oh y-e-a-h," replied Angela, immediately standing up and rubbing her belly. "I'm starving."

"Nice," observed Andrew, "a woman with an appetite."

"Feed me now," bellowed Holly.

As Phillip stood up, he spied Réginald scurrying through the Ballroom with a beautiful young lady on his arm. He pointed in their direction and looked at Andrew. "Do you think that is…"

"Yes, for sure that's Noella," he replied.

"Who?" Angela inquired.

"That's Regi's daughter," continued Andrew. "She's an intern in Paris, soon to be a Neurosurgeon," he explained.

Réginald took Noella straight to her mother who was relaxing in a lounger near the far end of the pool. Dominique's gaze shifted from the hypnotizing pool lights to the Ballroom entrance when she sensed a change in the air. A mother instinctively knows when her child is present. Dominique's hands shot to her face to restrain the excitement erupting inside.

"Well, that's fabulous she made it. Regi wasn't optimistic that she would," Phillip continued, watching the scene unfold.

"They look so happy to be reunited," added Angela.

"That is one striking woman," observed Holly. "Look at the confidence pouring out of her."

Andrew spontaneously reached over and pinched Holly's glamorous butt.

"Hey Mr.," she exclaimed, batting her eyelashes. "Do it again. Do it… right now," she insisted, and seductively angled her hips for him, albeit in a classy manner, of course, while glancing back at him with daring eyes.

"SMACK!" Andrew, the brave soul, used the opportunity to affectionately slap her on the bottom. The sound echoed across the hall and turned a few heads.

"H-E-Y!"

"Yup."

"Yup, what?"

"That's one gorgeous butt ya got there, sweetheart."

Somewhere hidden beneath the magic of the night, fate stepped in and dropped Andrew and Holly into the love bubble. Things were happening fast, too fast, but neither cared to slam on the breaks.

"Damned right, little man," replied Holly with her finger tapping his chest, "and if you're not careful, I'll squash you with it, too!"

Standing eye to eye, their noses touched. Andrew wrapped his arms around her waist and pulled her closer. Holly paused a moment, then wrapped her arms around the back of his neck, grabbing and massaging a pinch of hair between her fingers to satisfy her curiosity.

"You are one *Hot Lady*," he mumbled softly into her ear, blowing gently as he spoke and burying his face into her luscious, curly locks.

"Okay, love doves. Hungry here," Phillip blurted out.

"Yes, save the love dance for later tiger," replied Angela, who was suddenly accosted by Sophia, desperately anxious to show her the pool.

"Venez… venez avec moi, Angela," the little girl shouted, tugging her away from Phillip's grasp. "La piscine est là!"

Phillip reluctantly waved good-bye to Angela. He couldn't compete with a fervent six-year old.

The smell of meat, freshly off the French Chef's row of specialty BBQs (rotisseries, smokers, charcoal, gas, and so on), was beginning to hypnotize the boys. Hunger had set in and Phillip could not take his eyes off the food.

"Let's eat," he proposed.

"Not yet. Wait for Angela," replied Andrew.

"I'll grab her a plate. Let's go." The boys began to argue.

"You don't even know what she wants," Andrew shot back.

"Hoh, my goodness. Angela? She eats like a horse," said Holly.

"There, you see? I'll save her some time. I'm HUNGRY."

"Fine," said Andrew, surrendering.

Getting to the buffet tables, however, was another challenge in and of itself. Everybody wanted a bit of Phillip's time.

"Fabulous party, Phillip," replied one guest whom he did not even know.

"Love what you have done with the place, darling," shouted Madame Lapossie-Laporte, drink in hand with a couple gallant fellows on either side and husband nowhere to be seen.

"Excusez-moi! Où est la toilette?"

Phillip discreetly directed the guest to the washrooms around the corner.

"I never thought I would see inside this grand château. It is so... magnifique! Merci, Phillip."

The compliments continued throughout the night in every direction Phillip turned. The mood, like the music, was enriching and everyone was happily engaged in conversation. Some discussions were loud and hearty while others were refined and orderly. The Ballroom was a network of activity that radiated from the center of the room where couples showcased their dancing skills. In the background, foreground, and all the tiny spaces in between, were the heavenly sounds of the Bösendorfer Grand, an eighteenth century harpsichord, violins, violas, cellos, horns, woodwind, vocals, percussion... even a harp. The conductor's hair tossed and flung to and fro as he waived his arms in every which direction. Only a trained eye could unravel his magic.

Phillip mingled a bit at first, but now his attention was entirely focused on Angela, well almost; he hadn't eaten all day. *How, Good Lord, did Angela end up in my arms tonight*, he thought? *Oh yes, the invitation*, he pondered, and then momentarily wondered where I had gotten off to, before the hunger distraction set in again.

"We're almost there," encouraged Phillip as he led Andrew and Holly to the least congested buffet table. These buffet tables were continually replenished by frantic chefs passionately creating flavorful wonders on the BBQs and their assistants' running back and forth between the BBQs and the kitchen to keep the buffet tables, twelve in all, bursting with a delightful assortment of food. Andrew began salivating at the site and smell of the filet mignon steaks positioned row by row in the dome warmer. The cook's assistant noticed and immediately took his order.

"Rare, medium *ou bien cuit*... well done, monsieur?" asked the server.

"Still mooing," he replied.

"Pardon, monsieur?" he asked, leaning towards Andrew to make sure he heard correctly.

Phillip chuckled. "I don't think they speak Texan here, mate," he responded lightheartedly.

"Hold on, boys." It was Holly coming from the other end of the buffet table.

The boys immediately shifted their attention back to Holly.

"Sorry to pull you two away from your raw, red, mooing

meat..." she scowled, "but Angela seems to be motioning for us to join her over there," she continued, pointing in Angela's direction. "Looks like she wants us to meet at your Butler's table.

"Oh yes, I see. Okay, then... I guess Réginald is ready for us to meet Noella," sighed Phillip as he took one last look at the buffet table.

Knowing Phillip well, Andrew signaled for the server to follow them to the table to take everybody's orders for dinner. Phillip's hypoglycemia and high metabolism made him a very irritable individual if he missed a meal, not a good combination for this evening. Andrew learned this the hard way once and was not about to let it happen again. He quickly grabbed a couple buttered croissants from the table and handed one to his pal as they strolled over to the other side of the pool.

"Ah, thank you," Phillip said, taking the croissant. A smile immediately replaced the anxious look on his face.

"The server will follow us over to take orders for the entire table," Andrew advised.

"Good idea. We can all have dinner together."

The two men walked casually together behind Holly as she sped away to meet Noella. The two ladies had something unique in common, the Emergency Room. As it turns out, Angela also had something dear in common— her mansion.

"Where the hell is Pops?" Phillip blurted out.

They stopped and scoped the yard for me. I was sitting on my favorite bench in the Conservatory enjoying the events around the pool as they unfolded. Oh darn, so much for remaining invisible.

"There he is," Phillip gestured to Andrew, and then waved for me to come over. "The lazy bum," he continued, "sitting in the Conservatory away from all the action..."

"Smart man," Andrew replied.

I eased my way off the bench to join them. I had been waiting patiently for the right moment to meet Noella. It's a miracle how things just fall naturally into place sometimes.

I stopped at the side bar in the Ballroom to have my empty glass refilled with Cognac. I took one sip, grimaced, and gave it back to the bartender. It wasn't anything like Réginald's secret stash.

"I've changed my mind. I'll have a *Jack and Coke* instead, please."

Armed with my standby, I proceeded to Réginald's table where Phillip and company had gathered. Little Sophia and her playmates were lined up along the poolside, shoes and socks off, legs dangling in the pool. I made a little wager with myself. Someone was going to end up in the pool tonight and my money was riding on the brave young fellow tugging on Sophia's ponytail.

"Ouille! Arrêtez, tout de suite!" she bellowed and splashed him with a handful of pool water.

I sat down between Holly and Dominique, directly across the table from Phillip and Angela. Caroline's group was at the table next to ours, their party mode in full swing as Caroline, Maurizio, Sophie and her husband attempted to dance the Viennese Waltz. Gillian and Jake sat adjacent to our table with Ben and his wife. The Niles & Pikes lawyers had become very interested in French real estate during their visit and were talking about buying a seaside property in Marseille.

Angela, Holly and Noella were having a passionate conversation about architecture. It was as though they had been best friends all of their lives.

"I have admired this château ever since I was a little girl," Noella said reflectively, memories abounding as she scanned the place. "It is a great treasure I hold in my heart."

She paused for a moment, and then continued.

"I remember my birthday parties, right here at the poolside. The memories that I have are…" She paused in mid-sentence when something, someone, caught her eye.

Holly and Angela managed to follow the trajectory of Noella's eyes to Sebastian, his wife and David who were making their way towards the buffet tables from the Ballroom. Her breath froze instantly in her chest, eyes fully dilated as she watched her childhood friend stroll across the yard. It had been twelve years since she last saw him. Her heart swooned briefly, and then regained itself.

"… magnifique," she finished.

She captured everybody's attention at the table in that short, yet suspended moment. David was the high school sweetheart she left behind to pursue her dreams of becoming a Pediatric Neurosurgeon.

"Ahem," one of the servers intruded. "Can we take your orders now please?"

"You most certainly can, my good fellow," Phillip bellowed.

Over the course of dinner, many exciting stories were shared. Réginald shared a story about Noella's vocal aspirations. When she was a child, everywhere she went, she would sing a tune.

"How come you don't sing anymore, Noella? Sing something for me," Réginald pleaded and took his daughter's slender hand in his own.

"Oh Papa. You're drunk," she replied tenderly.

"Non, non, ma chérie. I am not." His passionate pleas, however, were not enough to entice the songbird.

Noella and Holly spoke passionately about their careers in medicine as the evening progressed. Part of Holly's Nursing training included the study of the brain and the nervous system, an area of medicine she found fascinating. She had a reasonable grasp of neuroanatomy, neurochemistry and behavioral neuroscience. Unfortunately, all the medical chatter almost put Phillip and Angela to sleep. They gazed dreamily into one another's eyes, becoming more adventuresome in their flirtations as the cocktails accumulated in their systems. Angela spontaneously reached out and stirred Phillip's *Jack and Coke*... with her finger. A sly smile formed on Phillip's lips as Angela teasingly dabbed the whiskey finger on her tongue.

"T-a-s-t-y," she whispered softly.

Phillip reached out and twirled a strand of Angela's locks around his finger. Her eyes slowly shut as his index finger then continued around the curve of her ear and down her cheek.

"That feels so nice."

"Fillet Mignon, monsieur?" queried the server, standing behind them with a few dinners in his hands.

"Yes," Phillip said, regaining his composure. "Mmm, that smells good," he added as his and Angela's dinner was served.

When dinner was over, Réginald and I decided to refill our glasses with the premium Cognac he had in his reserve. I eased out of my chair and stepped backward to make room for the little ones running off, and somehow managed to put my foot on the curved lip of the poolside. I panicked a bit, overcompensated and sure enough, ended up in the damned pool. Dear Lord, I just lost my own silly bet. Worse, the kids broke out in laughter thinking I had done it on purpose and, within seconds, every single kid on the pool deck was in the pool splashing around. Sophia was the first to my rescue. Supporting myself with one hand on the pool edge while Sophia wrapped her arms around my neck, I looked up at Phillip and Angela standing over me and uttered a few simple words.

"Can you get me another glass, old sport?" I looked down at the bottom of the pool to see where my whiskey glass had fallen. "Mine, unfortunately... is somewhere down there. Hah."

"Nice one, Charles. You seem to be winning all the ladies hearts tonight," observed Angela.

"Well, it certainly does come naturally," I replied.

"I saved you, Mr. Niles. I saved you," exclaimed Sophia.

"You sure did, my dear."

"Now you swim with me."

"Well... alright then."

When you're wet, you're wet. Nothing more can be done. So, I ended up playing pool tag with the kids... in my brand new tuxedo. The kids thought it was funny; a grown man in the pool with all his clothes on. They failed to realize that I wasn't alone.

Phillip watched me swim off with Sophia attached to the back of my neck. He thought it was all quite amusing. The sounds of Saint-Saëns' *The Swan* filled the evening air and blended quite nicely with the chaotic noise of children playing in the pool. Phillip slid his arm around Angela's waist and pulled her close. Their rosy noses touched.

"Are you a good dancer?" she asked.

"Have I stepped on your toes, yet?"

"You're not allowed to answer a question with a question."

"Okay, then. Yes."

Angela glanced down at Phillip's feet as his body swayed gently back and forth. Smooth Italian leather dress shoes. *He does have good taste. The footwork, on the other hand...*

"Hmm," she managed.

She knew how to dance, all right. Seven years of professional Ballroom dancing lessons and dance competitions from the *all grown-up* age of seven, I might add, had taught her all the right moves; moves that she had never forgotten.

"Prove it," she dared.

Phillip drew a blank expression.

"Prove it? I'm dancing, aren't I?" he retorted.

Angela paused for a moment then pulled her dress up a bit in preparation for her next move.

"I'll show you."

She stepped in close, wrapped her silky right leg around his waist and ran both hands up his chest around his well-toned neck.

Phillip felt some seriously arousing heat. Looking over Angela's shoulder, he saw Andrew and Holly swiftly wave good-bye and escape through a side door to the Conservatory. They had their own heat to generate.

Angela whispered softly in Phillip's ear, "Dance with me."

So he wrapped his arms around her shoulder blades and nuzzled his face in her neck. Working his way up to her ear, he blew several soft, warm kisses that spiraled around her inner ear canal and bounced off the delicate membrane within.

Angela's knees almost buckled.

"Well... I guess that's a start," she declared, "but I'm not completely satisfied yet."

Unleashing him from her leg wrap, she took one large step backward holding onto his arm for support, raised her right foot up onto his shoulder letting her dress naturally slide down towards her hips.

"Okay, *Mr. I can dance*," she said dauntingly, "show me your moves."

"That's pretty hard to beat, *Miss Moonlight Ballerina*," he replied and tenderly kissed her elevated foot, elegantly perched on his strong shoulder. "How about this?"

Phillip lowered his butt—back straight to avoid unnecessary strain—and in one uniform movement, slid his right forearm underneath her soft thigh, grabbed a hold of her firm right buttock and lifted her effortlessly up onto his shoulder.

Angela gasped in excitement. Catching her breath, she reached for the untouchable moon with her long, commanding fingertips.

"You're full of surprises, Phillip. What other secrets are you hiding from me?" she laughed from above, praising Phillip's rather bold dance move.

"How's the view up there?" Phillip whispered, as he proceeded to dance and turn uncomfortably close to the pool.

But unsavory memories of an unexpected and ill-timed pool adventure quickly entered Angela's mind.

"Don't even think about throwing me in the pool, Phillip," she warned.

"Hah ha," he chuckled and put her down. "The thought didn't even cross my mind. This did though."

Drawing her into his arms, Phillip gently placed his slightly open lips on her pillow soft, ribbons-of-ice-cream mouth. They were suspended in mid-kiss bliss when fate stepped in.

"Turn it down a notch, Romeo," Gillian whispered as she passed by on her way to the ladies room. "Six pairs of eager young eyes are glued to you right now."

Angela had forgotten about the kids in the pool and was shocked back into reality. The noise from the pool had seized as all the kids, including this old kid himself, were thrilled speechless.

At that moment, Réginald returned with our bottle of premium Cognac and a towel. I quickly made my way out of the pool. One shot of Cognac and I turned into a blast furnace.

"Thanks, old friend," I said to him.

I couldn't resist, though, with Phillip and Angela standing there like two deer caught in the headlamps.

"Thanks for the show, you two. The in-pool seats offered an *unbelievable* view. Well done."

"Well, of course, those seats do go at a premium," Phillip replied. "Glad to hear you were not disappointed with our... grand performance. Perhaps, come back later for the encore," Phillip teased, the thought of skinny-dipping crossing his naughty mind.

With a chuckle, I made my way back to the room to change into fresh clothes. *Perhaps a hot bath is in order*, I thought to myself. I can relive *The Moment* in peace.

"Might I interest you in a tour of the château, my dear?" offered Phillip, quickly searching for a way out of the spotlight.

"Absolutely, Casanova, show me the way," she replied, also eager to exit the stage. As they were leaving, they passed David standing alone under a pool lamp watching Noella from a safe distance. His heart was still broken. His eyes were glassy, yet hidden behind a brick wall five feet thick. They stared at one another, a whole conversation without a single word. When Phillip and Angela passed by, David turned towards them, smiled and walked alongside them back towards the bar.

"Nice party, Phillip," he managed.

"Thanks, David."

"Makes up for the ridiculous performance on the horse this afternoon... almost," he added with obvious disdain in his voice, before walking off.

"Yikes," observed Angela. "Is something going on there, champ?" she asked when David was out of earshot.

"He's pissed off I took Turbo out for a run. The horse is… too good for me, I guess."

"Hmm, maybe, but I think there is something much deeper there that has nothing to do with you."

"What might that be?"

"Did you notice how Noella looked at David this evening?"

"Yes, that was very intense. Maybe, oh… I know something."

"Spill it," whispered Angela, eager to know the inside scoop.

"Regi's father was the former owner of your mansion."

"No way!"

"Yes, it was their family home. There's more. Apparently, they had to move out. Regi didn't elaborate, just said they ran into some bad luck."

"Hmm, I wonder if that bad luck was the roof. At one point during the history of the home, the roof caved in on the Northwest side."

"Doesn't sound like anything too major, Angela," Phillip replied.

"Well, this actually was pretty bad from an architectural point of view. One load bearing beam and two crossbeams gave way, crashing through two floors and demolishing several rooms, including what would have been a child's room."

"Oof, that's bad."

"Serious enough that Regi couldn't talk about it. You'll have to be sensitive of this when talking with him," advised Angela, watching David get another drink at the Ballroom bar and saunter off to the Conservatory.

"Yes, for sure I will."

Phillip and Angela walked through the Ballroom together, casually stopping to talk to the guests as they enjoyed the evening's entertainment. Some were pleasantly drunk and having far too much fun. Others were dancing to the rejuvenating sounds assembled by the orchestra, currently John Stanley's famous *Trumpet Voluntary*. The horns in this composition were magnificent. I could hear them all the way upstairs where I was soaking in a scented sea salt bubble bath. More like bubble Jacuzzi tub, actually, given that about five people could fit comfortably in there. The water jets massaged my poor old back, nicely unraveling my tight muscles and moderately seized joints from the pool experience earlier in the evening. I reached for my vanilla hazelnut coffee, remembering my golden rule of no alcohol within twenty feet of a hot tub, especially when alone. The soothing pulsation of the water jets against my back sent my mind wandering. Gosh, everybody looked so ravishing tonight. I was so lucky to accompany Angela and Holly to the party and deliver them straight into the hands of my two fine young lads. If they blow this one, I'm going to boot them both in the arse with my imaginary bionic legs. I wonder how much a pair of those would cost? But I digress… back to my story.

Jake and Gillian were dancing in one another's arms at the center of the Ballroom floor to the spine tingling sounds of Cole Porter's *Let's Do It, (Let's Fall In Love)*. It was Gillian's first dance with Jake at their wedding. Her head rested on Jake's shoulder as they both weaved their way back to their wedding day. Fond memories darted across their field of vision. As the mist lifted, Gillian's eyes focused on Phillip and Angela, mingling with the guests at the tables close to the stage.

"Unless I'm mistaken," Gillian observed, "I believe we

have a new Princess in our midst."

"Yes, the lady next door," replied Jake with a touch of irony.

"More like the very ambitious renovator that won't be next door for long once her renovation project is complete."

"So, she lists the place, we buy it as per Phillip's instructions and everybody is happy. Fairly uncomplicated, I think."

"Except for the little part about *Princess in our midst*," Gillian interjected.

"Hmm. So they connect; the romance ignites and quickly fizzles out. Our Princess moves back to Toronto and finds another renovation project. Phillip returns to work. Win, win?"

"Uhm, possibly... More likely, though, that these two *fully* connect and begin building a life together."

"I don't see it," Jake said emphatically. "What does Phillip have in common with a Canuck renovator?"

"Look where you're standing, Sherlock. Renovation projects don't get much bigger than a massive four-century-old Renaissance château."

"Holy fuck!" Jake finally clued in. "Where's Andrew?"

"In the Conservatory," replied Gillian, "with Angela's best friend... Holly."

As the evening slid into night, Phillip and Angela finally managed to elude the Ballroom crowd and escape to the third floor library. Along the way to the library, Angela noticed the poor condition of the stairs and hallway floors, walls and ceilings. *The carpets are worn thin and coming apart*, she thought, *and the light fixtures make the hallways look... spooky*. When she stepped into the library, however, her mouth dropped in awe as she gazed at shelf upon shelf and wall to ceiling books, many of which were only reachable using the sliding ladders.

"What do you think?" Phillip asked.

Angela turned slowly, taking in the entirety of the large room. There were more books here than at her local library at home. The solid mahogany tables and chairs must have been centuries old. The ornate couches appeared to be from the nineteenth century. Then, when her eyes fell upon the spiral staircase leading to another floor, she could no longer withhold her excitement.

"Wow!" she whispered.

"Yes, the books are a little overwhelming."

"Where does the spiral staircase lead to?"

"It leads to the East Wing fourth floor main library. This part of the library is linked to the Master Suite Study and is more or less a resource of basic information. The heavy stuff is on the upper level."

"This room has a lot of potential," Angela replied, taking a seat on one of the couches and motioning for Phillip to do the same.

"What do you mean potential?" Phillip scoffed. "There's nothing to improve upon in this room," he argued, sitting down beside her, "is there?"

"Does it smell a bit musty to you?" observed Angela.

"A bit, I guess."

"Well, that can't be too good for your books. So, the ventilation needs work. Also, the lighting is awful. You need new lighting and new carpets. The wood flooring has come loose in places, too, I noticed."

"The lighting is fine. I can easily see the shelves on the other side of the room."

"Ah, yes, but can you read a book in here for any length of time without getting a headache?"

Phillip remembered his experience reading in the library

last week. He read for about fifteen minutes before his eyes fatigued and he left. Angela obviously knew what she was talking about.

"Maybe... not," he replied.

Angela crossed her legs and leaned over to straighten Phillip's tie, which she noticed was tied in a double Windsor. *That* she could appreciate. Shoes check. Tie check, check. Shoulders, checkity, check, check. Kiss, home run.

"You smell wonderful," he whispered and buried his face in a handful of her hair.

"Shampoo," she smiled.

"Fancy," he replied.

"Not really," she said playfully tapping her chest at the crest of her cleavage. "This fragrance, on the other hand, is f-a-n-c-y."

"Mmm, I know. I've been enjoying it all evening," he replied, placing his hand on her thigh and leaning over to inhale the fragrance.

"Aaah," he exhaled. "You smell like a field of wild flowers in the springtime."

Angela stared into Phillip's seductive eyes for a few moments, her arm draped over the back of the couch. When he began to lean in for a kiss, she stopped him by spontaneously placing her index finger in the center of his forehead. They both shared a muffled laugh.

"Show me the second part of the library," Angela demanded, pointing to the top of the spiral staircase.

"Right... Off we go then," he replied and reached for his cell phone to read another text message, this time from the Chief Operations Officer (COO) of the company.

"Anything serious?" inquired Angela.

"Nothing I can't handle," he smiled.

Phillip followed her closely up the stunning wrought

iron spiral staircase.

"It's quite the workout, isn't it," he commented, somewhat out of breath.

"Only if you're out of shape," she replied. Her long strides powered her up the stairs. She was anxious to see the landing above.

"Hey! I swim each morning, don't forget."

"But that's just plain fun, isn't it?"

"Well, yah, but it is also a strenuous workout."

"Hmm. Why don't you come over and help me tear up carpet, tile and wood flooring sometime? And then you can talk to me about what characterizes a strenuous workout."

Phillip, seizing the opportunity, promptly volunteered his services.

"What time tomorrow?"

Angela reached the top of the spiral staircase and gazed into the room. The architectural magnificence radiating from the library literally squashed Phillip's question completely from her mind.

"Whoa! Phillip, this is incredible."

"Yeah, it's pretty amazing, although I don't think it's a great idea having such a large fireplace in a room filled with so many books."

"It's fine as long as you keep the fire in the fireplace. Besides, the hearth is huge. Any sparks flying out will quickly burn out on the hard, open surface."

"I think one would get quite the workout hauling firewood up here," Phillip added, smartly.

Angela laughed.

"Not really, Phillip. That's what the wood elevator is for," she told him, opening the elevator door built into the fancy stonework around the fireplace.

Phillip peered in. *Great idea*, he thought.

"However, one would definitely get a solid workout

hauling wood to every fireplace at my home. Unfortunately, there are no elevators at Le Manior Portman."

Phillip jumped at yet another opportunity to help Angela.

"I would be pleased to help you with your renos, Angela. Besides, I could use a good workout," he said, charmingly.

"In that case, why don't you drop by tomorrow morning and help me with my railings, say around 10:30?"

"I'll be there."

"Excellent!"

"How are your renos coming along, by the way?"

Phillip was curious about Angela's progress and still wanted to purchase it if she was willing to sell.

"They are coming along nicely. I've finished the exterior walls, windows and shutters."

"Yes, I noticed. They look spectacular," Phillip continued as he led Angela out of the library towards the indoor pool and the walkout. "Love the black shutters, too."

"Thank you. I think they highlight the stone features of the mansion."

"Indeed, they do," he agreed, as they walked across the walkout to the banister and looked down upon the party festivities below. The pool glistened with the light from the patio chandeliers. Amazingly enough, the orchestra was still playing, even though many of the musicians were sitting at tables enjoying food and drink now.

"How come I hear the glorious sounds of Vivaldi's Four Seasons while the musicians sit around the pool deck toasting one another?"

"There must be ghosts in your castle, man. RUN!" she said quickly, pretending to be frightened.

Goose bumps tore across Phillip's back and his face turned pale white. Angela began laughing at him.

"I'm not that gullible," he said.

"Looks like the orchestra brought their very own DJ to mix it up a bit while they take a break," concluded Angela.

"Yes, indeed."

They stood in silence for a while, staring out across the orchard. Angela's mansion stood at the far end of the property. She had left the kitchen lights on.

"The truth is, Phillip, I have about six months of renovations left and about one more month of capital."

Silence ensued as Phillip processed Angela's revelation.

"Tell me, Angela. Do you want to keep that mansion or do you intend to sell it and move on."

"I have no choice. I must sell and I might have to list the property before I finish the renovations, which would really suck."

Angela had never left a project incomplete. It would be, for her, the worst kind of failure, but she was not about to tell Phillip that.

"Are you able to separate business from pleasure?" asked Phillip.

"Yes," she replied immediately.

"Then let's make a deal."

"Okay. What do you recommend?"

"I'll buy your mansion as it stands…"

"I want $1.5 million US."

Phillip's hand moved to his hip in one motion as he stepped back from the railing; an enlightening grin rolled across his face as he gazed into Angela's eyes.

"Is your next big renovation in the States, then?"

"Maybe… I don't know, yet, but I want 1.5 and not a cent less, firm."

"R-i-g-h-t."

When Phillip walked away, her heart sank. She wanted to call after him, but something stood in the way. Instead, she watched him walk calmly across the walkout towards the sliding doors. He was a shrewd business man, indeed, but he wasn't a mean man. He pulled a chilled bottle of white wine from the ice bucket sitting in the fridge near the sliding doors, grabbed two wine glasses from the cupboard and a corkscrew, and then returned to the railing. Angela's worried expression eased. He handed her both wine glasses and began to carve away the tin wrapping around the head of the bottle.

"A handshake is considered legally binding in California," Phillip said a few moments later. He continued to uncork the bottle of wine as he spoke.

"We're not in California," Angela replied.

"Does that mean your word means nothing?"

"My word is good and is as solid as the floor on which we stand."

Phillip looked down at the cement floor and smiled.

"Excellent. Are you willing to negotiate?"

Angela looked into Phillip's eyes. They were all business. "Let's hear your terms, Mr. Niles," she said, lifting her chin and pointing her nose slightly off center of Phillip while maintaining piercing eye contact. This was her *best not fuck with me* look.

Phillip proceeded to pour the wine into the two glasses in Angela's hands. He then put the bottle down and took a glass for himself.

"I will buy your home now and, in return, you will stay on and complete the renovations you originally planned for the mansion within the six month timeframe you previously indicated. The amount that I am willing to pay you for your mansion and six months of service and supplies for the renovations is 2 million US. Does that work for you?"

Angela paused to process everything Phillip had said.

When she smiled, Phillip stuck out his hand.

"Do we have a deal, Ms. Portman?"

"We have a deal, Mr. Niles," she replied, taking his hand and giving it a good hardy shake. They tapped glasses, took a sip of their wine and sealed it with a *disgusting* kiss… well, disgusting according to Sophia's younger cousin, Pierre, anyhow. The two curious kids managed to stumble upon Angela and Phillip while playing Hide and Seek. Sophia's giggles gave the two away.

"Who's there?" Phillip called out.

Sophia and Pierre stepped out into the open, realizing they had been caught. The two could not stop giggling. Angela smiled at them, but Phillip had other plans.

"You know there are Boogie Men up here, right?" Phillip said with a spooky calmness.

Their faces went from giggles to gasps in a tick-tock of the clock and screams could be heard as they ran back down the stairs to the Ballroom.

Angela smacked Phillip in the shoulder.

"That wasn't very nice," she scolded.

"Ah, my dear, have you not heard the ghost stories?" replied Phillip with a sly grin.

"Don't even go there, Buster."

"Right," he agreed reluctantly. "Shall we go find Caroline and Ben to have the terms of sale written up?"

"Can't it wait until tomorrow?"

"I suppose."

"Good, now where were we?"

Before they had a chance to recollect their conversation, a voice cut in.

"Ahem, excusez-moi!" It was Holly, leaning against the sliding glass doors.

"There you are," exclaimed Angela. "We were wondering where you got off to."

"Is that so? Appears to me you forgot us completely," came Andrew's snappy reply as he appeared from behind Holly with an elegant tray of assorted cheeses, crackers and another bottle of Bordeaux, this one from the Haut-Médoc region; Grand Cru Classé de Médoc, Château Cantemerle, 1989).

Alas, Andrew had hit a nerve.

"Reverse Psychology is simply *unattractive* and *illogical*," replied Angela calmly.

"Agreed," Phillip stated, detecting the sincerity in Angela's voice. "It's akin to running the quarter mile… backwards. Everybody watching is thinking *what the fuck?* and dismisses you outright, assuming that *the poor beggar's circuit board is fried.*"

"Easy now, we come in peace and friendship," Andrew replied lightheartedly. "See," he continued, pointing to the label on the bottle.

Phillip inspected the label and showed it to Angela with a gesture of approval.

"Okay, we'll forgive you seeing as you brought such a fine bottle," Phillip said with an easy smile.

"What a beautiful space up here," observed Holly, walking across the walkout to the railings and inhaling the evening air. "I will be sorry to leave it all behind in two days."

"I'm leaving on Monday, as well," said Andrew. "We should try and get the same connections, at least to Paris and Chicago, anyway."

"Sure."

"Give me your itinerary later and I'll take care of it all," Andrew offered while igniting the gas lamp burners near the table.

"Okay," she happily replied, and danced over to give him a kiss.

"Ah, that's better. Thank you for the light and warmth, Andrew," said Angela.

"You're most welcome."

They sat down at the table under the gas lamps and opened the next bottle of wine. With glasses in hand, they each made a toast as they went, in turn, around the table.

Holly belted out her toast first, "To love and happiness."

"To new beginnings and opportunities," continued Andrew.

"To keeping pleasure and business separate," toasted Angela.

Phillip was amazed at how easy the toasts rolled off of everybody's tongues. He took a moment to think about his own toast.

"I, uhm…"

He stumbled for a moment.

"I would like to make a toast to my loving grandfather, who's probably passed out upstairs in his bed right about now, dreaming of fast women and supercharged muscle cars. My grandfather, The Mountain; he is my balance in the forest of life. May his happiness be great and his quarter mile run in the *sleeper* Plymouth Acclaim next week, be hair raising and awesome!"

"To grandpa," replied the ladies, their eyes misting up.

"Good one, Phil," Andrew said and they all clinked glasses.

"I'm going with him to Infineon Raceway, by the way."

"Excellent idea, Andrew. I wish I could go too, but I have to arrange some things here before heading back to the office."

"I'll get it all on video for you."

"Thanks man."

"So, how long will you be in California?" Angela asked, trying to conceal her concern.

"I'll probably head back to California for a week each month, just to make sure they don't forget me back home."

"Jerome, our Chief Operating Officer is doing a good job filling in as the front man while we're here enjoying our time in France," Andrew told them, "but he is getting too comfy in the role. So, we need to head back and bring some normalcy back into the daily operations."

"All this talk about going home is killing my mojo," Holly complained.

Angela also expressed her displeasure. "Yah, smarten up boys. The weekend has only just begun."

"You're right. Let's plan something for tomorrow," Andrew suggested.

"Ideas anyone?" asked Phillip as he spread some Brie cheese on a cracker and handed it to Angela.

"Shopping," replied Holly, "somewhere out of town."

"Yes, good idea," Angela said in agreement. "Let's head south."

Andrew looked at Phillip. The possibilities were endless.

"We can call Akhila to see if the helicopter is available tomorrow," Andrew suggested.

"That's a thought," replied Phillip. "Or, we could drive… see southern France by car and discover a nice small town along the Mediterranean."

"Oh, how lovely," Holly said, nodding her head at Angela.

"Yes, that does sound like fun," she agreed.

"What do you think… the Bugatti Veyron and the Peugeot RCZ?"

"Sure, as long as we can swap cars on the way back?" Andrew asked.

"What? Now you want to play musical… cars?"

"I wanna drive both, man."

"Do you have your quad-turbo license?" asked Phillip

with a cheeky smile.

Andrew scoffed. "I'm certified on shifter go-carts, my friend." he replied swiftly. "I'm good to go."

Phillip turned to the ladies and made a subtle remark. "What's scary about this is that he is dead serious."

The ladies gave Andrew a suspicious look.

"It's a car guy thing," he calmly replied in his own defense.

"What about Charles?" Angela asked Phillip.

"I think he'll be too tired in the morning for a trip like that, but we can invite him anyway, just on the off-chance."

"Good idea," added Andrew.

Even though the starry night eased slowly across the Midnight threshold, the party was still gathering momentum below. The music played on, the dancing continued, the laughter and good cheer echoed throughout the hallways as people broke off into small, intimate corners of the château. In the stables, the horses looked at one another in amusement while the party folks strolled through.

Funny creatures these humans are.

At least they feed us.

Yah, that's a bonus, but they sit on our backs.

Yah, that part sucks. They should learn how to run around the place on their own.

Hah ha... on two short, skinny legs?

They're safer on my back, except for that yahoo this afternoon. He gets on me again and I'll drop him on the road instead of in the creek.

Easy now, Fireball! He just might be Le Grand Fromage... you know, The Big C-h-e-e-s-e.

Smelly cheese... Okay, the creek, then.

Perched on top of the open stable doors sat a plain white dove pensively absorbing the mood of the festivities. From this spot, there was a view of the orchards, the stables, the pool party and the events taking place on the walkout above.

...Things are coming together nicely.

"Anybody up for a little skinny dipping?" offered Phillip.

Oh my goodness, maybe not!

"Hmm..." Angela pondered.

The dove swooped in and landed on the railings, capturing everybody's attention.

"You know, Phillip, I think it has been a splendid night," Angela began. "We've probably had a little too much wine to be going skinny dipping, but I sure would like to take a rain check on that offer."

"My thoughts, exactly," Holly said, sending a huge smile Andrew's way and lovingly stroking his cheek.

Phillip watched the dove extend one wing using its leg as a base on which to stretch. *That's odd. He's not the least bit afraid of us*, he thought as he peered into the bird's peaceful eye. He remembered from his Sunday School teachings that The Holy Spirit, in the form of a Dove, descended on Jesus at the time of His baptism. Perhaps the dove on the railing tonight was a symbol of divine intervention?

"Yes, of course," he replied, finally regaining his sense of being. "Perhaps it would be a good idea to head downstairs and mingle some more."

Several sighs were heard around the table. It had been a long day for everyone and the cool night air was beginning to dance uncomfortably along the ladies bare shoulders.

"On second thought...we have a big day planned for tomorrow. Let's think about turning in before too long. Actually," he continued, "you both should go ahead and pick a vacant room on the third floor. Make yourselves cozy for the night. It's too late to take you back home now, unless you object, of course?"

"No, no... sounds perfectly fine, right Angela?"

"We could simply walk back through the orchard to get home."

"Don't forget about the Boogie Man," Phillip whispered.

"I am a bit tired, though," Angela confessed.

"And it's a long haul through the Boogie Man infested orchards."

"Oh alright, we can crash here tonight."

"Good," replied Phillip, now turning his attention to Andrew. "Shall we head down, let our guests know that they are welcome to continue the party and spend the night in the second floor rooms if they wish?"

"Good idea. We can also bid everyone goodnight and fade away to our own chambers, as well. I'm excited about tomorrow," Andrew said, looking deeply into Holly's eyes as he and Phillip stood up from the table.

Holly warmed him with her smile. "Me too, Snookums."

"Goodnight, my darling," Phillip whispered to Angela and sealed their departure with a tender kiss.

"See you in the morning, champ," Angela, said softly. "Great party, by the way," she said emphatically as the lads strolled away.

"It was indeed," he said to Andrew as they headed for the stairs. "Something tells me, however, that you and Holly didn't expect to find Angela and I on the walkout this evening."

"Ah, you know how it is. It all worked out fine anyway."

"I think so, too. Holly seems like a wonderful person, Andrew."

"She is quite remarkable. Did you hear her conversation with Noella at dinner tonight?"

"Yes, the part about saving the boy's life using the scissors from her nail file kit was incredible."

"The emergency tracheotomy, yes. Even the brainy neurosurgeon was impressed."

"Noella was impressed," Phillip continued, "but I think her mind was also elsewhere, on David, I think. Did you notice the heat there?"

"Yes, I did. There's definitely some obscure history between those two."

"Definitely something..."

Angela and Holly made their way to the third floor and picked a large guest room with separate sitting and study rooms, balcony and a very spacious ensuite bathroom. The King four-poster was large enough for both of them, but they were not quite ready to retire yet.

"Check this place out, Sugar," Holly said, dancing through the rooms like a Monarch butterfly in the summer breeze.

"The structure is absolutely beautiful, but I can see where it needs some careful attention and restoration," she replied, pointing to the loose moldings and some cracked tiles in the ensuite bathroom.

"Angela, you're too picky."

"Yes, but I would fix these things if I owned this place." *I would also make it a little more inviting, as well*, she thought to herself.

Holly wandered into the sitting room where there were three couches set in a cube fashion in front of the open fireplace.

"I can set up the fireplace in the sitting room, if you want to relax in comfort for a bit."

"That sounds splendid. I'll make some herbal tea," offered Angela, as she sorted through the basket of teas on the tea trolley.

"Anything good there?"

"Yes, we have Peppermint, Chamomile, Chocolate Chaï, Feeling Soothed, Feeling Restored, Dreamtime, Jasmine,

Green Tea, Black Tea and Ginger Peach."

"Throw two Chocolate Chaïs, one Green, two Restorations, one Peppermint and… one Ginger Peach in the tea pot. That should do it!"

"That's quite the brew you conjured up there, Miss Bubble-Bubble Double Trouble."

"Ahyahahah, sistah, we be brewing up a fine and dandy storm," Holly cackled.

"Shall I throw some bat whiskers and termite brains in the caldron then?"

"No thanks… just some sweetener and milk for me please," replied Holly in her normal voice.

"Awe, you're no fun."

Holly sighed. "The fire is lit," she said as she slipped out of her dress and stockings to relax in her slip.

"And the tea is steeping," replied Angela, also slipping out of her dress and stockings as she got comfortable.

Holly grabbed the pillows from the bed and hurried back into the sitting room, throwing herself on the couch in a display of ecstatic exhaustion.

"Phillip is a handsome, charming fellow," she observed. "What took you so long?"

"We didn't exactly hit it off in the beginning."

Holly stared at Angela, hoping she would be a little more forthcoming.

"I guess I was intensely focused on my renovations and didn't really want any complicated distractions."

"And now you do?"

Angela walked over to the tea trolley and poured two teas. The question stung a bit, but she knew it was coming from a good place.

"I don't know," she replied finally. "We just seemed to connect tonight, and it felt right."

"That kiss by the pool had everybody's jaws gaping wide

open."

"He has a way of making me forget my surroundings. When I'm in his arms, I don't worry about anything. I simply dance in the palm of his hand, like he was my King Kong or something."

"Nice analogy, Angela. You're... in love."

"He's buying the mansion and paying for me to stay on to complete six more months of renos, basically the entire project."

"That's fabulous news girl! How much dough are you getting?"

"Two million US," she replied, throwing her arms in the air and swinging her hips in celebration, "all said and done."

"Okay, sistah, I'm officially leaving the Nursing business for the lucrative home renovation business," Holly declared whimsically, leaping over the back end of the couch to give her dear friend a big hug. "Congratulations Angela. I'm so proud of everything you have accomplished this year."

"Thank you. You're such a good friend... helping me get to this stage in my life," she said with tears in her eyes.

"I haven't done much."

"Yes," *sniffle-sniffle*, "you have."

"Just been a friend, is all."

"That's everything," replied Angela quietly.

Holly pulled Angela in for another snuggle-hug. The two leaned on one another for a moment and began smiling. It was an emotional rollercoaster ending to a rather grand day. Something at the back of Holly's mind, an annoying alarm bell, kept going off though. She had to ask.

"Has the deal been finalized, yet?"

"No, not officially, but we shook hands on it."

Holly held back her concern. Instead, she smiled and nodded her head in a show of respect, but that little alarm bell at the back of her head kept sounding off; *A handshake! What the fuck are you thinking woman?*

"We're going to meet with Caroline and Ben tomorrow to get something written up. So, it will happen soon enough."

"Aren't we going on a road trip tomorrow, er... today?" Holly questioned subtly, glancing at her watch to confirm the early hour of the morning.

Angela looked shocked. "Yes, we are! Time to crash," she told her, jumping on the couch in front of the fire...totally missing the subtlety of Holly's question.

"Yes," she replied softly, fluffing her pillows and stretching out on the adjacent couch. "Let's get some sleep."

PART V

Peter Breeden

EIGHTEEN – UP WITH THE BIRDS

The next morning came quickly; at least it did for me anyway. Everybody else was still fast asleep. The relaxing Jacuzzi-massage bath I took before crawling into bed last night miraculously turned my old achy muscles into Herculean boulders, well… not quite, but somehow I felt much younger this morning. I rolled over to look at the clock. It was 6:59 AM. Knowing full well I wouldn't fall back to sleep, I crawled out of bed, opened the curtains and stretched in front of the bedroom window, wearing only my Dale Earnhardt Daytona 500 boxer shorts. *'The Intimidator,' the Master Drafter, the Bump, Tap and See Your Ass Later Racer. RIP my friend.*

My bedroom faced the front grounds of the château. In the distance, the morning mist hovered over the fields and gradually began to fade away as the sunshine poked its way through the wispy clouds. I opened the window and took a deep breath of fresh, Agenais morning air. I heard the birds chirping in a mad frenzy coming from all directions. And then I saw them, chasing one another through the fountain below, performing wondrous acrobats as they darted in and out of the rose bushes. They were mildly entertaining, but without my morning coffee, they were the precursor to a headache. From the corner of my eye, I notice something very disturbing. *Oof, that can't be the…*

"Gosh-dagnit! Who left the Rolls Royce outside all night?" I bellowed, slapping my hand on the window frame.

A voice from below replied, "I no find the reverse. It make funny noise."

I stuck my head out the window and saw the young valet standing by the steps, the same fellow who took my keys last evening. He had obviously stayed there the whole night worrying about the car.

"Je suis désolé… monsieur," he said, taking off his hat. He looked as though he would breakout in tears at any moment.

"I'll come down," I said waving my hand. "Stay there."

I quickly pulled on my pants and a shirt. I had to give the young lad credit for not driving it when he was unsure. *Did he say noise? The car made a noise? Please, dear Lord, let the transmission be unharmed.*

When I reached the front steps, he was there to greet me and personally hand over the keys. His name tag said, Jean-Luc.

"Ah, Bonjour, Jean-Luc."

"Bon Matin, monsieur," he replied with a smile.

We walked over to the Phantom and I immediately noticed that the car was half off the driveway and needed to be backed up to complete the turn. He must have had problems getting it into reverse gear. That can be tricky on this car or any manual car if one is unsure of the shifter. I motioned for him to get into the passenger seat and I took charge of the wheel. Looks like he stalled the car while in gear. I stepped on the clutch and shifted back into neutral. When I turned the key, the old girl fired up nicely. Jean-Luc watched each of my actions with devoted attention. I made eye contact to ensure he was watching, and then I stepped on the clutch and shifted into reverse. Gradually easing off the clutch and gently tapping the gas, we moved backwards without a hitch.

"Ah, dis is how de reverse go. Bon!" he said with eyes bigger than the moon.

I smiled and he was relieved.

"All is good, no?"

"Yes… all is good."

He smiled, double-tapped the dashboard and gave a hearty laugh when I honked the horn. It's not every day that one sees another's pyloric valve wobble through the frame of a diastema.

Shifting into first gear, we pulled forward and off towards the garage. *Wonderful, everything works*, I thought to myself. I glanced over at the young lad and could tell he was excited, despite staying up all night to ensure the safety of the car. That dedication deserves some kind of reward, I thought.

"Do you need a ride home?"

"Ride? Oui… mon sac!" he said, motioning for me to stop. He leapt out of the car and raced up the front steps into the château. Moments later, he reappeared with his backpack, leaping down the stairs three steps at a time. At the bottom of the stairs, his knee buckled. The backpack and his French chapeau flew in alternate directions and one shoe popped off as he barrel-rolled along the ground.

"Good Lord," I exclaimed and opened the car door to see if he was alright. By the time I twisted to move my ass out of the car, he had already picked up his belongings, put on his shoe and returned to the passenger side of the car.

We stared awkwardly at one another for a moment.

"Mon sac," he said, holding up the bag.

"Fantastic," I replied and smiled, but couldn't help thinking what a wonderful blessing it is to be young, agile and durable. I was a little jealous of his youth... his freedom. If I had crashed like he just did, I would most likely be dead. I put the car in gear and headed down the long driveway to the road.

"24," he responded hastily in his mother tongue, and then searched hard for the correct English words, "ehm, *twenty-four*, Rue St. Anne."

"What was that? 24 St. Anne Street?"

"Oui, St. Anne."

"Ah, where is that?"

"I show you. Gauche à la fin..." he said, pointing to go left at the end of the driveway. *This should be fun*, I thought to myself.

"Okay, turning left onto the main road," I said aloud, just to make sure we were both on the same page.

"Magnifique!" he replied and settled back to enjoy the multimillion dollar ride home in the Rolls-Royce Phantom.

Things were slowly coming alive at the château. Phillip was having a tough time getting out of bed this morning. It might have had something to do with a loud horn that went off around 7:30 AM, waking him out of a deep sleep. *Was that the... Rolls-Royce horn*, he mumbled to himself. *Grandpa, you can't be up already*. Indeed, I was 'up and at em' already.

Phillip tossed and turned for another hour before giving in to the persistent echo of the annoying ghost horn rebounding in his head. He decided to stick to his morning swimming routine despite the annoying elf tap dancing on his cerebellum , a subtle reminder of the fantastic time he had last night. He stumbled out of bed and walked to the ensuite bathroom in his NHRA Funny Car boxer shorts. *It runs in the family, I guess.* Grabbing a towel, he marched up to the pool, taking the shortcut through the library, and jumped in. A few warm up exercises and he was good to go. *Forty-five minutes of this*, he thought, *and I'll be as good as new.* He was right, too. Forty-five minutes of the front crawl had reinvigorated him. The headache was gone, replaced only by unrelenting hunger pains. When he stepped out of the pool, Réginald handed him a fresh towel and a glass of freshly squeezed orange juice.

"Thanks Regi."

"Pas de problem. Breakfast is almost ready. I assume you are hungry, non?"

Phillip thought about his response for a moment. It was no ordinary hunger he had this morning. It was more... primeval.

"Starving...like a horny Gorilla... caught between feasting on termite infested tree bark and surprising his lady-love doing summersaults in the luscious green grass beyond the stream."

Regi took a minute to process Phillip's wild, exercise-fuelled delusion, and then simply humphed.

"Very well, one order of Gorilla treats for you and a couple of sweethearts."

"Are the ladies up already... seriously?" Phillip asked, surprised that anybody in their right mind would be up yet.

"Yes, and Andrew," he continued. "They are having coffee on the walkout."

"Okay, I'll have a quick shower and be right up then," he replied and turned to go, but stopped when a rather melodic voice graced his ears.

"Oh, forget the shower, Rhett," stammered Angela as she marched through the sliding doors doing her best

Scarlet O'Hara impersonation. "We're hungry now!"

Phillip, standing tall with the towel slung around his neck, watched her every move.

"Well, hello there, Sugar," he replied, giving in and playing along, Rhett Butler style.

"Hello, Rhett," she replied with a toss of her shoulder. "All a girl wants is a little breakfast," she continued. "Why can't you just stop for a moment and be civilized?"

"I'm a bad man, Rose Bud, an outlaw, as uncivilized as they come."

"Well, 'fiddle-dee-dee' then you stubborn old… Cow Pie," she said tossing her hand and turning away. "I reckon I'll find me a real Buck… a Strong Hand of the land. One who knows when his lady needs a little breakfast," she turned to face him with a piercing look and both hands on her hips.

"Well in that case, my dear, breakfast is served," he said with a smile and taking her in his arms.

"A fan of the classics, are you, handsome?" Angela queried, running her finger down his damp, muscular chest.

"Yes, but an even bigger fan of a certain classy lady," he said, leaning in for a slow, tender, heart-embracing, mouth-smothering, knee-buckling… kiss.

Réginald, happy for their love, but embarrassed by the open display of affection, gently reminded them of his presence.

"Ahem, ehm…"

"Yes, yes, Regi, off we go," he replied, leading Angela back out onto the walkout and the warmth of the brilliant Agenais sunshine. "Come my dear, I am under the impression that you desire a little breakfast."

"Oh, whatever gave you that impression?" she replied with a teasing smile.

Angela and Phillip joined Noella, Andrew and Holly at the breakfast table. Warm croissants and the aroma of freshly brewed coffee on the table put everybody in a cheerful mood. The calmness of the morning soon turned into a loud, boisterous conversation at the table. Everybody had a story to tell and passionate conversations kept the fires stoked and roaring. The conversation took many unusual turns, but when it landed on the road trip to the Côte d'Azure, Noella's eyes dilated and opened wide. She loved her country with an enormous amount of zeal and could hardly contain herself.

"Road trip? I love road trips!" she exclaimed.

"Come with us then," Angela demanded. "It'll be fun."

"Ah merde! I would, but I depart in about twenty minutes. I have to return to the hospital."

"Regi told me you had to return first thing this morning," said Phillip. "It would have been lovely for you to join us today, especially with all the insight you have about the country we'll be driving through."

"Well, I do have some tips for you," said Noella. "I recommend that you head down to Agde via Narbonne and stop in Toulouse and Carcassonne along the way. This way is very scenic and you will enjoy it very much."

"Ooh, that sounds lovely," replied Holly.

"Stop in Toulouse for some shopping and a coffee break. There are many fabulous Cafés in town. Don't stay too long. Hop in the car and head to Carcassonne for lunch. There is a lovely restaurant that my dear friend owns called *La Vieille Vigne du Sud*. Stop there for lunch. The food is exquisite and the views of the vineyards are incredible," she continued, everybody's attention glued to her every spoken word. "Ask for André and tell him I sent you," she said with a twinkle in her eyes and an approving wink. "After lunch, make haste for Narbonne. Stop here for another café and be sure to see the Cathédral Saint-Just-et-Saint-Pasteur de Narbonne. C'est magnifique. Enfin, Agde. It is here where the sea turns your heart into butterflies."

"Sounds like magic, Noella."

"Yes, Andrew, Narbonne and Agde are quite magical. Stay in Agde for the afternoon and choose a nice restaurant for dinner that overlooks the Mediterranean Sea. You won't be disappointed."

"I want to walk along the beach in my bare feet," Angela replied, dreamily.

"I think you will be very surprised with what you discover at the beaches," Noella added with a bit of mystery in her voice. She chose not to reveal a local secret, but rather allow her new friends to discover a bit of France on their own.

"How long will it take to get to Narbonne?" Andrew asked.

"About two seconds in the Bugatti," laughed Phillip.

"Or, about two supersonic slaps from me," Holly scowled.

"And a week in the dog-house, Buster…" continued Angela, who leaned over and poked Phillip's shoulder.

"You will have plenty of time and enjoy the scenery much more if you drive at a safe pace," Noella continued. "The French, however, like to drive crazy fast in their small cars. So, take care."

"Well then," said Phillip, expecting to be freed from the anti-speeding law the ladies just laid down. Their glare, however, signaled his defeat.

"I recommend leaving Agde around 21:00 hours, a little after sunset, so you do not get back too late. Definitely watch the sunset from the beach. It is magnificent!"

I caught Phillip's eye when I strolled onto the walkout.

He wasn't overly excited to see me.

"Hello there, all," I said, walking up to the table. "Miss me?"

"Not if that was you honking the Rolls horn at 7:30 AM this morning," Phillip said hotly.

"Indeed it was, sorry." I chuckled.

Andrew pulled out a chair and I sat down. Holly poured a cup of coffee for me and I gratefully took a sip. I had just returned from dropping Jean-Luc off at home. *What a nice kid*, I thought to myself.

"Join us for a road trip, today?" asked Andrew.

The thought of a road trip was overwhelming. On one hand, it would be nice to see the country and some new places. On the other hand, I was wiped out. I needed some down time.

"Thanks for the invitation, but I have a previous commitment. Yes…" I continued, still thinking of my excuse.

"And what might that be, Mr. Horn Honker?"

"I uhm, I… well, the Jacuzzi tub was so fine last night, I think I will just relax today and maybe sometime this afternoon, hop back in… you know, for another go."

"Sounds like a wonderful idea, Charles," Angela commented and reached out to give me a hug. "Thanks again for escorting us last night. You are one classy gentleman."

"Oh sweetheart… you're too generous. Indeed, it was I who should be thanking you lovely ladies for making an old man young again."

"Awe," replied Holly, leaning in to give me a hug, as well. *I'm a 'chick magnet,'* I thought to myself. *This old guy ROCKS!*

"Your taxi has arrived," interrupted Regi, with pronounced sadness in his voice. He knew it would be a long time before he saw his daughter again, but he also knew she needed to return to the hospital. Her work was very important. He would sacrifice his own happiness for that of his daughter. That was his promise to himself and Noella.

"Already?" Noella said despondently.

"Oui, ma chérie."

Noella said her goodbyes to everybody and made her exit. Her mother and father saw her off and waved goodbye as the taxi drove off. It was a heartbreaking scene, but it held the promise of a rosy future.

Back on the walkout, Phillip was getting anxious to start the road trip.

"Let's get this convoy rolling, folks."

"Yes," said Andrew, "we're losing daylight here."

"Oh wait," Angela interjected. "We need to stop off at the house before heading out."

"Alright then, let's get going," Andrew said anxiously. He could hardly contain his excitement. He was about to drive two new sports cars that he had never driven before.

"Right... Let's pull the cars out then, Lug Nut," Phillip said to Andrew.

"We'll meet you two at the front in ten minutes then?" Phillip verified as they were leaving.

"See you in ten," Angela replied.

"Have a good day, Pops." Phillip gave me a big hug goodbye. I was forgiven.

"You too, son."

I look back on that day now with great envy. What on earth could be better than the combination of 'The Fountain of Youth,' newfound love, two hot cars and a road trip through southern France? There is a lot of heartfelt emotion and harsh truth about the saying, 'you're only young once.' Be smart and have fun while you still can. The future seems so far away and yet it too becomes yesterday shockingly quick.

Peter Breeden

NINETEEN – WARM, BUTTERY CROISSANTS

Agde is a beautiful seaside town about three hour's drive southeast of Agen on the A62 and A61. In my opinion, it's a bit far to travel for a one day adventure. Nothing seems impossible, however, when you are young and in love, not even a 636 kilometer / 395 mile day trip. Good thing the boys like driving. Perhaps the ladies like driving, too… Ha hah. We'll see if the boys are brave enough to let the ladies drive. At least they can stop and rest in some great places along the way, such as Toulouse, Carcassonne, and Narbonne, which is about 40 kilometers west of Agde. The splendid thing about this adventure is that it's a new discovery on two fronts: personal and recreational. Wherever they stop, there will be something fun to experience as the young couples ease their way into one another's hearts. Of course, the cafés and warm, buttery croissants are reason enough to stop, regardless of the need to empty one's bladder or stretch the legs. Alas, I digress… on with the story.

The boys pulled into Angela's driveway at about 10:15

AM with the expectation that they would be on their way by 10:30. However, when they were greeted at the door by *The Rowdy Threesome*: Heartbreaker (HB), Bodyguard (BG) and Dovely (the cat), they knew it would be a while before they set off.

Angela let the dogs out to unload their burdens in the backyard. Within minutes, the bouncy canines were back in looking for food. After feeding the dogs and cat, the girls disappeared to prepare themselves for the trip, but not before sending the boys out to walk the dogs. It was 11:02 when they finally pulled out of the driveway: Phillip and Angela in the Bugatti and Andrew and Holly in the Peugeot.

"Toulouse, here we come," hollered Angela.

"Nice of you to warn Toulouse about your pending arrival, CG," laughed Phillip. "I'm sure they are making preparations as we speak."

"And what does CG stand for, Mr.?"

Phillip smiled and remained secretive. "Go ahead and guess."

"Alright then, how about..." she hesitated a moment, "Calendar Girl?"

"Nope. Ha."

"Better not be Crazy Girl."

"It's not," he laughed again, shifted the Bugatti up a gear and loaded Donna Lewis' Agenais on the stereo system.

The game continued as they drove past downtown Agen and along the waterway on the main route, southeast towards Toulouse. Andrew and Holly were right behind them with the top down on the Peugeot. Phillip could see them clearly in his rearview mirror. Holly looked like a 1960s movie actress in her black shades and silky walnut hair tied down with a fashionable Hermès scarf. F-a-n-c-y... Look out Audrey Hepburn... and Grace Kelly, too.

There's a new show in town starring Holly T. MacGibbon, the wildcat Canuck with feisty Scottish blood coursing through her veins.

The countryside was magnificent and awe inspiring. The hills rolled gently off into the distance and occasionally a castle or church came into view sitting majestically above the valleys and groves of trees below. They passed many vineyards with row upon row of vines running like ribbons across the landscape. Aaah... the science of wine making is the art of the ages. Will this be a banner year for French wine? Who knows? In twenty years, we'll open a bottle of this year's vintage Bordeaux wine and indulge ourselves in the bouquet of excellence. My guess is, yes, it will most certainly be a fabulous year. French wine is simply heavenly.

"Cute Genius?"

"Nice try."

"Oh c'mon. I want that one."

"Sorry."

"Well, it must be Clever Girl then..."

"Nice, but no."

"Shit! Gimme a hint," she bellowed, and switched the music to a Rock and Roll legend.

"Okay... CG rhymes with squeegee."

Angela rolled her eyes and became transfixed with the beauty of the passing countryside. Phillip's car phone rang, interrupting the music.

"Hello."

"Hi Phillip," boomed the voice. "It's Jerome. We have a problem."

"Lay it on me, Jer."

"We've hired a ton of new contractors and we don't know where to put them all."

"Hmm. There was lots of space on the campus last time I checked."

"Yes, but where do we put them: with the full-timers or in their own separate area or place them according to their job description? What?"

"Hmm."

"And we've run out of contractor badges, as well."

Phillip looked out in the distance and saw a beautiful church sitting on top of a hill and a Sheppard with his flock of sheep below.

"Boss... you still there?" Jerome asked impatiently.

"Yah, I'm here. Why is it again that we have contractor badges?" Phillip asked.

"For the temporary employees," replied Jerome, surprised at the nature of the question.

"Hmm, but they are still working, doing an important job for us, right?"

"Yes, of course."

"Why then should they be treated differently, any less?"

"They are only temporary employees, I guess."

"Sounds outdated to me. Okay, here is what you do. Eliminate all contractor badges from the system. Reassign the same full-time badges to the contractors and limit their access according to their needs. There is to be no discrimination between full-time, part-time and contract employees."

"Okay."

"As far as placement goes, situate the new hires with the work group to which they are associated. That way, everybody on the same project is within immediate reach in the office."

"That might take some time, Boss."

"Make this work, Jerome, and we don't have much time. This new project needs to be *'Haulin' Ass'* this week."

"Okay, I'll make this work... somehow."

"Excellent, my friend," Phillip continued. "Give Andrew a call, as well. Let him know about the change of plans."

"I'll do that now, then."

"Thanks. Later."

Phillip smiled at Angela as she gazed approvingly at him. You can learn a lot about a person on a road trip. It usually makes or breaks a new relationship and is a quick way of discovering compatibility. Unfortunately, if things go bad, they really go bad. I don't think that is the case with these kids though. A lifetime of experience has told me that a couple must possess and cultivate a physical and cerebral attraction for one another to sustain the health and inevitably, the enjoyment, of a relationship.

"So, does CG stand for two words or is it one word that rhymes with squeegee?"

"Two words," replied Phillip. "I just threw squeegee in there because it rhymes. That wasn't really a hint, was it?"

"NO, it wasn't. Now you have to give me two hints for derailing my thought processes."

"Fair enough, your guesses are good, but..." Phillip was interrupted by the car phone ringing. It was Andrew. "Pardon me, CG."

"Hey, Andrew!"

"What the fuck?" Andrew exclaimed.

"Ah, you spoke with Jerome."

"Yes, I did."

"Okay, hear me out. Why do we favor permanent employees over part-time or contract employees?"

"That's an easy one. Our permanent employees have earned their seniority."

"So contract and part-time employees should be considered less worthy then?"

"Less valuable to the company, I would say."

Phillip paused a moment, and then continued with an even, unwavering voice.

"Everybody is equally important in our company. Here's why: what happens when any piece of a chain fails?"

"You stop going forward and depending on what's driving the chain — potential disaster."

"Right, let's look at that. Say for example, you are riding a bike and the chain breaks. You lose your balance and your foot slips off the pedal, possibly injuring your foot or worse, you fall off the bike or swerve into traffic. How about a timing chain? The chain breaks, the pistons hit the valves and... KABOOM!"

"That's a little farfetched, I think, Phillip," Andrew replied, dismissing the analogy as highly unlikely. "Chains rarely break."

"Not really. Look at governments, major companies and even nuclear facilities that have failed because somewhere there was a flaw in the chain. It broke and things crumbled."

"So what are you trying to do here, create the perfect chain... a perfect workforce?"

"Perfection is not realistic, but improving the efficiency and resiliency of our workforce by instilling equality within the workplace is essential. Productivity is based on the collective efforts of a synchronized and harmonious pool of workers. All of our employees are connected by this one chain that drives the engine of our success. If we teach our employees to look after one another, instead of treating some workers like 'outsiders' we can create an environment that fosters both creativity and empathy."

"You might be on to something, here. Give me a chance to process it all. Man, you're making me think on my vacation. Holly is scowling at me, too, for discussing business."

"Sorry. I just think it is time to balance things out a bit. Give Holly a kiss for me. I see you guys in my rear view mirror, by the way."

"Kiss back attcha, sweetheart," screamed Holly over the car phone.

"Hey, what about me?" hollered Angela.

"Oh, hi Angela," Andrew replied.

"We love you too, honeybunch," Holly added affectionately.

"I'm hanging up now," Phillip warned. "Oh, there's the ten kilometer sign for Toulouse. Follow me folks."

Andrew disconnected and said aloud, "Forget that!" and accelerated past Phillip in his sporty little Peugeot, Holly waving as they passed by.

The downtown core was alive with people when they arrived. There were Bistros at almost every corner with outdoor tables and waiters in proper attire. There were street performers making people laugh as they strolled by and sidewalk artists creating masterful illusions with various colors of chalk. The mood was jovial and there was romance everywhere to be seen. Couples of all ages were engaged in passionate conversation and people walking their pets enjoyed their alone time whilst being part of the natural chaos that is the French way of enjoying and celebrating life.

The boys parked on the street next to an outdoor flower shop, bought the ladies each a rose for their hair and pointed to an outdoor café with umbrellas shading each table from the beautiful, yet intense, midday sun.

"Is this outdoor café to your liking?" Andrew suggested.

"Fantastic," Holly replied.

"Works for me," Angela added.

The boys pulled out the chairs for their ladies and

gallantly adjusted their seats as they sat down.

"Thank you," Angela said when Phillip bent over and kissed her on the cheek.

"Oh my," Holly said enthusiastically. "Is that a shoe shop and a dress shop side-by-side across the street?"

"Indeed, it is," Angela replied, tilting her shades to get a better look. "Look at those heels, boys!"

"Afraid you'll have to try them on for us to judge them properly," Phillip hinted.

"Bonjour, tout le monde. Je suis Jacques est…"

"I'll order for everybody," Angela offered. "Tell me what you want."

"Oh, you speck Anglais? Non problem."

Angela quickly assembled some French words to communicate they needed another five minutes. "Cinq minutes de plus, s'il vous plait, monsieur."

"Bien sûr, Madame," replied the waiter who politely bowed his head and left.

"Okay, what do y'all want?"

"I don't know about everybody else, but I could sure use a caffeine boost," Phillip replied.

"Yes, and some warm, buttery croissants," Holly added.

"Sounds good to me," Andrew said in agreement.

"Excellent, I'll order some cheese, as well."

"Monsieur," Angela said, catching the attention of the waiter.

"Oui Madame? Êtes-vous prêt?"

"Oui, je suis prêt. D'accord, je prends trios Expressos, une tea herbal menthe, les croissants et du fromage Brie pour la table."

"Formidable! Le vin rouge, peut-être?" inquired the waiter.

"Un instant," she replied, holding up a finger to signal she needed a moment to confer with her friends. "Do we want wine?" she asked.

"We'll be back on the road in an hour or less," Phillip advised.

"Okay."

Angela looked up with a smile and politely refused the wine. "Non, merci."

"Bon!" replied the handsome waiter, who smiled and left to serve customers at another table.

"Excuse us gentlemen," replied Holly as the two ladies stood up to head to the ladies room.

"Certainly," replied Andrew, standing up.

"Leaving us already?" Phillip said teasingly.

"Fat chance, Mr. Niles," Angela replied. "Somebody has to make sure you two behave yourselves."

Phillip stroked his chin with his fingertips and smiled warmly as he and Andrew watched the lovely ladies disappear into the café. They turned and looked at one another, sat down and each picked up his glass of lemon ice water. Without a word, they tapped glasses and took a drink.

"Aaah. This is a happy spot," Andrew declared.

Wow, this is big, Phillip thought.

In Andrew's mind, there was only one official happy place and that was Disneyland. No other spot rekindled the warm memories of his childhood like the magic of The Park and the Disneyland Fireworks Display with Tinker Bell flying through the starlit night sky. Walt Disney was his hero. For Andrew to declare this spot a happy spot was something earth shattering.

"You've never said that about any place other than Disneyland before. Why here?"

"Remember that spot in The Park where I said I would propose?"

"Yes."

"I've found the woman that, in a year's time, I will ask to marry me."

"Holy… Holly? How did you? Andrew, it's only been two days."

"I know. My heart tells me she is the one."

They sat in silence for a moment. Phillip needed time to process Andrew's revelation.

"How do you know she's the one?"

"My intuition is God speaking to me and when God speaks, I listen. My gut feeling is that this wonderful woman is good for me. Holly builds me up and infuses energy into my tired body. She's the nitrous oxide that makes this old clunker a rocket ship in the quarter mile. Like your Grandpa's Plymouth."

"The Plymouth… where did that come from?

"I guess I'm trying to say that Holly breathes new life into me. Some mornings when I wake and stare at myself in the mirror, I feel old, Phillip. I want a wife and a family. It's time."

"You're not old, heck."

Phillip began thinking about his own situation. Angela was certainly a welcome addition in his life, but marriage was not in the cards for him.

"What about you?" Andrew asked after a moment.

"Me?"

"Yes you, Rufus."

"Marriage isn't for everybody; you know that from your Bible studies."

"Yes, I sure do. I also know you."

"And?"

"Hello boys," Angela whispered softly, Marilyn Monroe style. "We're back."

"Sorry to interrupt, please continue," said Holly.

Andrew looked at Phillip and exhaled. "Only time will

tell for sure, my friend," he concluded.

"Are you boys talking shop again?" Angela bellowed.

Phillip smiled and leaned closer to Angela. "Grandpa's running the quarter mile next week in his modified Plymouth Acclaim. Andrew claims the old clunker to be faster than a Vette, something about nitrous oxide breathing new life into an old engine."

"Well, I hope he wins," Angela replied.

Phillip leaned in to kiss Angela tenderly on the lips, much to the delight of the waiter who appeared out of nowhere with the drinks and food.

"Et voila!" he said, effortlessly placing the drinks, basket of warm croissants and cheese around the table.

"How come you don't spontaneously kiss me like that?" Holly bellowed, shocking the pants off Andrew. The waiter stepped back pensively caressing his chin with his index finger and thumb as everyone patiently awaited Andrew's response.

"Oh, he's more reserved… you know, not as adventuresome as I am," Phillip said teasingly.

Andrew, realizing the moment had come, stood up, took Holly into his arms and, leaning her backwards, kissed her passionately on the lips.

"Woo!" Holly exclaimed after catching her breath. "Now that's what I call a kiss."

"Bravo, monsieur," applauded the waiter.

The boys took the ladies shopping after their refreshments at the café. Angela and Holly modeled a number of sinfully hot dresses (LBDs and LRDs) for the boys. The open toe and spaghetti-strap heels were a big hit, too. *Darn it*, I thought in retrospect. *It would have been fun times if I had joined them for this trip.* Oh well, it was not meant to be. With their shopping bags full to the brim, they headed back to the cars and hit the road with hopes of being in Carcassonne at a reasonable time for lunch.

The scenery along the A62 to Carcassonne was breathtaking. Rolling hills and mountains spanned off into the distance. Patches of vineyards on the southward-facing slopes revealed row upon row of fertile vines loaded with grapes for the fall harvest, ironically the least touristy time of year in southern France. Cattle, dairy, sheep and goat farms appeared along the way. A lone Shepherd with his sheep standing in the shade of a large tree reminded Angela of the painting in her guest bedroom.

"The landscape is very romantic here," she observed.

"It's a beautiful day for driving," Phillip replied.

"Fromagerie," she mumbled, noticing the large sign in the farmer's field.

"That's a dairy cheese store," Phillip declared, proudly showing off his French skills.

Angela laughed.

"Yes, in this case, a local dairy farmer who makes and sells his own brand of cheeses. French cheeses are among the best in the world."

"What is your favorite cheese?"

"I like Brie, Havarti and Camembert."

"Mmm, I like those, too. Blue cheese and Gorgonzola are nice, as well, but I'm not a fan of Stilton. That stuff smells awful."

"My dad likes Stilton cheese. I leave the room when he opens it. I think it's gross… smells worse than a bad case of toe jam on a ripe foot."

"Ugh! How can anybody put that stuff in their mouth?"

"… and keep it down," Angela added.

"It gets worse… there is a so-called premium cheese that has maggots crawling through it when you eat it."

"Get out."

"No seriously."

"Thanks. I've completely lost my appetite."

"Sorry."

Angela suddenly had a desperate urge to change the topic. "Okay, trivia time."

"Nice, hit me."

"Name three Nicole Kidman movies?"

"*Dead Calm*, *Australia* and, wait for it... *Moulin Rouge*."

"Well done, Cracker Jack. Oh, oh, oh, turn it up. I love this song!"

Phillip's thumb jumped to the volume button on the steering wheel. "Increasing volume now," he replied, watching the volume bar on the satellite radio rapidly climb towards *very loud*.

"I know all the words," Angela exclaimed proudly. "It's called *My Backpackin' Holiday*."

"Sing it for me, CG."

"Okay, then... Here goes..."

School is done!
Time for a little fun.

Love ya Ma!
Love ya Pa!
I'm headin' for Heaven.
I'll be back when I'm done.

I caught a Big Ol' Bus.
I had a thousand bucks.
Nobody stoppin' me,
I've set myself free.

Had my headphones blastin',
My sneakers a tappin',
Rockin' down the PCH
Clappin' and laughin'/

Arrived in San Francisco.

Danced along Embarcadero.
Skipped a rock in the Bay,
And flew stand-by to LA.

(Chorus)
I'm on my...
Backpackin' holiday,
Daily grind getaway,
It's my Bootleggin', Bar-hoppin',
Friend findin' and Freeloadin',
Wave-ridin', Hikin',
Shoppin', Dancin',
JaM-bO-reE.

Landed in LAX on time,
Saw the shops along Rodeo Drive.
Kissed a friend behind the Bougainvillea
And pearled a gnarly under the Zuma sun.

Bought a cheap ticket on the Amtrak train
Rollin' Eastbound through the stormy rain.
Hello Colorado,
Hello Tennessee!

(Chorus)
I'm on my...
Backpackin' holiday,
Daily grind getaway,
It's my Bootleggin', Bar-hoppin',
Friend findin' and Freeloadin',
Wave-ridin', Hikin',
Shoppin', Dancin',
JaM-bO-reE.

Grabbed a coffee at a Bistro,
In a little town called Ashville.
The North Carolina morning set me free,
And the misty mountains grabbed a hold of me.

I made a new friend on Blue Ridge.
We biked across an old bridge.
Found a campground by a river bend.

Ran down the dock and leaped off the end.

(Chorus)
I'm on my...
Backpackin' holiday,
Daily grind getaway,
It's my Bootleggin', Bar-hoppin',
Friend findin' and Freeloadin',
Wave-ridin', Hikin',
Shoppin', Dancin',
JaM-bO-reE.

Then I got a call from Papa asking,
"When you coming home?"
I said "I'm camping by the river bend,
And freeloading off a friend."

Phillip laughed and jived with the beat as Angela sang every word of the song slapping her sexy thigh to the beat. He was having the time of his life with a wonderful woman he met through the simple act of throwing a dart at a wall map and following his intuition. As the song came to an end, he attempted singing the last few words with her.

Then I got a call from Mama saying,
"Catch the homebound train."
So, I'm heading back to Medford,
Dreaming along the way...

I'll be back again someday,
On a daily grind getaway.
I'll be back again someday,
On my backpackin' holiday.

"You can really sing, girl."
"Yeah," Angela bellowed. "That song cranks, man. It reminds me of a wild high school dance I attended. I rendered all the boys speechless with my Ballroom moves."

"Ah, but you still haven't cracked the code yet."

"Code... Oh, yeah, CG," she laughed. "I cheated."

"What?"

"I cheated. I asked Andrew... er, Charles rather. I'm your CG," she replied triumphantly.

"That's not fair."

"You're so cute."

"Do you know what a Coolant Gauge does?"

"Coolant Gauge? That sucks, Phillip. You're not calling me that."

"What? I thought... oh, I see, the old Poker Face trick."

"I'll polka dot your face, alright."

A few moments passed before Phillip could gather a response. He was envisioning waking up in the morning with polka dots painted all over his face.

"So, you're not buying that one, huh?"

"You're not giving me a nickname that describes a car part. Forget it."

"Okay then."

A few moments later the car phone rang.

"Hello Pops."

"Hey, Lug Nut."

"What's up?"

"I'm in the garage here with the Rolls. I can't seem to find the leather protector for the seats."

"Ah yes. It's in the bin underneath the car cover behind the car."

"Got it, thanks."

"Later."

"So what's so great about a coolant gauge?" Angela asked, her curiosity getting the best of her.

"A coolant gauge, also known as a temperature or water gauge, tells you how hot your engine is running."

"So, engine's run hot."

"Think of it this way. A thermometer tells you if you have a fever, right?"

"Yes."

"Similarly, a coolant gauge tells you if your engine is healthy or sick. If it is sick, it shows how serious it is and you can then deduce what precautions to take."

"So, a CG is like a Barometer then."

Phillip pondered Angela's response. A Barometer measures the atmospheric pressure, which is then used to gauge if rainy weather or a storm is coming.

"Hmm, well it is similar because a high coolant temperature has a lot to do with the increased pressure on various engine components."

"So, I'm a CGB then?" she responded favourably.

"Hah ha, if you like," Phillip chuckled. "I was thinking more along the lines of the Doctor who diagnoses and repairs the issue according to the results of the coolant gauge."

"Ooh, I like that. So, why not just call me Doctor then," she said mischievously.

"Ah, my dear, that's a good question. And the answer is… because the Doctor needs the instrument to diagnose the problem. No instrument, no solution, no problem resolution."

"Nice rhyming, brothah. You can call me CG. I feel the *l-o-v-e* connection."

"Oh my God, that's cheesy."

"I'm getting hungry, man."

Phillip glanced at the onboard GPS. "ETA, seven minutes to Noella's recommended Carcassonne restaurant. Are you going to make it, sistah?"

"My word, brothah, I feel the cabin pressure increasing. The coolant gauge is showing a fever coming on… Best get a move on so we can resolve this situation!"

Phillip laughed and gave the Bugatti a little encouragement.

"The Doctor's on it, my dear."

TWENTY – DESTINATION AGDE

The restaurant that Noella recommended was situated on the majestic *Le Sommelier et Le Verre à Vin* winery on the outskirts of Carcassonne. Noella's old college friend, André, from L'Université De La Sorbonne, ran *La Vieille Vigne du Sud* restaurant on the estate property and his family ran the winery that stretched along a rocky, south facing hillside situated above a lovely scenic valley below. When the winery came into full view, everybody went silent in awe as they absorbed the splendor of the estate. Phillip and Andrew pulled into the driveway, winding through trees and gardens on either side. They parked by the restaurant, which had a full view of the grapevines stretching up the hillside, and a picture perfect view of the wide valley below.

"Are you sure about the plumb-prune business, Phillip?" Angela asked as she looked out over the fertile valley to the horizon beyond. The wine business sure does look promising from my perspective."

Phillip chuckled, raised his hand to shade the sun from his face and simply gazed at the splendor in front of him.

"Wow," Holly said as she and Andrew sat on the bench overlooking the immaculate vineyard paradise.

"I've always wanted a vineyard with a view like this," Andrew let on.

"Buy this one," Holly teased. At the back of her mind she saw herself buying a vineyard one day if she could manage it financially. She was already in love with this one. Her nursing career had allowed her to save a nice amount over the years. Her two bedroom condo overlooking Lake Ontario and the State of New York in the distance was fully paid off.

"I have a place in mind," Andrew replied.

"Oh yah? You would buy a vineyard?" Holly asked.

"I sure would… and I would build a bee farm on the property."

"And where is this place you have in mind?"

"Napa Valley or Sonoma, haven't decided for sure yet, but California is where my heart lies."

"I've never been there. What's it like?"

Andrew looked at Phillip and smiled. Then he looked out over the valley to the distant hills and breathed a few words.

"It's a basket full of joy."

His words seemed to echo off the south facing vines and through the valley below. Even though the words were only a whisper, the basket full of joy travelled through each of their minds like a warm gust of ocean wind wrapped in brilliant afternoon sunshine. Everybody's mind went in different directions. Phillip reminisced about the good times spent surfing with Andrew at his favorite surf spot, The Rock in San Luis Obispo. Andrew's thoughts drifted to his envisioned vineyard and bee farm. Angela's thoughts carried her to a place she once read about called La Jolla (pronounced la hoya) near San Diego. Holly dreamed about owning a mansion overlooking Zuma Beach in Malibu and going for a swim in the ocean every day.

"Bonjour," burst a raspy voice from behind. "Welcome to our little piece of paradise," continued the young hostess, Michelle, who espied them from the restaurant and quietly approached the group of enamored tourists.

"Hello there," Phillip replied.

"Will you be staying for lunch today?"

"Yes indeed, if you have room for us."

"We certainly do. Come with me."

"Fabulous! Your restaurant came highly recommended from a friend of ours."

"Who is your friend?"

"Noella Beauchamp," Phillip continued.

"Oh yes, André and Noella are best friends. We know her well here."

The walkway to the restaurant was lined with finely manicured climbing roses, ivy vines and hanging baskets on either side. In the center of the walkway was a beautiful multilayer fountain with separate walkways on either side leading to open garden patios. The outdoor tables were elegantly set up with white linen and vintage oil lamp candles, one positioned at the center of every table. The guests didn't notice the new arrivals when they ambled by. They were too busy chatting and enjoying their meals to notice anything going on outside of the cozy garden oasis where they sat sheltered by a myriad of tropical trees, shrubs and plants. Continuing past the fountain and through the front entrance, the eager party arrived at the hostess' desk where they each signed the Guest Log.

"I love the cozy feel of this place," Angela commented as she grabbed on to Phillip's arm. "Look how the restaurant splits into a raised dining area on this side and a full bar and games room on the other."

"Very nice," Andrew agreed.

"And the garden theme carries on throughout the restaurant, too," Holly added.

"The views are even more spectacular from your table," Michelle replied as she motioned for them to follow her up the ramp to the dining room. The place was about half full as they walked past several tables towards the VIP Gazebo extension with a full panoramic view of the vineyard, valley below and rolling hills stretching to the horizon and beyond.

"Oh wow! Formidable. Incroyable..." Angela could hardly contain her excitement. Holly placed her hands together, as if praying, gleefully smiling like a school girl.

Becoming an angel is a miraculous gift, indeed. I have been touched by God's grace. All these adventures that I missed in my mortal life, the stories I tell you now, I discovered through my spiritual being as one of God's chosen angels. Eternal life is the greatest reward of all.

During the course of their meal, André stopped by and introduced himself with a complementary bottle of one of the vineyard's best vintages. He had nothing but the highest praise for his dear friend Noella, who had phoned him earlier in the day to advise of her friends pending arrival. He told them a few stories about times past and after lunch André gave them a personal tour of the vineyard, which included a rare viewing of the private wine cellars.

With two cases of premium vintage Carcassonne wine in their possession, they once again hit the road, this time headed for Narbonne with expectations of arriving in Agde shortly thereafter.

"Tell me something life-changing about yourself, Phillip," Angela asked rather spontaneously; "an event in your life or whatever."

"Alright CG," he said, glancing over to gauge Angela's mood. "You go first."

"Hmm, my father married a Catholic girl."

"And how has this been life-changing for you?"

"Well, my father is Jewish for one, a Dentist."

"Ah, that explains your stubbornness, hah ha… and dedication to your work."

"Well, yes, I guess I'm both of those things."

"Was that confusing, growing up in a Jewish-Christian family?"

"Well, I wasn't forced to be one or the other. We celebrated Jewish and Christian holidays. My Mom taught me the Catechisms and I had my Bat Mitzvah at the age of thirteen."

"You do enjoy your parties, don't you?"

"Hah ha, yes I do! Anyway, I haven't really chosen one religion over the other. I love both of my parents."

"Well, you have chosen, actually, you just don't realize it yet."

"What do you mean?"

"You're both Jewish and Christian. Does that make things easy for you?"

"That's a little confusing, Phillip," Angela replied with a suspicious glance at him. "The prophet Elijah who ascended into Heaven without dying is believed to be the promised Messiah in Judaism, whereas Jesus is the Messiah in Christianity."

"You are right. Give it some thought and perhaps, may I suggest stepping outside the box to see the big picture. There are Jews for Jesus and there are Christians who embrace their Jewish brothers and sisters through common Old Testament scripture."

"Maybe. Okay, enough about me, Buster… your turn."

"My life-changing story began over five years ago when I finally gave in and decided to read the Bible, front to back."

"You read the entire Bible, front to back?" she repeated. "Why?"

"Yes, I read the Old Testament and the New Testament from page 1 of Genesis to the very last page of Revelations in my New International Version Study Bible, which was a gift from Andrew, by the way. When he found out I was reading a pocket version of the King James Bible, he bought me an NIV Study Bible that very same day."

Phillip paused for a moment before answering Angela's second question. "I read it because I was afraid of going through life not knowing the answers, the teachings of the Bible."

"So, if you read the Bible you'll find all the answers?"

"Great question, Angela. I asked myself this while reading the Books. The answer is no. I reached a point in my Bible studies where I needed some of my own questions answered, questions that I had about some things in the Bible that were not clear to me."

"What did you do?"

"I went church hopping in hopes of finding a teacher, a Minister of the faith."

"Hah ha ha, you went... church hopping?"

"Yes indeed, my fair lady, I did."

"Why not just go to your parent's church?"

Phillip paused for a moment. The question about his parents would always be a tough one for him.

"Same reason you don't buy the first house you see. It's got to fit. Your heart must feel... at home. Besides, my Mom attended the United Church and my father is Anglican," Phillip continued, smiling at the ironic twist of their conversation.

"You don't talk about your parents much."

"No, I don't."

Angela decided not to push the subject.

"So, you're Anglican and United then," she concluded.

"Hah ha, it's not that simple, unfortunately."

"No?"

Phillip glanced over at Angela who had her bare feet casually resting on the dash of the Bugatti, her anklet sparkling in the sunshine. I know my boy and there was no way he was going to ask Angela to remove her sexy feet from the pristine dash of the Bugatti, even though feet resting on the dash of an expensive car was a major pet peeve of his.

"My church hopping landed me at a beautiful and welcoming old Presbyterian parish."

"Welcoming… I can't imagine any church not welcoming new members."

"You'd be surprised, then. I remember one occasion in particular. At the end of the service, I reached out to shake the Pastor's hand thinking he would notice the new face in his congregation. He shook my hand while engaging another member behind me, forgetting even to say hello and, of course, welcome. I never went back there."

"Wow that was pretty insensitive. Nobody's perfect though, Phillip. He could have been caught up in the moment."

"Business is business, my dear, and a church is a business. Not welcoming new customers, last time I checked, was bad business."

"Good point. So, you're Presbyterian then?"

"Yes, a Christian who also understands that Christianity blossomed from the roots of Judaism. The two religions are eternally connected. Embrace life with love, patience, kindness, understanding and especially tolerance. There are many complicated things in life we were never meant to understand. It is God in whom we trust to protect us. The way He does that is far beyond our comprehension. Love is what the Bible is really all about. That's simple enough for me to understand."

"That's a really cool perspective, Phillip. I should read the Bible."

"Reading the entire Bible is the equivalent of earning a University Degree, you know. It took me three years to read it and I'll spend the rest of my life learning, understanding and practicing its teachings."

"Okay, changing topics…" Angela declared.

"Okay, something else on your mind?"

"Yes, where do you stand politically?"

"Hah ha. You're jumping from one highly charged subject to another one. You really are brave!"

"That or just plain foolish."

"I'm Republican. You?"

"I'm more of a cross between the Progressive Conservative Party and the Green Party. I'm concerned about the environment and the damage we have done to it."

"Ah, in the US, Republicans are Conservative. The Democrats are Liberal."

"So, I'm a Green Republican then?"

"Hah ha, I wouldn't advertise that, although I think everybody is worried about the environment these days, regardless of political persuasion. We have to change our way of life to reverse the damages already inflicted on the earth and that is really tough job to accomplish."

"Well, we better figure out something soon or we'll not have a planet left."

"I've got an idea."

"What?" Angela replied.

Phillip dialled Andrew on the car phone.

"What's up, Homey?" Andrew answered, obviously in the middle of a good joke gauging from Holly's wild laughter in the background.

"Okay, pull yourself out of the 80s for a minute."

"You're killing my mojo, man."

"Sorry. Mojo? What the... I think they call it something else *nowadays*..."

"Now-a-days, huh? Nice, you might as well have said Whoops-a-daisy, Old-timer."

"Hey, I can see the Cathedral steeple in Narbonne. Let's go light some candles."

"Good plan, man. I'll follow you."

Phillip disconnected and turned to Angela.

"You light a candle and pray for the politicians to clean up the environment and I'll light a candle and pray for peace. Deal?"

"You're on, man. Take me to Cathédral Saint-Just-et-Saint-Pasteur de Narbonne!"

"Wow, you speak French very well."

"Thank you, Lug Nut. Must be the wee bit of French blood in my lineage..."

The boys drove into Narbonne using the soaring steeples for direction. The city was alive with people going their different ways carrying shopping bags, grocery bags from the market or food from the street vendors. Many were out for an afternoon bike ride and the parks were overflowing with families' barbequing and kids playing under the afternoon sun. A group of teenagers shared a basket of French fries near a public fountain while a small restaurant served up some steamy bouillabaisse on the outdoor patio. The city was adorned with beautiful vines spread across fences and buildings. Flowers, trees and shrubs decorated the sidewalks and parks. The ancient

Gothic-style cathedral with its pointed arches and breathtaking architecture was easy enough to find. It was the jewel of the town and prominently marked the city center.

They wasted no time parking the cars and making their way through the main square gate to the cathedral. It towered above an ancient city wall, which seemed to be part of the cathedral itself. When they entered through the massive doors, the majesty overpowered them.

"It says that the first stone was laid in the current chapel of the Sacred Heart by Archbishop Maruin on April 13, 1272." Angela said as they strolled by some plaques. "The cathedral was never completed," she continued.

"How come?" Holly asked.

"Looks like politics and a lack of funds to complete the job."

They continued walking slowly through the narthex admiring the artwork along the walls and the vintage furniture. The floors, steps and pillars were made of solid French marble dating back many centuries. In the sanctuary, the beautiful stained glass windows, each with a biblical story of its own, stretched high above their heads to the dome ceilings above. The magnificent window and roof arches, pervasive throughout, held everything together and reassured visitors of its fortitude. The pews lined up row upon row on either side of the spacious aisle leading toward the altar, which sat draped in a red cloth.

"Check out the pipe organ... it's huge!" Angela observed.

"Focus people, we're here to light candles, remember?" Andrew advised.

"Not before I take a few pictures," Holly said, pointing her camera at the stained glass windows and snapping a few shots.

At that moment, the pipe organ came to life and startled

everybody. "Someone's practicing today," Phillip said.

"Or it's a GHOST," Angela replied, raising her eyebrows and winking at Holly.

"Let's just light the candles and go," Andrew said impatiently. He wasn't a fan of gothic cathedrals, or anything spooky for that matter.

One of the attendants pointed them to the prayer candles near the front of the cathedral. They emptied their pockets of change in the payment box and, one by one, they lit a candle, bowed their heads and prayed.

The relatively short drive to Agde was very scenic. The Mediterranean Sea snuck up on them as they drove down the A61, making them all the more anxious to be in Agde or Le Cap d'Agde to be precise. The warm summer air flowed through the open windows and carried with it a wonderful combination of fragrant flowers and salty beach aromas. The sea opened up to an awe-inspiring, panoramic, sapphire blue playground as they rolled into Agde. Euphoric expressions spontaneously rolled across their faces.

"Oh my God, that's beautiful!" Angela shouted, sticking her head out the window for an unobstructed view.

The seashore was speckled with sun worshipers and beachgoers. Kids of all ages were chasing one another along the pristine shoreline and playing in the water. Several mega yachts sporting hot bikini clad ladies and buff men were anchored a safe distance from shore. Ah, the serene lifestyle of the affluent with their expensive shades and Martinis in hand. The worry-free facade is very convincing, but the reality of their lives is often less than glamorous.

"Do you own a yacht like that in California?" asked Holly as she turned towards Andrew and noticed that he was also transfixed on the mega yachts instead of the road. "Hey, eyes on the road, Buster!"

"Yes, eyes on the road, not the big boats with helicopter pads."

A moment of awkward silence passed between them.

"No, I don't own a yacht. Those things cost a fortune in addition to a loaded bank vault to maintain."

"Yachts with helicopter pads..." she scoffed. "More like yachts with bikini clad supermodels."

"Where?" Andrew said, squinting his eyes and pretending to get a closer look.

"Actually, they're everywhere... and holy jumpin'..." she continued, pointing to the beach, "some are nude! Look there... no don't!" she said reaching over to shield his eyes from the nude couple walking along the beach. "They're buck naked!"

"I'm driving, remember?" he replied, and then snuck a peek at the nudist beach. "Nice!" he said, chuckling.

Pleasure boats ran up and down the coast towing parasails, inflatable water toys and wake boarders. The marina was bustling with busy boaters excited about the all-encompassing sunshine and warm gentle breezes. Sailors in sailboats of all sizes were tacking along the coastline, their telltales guiding the way. Boaters enjoyed the big picture perspective of Agde from the water, while beachgoers gazed at them with envy. The town, itself, sat on a bluff above the shore similar to the bluffs scattered along the coast of California. It offered a trillion dollar view of the bejewelled Mediterranean and the luxurious cruise ships passing by with their worldly travellers. The excitement of it all made Angela and Holly desperate to change into their bikinis, sarongs and beach sandals they purchased in Carcassonne.

"Park the car already," Angela bellowed and called Holly

on the car phone.

"Easy Duchess, there aren't a whole lot of spots available."

"Yes?" Andrew answered.

"Hi Andrew, is Holly there?"

"Hell ya, I'm here," boomed the voice over the speakers.

"Let's change into something a little more comfy."

"Agreed," she replied, looking intently at Andrew. "Will you park the car please? I want to get out."

"Whoa Superstar, there aren't a whole lot of spots available," Andrew replied.

"My sentiments exactly," said Phillip. There are no spots."

"Let's find a restaurant where we can rehydrate and change into some sexy beachwear," Angela said flirtatiously, but with the sole intention of getting them out of the car quickly.

The lads found a parking lot beside a café within two minutes flat. It's amazing how the male psyche works... You mention 'sexy' and 'beachwear' in the same sentence and they become obedient real quick, like children anticipating a trip for hot fudge Sundays.

The lads waited patiently for the ladies to return, leaning on the banister of the café patio overlooking the beach.

"I don't wanna leave, man," Andrew blurted.

"Don't think about it then."

"It's hard not too when my flight departs tomorrow evening."

"Focus on the magic of the day instead of wasting it thinking about, or dreading, tomorrow."

"Ya, ya, ya... whatever."

"Cheer up old friend."

"Holly flies with Charles and me as far as Chicago tomorrow. Then we say our good-byes before heading back to San Francisco."

"Poor Mr. Mopy Head."

"Well you're not much help."

"Give it some time. Talk on the phone and plan something if it feels right."

Andrew nodded, but their conversation did little to remove the knot in his stomach. Not even his best friend could reassure him that things between him and Holly would turn into something wonderful and everlasting.

The ladies reappeared, walking casually across the patio towards the men in their fashionable sun hats and 'red alert' bikinis. Andrew's knot tightened a little further and his heart red-lined. *My Lord*, he thought to himself. *This must be what Heaven feels like.* Angela was wearing a pink sarong that split open as she walked, revealing a luscious, silky smooth leg. Holly's sarong was transparent white, revealing the satin blue lace bikini underneath. *I want to tug those lace bow ties off with my teeth*, Andrew thought shamelessly.

"Can you retie my sandal strap for me, big boy?" Angela asked, placing her foot on the chair for Phillip. "It's a little loose..."

"Certainly," Phillip replied, bending down to retie the lace strap around her lovely ankle. *My Lord, her legs are gorgeous.*

"Damn, my bikini strap is too tight. Be a darling, Andrew, and retie it for me?" Holly asked politely, batting her eyes in the process.

"Sure." *I like this game.*

"Oh, not there honey," she said, moving his hand from her bikini top to her left thigh. Right there, big fella," she continued, pushing her sarong down a bit to reveal her silky smooth thigh.

Andrew blushed as he retied her bikini thong lace. *I'm a lucky, lucky man.*

"How's that," he asked, with his fingertips still resting on the bow tie and lightly touching her thigh.

"Much better, Handsome... thank you." She leaned over with one hand on his blushed cheek and gently kissed his lips.

"I'm craving ice cream!" Angela said aloud. "Anybody else?"

"Oh yeah!"

"I could go for a little something to cool me off...."

"Me too. I'm overheatin' here..."

It was unanimous. The lads followed the ladies inside to the ice cream counter.

"Mmm, they smell like honeysuckle and lavender," Phillip whispered.

"It's driving me crazy. Is that sunscreen? Who makes sunscreen smell so good?"

"Don't know, but I sure do like it... a lot."

"I'm so fucking horny now."

"No shit!"

Angela placed the order for everybody, and then undid a couple buttons on Phillip's shirt while they waited.

"Loosen up, Phillip. You're in the French Riviera now."

"Yes, Mr., you too," Holly added, promptly undoing all the buttons on Andrew's dress shirt and pulling the shirt tails out of his jeans.

The ladies followed the men as they walked out of the café enjoying their ice cream. The two lads unconsciously rolled up their shirt sleeves.

"Now that's a mighty fine ass on my man," Holly whispered.

"Yes, lucky you," Angela agreed. "Phillip's got a tight, hard butt, too."

"Yes, he does and broad shoulders, too. Lucky you."

Angela and Holly teased one another as they compared

the attributes of their men. Women after all, are just like men when it comes to admiring physical attributes. They just don't advertise it. Oops, I evened up 'the playing field'. My bad, Hah ha. Sorry ladies.

Phillip and Andrew rolled up their jeans and walked barefoot along the watery edge of the beach while the ladies talked, danced and did the occasional cartwheel in front of them. Somehow along the way, they managed to attract a group of kids who began doing cartwheels and chasing one another through the water.

"Try one," Angela dared Phillip.

"What? A cartwheel...?"

"Yes, gymnasts do them all the time. It's easy, see?" Angela proceeded to effortlessly complete two perfect *splashtastic* cartwheels finishing with her arms in the air, standing in half a foot of water.

"Very nice. Do it again," Phillip said, amused.

"I'll do it again alright, Buster," Angela replied, splashing water on him with her foot. The kids laughed and watched Phillip for his reaction.

"Hey," Phillip bellowed, and made his own splash, which was enough to start a war, at least from the children's perspective anyhow. A 'no holds barred' water fight began that resulted in soaking wet sarongs and jeans. The kids automatically sided with the ladies, who in turn splashed up a storm on the seriously outnumbered fellows. Poor Andrew and Phillip... Even when they were down in knee deep water, the mad water frenzy continued. The only way to stop it all was to pick up the ladies and carry them out to sea.

"Put me down," Holly demanded.

"I will," Andrew replied, "when we get a little deeper, guaranteed!"

Angela loved every moment as her valiant Knight carried her out to sea.

"Kiss me now, fool," she demanded, flapping her feet like a helpless mermaid. Phillip laughed and kissed her belly.

"Ready?" he asked.

"Do it," she replied, and under they went.

When they resurfaced, they were embraced in a passionate French kiss serenaded by the melody of kids' splashing and laughing in the background. A little further out, Holly and Andrew were swimming and frolicking together like two young dolphins. *Is this really happening... to me?* Andrew thought to himself. *Thank you Lord for this beautiful woman you have put in my life.*

The sun dried their clothes as the four love-struck explorers continued walking down the beach, this time, hand-in-hand. Salty kisses and bottom pinches were intertwined with plans for dinner. A local recommended the beach party happening that evening at one of the popular beachside restaurants. Dinner, desert, live music, entertainment, dancing and a bonfire were all included in the evening festivities. It was an event that many locals attended each year and was guaranteed to be a good time.

"Well, we won't need to change clothes," Andrew advised them.

"And it's a buffet, so we can eat all we want," Phillip added, patting his stomach.

"Dancing... I'm in," Holly declared, doing a little hip-swing dance.

"Yay," Angela cheered. Unable to contain her excitement, she slapped Phillip on the ass.

They made their way to La Plage de Tête beachside entrance, which was prominently marked by a large bonfire surrounded by kids, adults and old timers alike. Everyone was in good spirits and some were already dancing under the cabana to the lively sounds of a popular local band.

Well prepared food is often a great conversation initiator. The lengthy and overflowing buffet table underneath the cabana was no exception to the rule this evening. People were shoulder-to-shoulder loading their plates and conversing leisurely with family, friends and strangers as one. It wasn't long before the foursome had made friends with several other young couples.

A cute French couple were highly amused by the horny Americans near their table, not the foursome, but another couple that seemed to keep everybody entertained with their adlib Karaoke and steamy dancing. They certainly were part of the standouts, but definitely not the center of attention as there were many couples having a good time out there.

Phillip and Andrew concluded that they were stage performers on holidays; however, they weren't. They were actually undercover federal agents investigating two individuals associated with a cartel operating along the French Riviera. The boys had stumbled upon tomorrow's headlines.

Later that evening, the 'high on life' Karaoke duo were invited to one of the mega yachts anchored offshore where they hoped to make a big narcotics bust and weaken the cartel, but the ensuing gun fight ruptured the propane tanks, which in turn detonated the explosives stored on the deck below. The propane explosion collapsed the top two decks and turned the yacht into a fiery mess. The TNT, on the other hand, blew the entire back end off the boat, including the helicopter pad with a thunderous roar that shook the whole town. The undercover Karaoke duo dove into the water just before the big blast, escaping in grand fashion as the explosion lit up the sea behind them. They were picked up by the Recovery Team as they swam ashore under the fire swept moonlight. The suspects managed a narrow escape in their twin supercharged speedboat; the same wave pounding race boat that brought the Karaoke duo to the yacht earlier.

Although their cover was blown and the agents slouched in defeat, the recovery effort at the crime scene the following day yielded some pleasant surprises. At the bottom of the sea sat 500 million dollars' worth of cocaine, an undamaged, air tight safe holding six bricks of pure gold and a black velvet box packed with blood spattered, fingerprint-loaded, mini zip lock packets of brilliant white and pink diamonds. That twin supercharged speedboat wasn't heading back to headquarters, that's for damned sure! But I digress... back to the story unfolding earlier in the evening, where raging hormones underneath the cabana were colliding with romantic views of beach torches and the sparkling sea.

Phillip leaned back in the wicker couch with his feet up as the party continued around him. Angela was nestled by his side, his arm swung around her shoulders. The sun was sinking below the horizon between two towering, open-flame beach torches framing a beautiful yacht anchored in the distance. The sky became a magnificent crimson-indigo as ribbons of red, pink and orange bounced off the bottom of a couple wispy clouds spread across the horizon. The sea sparkled like a bed of diamonds. A charming Agde couple were beside them, starring amusingly into one another's eyes, interspersing gentle kisses with tender caresses. Holly and Andrew were still on the dance floor pretending to be carefree teenagers. The Karaoke duo had strategically linked up with another group of happy dancers.

"Where do they get all that energy?" Angela wondered as

she glanced over at the American duo tearing up the dance floor.

"They might be running on a different type of fuel, honey."

"Ah... Oh! You think?"

Phillip smiled and flicked her nose with his finger. "That's one helluva sunset, huh?"

"It's pretty."

"We call it *le coucher du soleil*, or more elegantly *le crépuscule d'amour*," Chantelle replied, sending Angela a wink before turning her attention back to her fiancé, Marc.

"That's very romantic," Angela whispered, raising her chin to kiss her man.

"You're missing the sunset, man," Phillip hollered when he noticed Andrew and Holly returning from the dance floor.

"Waddya mean? It's right there!" Andrew shot back.

"That's beautiful," whispered Holly, sinking backwards into Andrew's chest.

"We ordered coffee to jazz us up for the return trip," Angela said, smiling at Holly and pointing to the carafe on the coffee table where Phillip was resting his nicely manicured bare feet.

"Oh, perfect. That should keep us awake while we drive the boys' home."

Andrew and Phillip instantly looked at one another with completely baffled expressions. *This was news. Did the ladies plan this? Une conspiration, n'est-ce pas?* A myriad of thoughts ran through their minds.

Noticing their shocked expressions, Angela added some clarification. "You didn't think you could hog all the driving, did you... sweetie-pie?"

"Ya, you weren't planning on keeping us in the passenger seat for the whole trip... were you?" said Holly, looking intently at Andrew.

"No! No, absolutely not," he replied innocently.

Phillip laughed, but underneath it all he wondered if Angela knew the Bugatti was a *1200 horsepower, quad fed Dragon...* the type that inhales pressurized gasses and throws thunderous flames out the back. As the ladies reached for the coffee, his attention changed to the Karaoke duo and some other party-goers walking towards the Baja speedboat he had been watching enviously all evening. The Baja, *Always Early* elegantly painted across the stern, arrived at the dock from one of the mega yachts anchored a short distance offshore.

"Is that the American couple that were keeping us entertained earlier?" asked Phillip as he nodded his head in the direction of the group walking down the beach.

"Looks like it," Andrew replied pensively.

A gut feeling sent shivers up Phillip's back. Something wasn't right.

"They must be taking the party out on the water," Holly added. "Nice," she continued, flirtatiously raising her eyebrows at Andrew. She loved boats, especially the big ones.

The sun was just sinking below the horizon when the group pulled away from the dock and headed towards the yacht, the sleek one with the helicopter departing from the stern. The bonfire on the beach was roaring and the band continued to play under the cabana. The stars began to appear, lighting up the night sky with their mesmerizing beauty and mysterious nature.

Is there life in the distant reaches of the universe where the stars dance and the planets spin? I know you want to ask me that question, seeing as I am an angel sent by The Almighty, Himself. I can tell you that 'God created the universe, not just our galaxy, but the entirety of the Heavens, and on the seventh day, He rested.' I know I know... prove it. It's in the Bible. Faith, my friends... and Hope with a couple shakes of Patience, but most of all, LOVE. If it's God's will, it will be and if it's not then, as the Beatles song goes, 'Let it be.' Think of it this way, if perchance there is no life out there, there may very well be someday. Ah, yet again, I have digressed... back to the kids.

The weight of the lengthy drive home was beginning to weigh on everyone's mind.

"If we leave now, we can be home around midnight," Phillip suggested. The way he angled his head and smiled at Angela was endearing.

Twenty minutes later they were back at the cars and on their way. As the ladies drove out of town, the sky lit up in the background.

"Shit! We missed the fireworks," Angela exclaimed, looking back in her rear-view mirror. Then the TNT exploded on the yacht sending a rolling thunder along the coastline.

"That's some show," Phillip said, pretending he didn't know what was actually happening.

"Awe, we missed the fireworks," Holly whinged. "Let's park and watch from here?"

"Nah, let's keep going," Andrew replied. "I'll take you to the most magical of all fireworks displays when you come visit me in California. Deal?"

"Deal!"

It was a day that would last forever in their minds.

The ladies made record time returning to Agen. They dropped themselves off at the mansion and kissed the lads goodnight. When they were safely inside, the boys pulled away. They didn't expect to find me in the garage when they returned to the Château, but I was there, sitting by the Rolls smoking a cigar with a big grin on my face.

"So ya made it back in one piece, did ya?" I bellowed as Phillip stepped out of the Peugeot.

"Since when did you take up smoking?" Andrew asked.

"Oh, this? A little celebratory spoke, er… I mean smoke."

"Hah! Whatcha celebrating, Pops?" Phillip asked curiously.

"You two… welcome to the beginning of something new and wonderful," I said, referring to the successful trip that they all shared together.

Phillip smiled and said, "Gimme a pound," as he and Andrew tapped fists in celebration of the occasion. Then he reached over for the cigar, taking a puff before handing it over to Andrew.

He gagged and did the funky heave-ho in between coughs. "Damn, that's strong," he blurted, finally catching his breath.

"You're supposed to take a small puff," I said comically.

"Are you teaching me how to smoke?" Phillip shot back and noticed Andrew was laughing at him.

I smiled and took the cigar back. "Nope."

"Whatever… I'm beat. Time for bed, Pops," Phillip said, unable to focus any longer.

"You boys go on ahead. I'm going to check the oil levels in the Bugatti and Peugeot."

As the boys headed off to bed, I stood up and watched them stumble through the door. I lifted my cigar one last time for one last puff.

Peter Breeden

TWENTY-ONE – HOMEWARD BOUND

The next day was an exercise in chaos as Andrew, Holly and I prepared for the return trip. After gathering our belongings together, we all relaxed and ate lunch by the pool. The water glistened underneath the golden sunshine and the blue sky stretched lazily over the stables, orchards and mansion to the horizon beyond. Nobody noticed the beige dove on the pool lamp above my head or the white dove perched on the stable doors. But I did. I saw them. Their serene eyes seemed to soothe me as I sat through lunch barely touching my food. I wasn't hungry.

Angela and Holly became teary-eyed when Akhila landed the helicopter on the front lawn. She waved to us all from the cockpit as we stood by the fountain. I could tell that Akhila recognized Angela by the overextended, omnipotent smile spread across her face. *Ah, yes! That's the lady who was frolicking in the field on our last trip*, she mumbled to herself.

Réginald and his wife, Dominique, were there to say good-bye as were Phillip and Angela, of course. Regi had a message from Noella to relay to the group, something about a future trip to California that got everybody excited.

I was busy recording everybody's good-byes from a trellis within the rose gardens. *I'm going to miss this place*, I thought to myself. *I'll return... Yes, I'll come back in a few months to tend the horses, run the cars, and check on Phillip, the good Lord being willing, of course.* I mumbled a few words about how incredible this place was and how much I loved everybody, especially Phillip. I am really proud of him, the inimitable Phillip who is and always will be my kid grandson.

"What are you doing hiding over there, Charles?" Angela asked. "Come on over here."

As I approached, she reached out and gave me a big hug good-bye. That was very comforting. I shook hands with my old friend, Regi, who slipped a bottle of premium Cognac in my bag.

"Just so you don't forget me, non?" he said.

"I won't forget you, Regi. I won't forget," I said reassuringly.

We reluctantly made our way to the helicopter. Phillip helped me in and told me not to flirt too much with Holly on the way back to Chicago, our last hub before heading on to San Francisco.

I reassured him I would, hah ha. *That's what old men do best... keep the ladies laughing.* Holly is a wonderfully talented gal. Andrew is a lucky man, indeed.

Phillip then leaned into the cockpit to say hello to Akhila, who was looking straight at him with huge honey brown eyes and a wicked smile.

"So, who's the cutie-pie, Phillip? She's got hot legs!"

"Hah ha... you're right, Akhila, she does."

"Have I seen this one before, somewhere, perhaps in a nearby field?"

"Ahem, maybe," he replied, trying to conceal his

embarrassment.

"Oh, don't be shy, Phillip. I'm only just curious. Maybe, I can fly you and hottie…"

"Angela."

"… and Angela, thank you, to a secret lagoon hideaway where you can make many babies and I can be the god mommy, hmm?"

"Hah ha, we'll see, but for now, I leave these good people in your capable hands…"

"Oh, my capable hands," she replied, displaying her beautiful Henna artwork. "You have no idea what I can do with these babies."

"I can well imagine," Phillip replied, bashfully.

Akhila reached over and pinched his cheek, "You're such a mischievous boy, Phillip." Peeking back at her passengers to make sure they were all safely buckled in, she continued with her trademark style, the light-hearted, half-crazed Indian helicopter pilot.

"Right then, are you ready for blast-off?" she bellowed from the pilot seat. "It's a mighty fine day for a tour through Bordeaux."

"You mean lift-off, right?" Andrew clarified, with a somewhat concerned expression.

"Oh sure, honey… lift-off, blast-off, throttle-up, hammer-down, same thing, right?"

Andrew, detecting the light-hearted nature of the pilot, decided to push his luck.

"I'm ready," Andrew hollered through his headset. "How 'bout letting me fly for a bit?"

"Oh, you're a bad boy, aren't you?" she replied with her best Bollywood face. "You tighten that belt buckle Mister and stay securely planted in that seat."

Andrew laughed. "What's your call sign?"

Akhila looked at him suspiciously. "Who's asking?"

"Andrew, Andrew Pikes. Nice to meet you," he replied, extending his hand.

She smiled and, with that abundant Indian warmth, reached back and shook Andrew's hand: "Sunset, as in Sunset Boulevard."

"Well, Sunset, do you think you can show Holly, Charles and I a little something special before "touching down" at the airport?"

"You bet your ass, Malibu."

"Hey, is that my call sign?"

"It's official! For the duration of this flight, Andrew Pikes will be known as Malibu, as in Malibu Beach."

"Cool!"

As the helicopter lifted off, I waved to everybody below. My stomach heaved, not with flight anxiety, but with the dread of leaving a big piece of my heart behind. Angela and Phillip leaned on one another as they waved good-bye. Akhila circled around the fountain, and then rose slowly above the Château. Regi and Dominique watched as we circled around them. Regi acknowledged by good-bye salute with one in return. Dominique blew me a kiss. What a sweetie-pie. My heart slumped in grief as we departed.

Even though my heart seemed to sink into the abyss of perpetual loneliness, there was still a faint glimmer of light, a sliver of happiness in all the darkness. My sweet Isabella was waiting for me. I have two days to prepare her for Wednesday night drag races at Infineon Raceway. Sonoma, California, here I come!

"We're still on for Wednesday, right?" I said to Andrew.

"You bet your ass, Pops!"

PART VI

Peter Breeden

TWENTY-TWO – BUBBLE BATH

Akhila took us on a wonderful tour of Bordeaux before dropping us off at Médoc International for the return flight home. She even allowed Andrew to sit in the co-pilot seat for a bit, which made his day.

The long flight back to Chicago was doubly tough. Both Andrew and Holly were dreading letting go of one another and it made their in-flight conversation awkward. Life has a heart wrenching way of reminding us that the good times inevitably come to an end.

I gave Holly a warm hug after we landed at O'Hare. I invited her to California, as did Andrew, of course, and thanked her for being such a good sport. Then Andrew walked with her to the Toronto Departures Gate while I sat slouched in my seat, staring pensively at our Boeing 767 docked outside the Gate windows. Toronto seemed so far away to him. *Canada, after all, was that rugged, frozen, sparsely populated tundra north of the 49th*. The misapprehensions about the country continued to plague him as they walked along, hand in hand. *Niles & Pikes Inc. didn't even have an office in*

Canada. It's too blooming remote and cold too, dammit! Ferocious wild animals roam around freely in the neighborhoods: moose, polar bears and, oh my god, beavers—the destructive beasts!

Inevitably, life unfolds and takes hold of you. Home is wherever your heart pulls you. Happiness grows on trees and waits there patiently for you to look up and grab hold of it.

Gate H11 appeared and Andrew's stomach sank a bit deeper. Holly was anxious to get home, but also emotionally wound up about saying good-bye. They kissed and hugged one another passionately. Andrew somehow gathered enough courage to begin walking backwards, waving good-bye as he went. They both made fools of themselves blowing kisses. Then Holly turned and walked up to the counter to verify her departure time; Andrew leaned on a pillar for a moment watching her slip out of his reach, and then turned away when his eyes began to flood.

When he arrived back at our departure gate, he said only one thing: "I'm buying a fucking Gulfstream."

I smiled and gave him a reassuring pat on the back.

Before we knew it, we were back in California and I was back on the farm. It felt good to be home, to see Velocity running alongside the truck as I pulled up to the fence.

"Hey Velly! Good to see you again, old sport. Phillip's still in France, but he'll be back soon," I said, reaching out with an apple in my hand. "Yes, the young pup finally found a mare to hump."

I saw Jeffrey, my senior farm hand, waving as he emerged out of the field in the trusty old John Deere. I parked at the front door as he pulled up, dusty as the Mojave Desert stirred up by the Santa Ana winds, and smiling like a hyena.

"Glad you're back, boss!"

"Good to be back, Jeffrey. The artichokes look mighty fine."

"You knows it, Charlie. You knows it."

"Where's that well-behaved son of mine?"

Of course, I wasn't surprised to hear he was MIA for the last two days, out chasing women and having a good old time.

"He ast me, *Do I knows who's I is?*" Jeffrey continued, obviously upset. "I only ast him to help out a bit, spray the crops and stuff. I said, *I knows who's you is. You's Mr. Niles' lame mule-ass son um a bitchin, freeloadin', manure pattie. That's who you is.*"

"Hah ha... Good for you, Jeffrey."

"He took off. He's gone two whole days... two whole days now!"

I thank the Good Lord for Jeffrey. He's a hardworking, sincere southern lad from a family that's been working this artichoke farm for the last four decades. Without him running things, my farm would be a disaster zone.

Jeffrey went back to work, driving the tractor back into the field to hookup the trailer his two sons had loaded with refreshments and food for the field hands. I dropped my baggage on the steps and walked to the barn. I approached the open barn doors with great anticipation. I even took my Dodgers ball cap off so I could see her in plain view. There she sat, wrapped in a black NASCAR car cover and a dozen chickens on the roof.

"Drat! Scat!" I flung my arms to disperse them. Then I slowly pulled off the cover.

"My word! You're a damned fine sight for sore eyes, Princess."

A few moments passed as Isabella and I got reacquainted. I had just popped the hood when the barn phone rang. Reluctantly, I picked it up.

"Hello?"

"Dad, is that you? You're home already?"

"Yes, I'm home. Did you not read the letter I left for you?"

"Yes, of course I did."

"Then you knew I would be home today."

"Yes. Hi. Hey, can you come bail me out? Damned CHP pulled me over. I wasn't even drunk, just had a few. The bastards said I resisted arrest, too."

I took a moment to process it all. It was a shock, of course. I never lost hope that my son would eventually see the light.

"You're still a child, boy. Forty-eight years old and you can't even take care of yourself."

I was so pissed-off I hung up the phone without asking which jail his sorry ass was stuck in.

I made my way back to the house to make a few phone calls. This was just what I didn't need to come home to. FUCK! Then I noticed the opened envelope that I addressed to him sitting on the kitchen table. *You cashed... the fucking 'Emergency Supplies Fund' for the farm and never even read the letter I wrote. You rotten hunk of parsnip!* The letter was still unfolded, sitting in plain view on the table adorned with several round coffee mug stains. I picked up the phone and called my old friend Bernie at the local jail. Sure enough, that's where my superstar son was.

"What did he do, Bernie?"

"Luckily, he didn't hurt anybody, Charles."

I breathed a huge sigh of relief. "Thank goodness."

"We caught him driving, loaded none-the-less, down Cannery Row. Apparently, the party he was at got trashed. He had a couple happily plastered ladies with him too."

"Wonderful."

"Yup, they were heading to Lover's Point to continue

the party and missed all the red lights along the way. Hah, whoops!"

"Well, thanks for stopping him. Wanna keep him for a while?"

"Not really..."

"Not even overnight?"

"Not after all the verbal abuse we took last night."

"Okay, I'll send Jeffrey to bail him out. That should really make his day."

"Good plan, Charles. Hey, how was your trip?"

"Fabulous, Bernie, had the time of my life," I replied and hung up the phone.

Andrew immediately headed for the den the moment he stepped through the grand acacia wood doors at his home in beautiful Palo Alto. He fired-up his laptop and clicked the Gulfstream bookmark in his Favorites list.

"That's the one," he said aloud, selecting the G650 model photos. "Hoh ho, look at that interior."

With a picture of the warm interior of the aircraft displayed in front of him, he sat back and dialled the Gulfstream Aircraft Sales number for Southern California.

"Gulfstream Sales, Ron speaking."

"Hi Ron, Andrew Pikes here."

"Hi Andrew, good to hear from you."

"I'm caving, man. Wrap me up one of those G650s with the floor plan we discussed, and I guess I'll need a couple pilots, as well."

"Fabulous. I'll take care of everything, Andrew."

"Excellent, Ron. Send the 'all-said-and-done' amount to Jake and Gillian. We'll have a check in the mail for you this week."

"Sweet Jesus, my boy. I like how you do business."

"Let's get her done then. I hope to see that G650 on the

blacktop ASAP."

"I'll get right on it then."

"Okay. Later."

Leaning back in his butter-smooth leather chair, he breathed a sigh of relief and finally relaxed. A thought popped into his mind and a smile stretched across his face. Behind him, a map of California hung on the wall. A set of darts was tucked away in his desk drawer. Spontaneously, he reached for the darts in the drawer and without looking behind at the map, he threw the dart. There was a thud against the wall and another as the dart fell to the floor.

"Dang!" he muttered and took another dart. This time, he covered his eyes and faced the map. Then he threw the dart with such a force that made him combust out the other end.

"Hah ha, old fart," he muttered.

The dart hit the map with a thud and stuck halfway into the teak wood panel behind. He spread his fingers just enough to reveal where the dart landed.

"No shit! Malibu!" he said running over to the map for a closer look.

"Dab smack on Zuma Beach, too. Nice. Akhila got it right, in more ways than one. What a gal."

Across the pond, Phillip was busy in his study working on company business plans. His study was more like an operations room with multiple monitors and laptops open and displaying key information about different projects on the go at Niles & Pikes Inc. The company was doing really well. Software revenues were growing beyond expectations each quarter. The stock was up 150 percent this year. It was time to think about a stock dividend as a reward to loyal shareholders. His train of thought was so intense; he did not hear the first few beats of his cell phone ring tone.

"Hey there, Supercharger."

"Hey CG girl."

"Whatcha wearing?" Angela asked.

"What? Are we engaging in phone sex?" he whispered.

"Maybe. Is that a bad idea?"

"Ahem, I'm wearing, ah..." thinking of something sexy other than his jeans and SR-71 Blackbird T-shirt, he responded, "Boxers."

"Oh my, darling. Are they baggy or tight?"

"Hmm, I think it is your turn, non? What scandalous outfit avez-vous ce soir?"

"Oh, I see the Agenais lifestyle has turned you into a horny French man."

"Ce n'est pas possible."

"It is true! Naughty boy."

"Are you going to make me wait all night?"

"Non! Je ne suis pas désagréable. I'm walking into the master ensuite as we speak and turning on the tap for a nice, hot, bubbly bath."

"Keep going."

"I'm putting you on speaker phone." Angela placed the portable phone on the window sill, reached for the Lilac and Lavender bubble bath and sat down on the lip of the vintage claw foot tub in her skin tight jeans. "Still there?"

"Ah... y-e-a-h."

"Good. I'm pouring in the bubble bath now. Oh, it smells so lovely."

"What does it smell like?"

"Like a warm, summer afternoon wrapped up in tall lemon grass held together with ribbons of lavender and lilac."

"I'd jump into that. Want some company?"

"You're bold, tonight."

"Yes, I am."

"Uhm, no, I don't want to share my tub tonight. Maybe another night…"

"Fair enough. So, you're naked then?"

"Not yet. I believe it's your turn."

"Cotton, form-fitting boxers," he replied, pulling the waist of his jeans to verify his underwear.

"Color?"

"Plain white… nothing fancy."

"Very nice."

"And yours?"

"I'm still in my jeans… you know, the skin-tight ones?" She stood up from the tub and inspected her butt in the full length mirror, seductively running her left hand down and around her derriere.

"Yes, I vaguely remember those," he replied.

"I like this pair. They curve snugly around each buttock."

"Ah, yes indeed, for complete support."

"Well, it's not like I've ever lost a hip before…"

"Thank goodness!"

"A good pair of jeans feels sexy, too. They not only accentuate the curves of my ass, but also showcase my long, luscious legs." She continued, unbuttoning her pants in front of the mirror and slowly shimmying out, one leg at a time. Phillip was hard as a barbell.

"Yes, your body is hot, er… I mean those jeans are hot."

"That's okay, big boy. I know what you meant. Tell me, what else are you wearing?"

"Well, actually, I'm wearing jeans, too."

"Dammit man! Take them off."

"Off they come, right now, as we speak." He frantically pulled down his jeans, stepped out of them and sat back down.

Angela, wearing only her black silk panties, matching bra

and three inch heels, walked casually over to the tub.

"Tell me something sexy," she demanded, crouching down to shut off the water and run her hand through the bubbles.

"Hmm, well my shoulders and chest are swelling from the workout I had earlier."

Angela's nipples went hard.

"And my biceps feel like chiselled boulders."

"Oooh… imagine, mmmm… my tongue travelling up your rock hard bicep, ahhh… your deltoid squeezed between my luscious, juicy lips."

Phillip was on the verge of an orgasm.

Angela quickly kicked off her heels.

"I'm removing my black lace panties and flowery silk bra."

"Imagine my mouth around your beautiful breasts, my tongue dancing on the tip of your nipples," he replied.

Angela climbed into the bubble bath and sank into the bubbles. Her breasts were swelling and her chest heaving with arousal. She touched herself and felt her legs constrict.

"Oh my God, Oh My…." she exclaimed, as thoughts of Phillip's face buried in her tits sent her reeling over the edge.

Angela's throaty Mmmm's, Ohhh's, Ooooh's and Aaaawe's of pleasure leading to her spontaneous climax sent Phillip on a wild adventure of his own.

Ah, the joys of young, innocent love…

Peter Breeden

TWENTY-THREE – HAMMERHEAD

I watched Jeffery pull up the driveway with my distraught son in the passenger seat yapping some kind of foolishness. Obviously, the world was at fault, not him. I reached for the lemonade sitting on the side table, took a sip and leaned back in my rocker. The view from the veranda always brought me peace of mind, even on days like today. I gazed out across the fields to the hills beyond. A crop duster pilot was working her magic on the adjacent farm, flying low over the crops, and then pulling vertical climbs and hammerhead turns at the edge of the property lines.

That's Margo. She's only seventeen. She'll be a deep space astronaut one day, commanding missions that take her and her crew far beyond our solar system. The Space Shuttle fleet, now an iconic relic of the Age of The Climate Change, sits proudly in museums across this great land. At the California Science Center sits an outcast, pimple-infested adolescent on a bench in full view of the Space Shuttle Endeavour, sketching the solar powered inter-burst steam driven, counter oscillating, quad power plants and oxygen generating system of what will eventually become an integral part of the new and massive International Deep Space Interplanetary Transport Ship (IDSITS). Across the globe, another young scientist is designing the interplanetary oxygen harvester while his best friend brainstorms the possibilities arising from a Zero Gravity Green House fed by 24-hours of redirected sun-star-light.

Alas, let the truth be told. It's been over half a century of blasting into space and we have yet to physically transport a human beyond the proximity of the moon. I think Columbus had a better exploration track record and *his ship* was powered exclusively by the wind. Yes, it is true. Our mission to explore space has failed because we have not yet built an intergalactic spaceship, a massive endeavor that undoubtedly requires the collective efforts and resources of all countries, not just a few. Instead, we have spent our time fighting over natural resources that don't belong to us. They belong to God and are on loan to us. We didn't create them and our behavior indicates that we are certainly unworthy of them. So, how will we ever discover new worlds? I tell you the truth; we will not advance as a human race if we don't start sharing God's resources freely and responsibly. Only then will we have our massive intergalactic spaceship, one which can only be built on the moon. Heck, we haven't even started production of the Lunar Spaceship Manufacturing Plant necessary to build the IDSITS. Well, actually... a 14 year old has and her design, a hobby inspired by the first female Chinese astronaut, will eventually be used to build the blueprints for the plant. But I digress...

My son climbed out of the truck, hiked over to the steps and promptly gave me a piece of his mind.

"Why send him to pick me up? That's humiliating. The farm hand," he continued with exaggerated facial, body and hand expressions, "bails out the son of a reputable artichoke farmer… again! What the fuck, Dad?"

I had no response for him. The real question was *how far beyond the edge are you willing to go to save your kid?*

I briefly caught his eye and made an effort to smile in a way that conveyed patience, compassion and unconditional love. His eyes were full of anger. I poured him a glace of chilled lemonade made from scratch by Jeffrey's lovely wife, but he only scoffed and huffed. He wasn't interested.

"I spent it all, you know… two weeks of pure bliss. The best part was escaping this shit hole."

He put his cigarette out before entering the house. At least there was a glimmer of hope, a hint of respect. I watched the butt smolder on top of the ice in the jug of lemonade and thought about what he would feel if he knew the money, the *'Emergency Supplies Fund,'* he spent was Phillip's, his son's contribution to my welfare while in France. I didn't have that kind of money. I'm a farmer.

There's only one answer: *All the way.*

I've obviously got some work to do. I can try harder.

"This is not yet a *faits accompli*," I mumbled, chuckling as I recalled a heated discussion with Caroline about French expressions at the Château party last week. My, how time flies.

The hummingbirds darted back and forth between the hanging baskets on the veranda as I leaned forward for a better view of the crops. The sound of their wings pulsating put my mind at ease. I lifted my cap, scratched my scalp and exhaled the pent-up stress in my chest.

"Perhaps the boy needs more work… or inspiration to work harder. Maybe he thinks I don't love him," I mumbled as I pulled myself up from my comfy seat. "We'll fix that," I blurted. "Time to call Takeisha," I decided as I strolled off to the cozy green couch in the den.

Peter Breeden

TWENTY-FOUR – DIGNITY

His eyes shifted from the time on the SR-71 Blackbird / F-15 Eagle Formation desk clock in the Oval Office, which displayed 16:14 hours in the fiber optic entanglement of the aircraft's afterburners, to the view of the lush green lawn from the window. The lawn was a virtual canvass where the President of the United States often painted his ideas for the country. His current masterpiece was somewhat abstract and represented a brainstorming session on how to rebuild the shattered US economy. The worry of it all pounded between his ears like the relentless crashing of waves against a storm wall.

"Where have all the jobs gone?" he mumbled, tapping his fingers on the desk as he watched the birds flap about in the bird bath.

He crossed his ankles and leaned back further in his leather chair. Out of nowhere, a falcon appeared, slicing through the sky. It snatched an unsuspecting robin from the bird bath and disappeared almost as quickly as it had come. The ambush had turned the lawn into a ghost town. An eerie silence overshadowed his thoughts.

"Golly." He shook as a shiver ran up his spine.

"That's where all the jobs have gone," he whispered, looking out the window once again for some indication of life. "Fear…"

"I've got to get corporate America hiring again," he bellowed, sitting back down in his chair and tapping his fingers on the desk. He opened the top secret file containing the most recent contact information for the top 500 corporations. His eyes immediately shot to the top of the list; Niles & Pikes Inc.

"Barely out of College and they create the largest software company in the world," he mumbled to his canine companion, Jupiter. "Barely out of diapers…"

He clicked the link to access their most recent quarterly results and gasped at the unbelievable numbers.

"BRATS!"

"Woof!" barked Jupiter.

"Genius Brats!" he continued, looking at Jupiter for more feedback.

"Rrrrrwooof, woof!"

"Look at these sales and revenue figures."

He picked up the multiline phone and dialed the direct lines of Phillip in Agen and Andrew in Palo Alto. He knew exactly where they both were. Thoughts of JFK's infamous words echoed through his head as they did each and every day of his term in office: "Ask not what your county can do for you, but what you can do for your country."

My Heavenly perspective on the matter is a little more elaborate; *ask not what countries can do for themselves, but what they can do collectively.*

"This is Phillip."

"Yes, I know who you are, Spanky," replied Andrew, "wazz up?"

"Nothing's up… you called," Phillip continued,

somewhat perplexed.

"Huh? I didn't call."

"Are you boys 'bout done?" boomed the voice of the President.

Immediately recognizing the unmistakable voice of the Commander-in-Chief, they both froze, damned-near shitting their pants in the process.

The *FALCON* has arrived.

"Ah, yes Mr. President."

"Good," he bellowed. "Congratulations on the stratospheric success of you company."

"Thank you, Sir."

"Your innovation astounds me, boys, and those quarterly results are some impressive numbers."

"Yes, we are doing well this year, for sure," Andrew agreed.

"Well, that's the purpose of my call today, lads. I need your help."

"Absolutely," Phillip said, prematurely committing himself and Niles & Pikes Inc. to whatever the President had in mind.

"As you know, the economy is the shits… worst case of pecuniary diarrhea imaginable. We've got to get Americans back to work."

"Yes, we've just hired 436 new employees for a new joint hardware / software project," Andrew said triumphantly.

"We call it the Single Unit Device or SUD for short with SuperNova and HyperNova software versions," Phillip continued. "There will be two fully integrated multi-media / multi-electronic gadget hardware options: one for personal use, the SUD-Personal, and one exclusively for business use, the SUD-Business."

"Excellent. I know what you are up to and I think it is

ingenious. However, I need you to hire an additional 50,000 workers."

Silence seized the conversation. It was obvious the President wasn't making a joke.

"Uhm... even if we did hire that many people, we don't have the space to accommodate..."

"I've given that some thought, as well," continued The Commander-in-Chief. "You can pick up some vacant office space in Texas, North Carolina, Los Angeles, Chicago, Toronto and Seattle."

"What would you have these people do, Sir?" Phillip replied, somewhat concerned at the President's shockingly ambitious request.

"You boys are the geniuses. I'm sure you can figure out a clever way to turn the talent pool into hoards of revenue. Invent some new software, a gadget or something incredibly smart. Impress me."

"Did you say, Toronto, Mr. President?" Andrew inquired.

"Yes, there's an empty office building up there we need to fill up."

Silence once again enveloped the phone line. Andrew began tossing around a few ideas, possibilities directly related to his inmost desires to see Holly again.

"Ah c'mon. You're sitting on 950 billion in cash. Stop fartin' around with castles and fancy cars and get back to work. Retirement living is for seniors. They've put their time in... you two have not."

Another moment of awkward silence apprehended the line.

"All right," Andrew replied hesitantly, not knowing what to think about the retirement living comment. He knew what long hours and sleepless nights were all about.

"We'll make use of the vacant office space, Sir," Phillip

said reassuringly.

"So, I can sign you up for these buildings then? I can count on you both to come through for me?"

"Yes," Andrew replied.

"I believe so," Phillip concurred.

"Fantastic! You boys are just what this country needs; role models who remind each and every one of us that we cannot be crushed by the volley of storms that come our way. I like it! Now, excuse me while I call some Black Gold CEOs. We'll get this economy rolling again, even if it means creating a new Graduated Economic Recovery tax on all top luxury items… including castles, er uhm, Châteaus. It doesn't make sense to me to see the super-rich flying around in their luxury jets while the average American has his head buried in his hands because there are no jobs out there."

"Agreed," replied Phillip. "We need to restore dignity…"

"Yes, boy. DIGNITY. It makes more sense for the super-rich, who fly around in their luxury jets between their lavish homes, to better protect the stitching that holds everything together."

The President hung up and left Andrew and Phillip on the open, secure… line.

"Hello?" Phillip queried. "Mr. President?"

"He's gone… I just bought a G 650," Andrew threw in for good measure.

"Nice! Is that the model with premium leather interior, reclining couches and full galley?"

"And berthing for six!"

"Any workstations?"

"Yes, five workstations and comfortable seating for fifteen."

"Good call, man. That's forward thinking… you must be

a genius."

"That's right, g-e-n-i-u-s," Andrew replied with a chuckle.

"Yeah, well, don't expect any more ego boosters for a while."

"On that note… Charles and I are headed to the track tomorrow evening."

"Hah ha, *n-i-c-e*… Wish I was there with you. I love Wednesday night drags."

"So come, then. We're going to give the Comp Rod class a little ground pounding surprise!"

"I bet you are, but I can't. I've gotta hot date tomorrow. Angela's making her world famous Tiramisu, which, by the way, I get to sample if I'm a good boy. Jealous?"

"Lil' bit."

"Good. We can't let you have all the fun with that lil' business jet of yours, now can we?"

"Awe, don't worry, Lug Nut. I'll share my new *a-i-r-p-l-a-n-e AND* the GER tax with you."

"Gee, thanks man."

TWENTY-FIVE – TIRAMISU KISS

The drive from Monterey began with a soothing scene of rolling waves massaging the beaches along the PCH coastline and continued past rolling fields of luscious strawberries down the 156 to the I-101 where Cypress, Redwood and Eucalyptus trees lined the hills and valleys on our journey towards Gilroy, or what I like to call Garlic County, USA. The invigorating smell of garlic and accompanying collection of fond memories from past Gilroy Garlic Festivals hovered like a mist over my mind until Andrew merged onto the I-280, the Junipero Serra or *"The World's Most Beautiful Freeway,"* as the sign along the roadway clearly states. I've admired this stretch of road since day one over half a century ago; 1955 to be exact. It is sandwiched by God's beauty on either side. Like the solitary hue of the Milky Way strewn across the Heavens above, it runs the length of the San Francisco Peninsula between San Jose and San Francisco. On one side, the tree-covered mountain ranges stand in the distance, immovable and graceful. On the other, a volley of rolling hills spans the length of the peninsula connecting one Bay Area city to the next. Every now and then, a stately home, or one with an amusing architectural flare, peeks through the trees. The tranquility of the Crystal Springs Reservoir tempts passers-by to pull off the freeway and sit by the water's edge for a moment of peace. If you're keenly discerning, you can even see the airliners on approach to San Francisco International as you drive into the city. We passed through Golden Gate Park on 19th Avenue where more fond memories of my wife and I having fun riding the paddle boats and eating ice cream came to mind. This land is the very bones and flesh of my being, the entirety of my mind.

"There it is… at last," exclaimed Andrew as we entered and crossed the Golden Gate Bridge. Through the rear view mirror or a quick turn of my head, I never failed to glance backwards at the inspiring view of San Francisco through the suspension wires of the bridge.

"Bella Donna," I said.

"You have an old girlfriend back there I don't know about?" Andrew asked.

"Yes…" I said, pausing for a moment of old timer's reflection, "on the observation deck of the Transamerica Pyramid, many years ago. We hopped on the cable car afterwards and spent the whole day celebrating our 25th anniversary strolling around the Embarcadero."

It was 2:45 pm when Andrew and I finally pulled into the entrance at Infineon Raceway in Sonoma with the Plymouth in tow. *A beautiful day for racing*, I concluded as we pulled into the lineup at the gate. The temperature sat pleasantly at 89 degrees. There was no wind or humidity to speak of and a few wispy white clouds etched across the otherwise blue California sky.

Across the pond in Agen, the nine hour time difference put things at 11:45 pm or fast approaching the witching hour. A full moon floating on a cloud of haze lit up the night sky; in the distance, a creature of the night cut the silence with a bone chilling howl.

"Dammit!" Phillip steamed, checking the time on his Hamilton wristwatch and shaking his head. He hurried up to the front entrance and lost his balance on a rather large dog bone sitting in plain view, but managed to avoid wiping out altogether. A cozy glow from the chandelier reached out through the leaded glass windows, inviting him out of the darkness. Wrapping things up at work had made him half an hour late for his date with Angela.

He knocked on her door holding a bouquet of red roses in one hand, a fine bottle of Cabernet Merlot in the other. A check for 2 million US was tucked nicely away in his wallet.

The door swung open… "Hello there, handsome."

"Hello doll."

They stood in admiration of one another for a few moments before Phillip leaned in for a kiss.

"Nice chandelier, my dear."

"Early 1900s…"

"Bavarian?"

"The crystal, yes, but everything else is authentic Spanish design including the ornate bronze sculpting."

"Magnificent!"

"Thank you!"

"Flowers for a lovely CG," he continued, handing her the fragrant bouquet of roses, "and spirits to cheer you up when you lose."

"Hah, I rarely lose when I play pool, mister. I hope you brought your bag of magic tricks. You're late."

"Sorry," he apologized, quickly changing the topic. "I won't be needing magic, my dear. It's all about technique and diversion."

Phillip noticed the wrought-iron railings as soon as he stepped into the foyer.

"So this is what you've been up to for the last week."

"Yup."

"Wow, it looks fantastic. Nice job."

"Thank you. Don't try sliding down them though. They're not slide proof, yet."

"What, am I nine years old?"

"Uhm, no," she replied with a smile. "Maybe, twelve, though. You're still preoccupied with cars, and you make funny engine noises when you think nobody is watching," she continued, giving him a flirtatious slap on the bottom as she turned towards the kitchen.

Look at those long, shapely legs, Phillip admired, reaching out to pinch her beautiful curvy ass. *Those G-string panty outlines… in skintight jeans,* he mused, trying to remain cool. *Looks like Angela is the Queen of Distraction tonight*, he concluded.

Angela gave a little gasp and a pretend look of shock as she stared back at her man and seductively whispered, "You naughty boy."

"Yes I am."

"Behave then… or there will be no Tiramisu for you," she replied with a smoldering look of passion. Then, crouching down, she gave Dovely a nose kiss, revealing a glimpse of the scandalous transparent lingerie showcasing a shapely pair of silky soft breasts beneath her loose shirt.

Back at the racetrack, the gates finally opened allowing us to join the lineup for mechanical inspection. I noticed quite a few bewildered glances directed our way as we pulled into the lineup.

I overheard one young fellow as I climbed out of the truck.

"Wow, look at that *rocket*," he said mockingly.

He was standing with a group of friends beside his shiny new Mustang GT. I tossed a sly smile in his direction just to let him know I had a big secret, and then I climbed onto the trailer to prepare the Plymouth.

"Pop the hood," Andrew said.

I slipped in the driver's seat and pulled the hood release. As soon as Andrew lifted the hood, the GT kids came over to humor us, climbing up on both sides of the trailer to peer inside the engine bay.

"Is this the Hot Dog Taxi?" one cheeky fellow asked as he climbed aboard.

Andrew pointed at the engine and simply replied, "No, but she's tamed a few mustangs in her time."

I chuckled. Indeed, Isabella had surprised many overconfident muscle car owners in the past.

I couldn't see their facial expressions from where I was sitting, but I sure did enjoy hearing the shock in their voices as they beheld the highly modified 3.0 liter V6 engine. *Ah, sweet justice*, I mused.

"Awe, cool! Where did you get the RAM Air kit?" replied the same snarky fellow whose comic remark a few moments earlier was coming back to bite him on the ass.

"We built it to *ram* the *nitrous* through the runners," Andrew replied.

"Nitrous? No way!"

An aloof teenage girl, who kept staring at me like I was some bizarre amusement attraction, jumped on the trailer and peered inside the driver's side window where I was sitting. After scoping out the cockpit, she finally blurted out, "Your momma know you do this shit?"

I didn't quite know how to respond. I shrugged and tried to find some words, but she continued before I could find any.

"I like this car. It's... S-E-X-Y," she continued, slowly nodding her head to show appreciation as she scanned the AutoMeter speedometer, tachometer, fuel pressure, water temperature, and oil pressure gauges.

Again, I was left speechless.

"What's that red lever for?"

I somehow found my wits and climbed out of my state of shock. I looked in the direction she was pointing.

"That's the switch guard for the fogger system," I replied, flipping it open and flicking the switch to engage the nitrous system. When the red light lit up, her eyes nearly popped out.

"Whoa, that's cool!"

"This blue button here is for the nitrous purge," I continued, pleasantly surprised to see the interest the car was receiving from the younger generation. In my mind, I was 20 years old all over again and equally as excited as these young kids were. I listened to them hoot and holler over the engine modifications, each of them predicting what Isabella would run in the quarter mile. In my rearview mirror, I saw the track official approaching us for the mandatory mechanical inspection. Everybody returned to their cars a few moments later.

Andrew ran through all the modifications in detail with the track official. The inspector verified the nitrous bottle blow-down tube was properly vented outside the vehicle. He also checked the drag tires, disc brakes (slotted and drilled for maximum cooling), solid engine mounts and 5-speed manual transmission.

"Looks good," he said. "Let's see your helmets."

"Sure," Andrew replied, reaching for our helmets in the passenger seat.

The inspector, an older fellow with white hair, track cap and vintage shades, missed nothing. If your car didn't pass his inspection, you didn't race.

After inspecting the helmets, he gave us a nod of approval and wrote *Comp Rod* on the top corner of our windshield to identify our race class. The Comp Rod class is comprised of cars that are not street legal due to their modifications and setup. *Tonight, we run with the Big Boys*, I thought to myself.

"Okay, you guys are good to roll," the inspector said at last. "Have fun."

"Thanks," I said, from behind the wheel.

Andrew pulled the trailer ahead with me still sitting behind the wheel of the Plymouth. He drove into the Staging Area where all the cars that passed mechanical inspection were lined up for an evening of drag racing. The first cars of the evening, Chevy vs. Ford muscle, rolled through the Burnout Box and turned the peaceful valley into rolling thunder as they smoked out the place. The double-yellows lit up on either side and the engine revs roared. When the green lights lit up, the age-old rivalry between the two highly competitive automakers could be heard across the valley. The highly customized engines unleashed something furious on the rear slicks as they sped down the track.

There was something different about the Tree Lights this evening: yellow, yellow, yellow, GREEN. *They looked cleaner, brighter... very nice*, I thought. I chuckled as a nine second quarter mile run had the Porsche 911 Carrera GTS genuflect in homage to a highly modified turbo Honda Civic. *You can't judge a car by its skin*, I thought to myself. *You know nothing substantial if you don't know what lies beneath.*

"Let's role Isabella off the trailer," Andrew said eagerly.

"Sure, Boss, she's all yours," I replied, handing him the keys.

Andrew fired up the V6 and tapped the gas. The dual

three inch open exhaust pipes erupted with a thunderous roar sending heads turning from all directions.

"Hah ha," he chuckled and waved as he drove back to the gas pumps to fill the tank with some high octane race fuel.

Last winter, we decided to reduce the exhaust pressure, and thereby increase the horsepower output, by removing the resonator, catalytic converter and muffler, replacing it with a three inch pipe at the header collector from above the heavy duty subframe running back towards the back where it split into dual three inch pipes in front of the rear wheels. The results were my kind of Rock 'N Roll. Now, all we have to do is run a damned near perfect quarter mile to see our true performance gains… easier said than done.

"I'll park the truck," I hollered to Andrew when he returned, but I don't think he heard me. I watched him drive off to the staging area and join the Comp Rod class. I don't know who was more excited, him or me, but I certainly knew at that moment we were going to have the time of our lives.

I drove the truck back to the parking lot on the other side of the crew pits. The emotion of it all hit me hard. This was my fifth decade of running drag cars in Sonoma, California. At least one of my boys was here tonight. I parked the truck and said hello to my old friend whose racecar was sponsored by a local casino. It was an eight second quarter mile 1950s corvette. What a beauty. I glanced over at the hot dog stands, but decided to wait a while. *Let's get a few runs under our belts first*, I decided. I walked up pit lane towards the stands. *Those hot dogs sure smell good*. I pondered and drooled as a group of kids passed by with boxes of dogs, fries and drinks in hand. *Wait for it*, I thought, and continued towards the staging area. When I saw Andrew was already in line for the burnout box, panic flew across my face.

"Gosh dagnit! Was I gone that long?" I removed my hat and wiped the sweat from my forehead with my forearm. *The view of the track will be better in the stands*; I decided and eased my way into the lower level of the grandstands.

"Sit down, old fart."

"Oof, sorry… my apologies."

While in the process of finding a seat and dodging the occasional obscenity from irate spectators, I stopped to watch Andrew do his burnout.

"Easy, old boy… save some rubber for me," I mumbled.

"What the fuck? Is that a K-car?"

Another spectator replied, "It's an Acclaim, a Plymouth Acclaim. Hah!"

To my horror, a fully blown 1960s Ford Fairlane pulled up in the left lane. It was loaded with sponsor stickers. Even worse, his burnout turned the entire Burnout pad into a thick cloud of smoke.

"Uhg! This is going to be ugly," I muttered. Then I realized Andrew hadn't purged the nitrous system.

"Sit here old man," a spunky southern belle said, kindly tugging my arm to get me down. "You know that car out there?" she asked, pointing at the Plymouth.

"Ah," my hesitation saved me.

Yellow, yellow, yellow, GREEN.

The Fairlane charged down the track and nailed the trap at 169 mph… leaving Andrew sitting pretty at the Tree. He not only stalled the car, but forgot to purge the nitrous system.

"Damn, that Ford's fast!" the southern belle blurted.

"Hah ha, looks like the Plymouth has stage fright!" someone shouted from behind us.

"What a piece of shit!" another disappointed hot rod enthusiast proclaimed.

Andrew, beat red and furious under his helmet, fired up the car and hit the gas. It bucked a few times, and then grabbed when he hit wide open throttle. Isabella lurched forward and spun the tires halfway down the track.

"Excuse me," I said to the southern belle. "I have to go fix a severely bruised ego."

"Awe c'mon CG, just one bite," Phillip pleaded.

"Ah, the sweet pleasure of hearing the agony of failed self-gratification," Angela said, placing her Tiramisu masterpiece back in the fridge.

"You're a mean feline."

"You'll savor it more if you wait a bit longer," she told him, placing her arms around Phillip's neck and smiling at his childlike mope.

"Even my Great Danes know restraint. See how well they're behaved sitting over there by the sliding doors?"

"If I pulled a cookie from my pocket, they would be right over here in an instant."

"Yes, they would," Angela agreed, "but they would sit there nicely until you handed it over."

"Hah ha, okay… point taken."

"Let's head to the pool room. Here, take these," she said, handing Phillip the bowl of spicy hot chicken wings. "I'll bring the dipping sauce and veggie tray."

"How 'bout the wine, sweetheart?"

"It's on the bar. I'm in the mood for Chianti tonight."

"Italian?"

"Si."

"Very nice," Phillip approved and headed off with the chicken to pull the cork.

Andrew pulled behind the last car in the Comp Rod lineup. I could see the frustration in his actions as he parked the car and climbed out, tossing his helmet on the driver's seat.

I looked at him with a wry smile and couldn't resist cracking a joke.

"I don't suppose you caught that there run on video" I said, referring to the onboard video camera that records all of our runs, but only if we remember to start the video.

"Shit... YES," he said, and ran to the passenger side to stop the video recorder.

"Hah, let me get this straight, now. You remembered to record your run, but forgot to engage and purge the nitrous system..." I said, trying not to laugh in the process.

"Shut up!"

"I'm just sayin'... little odd, ya know, for someone who knows so much about cars and all," I continued.

"Ya, well I had a brain fart, okay?"

"And perhaps a pedal-clutch fart, too..."

"Yes, yes, just call me Buckaroo."

"Don't worry, kid. Pop the hood. You'll nail it on the next run."

Poor fellow, I thought. There's nothing more I want for him than to smoke some hot shot's car tonight. Oh, and marry Holly. She's a doll.

"I don't know what happened."

"You forgot to *follow the list*," I reminded him.

"You're right. What was it, again? Activate nitrous system, start video, drive through burnout box, engage parking brake, burnout, disengage parking brake, purge the nitrous system, stage to double yellow, purge again, rev to 3500 RPM, feather the clutch and leave on the second yellow."

"That's it! Simple, huh?"

"Piece of cake, Pops! I'll get it right this time."

"Yes you will, boy," I said reassuringly. "Arm the nitrous

system."

Andrew stuck his head in the car and flicked the switch. "Done."

"What's the bottle pressure?" I asked.

He leaned over the open trunk to read the nitrous bottle psi gauge. "She's pushing 1000 psi."

"Hmm, well the bottle warmer should give us another couple hundred psi," I said. "That should do the trick, I think."

Andrew, a little stressed out, ran his hand through his hair and bellowed, "So I just stomp on it... right?"

"Wide open throttle, little buddy."

Dovely jumped up on the bar to inspect the chicken wings, which seemed to bring back favorable memories of some yummy treats he once found in a paper bag beneath a park bench. He kept a close eye on Phillip. Something fishy was going on. *Is he worthy?* Dovely pondered for a brief moment then clawed out a chicken wing, bit into it and took off.

"Hey cat!" Phillip blurted in the direction Dovely had run, and went back to setting up the pool table for 8-Ball. "Thief," he grumbled.

Okay, he'll do, Dovely decided, gobbling down the spicy chicken wing.

"Ready?" Angela queried as she entered the pool room.

"Almost," Phillip said, pouring two glasses of Chianti. "Your cat stole a chicken wing."

"Way to go, Dovely," she cheered, placing the veggies on the bar and sliding herself onto a bar stool.

"What? You approve of such behavior?"

"He's a cat, Lug Nut. If you leave food out unattended, he'll help himself."

Dovely strolled back into the room pretending nothing

unusual had happened. He stopped by the bar and began grooming his shoulder blades, the one true sign of a happy cat... or one who just committed a crime.

"That's a narcissistic, pompous feline!"

"Aren't they all?"

Phillip pondered this for a moment. *Perhaps the little guy just wants to hang with the grownups.*

"Well, I'm moving the wings over here where I can keep an eye on them."

"Veggies and dip will be fine here on the bar." Angela lifted her wine glass to make a toast.

"To crazy felines and spicy hot wings!"

Phillip chuckled, tapped glasses with Angela and took a sip.

"Mmm, that's good stuff."

"Yes, very smooth."

Phillip leaned over and kissed Angela's neck.

"You smell like a gentle, early morning wind dancing along a meadow of fragrant, rain-soaked flowers."

Angela smiled and took another sip of her Chianti.

"It's my auntie's stock from her vineyard in Italy. Would you like to visit her, maybe this weekend?"

"Absolutely! Whereabouts in Italy?"

"Tuscany, near Sienna."

"Ah, beautiful, sun ravaged Tuscany. I'll call Akhila tomorrow to book the helicopter."

You can ravage me anytime, big boy. Angela's thoughts ran wild as she toyed with her fantasy. *I'll ride those mountainous shoulders of yours, wherever you take me.*

"Awesome!" she said with a little bounce on the bar stool that made her wine splash and land on the supple white flesh of her right breast.

"Whoopsy," she laughed, undoing another button on her loosely buttoned shirt.

Phillip gazed dreamily at her glistening boob.

Angela leaned seductively towards Phillip, her cleavage and breasts slipping further out of her silky tight, barely there lingerie body suit.

"Go ahead, Phillip. Have a little taste of Angel Ambrosia," she whispered, sliding off her stool and onto Phillip's lap.

"Mmm," he managed as he buried his face in her breasts and ran his tongue where the wine had spilled, boldly going beneath the silk lingerie for a brief moment.

"Whoa, Mr. Nitrous... I said a *little* taste. The chicken wings are over there," she said teasingly and pointed at the wings. "Mangia, mangia!"

"Awe, c'mon."

"Let's play POOL," Angela bellowed, grabbing a chicken wing as she spun around the table to pick up her cue. "Do you know how to play 8-Ball Strip?"

Back at the track, I watched Andrew pull up to the Burnout box and purge the nitrous system. The look on his face was intense. He rarely failed at anything, not because he was a genius, but simply because he chose not to give up. If he did fail, he went right back and corrected his mistakes until he was a success. There was no such thing as surrender in his book of life, but rather a relentless desire to succeed, even if that meant overcoming presumably impossible obstacles along the way. In his mind, there was always a solution to a problem and if he couldn't find it himself, he wasn't too proud to ask for help.

"Unload that beast!" I shouted from behind the concrete barrier. The crowd around me laughed, but Andrew looked straight at me with a huge grin and pointed his finger down the track to show he was ready to get the party started.

The track official signalled for him to pull through the

box and start his burnout. I watched as he inched the front wheels forward into the wet pavement, engaged the parking brake and hit the gas in second gear. The front tires, 15 inch MH slicks, spun madly throwing melted bits of rubber down either side of the car. He probably shouldn't have hit the nitrous during the burnout, but he did anyway and turned the place into a cloud of smoke.

"Goof," I chuckled.

The competition pulled up, a twin turbo V8 El Camino... the Dragon. *Poor Andrew...* Even if he did everything right, he still would not win this one. The El Camino's burnout made Isabella's look like child's play. *Oh well*, I thought to myself. *Let's just get a good run in.*

Both cars inched up to the line and illuminated the double yellows on the tree. Andrew's engine revs were swallowed by the monstrous roar of the El Camino spooling its twins. Andrew managed one final nitrous purge before the lights fired-off: yellow, yellow, yellow, GREEN.

The Dragon spun wildly out of the gate, but then his tires stuck and he pulled away like a steal ball bearing shot from a high powered sling shot. Andrew's launch was his best ever with a reaction time (RT) of .009. *That should make him happy*, I thought. The Dragon hit the trap with an elapsed time (ET) of 7.88 seconds. He must be running rocket fuel! Andrew, not terribly far behind, hit the trap in 11.01 seconds. *Well done, Andrew.*

Andrew shouted out the window, "She's overheating," as he pulled back into the line up behind a beautiful mint condition 1969 Camaro. *Hmm, I hope I race that Camaro.* I've never managed to beat one my entire life. I came close once, in my old bored out Hemi Barracuda. Damn that would be sweet... 1993 Plymouth Acclaim trounces '69 Camaro; headlines in tomorrow's newspapers. Hah ha.

Angela strategically positioned her butt on the rail of the pool table to make the final shot.

"Eight ball, corner pocket," she declared confidently as she leveraged herself across the felt. With one fluid motion, the pool cue slid over the soft bridge of her thumb sinking the 8-ball and placing the first game in her favor.

"Off with pants, Buster," she said triumphantly.

"What?" Phillip exclaimed. "I'll give you a sock."

"Hah ha, no... Winner's choice," she declared, motioning him with her finger. "Drop the pants, Casanova."

"I need to have a look at your rule book," he replied, awkwardly sliding out of his jeans.

She tilted her head for a better view using the pool cue for support. "What's that say on your boxers?" she asked, lifting her glass for another taste of her Chianti.

Phillip posed with a smile, "Fully Blown!"

"Is that referring to your ego?"

He humphed and proceeded to chalk up his cue tip. "Rack em up, sistah. You're about to have your ass handed to you."

"Is that so?"

"Oh y-e-a-h," Phillip replied, tossing the cue chalk aside.

"Well then, Mr. Fully Blown, let's get these balls rolling."

"Rack em up," he repeated, enthusiastically rubbing chalk all over his hands, smacking them together and slapping his face just for good measure. The dust cloud caused a gagging reflex.

Angela stared incredulously as Phillip tried not to choke on the dust, but failed miserably.

"That was quite the show."

"My other pair of Hot Rod boxers says *The Intimidator*," he barely managed after regaining his composure.

"Okay then, Mr. FBI... Fully Blown Intimidator," she laughed, breaking the racked balls, but failing to sink any.

"My turn, Honey-bunch," he replied pompously.

"Yeah, just remember that the ball needs to go *into* the pocket, not on some wild journey across the floor."

It was shaping up to be a spectacular sunset in Sonoma. The wispy clouds in the West looked like crimson brush strokes across an otherwise blue sky. Andrew coasted through the burnout box and lit up the tires for his third run of the evening. The smoke curled upwards, carried away by the wind like it had been summoned along with the inevitable departure of the sun. His competition: a candy cane red, split window 1963 'Vette with white racing stripes. The driver was laughing as she pulled through the burnout box, undoubtedly thinking this would be an easy win. I watched her father run high twelve's in the 'Vette earlier in the day against the kids with the Mustang GT. It was a close run, too. Andrew, all being well, should win this race, hands down. *Thank you Lord.* A win for Andrew meant I could finally get behind the wheel. *Don't mess this one up Andrew*, I thought impatiently.

Sure enough, he nailed it, taking the 'Vette from the lights and never looking back. Well, perhaps he did through his rear view mirror, much to the chagrin of his competition.

I watched him pull back into the lineup with the biggest smile I had ever seen on a young lad, plastered across his face. *Good, he's happy. Now it's my turn*, I thought excitedly.

"Don't miss this one, Spanky," she advised. "Otherwise, you're going to be walking around here bare-assed."

"No I'm not," replied Phillip confidently. He carefully lined up the cue ball with the 8-ball, an easy shot to the side pocket. Sliding the cue fluidly along the bridge stick, he sunk the 8-ball with ease.

"Nice, one."

"Thanks, off with your shirt, CG."

Angela's omnipotent smile had him a little worried. She slowly and seductively edged towards her man with a lock of hair curled up around her finger. After a momentary pause, she leaned over and whispered intimately, "How about you take off your shirt and I'll rack em up for another round, Mr. I-Forgot-To-Call-Out-The-Pocket."

"Shit!"

As Phillip removed his shirt and threw it to one side, Angela unconsciously undid another one of her shirt buttons. *Awesomely chiselled chest*, she thought as she gathered the pool balls. *My fingers are going to dance all over those pecs, squeeze those hulking shoulders and pinch... no, I'm going to bite that incredibly hard ass.* Her wild thoughts continued to demolish her heavily fortified walls and peak her arousal.

"How about we double the stakes?" Phillip offered in a last attempt of desperation.

"Mr. Risk Taker," replied Angela, leaning over for another veggie dip and running her hand casually down her backside, just for the sake of driving Phillip insane. "You know that socks count as one, right? If you lose, you remove the boxers and the socks."

"I'm still wearing my watch."

"Uh huh, that's jewelry, not clothes. It doesn't count."

"Fine, if I win, you remove your shirt AND your pants."

"If you win," laughed Angela. *Either way, Château Boy, I'm going to straddle that mighty fine chest of yours and have my way with you*, she fantasized.

Andrew was full of advice as I prepared for my run.

"Make sure to purge. Don't forget to hit 3500 RPM before dropping the clutch. Don't hit the nitrous too soon."

"Cork it, Crank Case! Let me focus here."

"Oof, sorry," he apologized and handed me my helmet.

"Check the bottle pressure."

Andrew ran back to the trunk to read the pressure gauge, "1230 psi. The bottle is HOT."

"Belts?"

He ran to the engine bay and verified the belts and pulleys, "Good."

"Hoses and wires?"

"Check and check," he continued, and then shouted, "Hold up!"

"What? Find something?" After a few moments of disturbing silence, Andrew replied.

"Yup, the RAM Intake assembly has come loose."

I jumped out of the car and stuck my head in the engine bay.

Andrew pointed to the throttle body inlet. The fastener around the connector hose had come loose.

"Good catch."

"I followed the RAM piping down to the scoop and noticed that one of the frame bolts anchoring the scoop has broken off. See here?"

"Damned bolt head broke right off. I must have over-tightened it."

"Can we fix it?" Andrew asked.

"Yes, grab the electric drill and the spare bolts from the truck. Oh, bring the screw driver set and the digital tire pressure gauge, as well."

"Be right back," he replied and ran off to the truck.

A few moments—and curse words—later, a familiar voice wafted over my perturbed state of affairs.

"Having mechanical issues?"

I peered out from under the car. The aloof teenage girl was back.

"Yes, but nothing we can't fix."

"I saw your last run... pretty awesome."

She sounded a little out-of-sorts.

"I like this car best of all," she continued.

I could tell she was sincere. I'm a good judge of character especially when it comes to kids who are a little different than the rest.

"Find yourself a helmet and let Tom know your riding shotgun with me on the next run," I said, pointing to the track official at the burnout box.

"Really?" she screamed and spun around like a little girl. "Cool, I'll be right back."

Andrew returned a few moments later with the tools. "I'm back. Here's the drill."

"Excellent, thanks! Okay, go ahead and tighten the connector hose around the RAM pipe and throttle body. I'll drill out this old bolt."

"Got it."

The aloof teenager returned just as I was sizing replacement bolts for the scoop frame assembly.

"Need any help under there?" she asked, kneeling down to inspect the air dam.

"I think I got it."

Andrew looked at the girl holding the helmet. "And who might this be?"

I was a little stumped as I didn't even know her name myself.

"Melissa, but you can call me Quarter Horse. That's my mustang back there. My dad won't let me drive it until I pass my driver's test."

"So, who's driving it then?" I asked.

"My obnoxious brother," she replied with a frown.

"Ah, I see... well then," I said, grabbing the pressure gauge and handing it to her. "Make yourself useful."

"Cool... what psi are you looking for in the tires?" she asked.

Andrew interjected. "We should have 15 psi in the front slicks and 32 psi in the rear tires."

"Actually, I'm making a small adjustment for this run," I said, much to their surprise. "Reduce the pressure in the front slicks to 10 psi. Keep 32 psi in the rear tires."

"Got it, Boss," Melissa replied, going straight to work.

Andrew looked somewhat baffled. "That's a little low for the slicks, I think."

"Naw, it's perfect. I need her to grab hard when I launch."

"Is this a new trick?"

"Nope, just something I've been saving for..." Andrew watched my eyes dart over to the '69 Camaro. "I can't teach you everything all at once, Andrew."

"It's the Camaro." He counted the cars down the line to see if the Camaro would indeed be running against Charles. "Nice, you get the Camaro this run."

"Yes, I do."

"You gonna win?"

"You bet your ass!"

"Well let's get Isabella fixed then. We run after Street and they're almost done."

"Yes, all it takes is one small oversight to ruin your whole day," I remarked. "If you're done with that fastener, go ahead and inspect everything up top and I'll check down below after I finish wrenching this new bolt."

"I'm on it, Pops."

Melissa was happy to be part of a team. She walked around the Plymouth, humming while she checked the tire pressure and made adjustments to the front slicks. It was a welcome change. Her brother hogged the Mustang GT. When she asked to help with something, she always got pushed aside. It wasn't really fair given that she graduated with an A average, hence the nice graduation gift, while her twin brother barely scraped through his final year. All the glory seems to go to the quarterback of the football team, it seems.

"Okay, I'm done," she bellowed from the back of the Plymouth, "ten pounds per square inch in the slicks and 32 psi in the back."

"Excellent, thanks Quarter Horse."

"You're welcome."

"Okay, people, saddle up. The line's moving."

"You cleared riding shotgun with Tom?"

"Sure did," she replied exuberantly.

"We'll be disqualified if you're lying to me."

"I wouldn't do that. Besides, Tom is actually Grandpa Tom," she said, laughing as she pulled her helmet on.

I looked up the line at Tom standing at the burnout box. He gave me the thumbs up. I smiled and nodded my head. Racing really does run in the bloodline.

"Good Lord, you missed," Phillip exclaimed, breathing a huge sigh of relief.

"Shut up."

"I'm just saying..."

"Two balls short of sinking the 8-ball, too, Dammit!"

Phillip stood smiling in that cocky way of his.

"My turn."

"Don't miss."

"Oh, I won't Deary."

"Hah hah, my grandmother calls me Deary."

"Well then, here's to Grandma. Number one ball, side pocket," he declared and sunk the ball in one smooth poke.

"Lucky."

"Skill, Baby, skill."

"Right..."

"Six ball to 4-ball, corner pocket."

Angela watched the 4-ball drop in the corner pocket. "Smooth."

"Getting nervous?"

"I have a few tricks up my sleeve, yet, Lug Nut."

"You might wanna pull a few of those tricks out right about now."

"Are you gonna sink that 7-ball or what?"

"You bet I am, sweetheart; 7-ball, side pocket."

Angela watched the 7-ball slip into the side pocket knowing that she was only one ball away from removing her shirt and skin tight jeans. Dovely, sensing the increased level of anxiety in the room, jumped up on the pool rail to give Angela a little fan support.

"Eight ball, side pocket," he barked triumphantly.

Angela scratched Dovely's head as she watched the 8-ball lightly touch the side pocket bumper and drop into the hole.

"Well done, Handsome," Angela conceded, *walking the walk* around the table in her four inch heels and drowning Phillip with a suffocating, sensual, open mouth French kiss. Having sympathy for the little man, she let him come up for air.

"Whoa," he burst out, gasping for air.

Angela grabbed his hair and pulled his head back for another kiss; her transparent body suit wrapped snuggly around her breasts did not stop them from bursting forth through her loosely buttoned shirt and around his cute face. Her mouth hovered above him, the bottom lip pinched between her teeth, "Go get the tiramisu little man; it's desert time."

Allowing Phillip to escape her grasp, she checked out his

bottom as he took off to the kitchen.

"Hurry back, Phillip," she hollered, "I've got a big surprise for you."

Phillip spun around just in time to see Angela slip out of her shirt, revealing the cognac satin see-through body suit that had been driving him nuts all night.

"Holy Moly!"

Angela tossed him a naughty look as she unbuttoned the top of her jeans and kicked off her heels. "Don't forget the forks and plates."

"Right... forks and plates."

With her pants fully unbuttoned and hanging loosely around her hips, she shimmied onto the pool table where Dovely was positioned like a Sphinx protecting a priceless treasure. "Hey there, Handsome. Do you think he knows what he's in for, hmm? I hope not..."

Dovely stretched his paw out and looked at her with deep admiration.

"I'm counting on shocking him into blissful submission."

I watched him pull through the burnout box in his mint '69 Camaro. He only glanced at me once, nodded his head and proceeded with his burnout. All eyes were on him as the V8 woke up and smoked the tires. It was solid black except for the twin racing stripes that stretched like jet streams down the hood to the rear spoiler. What a beauty. I never bought the car I loved the most... still don't know why. Ah, a 4-speed 302 with a wallop that made me weak in the knees.

"Hey, Gramps, we have a race to win here. Unload this beast!"

"You're right, Quarter Horse," I replied, snapping back to the task at hand. "You ready?"

"Purge and burn, baby!"

I laughed and purged the nitrous as we rolled through the burnout box and wet the slicks. "Let's get her done!"

With the parking brake engaged, I hit WOT in second gear. Isabella belched something wicked as the tires lit up and shot flames out the 3 inch pipes on either side of the car.

"Yeah hah hah HAAAH, baby," Melissa screamed.

"I want you to promise me one thing before we roll, Quarter Horse."

"What?"

"Racing is for the racetrack. Public roads, highways and such are for driving safely according to the law."

"Anything else?"

"One more thing," I said with direct, unwavering eyes.

"Don't drive angry. Stop for coffee... cool down or hand the wheel to someone responsible."

"Nobody's perfect, Gramps."

"But promise me you'll try anyway."

"I promise."

Mission accomplished, I thought with a feeling of deep satisfaction.

I pulled up slowly to shallow stage the car and revved Isabella to 3500 RMP.

Yellow, Yellow... And we were off.

The Camaro immediately pulled a full car length in front of us. His 0 to 60 time was an impressive low four seconds. I hit the nitrous at the top of second and shifted into third. It felt like we had just been unhooked from a high powered sling shot. I power-shifted at 6200 RMP into fourth gear and chirped the tires. The gap between us and the Camaro was shrinking quickly. We were *all out*. It was war.

"Don't you fucking let him win," screamed Quarter Mile.

Isabella's fourth gear, matched with the nitrous, was like a catapult launching a fighter aircraft with full afterburners engaged from the deck of an aircraft carrier... totally AWESOME.

"Not a chance! Kiss my ass, Bow Tie," I shouted as we snuck ahead of Mr. Camaro and blasted through the trap.

"You won! You smoked that Camaro."

"Well, not quite smoked," I said jovially, pumping the brakes, "but we did win by at least half a car length."

"That was AWESOME. Let's go again. I wanna drive this time."

"Hah ha, in time, Quarter Horse, you will in time."

The Camaro arrived first at the time slip booth with us directly behind. We watched somewhat impatiently as a tallish, lanky lady with curly auburn-brown hair jutting out from underneath her cap leaned out of the ticket window. She seemed to know Mr. Camaro on a more intimate level. They exchanged a few pleasant words and, after what seemed a lifetime, she handed him the time slip. He drove off and I pulled up and peered through the closed ticket window. That was odd. She seemed preoccupied shuffling time slips around, almost as if she had misplaced our time slip. *Oh, Good Lord*, I thought to myself. *Nobody will believe I trounced a Camaro without an official time slip. Shit, shit!*

"What's taking Molly so long?" Melissa bellowed.

"I don't rightly know, but I sure hope our time slip is somewhere in that pile of papers."

"Oh, I know what's going on here," Melissa laughed. "You spanked her boyfriend."

I looked over at Quarter Mile with a raised eyebrow, and then nodded my head when my old-time gears connected.

Molly opened the window and greeted us, "Nice Run! You got lucky, though," she said and handed me our time slip with a happy face stamp.

"No we didn't. We blew his ass off!" Melissa exclaimed.

I was caught in the middle of what was turning out to be the makings of a battlefield.

"Thank you," I said with a polite smile and slowly pulled away.

"Did you hear what she said?"

"I did, indeed."

"What a *B-i-t-c-h*."

"I'm going to frame this," I said, almost in tears.

Melissa watched me holding the time slip between my fingertips as I steered Isabella back into the staging lanes.

"Well done, Charlie," she said, noticing my name embossed on my helmet.

Andrew guided us back into the lineup, doing a funny checkered flag dance and sporting a double-thumbs-up act that was, quite honestly, a tad embarrassing.

"You did it," he shouted, opening the driver's side door. "You ran down that Camaro like a falcon outgunning its prey."

"Yes, I did."

"And your ET... Wow, 10.89 seconds. That's Isabella's best ever, right?"

"A record run, my boy," I said as I pulled off my helmet and shared a fist pound with Quarter Mile and Andrew. Her friends and brother came over to help celebrate the victory.

"Were you scared?" queried her brother.

"Shut up, Boner. You're just jealous I was the first to run 10 seconds."

Ah, sibling rivalry, I thought as they continued their spat.

I hadn't yet moved from the driver's seat. My energy level sank and a feeling of fatigue, probably from hunger, set in.

I caught Andrew's attention and he peered into the

cockpit. "I'm feeling a little famished, a bit dizzy with all the excitement, actually. Are you making a run to the hot dog stand?"

"I am now. What can I get you?"

"Something to drink; I've got a dry throat."

"Are you okay?" he asked.

"Ah, I'll have two Cokes, two fries and four dogs. That should do the trick..." Andrew gave me strange looks.

"Hungry?"

"Yup, that's for me and Quarter Mile. I like her style."

"Alright, then, you stay put and I'll grab us some grub."

"You're awesome, thanks Falcon."

That's the first time he's called me that, Andrew thought to himself.

"Hey, Charles, pop the hood, will ya?" Melissa asked.

So, Andrew headed for the hot dog stand and I popped the hood. The kids' voices faded into a dull murmur as they gathered around the engine bay to see what it was that made Isabella tick. I reclined the seat a bit to rest my head and absorb the wonders of the day. I was tired. The excitement had completely wiped me out. In the distance, I could see the miraculous artistry of the setting sun. *Ah, what a Heavenly scene.* I felt myself being pulled from the darkness into the brilliant colors of the evening sky.

When Phillip returned to the pool room, Angela was sitting in the center of the pool table, legs stretch out with ankles crossed and leaning backwards on both hands. Phillip paused for a moment to appreciate Angela's Vargas Girl pose. The nylon bottoms of her feet had a line running down the center. The thought of that line running along the back of her calves and thighs had him so horny he couldn't speak properly. Her nipples were sensuously visible through the sultry lace design of her nylon body suit, which wrapped like a figure eight around a beautiful pair of satellite moons.

"I ah... I, ahem hmmm. I've tits a misu. Shit! I mean I brought the tits, flates and porks." Phillip's face turned crimson red.

Angela smiled. Her plan was working.

"Don't you drop that... come over here, Puddle Jumper."

Phillip brought the tiramisu over and placed it on the rail of the pool table, nearly dropping it and the plates in the process. Angela crawled over toward Phillip, moved the tiramisu onto the bed where it wouldn't fall, and sat on the rail.

"Pull," she whispered, extending her legs outward. Phillip grabbed the cuffs of her jeans and slowly tugged them free. He stood there with mouth ajar as she moved her bottom sideways across the rail, crossed her beautiful legs and seductively arched her back.

After a moment of steamy silence, Angela motioned him forward, pulling him closer by the waist of his boxer shorts and wrapping her mile-long legs around him. When Phillip moved in for a kiss, her moist, pouty-soft lips enticed him to jump in. She leaned backward, as he moved closer, stretching out across the pool bed to grab the remote sitting on the rail.

"You're teasing," he murmured.

"Such a child," she replied and pressed play. The acoustic, live version of Heaven by Bryan Adams filled the room.

Heaven is exactly where I'm at, Phillip thought. *How did this beautiful woman fall into my arms? I'm so damned LUCKY.*

Phillip clasped her hands and pulled her back up. Again, he moved in for a kiss. Angela dodged it, instead reaching for a fork.

"You're forgetting the most important part, Mr. Horny Shorts."

She uncovered the tiramisu, scooped some up and lifted it to his lips. The smell of coffee, cream and Kahlúa aroused their senses. Phillip opened his mouth. *Nice juicy pink tongue,* Angela thought as she slid the tiramisu in. Phillip's lips closed around the fork. She pulled it out, stuck it in the tiramisu and flung her arms around his strapping neck.

"Now ravish me, you half naked man," she whispered. They locked lips, sealing the tiramisu with a smothering French kiss. The fire in their loins began to intensify as their mouths danced the Merengue. Phillip attempted to pick Angela up off the pool table, but her weight when she straddled him combined with his tipsy head had them falling backwards onto the sofa. They laughed together with eyes full of love and naughtiness.

Angela stood up, did a little pirouette for Phillip's pleasure and returned to the pool table where she dished out a bowlful of tiramisu.

Phillip watched her every move from the sofa. Her luscious body wrapped in the sexy nylon body suit had him unbearably horny.

"Awesome tiramisu, Bella Donna."

"Grazie, giovane."

She returned to the sofa and eased herself down on Phillip's belly, bowl in hand.

"Want some more?" she asked, seducing him with a spoonful of tiramisu, and then playfully inserting it in her mouth.

"Hey," he complained and sat up. Gently, he pulled her in for another Kahlúa intoxicating kiss. Their tender lips ravished one another, while Dovely watched from the bar. *This is all very entertaining,* he thought. *There better be some tuna cake in this for me at some point.* I am The Guard Cat after all.

Phillip's cell phone buzzed and beeped indicating he had received a text message. Angela froze. "Is that your cell?"

"Yes, it can wait," he said, desperately hoping it wasn't Andrew sending him a heads-up message that would shortly be followed by an emergency phone call about pressing company business. Or the President...

Angela put another spoonful of tiramisu in his mouth and leaned forward to give Phillip a prime view of her satellite moons. Underneath her, she felt the swell of his manhood lifting her like a surfboard on the crest of a wave.

Their lips touched... the cell phone rang.

Phillip looked over at his pants on the floor. "Probably nothing," he said, but calmly reached over to read the caller ID.

"It's Andrew," he said with a bit of frustration in his voice. "I better get this."

"Hey! What's going on?"

Andrew answered with a shaky voice. "I've some bad news, Phil, some really... bad... news."

Peter Breeden

TWENTY-SIX – SLEEPER ARTICHOKE TAMES THE LEGEND

As I look down upon my own funeral, I can't help wondering why God chose to scoop me up when He did. It was my time, I guess. He never justifies his decisions. We're just expected to accept them with the understanding that things might begin to make sense to us as time passes. It is the way He intended it to be. Everything eventually gets bundled together with a pretty ribbon.

Bear with me here, I'd like to elaborate a little more.

Dying is like a strong undertow that pulls you away from your safety blanket. You can fight it or surrender to it. Either way, you're powerless against it. Death ultimately conquers our mortal lives—except for Elijah who flew to the heavens in a fiery chariot—every single time, but it is not the end by any means.

Comprehending and coping with death, whether it is our own destiny or that of a loved one is the most difficult course to navigate in life. No matter how hard we try, that rough terrain always seems to get the best of us. We have no control over our eventual demise, and the mystery that surrounds it frightens us to the very core of our mortal and feeble existence. Being separated from everyone we love frightens us.

We grieve our losses in our own individual ways. Some people, me included, deal with the pain internally and speak little about it. Losing my wife changed me forever; life's music had lost its melody. Other individuals require social reassurance and comfort to help get them through the rough terrain. Either way, a broken heart inevitably manifests itself across the face. It cannot be hidden.

The shock of prematurely losing a loved one is akin to the derailment and ensuing wreckage of a commuter train. Something mechanical, human or otherwise breaks and the disruption turns into chaos. Something implausible has happened. Your normal day turns into a nightmare that paralyses your entire being much like a hypnagogic or hypnopompic hallucination. The train derails and disintegrates. Obliteration! The wreckage is catastrophic. So be the mind of a person whose daily routine is broken by the news of personal tragedy.

It was the worst possible timing. Why I had to die during Angela's and Phillip's special moment, the one that would connect them for all eternity was beyond me. But I shouldn't complain… I did, after all, get my quarter mile victory. The front page headline of the San Francisco Chronicle the following day read: "Sleeper Artichoke Tames the Legend." Yes, indeed. The old Monterey Bay Artichoke farmer drives his sleeper sedan to victory over the legendary '69 Camaro, a powerhouse in the automotive world of muscle cars… and dies of natural causes shortly thereafter still buckled into the driver's seat.

Looking back to my final moments is difficult. When Andrew returned to the Plymouth with the hotdogs, cokes and fries I had already passed. He cracked a few jokes about me taking a nap and sleeping on the job before he realized what had happened. He buckled over like he had been hit in the gut with a baseball bat. It never occurred to him that I was old. I guess that's a huge compliment for me, but my death was unfortunately a train wreck for him. I was such a huge and influential part of his life. Looking at him now as he stands grief stricken by my casket with Holly by his side, the runny nose and tears falling from his eyes are a testament to that love.

Someday, he'll find the courage to get back in the Plymouth and feel the exhilaration of the wheels on the Black Top one more time, but not anytime soon.

When Phillip received the news of my death from Andrew, his world caved in. Unlike Andrew, though, Phillip retreated into his own pain and dealt with it internally, refusing to talk about it with anyone. Angela, at first, did not understand his uncharacteristically introverted behavior. She had been shut out of the most guarded parts of his life and this was painful for her to endure. Nevertheless, she set aside her feelings and was there beside him at my funeral with her own broken heart to mend. Réginald and the rest of his family including Noella, Madame et Monsieur Lapossie-Laporte, Caroline and her family, Jeffery, Takeisha and even my angry son all attended my funeral.

The reception afterwards was unfortunately not a celebration of my life as Walt Whitman would have it, but rather a quiet gathering of a bunch of people who thought I would live forever. Well, needless to say, the reception lasted only a couple hours before everybody said their good-byes and went their weary ways. Angela returned to Agen to give Phillip some breathing room. Holly stayed with Andrew a few more days before she too became weary and headed back to Toronto. It was time to clean up the wreckage and rebuild, a process that could take months… or a lifetime.

The reading of my will took place at the lawyer's office, which was ironically located downtown San Francisco in the iconic Transamerica Pyramid. There were five people in attendance: Phillip, Andrew, my rather pale and guilt-ridden son, Jeffery and Takeisha. It was a beautiful office that overlooked the Golden Gate Bridge and Marin County in the distance.

"If everybody is ready, I'll begin," stated the lawyer.

The silent nodding of heads was acknowledgement enough for him to begin.

"This is the will of Charles Mac Clifford Niles," he continued. "To my dear grandson Phillip, I leave the video of our day on the helicopter sightseeing tour. I'm so proud of you, Lug Nut. You are an amazing fellow. In addition, I want you to have the family photos including the picture on the mantle and Velocity, our full-blooded black stallion."

A few tears fell from Phillip's eyes. Even though he said nothing, his grief pierced the hearts of everyone in the room.

The lawyer then looked at Andrew. "To Andrew Pikes, my unofficial, but equally as important grandson, I leave my Dodgified Plymouth Acclaim. I know how much you love this car and the time we spent together in it. Now you can race against Phillip and his Sassy Black Camaro at the track. Do this for me in celebration of my life."

Andrew wiped the tears from his eyes and buried his head in his hands.

The lawyer continued. "In addition, I want you to have my Hamilton pocket watch."

This pulled even more on his heart strings. A man's life can be held in the history of his watch.

"To my loyal farmhand friend, Jeffery Winston and my dear friend Takeisha Houston, who my wife rescued many years ago from a rogue swell at Lover's Point, I leave the two field-hand farmhouses: Northwest corner house is for Jeffery and the Southeast corner house if for Takeisha. You are both responsible for managing and running the artichoke farm. You take direction from Phillip Niles and Andrew Pikes who will inherit the farm equally. With God's good graces, the farm will someday have Niles and Pikes younglings running through the fields, my great grandchildren. The farm should be passed on to them in equal shares. I might be jumping the gun here, but I foresee this future happiness for Phillip and Andrew."

Jeffery and Takeisha hugged one another. Their friendship had grown over the years partly based on their mutual distaste for Brandon.

"To my only son, Brandon Niles, whom I love dearly and deeply wish to save from self destruction, I leave the adjacent Kindly Orange Grove and the crop duster. I purchased this grove for you on your thirtieth birthday and have been patiently waiting to hand it over to you since that day. The timing just wasn't right, I guess. Please continue to crop dust the artichoke farm, if your heart is still there. All my love and best wishes to you all. Dad."

Peter Breeden

EPILOGUE

When you crash, you get up, shake the daze from your head and eventually get around to picking up the pieces. Such was the case with Phillip and Andrew after my death. Their business lives kept moving forward thanks to a great team of lawyers and a highly competent Board of Directors. Their personal lives, however, had somehow disintegrated.

Brandon? Well… his life hit a pothole and barrel rolled into the center of a crossroad. I imagine he'll sit there scratching his head for a bit while he puts things together and decides where he wants to go next. Takeisha and the Kindly Orange Grove were unexpected albeit pleasant surprises for him.

The Plymouth sat at the back of the barn hidden behind a wall of hay bales. The family photograph on the mantle with me in the overalls holding the hoe was still on the mantle… it was too painful for Phillip to display in his Palo Alto home or at the Château. Angela continued her renovations of the mansion and also took over managing the Château alongside Regi in Phillip's absence. Phillip couldn't face the Château without nausea heaving his insides. Too many good memories... Holly continued nursing in Toronto and waited each night for Andrew to return her calls. There was nothing she could do or say to take his pain away.

Only the passage of time lessens the pain, but the sense of loss always returns on occasion to haunt the soul much like the serenity of the ocean turns to fury when a storm moves in.

It wasn't until a few months later when a Western Scrub Jay flew into Phillip's office window that things began to change. He bounced downstairs and into the garden below his window where the bird had landed in a patch of bougainvillea vines. Andrew, seeing Phillip run from his office, followed right behind.

"Is it dead?"

"I don't know," Phillip replied, bending down to pick up the motionless bird. "It's heavy."

"Probably drunk on berries," Andrew replied.

"And solid... this is a powerful bird!"

"Here, let me see," Andrew said, taking the bird in his hands. "She's still alive. See? She's moving her head."

"Oh, how 'bout that."

The bird's eyes began to show some recognition of its surroundings. It stared at Andrew, head still bobbing and body completely lounged out.

"Man! That must have been one hard hit. She's only just coming around now."

Andrew began blowing on its beak to help the bird regain consciousness. It was working. The bird perked up and rolled onto its belly. It kept looking at Andrew and Phillip with a sense of wonder and confusion, undoubtedly still scatterbrained. Well I should say *I kept looking at Andrew and Phillip.* Yes, the Blue Jay was Blue Charles and yes, I knocked myself out flying into Phillip's window, purposefully. I couldn't bear watching my boys' waste any more time feeling sad and God decided it was time for the next phase in their lives.

After taking a few minutes to regain a measure of consciousness and having received some persuasion from Andrew, I flew awkwardly to the closest branch where I perched and collected my senses. As I sat there staring at the two young men, I knew my job was done.

"Looks like the little fellow is going to make it," Phillip observed.

"Little missy, actually, will make it just fine. It's a girl."

"Well, excuse me Mr. Ornithologist!"

"Look!" Andrew pointed, "She's already back to BAU."

BAU or Business as Usual was exactly the message we were trying to send.

"Yeah, I need to get back to business… and Angela."

"Yes, it's time for us to step out of this funk, man," Andrew said in agreement.

After a few moments of silence, he said it; "I think Holly is the one for me."

Phillip looked at Andrew meaningfully and nodded his head. "Go get her then, Bubba. She's a good kid. Pops liked her."

"What about you and Angela?"

"She understands me. She's real about everything she does and isn't afraid to lay out the facts. I like that. She has my wellbeing at the center of her heart. So, there's much more than physical attraction there."

Andrew nodded as they both turned to head back in the building.

"Well then…" he said warmly, putting his arm around Phillip's shoulders, "go get her, Bubba!"

The next day, after a long flight from San Francisco, Phillip arrived at the Château, but did not immediately pull into the tree-lined driveway entrance. He paused for a moment, sensing that Angela might instead be at the mansion. He drove onwards to the mansion. The sun had just set. There were doves cooing on the tree tops and in the background the moon cast its illumination over the orchard. Phillip noticed the master bedroom lights were on and the hallway entrance chandelier shone brilliantly through the windows.

He knocked on the door, but nobody answered. Stepping backward for a better view, he peered into one of the windows. *Holy Poppa Wheelie*, he thought as he gazed upon the magnificence that Angela had created with the hallway entrance. The grand staircase was a work of art.

"Where is that girl?" he mumbled with one hand on his hips and the other holding roses.

Angela had watched him pull into the driveway from the tree swing she built from scratch in the side yard. This had become her favorite spot to watch the sunset and have her last cup of coffee before packing it in for the night. It was her peaceful escape from an otherwise busy day and distraught state of mind. When she saw Phillip pull in, a state of shock briefly walloped her heart, and then a big smile lit up her face. Her eyes filled with teary happiness as she casually walked up behind Phillip who stood patiently at his front door, confounded by the silence. She leaned on the banister for a moment or two, collecting her thoughts as she gazed upon the man with whom she had fallen deeply in love.

"I'm sure she's around here someplace… if you look hard enough."

Phillip almost jumped out of his pants.

"Oh! Hello Doll."

"Hey Handsome."

"Hi… er, I said that already…" he blushed. "I missed you," he continued, and handed her the flowers.

Angela smiled and smelled the bouquet of roses. When she looked up again, Phillip's eyes were glistening as he reached out and stroked her cheek with his thumb.

"Sorry I took so long," he whispered.

Angela blinked and wiped away a tear. "I understand, Phillip. A wrecked car needs some time in the garage before it can race again."

Phillip, amazed at how well Angela understood him, took her in his arms, confessed his love for her and sealed it with a tender kiss.

"I love you too," she whispered, running her hands through his hair. It was then that she remembered my video of the day of the helicopter tour. "Have you watched the video yet?"

"No. I thought we would watch it together."

As they walked into the brightly lit foyer, Phillip pulled a memory card from a treasure chest locket hanging around his neck and handed it to Angela. He had carried it with him since the reading of my will and only now had the courage to watch it. Angela, after all, would be there beside him as she had been all along.

"So, this is Charles' final message?"

"It is."

"Well, Big Boy," she replied, taking his hand and leading him up the grand staircase, "let's see what mighty Charles had on his mind."

"My God, you did an awesome job on this staircase."

"I was wondering how long it would take you to notice."

"Hey," he replied with a pinch on her bottom. "I noticed your genius from day one!"

Fin de la Première Partie.

ABOUT THE AUTHOR

Peter Breeden is thankful to have had numerous opportunities working as a Technical Writer for a diverse range of international IT companies in the Bay Area, California, as well as Toronto, Ontario where he currently resides with his wife. These experiences have been both inspirational and, in many ways, eye-opening for him. "Learning means doing," according to Peter's outlook on life and, as such, he continues to learn from his peers and mentors in his chosen profession. Peter is currently working on the second part of *The Niles & Pikes* series.

Made in the USA
Charleston, SC
28 July 2013